Advance praise for Meri Weiss and
CLOSER TO FINE

"Characters so beautifully crafted and realistic, you'll spend the rest of your life looking for them on the streets of Manhattan. This brilliant first novel by Meri Weiss is a comic masterpiece which bravely deals with the stark emptiness of tragedy and the ultimate redemption through friendship and the power of trust."
—Simon Van Booy, author of *The Secret Lives of People in Love*

"Meri Weiss has written a touching and perceptive novel about a young woman's growing understanding of love and loyalty in the complex and tangled web that is family and friendship. In the tradition of fast-paced New York novels such as *Bright Lights, Big City*, here is a new and refreshing look at a theme as old as humanity itself."
—Kaylie Jones, author of *Speak Now*

"Meri Weiss writes beautifully of love and death in a family, which, in her careful hands, becomes everyone's family. And the heart that beats beneath her cool wit is everyone's sacred heart. Enter a full-blown novelist."
—Roger Rosenblatt, author of *Lapham Rising*

"*Closer to Fine* is set in mythic New York of twentysomethings, close friends in wonderful–awful downtown apartments, pursuing careers in the arts, escaping for weekends up the Hudson. Haunted by loss, Alex muddles through with her best friends from childhood by her side. Though their struggles are real, the novel is an ebullient celebration of a bohemian world where friends become family."
—Anne Fernald, author of *Virginia Woolf: Feminism and the Reader*

"In Alexandra, Meri Weiss has created a character of charming—and sometimes alarming!—honesty and courage. It's impossible not to cheer Alex on her journey of self-discovery and impossible not to applaud her when she achieves her hard-won goal of true personal happiness. Written with verve, intelligence, and above all, with heart, *Closer to Fine* will appeal to any reader in search of a story that reaffirms the precious nature of family and friends."
—Holly Chamberlin, author of *The Friends We Keep*

"In *Closer to Fine*, Meri Weiss explores the nature of friendship and family with a gentle, forgiving touch. This is a sweet, funny, sad and wise book, and you'll find yourself missing the characters when you're done reading it."

—Bart Yates, author of *The Distance Between Us*

"In this honest and heartfelt debut about the pain of loss and the thrill of love, Meri Weiss takes subject matters as bleak as suicide, illness, and the death of loved ones, and by the end magically restores color to a world drained by grief."

—Robert Westfield, author of *Suspension*

"This charming novel is a love song to friendship, a funny, moving, and refreshing story about the shared laughter, misunderstandings, and revelations that occur when you know people for so long that living without them is unimaginable. Anyone who has ever picked up the phone at two in the morning to comfort or seek comfort from a friend will immediately fall in love with these characters, because you are almost certain to know or be one of them."

—Michael Thomas Ford, author of *What We Remember*

"*Closer to Fine* presents a very modern tale of life, death and love, and a very modern protagonist in Alex, who doesn't know what she wants yet isn't afraid to search through the familiar psychic minefields that accompany life in New York. Alex's quest to discover her "missing piece" is both heartrending and compelling in this impressive debut novel from Meri Weiss."

—Robert Reeves, author of *The Eulogist*

Closer to Fine

MERI WEISS

KENSINGTON BOOKS
http://www.kensingtonbooks.com

For my sister, my first and favorite friend
And
For my parents, for their endurance

Acknowledgments

Most of this novel was composed while listening to the same six CDs, thus it seems natural to thank the artists who inspired and oversaw my writing process, despite the fact I don't know you personally. So thank you to Melissa Etheridge, Sarah McLachlan, Bob Dylan, Jeff Buckley (RIP), Indigo Girls (Amy Ray and Emily Saliers) and Peter Gabriel. Special thanks to Melissa Etheridge, Amy Ray and Emily Saliers, for your continued activism, and for insisting the rest of us do what we can to save the planet, and each other. Extra special thanks to Amy Ray and Emily Saliers, for title inspiration.

Though I do not know you personally, I must offer a lifetime of gratitude to Madonna, for the innumerable ways in which you have inspired me and countless others.

To Ellen Levine at Trident Media Group, for your confidence and patience, and for believing in this novel.

To my editor at Kensington Books, John Scognamiglio, for your enthusiasm, your helpfulness, your remarkably attuned suggestions and, mostly, for making me feel at home in your House.

To Peter Senftleben at Kensington Books, for loving my novel and passing it on; for adoring my characters; and for your sweet demeanor, your stellar attention to details and your serene support.

To Professor William Roberson, for teaching me to teach, and for illustrating, by example, what an intelligent, dignified educator looks and acts like. If I turn out to be half as inspirational to my students as you have been to yours, I will consider myself a successful instructor. Thank you for reigniting my love of literature, supporting my literary endeavors and listening to me vent about the Yankees. You epitomize the word *gentleman*.

To Alice Flynn, for your continued support, which I cherish.

To Stacey and Siggy Scolnik, for all the love and affection over the years.

To Nicole Sachs, for years of unwavering support, faithful encouragement and uncomplicated friendship—your hugs have continually stabilized me.

To Laura Baudo Sillerman, for exemplifying grace under pressure and reminding those around you what is really important in life; for supporting not only the arts but also individual artists; for your humility, your generosity and your friendship. I am honored to know you.

To Angela Medwid, for fervently teaching me about life and love, and for championing my educational and literary pursuits. Our relationship has lasted far longer than either of us anticipated, and I thank the universe for placing such a fierce, passionate presence in my life. Thank you for introducing me to Diana, Holly and Molly—their music has improved my life. Your music—your ideas, your poetry, your energy, your friendship and your love—has improved my soul.

To Mike Matejka, for showing me a world without proper punctuation. You are such a smart, authentic man, and I am so thankful for your friendship and support. We are forever bonded by that sunny Tuesday morning.

To Debbie Pearl Siegel, who has been my loudest cheerleader from the moment we met—your enduring friendship and encouragement have both inspired and supported me. Your wisdom, creativity and originality light you up from the inside out—you make me laugh, you listen to me whine and you completely understand my connection to the sand, sun and stars of the East End. You are kind and generous, and I cannot explain how much I value our friendship.

ACKNOWLEDGMENTS

To Jamie Schenk DeWitt, my beacon of light amid the gray midwestern skies. James, you and I have traveled far and long together—our visits are few and far between—but here we are, sixteen years later, our friendship unbroken, our bond resolute. You are a steady, stable force in my life—you continually offer love, creativity, inspiration and, when I need it most, laughter. I admire your dedication to art, to ideas, to concepts that connect people. I thank you for your faithful friendship and your ardent support.

To David Spector, for your fraternal friendship.

To Lexi Spector, for brightening my world.

To my grandma, Rose, for reading all my work (no matter how racy), and for bragging about me to your friends.

To Steven DeVall, my babycakes. I really have no idea how I functioned before you began to play a starring role in my life—I cannot fathom existing without you. Thank you for letting me borrow pieces of your life, and for inspiring such a lovely, loving character. Thank you for catching me when I fall; for pushing me toward my aspirations; and for celebrating with me when I succeed. Thank you for your grace, your generosity and your inherent goodness. You are my touchstone, Steven, always.

To my parents, for supporting me in every way possible. Thank you for encouraging all my ambitions, and for honoring all my successes. Thank you also for presenting to me, on a daily basis, such a shining example of marriage.

To Kaylie Jones, you are everything a writing teacher should be. You forced me to write from the heart, which is so much harder and, ultimately, more gratifying. The quality of my prose is a direct reflection of your dedication and honesty as my guide and my exemplar. Thank you, Kaylie, for inspiring, motivating and leading me. This book could not have been written without you.

To Renee Ronika Klug, you are the wisest, most talented non-professional editor I know. I am so very grateful you are my friend—together we've laughed, learned and grown, and I cherish both our soul-baring conversations and our silly (but not really) debates about the nuances of "cacophony." You were the first to fall for Jax, Jordy and Alex, and I thank you for reading draft after draft. Quite simply, this book would not exist without you. Thank you for believing in me—your friendship and love sustain me, and your faith in me astounds me. You are bold; you are brave; you are beautiful.

To Allison, my sister, for helping to shape me. You've taught me basic skills (tying my shoes), important skills (studying for exams), necessary skills (negotiating NYC subways), and skills I still haven't quite perfected (balancing my checkbook). You have always protected and guided me, and for that I thank you. You are my favorite roommate of all time—the memories created by the Bean family occupy a vast section of my heart. Thank you for encouraging me to apply to schools, to move to HB, to write my way out. Thank you for supporting me, literally and figuratively, while I learned and wrote. You have always been my strongest and most trustworthy ally—I cannot create a sentence that accurately conveys my gratitude. With all my heart, I love you.

To Jenn Smits, for the laughter and love you have infused into my life. Yours is the only hand I want to hold.

Vincent Frein
In Pace Requiescat

1

My day is shot before I even walk into the minimalist, pretentious lobby of my brother's building. First of all, it's nine o'clock on a Sunday morning and there are several places I'd rather be—specifically my bed. Second, I'm on the Upper West Side, which may as well be China to someone who rarely ventures above 14th Street. Third, I've been called upon to care for someone I barely know. I know him, but not in the way you're supposed to know someone who is ill. I haven't seen him in six months, and he told me he was sick only four weeks ago.

Plus, I can't find my favorite shirt; there's a hole in my drawer. I turned my apartment upside down but there's still no trace of it. I've had that shirt for ten years. Needless to say, I'm way beyond pissed when the elevator man lets me into the penthouse apartment.

The monstrous space is unabashedly clean and tidy, as it has been on the few other occasions I've been here. It's the smell that alerts me to the changes. I recall the scent of lemon—not industrial, cleaning solution–type lemon, but sweet, soothing lemon—and today it's barely noticeable. I also vaguely remember the aroma of expensive candles but that, too, is hardly apparent. It smells sterile and cold, like dead air.

The living room and kitchen are spotless, but they are more than just unsoiled; they seem lonely, as if few feet have traversed their floors of late. All the shades are drawn, lending the room an eerie quiet. The words *quiet* and *Ashley* simply do not go together, at least from what I remember.

I hear footsteps emanating from somewhere down the hall, so I head for the fourth door on the right—so many doors, so few inhabitants—and knock twice. The door opens and a woman in white—white shoes, white button-down shirt, white pants—smiles at me. Her blonde hair is pulled into a tight bun at the base of her neck.

"You must be Alexandra, Ashley's sister. He told me you were coming to spend the day with him. I'm Sally."

She extends a latex rubber–gloved hand. Her handshake is extremely firm.

"He's just waking up from a nap. Will you fetch him some juice so he can take his pills? After he takes his medicine, I'll leave you two alone."

I nod, back away from the door and walk back to the kitchen. I drop my bag on the gleaming counter and open the refrigerator. I grab a carton of orange juice and search for a glass, opening and closing four cabinets before I find one. I pour the juice, spilling some over my fingers. As I wash my hands, it occurs to me that now is the time to escape. I can hand the juice to Sally, explain that I'm not qualified to be here—neither as a sister nor a caretaker—and run away, back downtown, where I belong.

But Ashley told Sally I was visiting. Does that mean he's looking forward to seeing me? Maybe he tells his nurse everything, like how long it's been since he and I shared a meal, or even a laugh. When I saw him last, it was because my mother instituted mandatory attendance at Thanksgiving dinner—whoever didn't go would be cut out of the will. None of us thought she'd follow through with her threat, but we realized if she was going to such lengths to get her kids around a table, we may as well show up, eat some turkey and make nice. Ashley hadn't looked sick—thin, maybe, but not sick. He and I had talked about what restaurants we frequent in the city and what movies we had seen.

I walk back to his room and knock on the door.

"Come in, dear," Sally answers.

When I open the door, she is leaning against the threshold, blocking my view of my brother. She glances at the juice and shakes her head.

"Oh no, not orange juice—he doesn't like orange juice."

He doesn't? Then why the hell is it in the fridge? I wonder.

"It's for guests," Sally continues. In addition to hospice work, she must also read minds.

"The apple juice, dear. On the left side." I turn to head back to the kitchen. "On your way back, could you grab a fresh pillow-case? He had some trouble while he was sleeping."

I nod, wondering but not wanting to ask what *trouble* means. I dump the orange juice, put the glass in the dishwasher and pour some apple juice into a clean glass. I begin to open and close doors in the hallway, hunting for the linen closet. I'm try-ing to be quiet, but apparently I'm not doing a good job, be-cause Sally's head pokes out from Ashley's bedroom.

"What are you looking for?"

"The linen closet."

She points to a door near the bathroom. "Have you ever been here before?"

I slowly stroll down the hallway, careful not to spill the juice, which I'm carrying with both hands, like a child. "A long time ago."

A long time ago explains so much about Ashley and me.

I hand the glass to Sally, remove a perfectly ironed white pillow-case from the linen closet and enter my brother's bedroom.

"Hi, Alex."

"Hey, Ashley. How are—" I am very rarely speechless, but as I absently look up, my words catch somewhere between my stom-ach and my throat.

"I've been better. How are you?" Ashley responds. The man lying in bed sounds like my older brother, but it can't actually be him. He is gaunt and frail and pathetic-looking. He looks like a withered balloon after a raucous birthday party.

"I'm OK," I manage to utter.

"Can I get a kiss from my youngest sister?" Ashley asks. "You can kiss my hand if you want."

I envelop him in a hug and kiss him square on the lips.

Sally takes the pillowcase from my hand and puts it on a large, fluffy pillow.

"Now make sure he stays in bed," she instructs. I turn around to face her so I won't miss any of her directives. "He can, and should, eat and drink anything he wants, except alcohol, of course. Give him plenty of hot tea, water, milk—lots of fluids, and lots of rest. I'm sure you two want to talk all day, but he really should sleep as much as possible."

So Ashley doesn't offer Sally much personal information. I nod effusively. Sally rolls the rubber gloves off her hands, drops them in a wastebasket and pats Ashley's shoulder.

"I'll see you tomorrow."

"Thanks. Bye."

We watch Sally leave and listen as the elevator doors open and close. And then it is just us.

"So how are you?" he asks.

"I'm OK," I reply, leaning against his night table. Pill bottles rattle, along with my nerves.

"Thanks for coming. I'm sorry if Mom forced you."

My palms begin to itch. "She didn't. Not at all." Liar.

"Mom and Dad usually spend Sundays with me, but one of her friends invited her to a luncheon of some sort, and I made her go. She could use a week off. I'm sure she just felt guilty about me being alone. You can leave whenever you want. I won't tell."

"I don't want to leave." Two lies in two minutes—good thing I'm not a Catholic.

"Alex, you're halfway to the door already. It's OK, really. At this point, I'm way past bullshitting. I can read the paper until Stella stops by later—it'd take less energy than trying to converse with you."

He sighs and leans back into his array of pillows. My eyes sting but I command them to stay neutral.

"I was just wondering where I left my bag. Let me go check."

I'm out of the room in three-and-a-half steps. I march into the kitchen and find my bag. I also find Ashley's stocked bar. A bottle of vodka is in my hands before I realize it's way too early to imbibe liquor. I unscrew the cap, tilt the bottle into my mouth and swallow. Then I open my eyes and exhale.

I bite down on several Tic Tacs as I amble back down the hall, my bag in hand. I feel more awake now. Ashley is staring at the doorway as I enter. I stand still for a moment, then drop my bag and approach the bed.

"Ashley, what the fuck is going on?"

"I'm dying," he answers matter-of-factly.

"But . . . how . . . why so . . ." I can't gather my thoughts.

"Why so fast?"

I nod.

"Kind of like cancer; the later you're diagnosed, the more screwed you are."

"But aren't you really into health and exercise? How'd you not notice?"

"I've always been anemic, so I have about ten colds a year. It didn't really strike me as odd. Plus I was on location for most of last year. It wasn't 'till I had bronchitis for two months straight that I thought something was amiss."

I nod, understanding without comprehending.

"So really, how are you?" he demands.

I want to know more but his eyes narrow as he waits for me to answer.

"I'm annoyed, actually." I'm surprised I'm telling him the truth—I don't think I've *told* him anything since I was in elementary school, and odds are he didn't even listen then.

"Why, because you had to schlep to the Upper West Side?" he asks.

"That, plus I seem to have lost my favorite shirt."

Ashley motions for me to sit, so I pull up a strange-looking (no doubt expensive) chair and plop down. The chair's arms stick out in different, unparallel directions.

"Deceivingly comfortable chair, huh?" he asks.

I nod.

"So tell me about the shirt," he demands.

"I've had it since senior year of high school. It's soft and totally molded to my body. Maybe you've seen it—a white T-shirt with purple flowers."

"I can vaguely picture it. It's a hippie sort of thing, right?" he asks.

I roll my eyes. "Don't start with the hippie references, please."

"OK, OK. So why do you love it so much?"

I sigh, pondering how best to explain my attachment to this shirt without inviting Ashley's ridicule. And why does he want to know? What right does he have to know? If I don't answer him, though, the air will be full of awkward hostility.

"Well," I begin. "It feels like second skin. I'm totally myself when I wear it. And I've worn it in so many places over the years, on most of my favorite days. It's there, in all my great memories."

"Tell me about them," Ashley says.

"About what?"

"Your favorite days. The ones you wore the shirt on."

"Why do you care?" I ask.

"I want to hear about your favorite T–shirt–wearing memories," he says impatiently. "As if we have anything else to talk about?"

I glance out the window, considering his request. It's a bit too late for this. I shouldn't even be here. I should be at home with my best friend, Jordy, reading the paper and eating bagels. This is my time with her and Ashley is stealing it.

Ashley reaches over and touches my knee. I gaze into his eyes, which look, but don't feel, familiar. "Please, Alex?"

I don't really want to tell him—as my older brother, he should know these things already—but he's right. We don't have much else to talk about. I sigh. "OK."

"Good. Now go," Ashley orders.

I describe for Ashley the experience of my first Dead show, and my third show, where I heard my favorite song, "Cassidy." I tell him about my last-minute decision to drop acid with Casey and Brooke on a bleak, frigid night during sophomore year of college. I reminisce about the Dead shows at Deer Creek—the first ones I attended with a boyfriend. I laughingly recall the Dead show at Red Rocks, when Hannah and Kate got screwed with counterfeit tickets and tried to sneak through the boulders behind the massive stage. They didn't get in, but they did get covered in vicious scratches. In the car, everyone crashed and I ate three boxes of white Tic Tacs to stay awake while creeping along in the postshow traffic jam. I recount for him the last day of junior year, when finals were over and the stubborn sun finally showed itself, and Casey, Brooke, Jules and everyone else sat in the garden of Dimitri's, the prettiest bar on campus, and drank cold, delicious daiquiris.

I stop for a second and watch Ashley. He's leaning against the headboard, his eyes closed, a small smile spread across his face. I take a breath and continue to unspool my memories. I relay the enthusiasm I felt the first time I saw Aimee Mann, at The Beacon, and then at Town Hall and The Supper Club. I attempt to encapsulate the pure, complete joy I experienced at The Rolling Stones concert at Madison Square Garden. I describe the lazy, perfect days in the Berkshires with Jordy, who's been my friend, seemingly, forever. I remind him about my high school graduation celebration, the last time anyone threw a party in my honor. I tell him about the most recent day I wore the shirt—in late July—when Jordy got a tattoo. When I'm finished, he opens his eyes and stares at me for a few moments, and then counts on his fingers, shaking his seemingly tiny head.

"How many Dead shows in total?" he inquires.

"Eighteen," I answer defensively.

"Wow," is all he says, frowning. "I wonder where you got that from."

"Have you been to any?" I ask.

"One, at the Meadowlands, for the experience," he answers, quoting the air.

"Figures," I respond.

"And I sat in a luxury box!" he laughs.

"Loser," I say.

Ashley chuckles. "Do you see why I made you talk about all those shirt-related memories?" he asks, serious again.

"Because you're bored?"

"No, to show you it's all right if you don't find the shirt. You don't need the shirt. It's all inside you," he says.

I roll my eyes. He seems a bit uncomfortable, so I get up and rearrange the half-dozen pillows behind him, careful not to jostle him.

"Jesus, Ashley, nice bedding." I don't think I've ever touched such silky, soft sheets.

"One thousand count, from London. Quite pricey, and relatively annoying when I miss the piss bottle and pee on them."

"I brought Star Wars Trivial Pursuit; we can play later if you want," I tell him.

"OK," he replies. "Did you know that in *Star Wars*, when they land after the big battle, Mark Hamill yells out 'Carrie!' instead of 'Leia?'"

"Duh, I told you that."

"Oh yeah, right."

I feel like I'm supposed to be doing something helpful. "Do you want or need anything?"

Ashley cocks his head, as if distracted by the music, and then states, "'I would like a nice, mind-altering substance, preferably one that will make my unborn children grow gills.'"

"The movie-line game? Now?" I ask him. "It seems a bit inappropriate."

Ashley shrugs. "It's what we do; isn't it?"

I look at my fingernails, then out the window—anywhere but in my brother's weary eyes. He's right—it's what we do; it's how we fill the vast void between us.

"Yeah," I answer, finally meeting his gaze and accepting the challenge. "*Party Girl.*"

"Way to go, Alex. I thought I'd nail you on that one."

"Try picking a line that's not from one of my favorite movies. Do you want anything or not?" I ask.

"A cup of tea would be lovely," he says in a sugary voice.

When I return with Ashley's tea, I realize the CD has ended, tossing us into silence. I quickly move to the stereo, which looks as if it might cost more than my monthly rent. I scan the racks of CDs, relieved to see they're organized in alphabetical order. I grab one, slide it in and sit down. The song is familiar and reassuring.

"Ooh, Sophie B. Hawkins. Good call. I like her," he says.

"Me, too. Cool songs, good lyrics. Plus, she's hot."

Ashley nearly chokes on his Earl Gray. "What?"

"Don't you think she's pretty? And sexy?"

"Sure, but I didn't know you thought about women that way," he says.

"Ashley, a woman can consider another woman empirically attractive without being threatened. We're not petty, like you boys. Or catty, like you personally."

Ashley stares at me, his bullshit meter on high. "Alex?"

"What?" I answer.

"Have you ever . . . um . . . you know?"

"Been with a woman?" I finish his question, although it is a treat to see him blush. He nods—embarrassed at the fact he was too embarrassed to articulate the words. "It's none of your business," I tell him.

"Oh, come on, Alex."

I don't answer. He looks at the ceiling while I direct my gaze at my shoes (which need to be re-soled). A minute passes, then another. Our eyes meet, and he speaks.

"Yes, I've been a shitty brother. You're not winning any awards in the Best Sister category. And we both know I'm going to die."

I see Ashley—really see him—for the first time in years. He's right, on all three counts.

"So, have you been with a woman?" he asks.

"Yes."

His sallow face fills with delight. "And?" he inquires.

"It was . . . fun," I answer.

"Fun? That's your response?" I nod. "More fun or less fun than with a guy?" he asks.

"I don't know. I'm not sure what—" to say to him.

"Wait a sec, Alex. Are we talking about one drunken smooch or—"

Why should I reveal this? I haven't even told Jordy. Ashley has not earned the privilege of knowing this part of me.

"The 'or' scenario, in college," I answer.

Ashley's face goes perfectly still, as if he's savoring every sentence—every word—of this conversation.

"Do you think you might be—" I can see the smile creeping across his lips.

"I don't want to talk about this, Ashley," I almost yell.

"I wasn't implying you should know for sure. I'm just wondering if the thought crossed your mind. Just go with the flow," he says softly.

"'What a waste . . . oh the humanity,'" I reply, hoping to distract him.

"*Heathers*. So you been with anyone I know?" His smirk is just screaming for a slap.

"Can we please change the subject?"

"No. Why don't you ask me something personal, to even the score?"

I don't even have to think. "When did you first know?" I ask.

Ashley laughs. "Fourth grade, Fire Prevention Week. Stan the fireman showed me how to stop, drop and roll. He put his big, calloused hands on my back and I got a hard-on."

Of course I'm drinking when he says this, so the soda shoots up my nasal passage and sprays his luxurious sheets. "You did not!" I scream.

"Indeed I did. It was the only time I was glad Mom bought me clothes two sizes too big," he says, smiling.

"But you dated that cheerleader in high school. You took her to the prom!"

"Things were different then, Alex. No GLAAD, no AmfAR, no PFLAG. 'Hmm, PFLAG . . . Parents and Friends of Lesbians and Gays . . . I'm beginning to like the sound of that.'"

"*Reality Bites*. Did you have sex with her?" I ask.

"Yep," he replies.

"How did you . . . you know?"

"I pretended I was screwing Rob Lowe."

Again the soda stains the sheets. Ashley gracefully ignores it and continues, but I shudder at the thought of the dry cleaning bill. "She thought I was a pro, too. Not that she would know the difference, since I popped her cherry!" Ashley thinks this is hilarious.

"You shouldn't use that expression," I scold.

"Why not?"

"First of all, it's disgusting and degrading. And if anyone feels the need to say those words, it should be a woman, in reference to herself," I declare.

"You use the word *fag*," he counters.

"That's because Jax gave me permission. I'm also allowed to say *queen, fagotini* and *FIT*," I tell him.

"No way! A woman cannot point out a Fag in Training!" he complains. "Even if her gay friend says she can." We laugh. "So you get to take advantage of the rules without being in the club?" Ashley smiles from ear to ear. "Can you do me a favor and change the CD?" he asks, a split second after I notice it's skipping.

I pick another, careful to replace Sophie B. in her designated slot. When I turn around, Ashley's eyes are closed. I creep toward the door, imagining how good a cigarette would taste, but his eyes pop open as soon as the music fills the room.

Ashley smiles sleepily. "Excellent. Madonna. And you even picked *Erotica*. You know the press screwed her on this one, right? It's actually a fantastic album."

"I know. You should get some sleep, Ash. Take a nap." I head for the door.

"I don't want to nap. Sleep is a waste of time." I know what he means, but I also see how exhausted he looks.

"What if I want to nap?" I ask.

"Come in here with me." He pats the bed. Not exactly what I had in mind, but maybe he'll doze off after a few minutes. I slide my shoes off and crawl into bed with my big brother. It's been at least a decade since we've sat this close to one another.

It takes our bodies a few minutes to acclimate to the feeling of intimacy. Neither of us says a word for a while.

"Alex?" Ashley breaks the uncomfortable silence.

"Yeah?" I answer, terrified of the question. I never thought he'd be so forthright with me today.

"Would you have sex with Madonna?" Relief seeps out of every pore.

"Definitely; would you?"

"In a nanosecond. You know, I think she's the only person on the planet who transcends gender. Every gay man I know would sleep with her, every straight man I know would sleep with her, every gay woman I know would sleep with her and half the straight women I asked would sleep with her as well."

"Jesus, have you worked up a scientific formula yet? Did you poll your entire neighborhood?" I don't disagree with him but I can't miss this opportunity to poke fun.

"Shut up. 'Go back to your playpen, Baby,'" Ashley says.

"*Dirty Dancing,*" I reply. As Ashley laughs, the fluid in his chest rattles. I really need a cigarette.

His balcony is bigger than my kitchen. I lean over the silver steel railing and stare down at a part of the city that means nothing to me—it's barely recognizable. I consider spitting and watching it float toward the unnaturally clean sidewalk, but manage to keep my immaturity in check. I light a cigarette, using one hand to shelter the fragile flame. It feels odd to spend time with Ashley without wanting to be elsewhere.

When I re-enter the room, Ashley is staring out the floor-to-ceiling window. He looks old and young at the same time.

"You know what I was just thinking?" he asks, turning to me.

"How much you'd like a cigarette?" I ask as I sit down.

Ashley laughs. "That, and how little I really know about you. Growing up, I was close with Teddy and you were close with Teddy, but you and I never hung out. It was almost as if I only had one sister. The five years between me and her and the five years between you and her were never an issue, but the ten years between us are really a huge wall, aren't they?"

I nod. "How come we never spent time together when we were kids?"

Ashley shrugs. "It wasn't like I avoided you on purpose, though you were a pain in the ass. It was the age difference, mostly—we were always at totally different stages of life."

"It seems stupid now."

Ashley nods. "Yeah, but when you were six and I was sixteen, we had nothing to talk about, and when you were ten and I was twenty, we didn't have much in common either. The only time I remember us hanging out or talking was at Uncle Carchie's cabin. That's where we started playing the movie-line game."

"So now I'm twenty-four and you're thirty-four, and we barely know each other." It sounds even worse than it did in my head.

He nods and blinks away the mist.

"So what do you want to know?" I ask.

Ashley readjusts his position in bed and grins. "If you could kill two people without getting punished, who would you kill?"

"Mariah Carey and John Travolta," I answer immediately.

"What's your beef with Travolta?"

"He's annoying—flying his planes all over, that cleft in his chin, his ruddy face. He's so not worth the money they pay him. I just want to bitch-slap him."

"OK, OK, I get the point," Ashley says. "Who would you bring back to life if you could? Whose death deprived the world of pure goodness or talent, in your mind?"

I answer immediately. "Audrey Hepburn and Princess Diana. You?"

"Jonathan Larson and John Kennedy, Jr. What are your three favorite CDs?"

"Bob Dylan's *Blonde on Blonde*, Grateful Dead's *Without a Net* and Tracy Chapman's self-titled album. You?"

"Madonna's *Like a Prayer*, Erasure's *Pop* and Nina Simone's self-titled album. Three favorite songs of all time?" he asks.

"Dylan's 'Desolation Row,' Melissa Etheridge's 'Sleep' and Peter Gabriel's 'In Your Eyes,' I announce. "You?"

"Jeff Buckley's 'Hallelujah,' Cher's 'Just Like Jesse James' and Van Morrison's 'Into the Mystic.' "

"Good choices."

"Who's your favorite drunk?" he asks, grinning.

I laugh. "Fitzgerald, hands down. You?"

"Dorothy Parker. Do you believe in God?" he asks, quietly.

"No."

"Me neither," he replies. "Are you hungry?"

"Yeah. You?" I ask.

"Yeah. Pizza?" I nod. "Number's on the fridge; money's *in* the fridge." I give him a look. "I keep forgetting where I put it, so I figured I'd eventually find it there."

The pizza arrives ten minutes later. Ashley eats in bed, and I balance a Royal Copenhagen plate on my lap. I eat slowly, staring out the window, because it hurts too much to watch Ashley's pained face as he struggles to swallow each bite.

"Jesus, what a view," I declare.

"It's yours," he says.

"What?"

"It's yours—the view, the apartment, all my money." Ashley is full after four bites. When we were little, Teddy and I would sneak him food under the table so it looked as if we'd cleared our plates and would therefore be served dessert. I remember one time he ate four hamburgers, with buns. Teddy used to call him Rover, because instead of feeding the dog the food we didn't want to eat, we fed it to Ashley.

"No, Ashley, please don't . . . give it to Stella or Teddy," I plead.

"It's done. Stella is my best friend but she's got millions. Teddy doesn't need money either—she's done really well for herself. I always knew her weird obsession with numbers would pay off. I'm leaving Mom and Dad the rights to my documentaries. From what I hear, your bedroom is really half the living room and you can't cook a decent meal because your kitchen is so small." He hands me his plate.

"I don't know what to do with that kind of money," I complain.

"'Greed, ladies and gentleman, is good,'" Ashley says.

"*Wall Street*. Seriously, Ashley . . ."

"I'll make sure my money guy checks in on you. He'll help you invest and save. Teddy will, too. But first have some fun. Buy a car or something. But don't you dare establish a foundation in my name. No little ribbons," he orders.

"I live in Manhattan. What do I need a car for?"

"So take a trip. Take Jax and Jordy to Italy. Go shopping. I don't know, put away a chunk of money for your kids," he suggests.

"Who says I'm having kids?" I ask him.

"You don't want children?"

"I don't think I'm equipped," I answer.

"What? You'd be a great mother."

"I'm not sure about that. I'm pretty clueless when it comes to kids. I'm sort of self-absorbed, and I can be very moody." This is new, admitting my flaws out loud, to my brother, of all people.

"Everyone's clueless about kids until they have them. Then the parenting gene kicks in. The self-absorption should wear off when you turn thirty. And you can always take a pill to control your mood swings." I crack up, as does Ashley. His laughter very quickly morphs into a coughing fit. I turn away so I don't have to watch his lungs battle for air.

"I'm just not sure—" I say when he's done coughing.

"Everything they say about kids is true, Alex," he interrupts, serious again.

"How do you know?"

"I have a godchild, remember?"

"Oh yeah. How is Stella's baby?" I exclaim.

"Stella's baby? Harry's almost six!" he reminds me.

"And you haven't lost your godfather position yet?"

Ashley laughs. "I almost retired my post after the porn incident," he says.

"The what?" I ask.

"I didn't tell you about the porn incident?"

"I think I would remember," I tell him.

"Oh God, you are going to *love* this! So I'm babysitting Harry, this is about a year ago, and he tells me he's never seen *Frosty the Snowman* on TV. I remember taping it one year, so I go through all my VCR tapes and, sure enough, I find the *Frosty* tape. He's all excited, and I'm thrilled to be the one introducing him to this pure, wonderful character. I imagine him, in twenty years, reminiscing about the first time he saw *Frosty* with his Uncle Ashley. I pop the tape in, and we settle on the couch. I hit PLAY, and all of a sudden these huge cocks fill the screen!"

"No way!" I shriek.

"Yes way! Apparently I taped over *Frosty* in favor of gay porn. I can't remember doing it, but Frosty sure as hell wasn't hung like the guys on screen!"

"What'd you do?"

"I scaled the coffee table and hit EJECT!"

"What did Harry say?" I ask.

"Nothing. He just stared into space for a few seconds. I think he was trying to process the image. Then he said he was hungry, so I made him a peanut butter and jelly sandwich."

"Did you tell Stella?" I ask, laughing.

"Fuck no!"

"You didn't tell her?" I yell.

"What was I going to say? 'Stella, better put money aside for your son's future therapy, because I just traumatized him with gay porn'?"

"Good point," I say. We sit in silence for a bit, smiling at one another. "Good story, Ash, really good story," I say softly. I feel like hugging him.

"I know. Only to me, right?" he says, shaking his head.

"Only to you," I reply.

I can't believe how many pills he takes—ten altogether. Some pills counteract the negative effects of other pills, and some pills prevent a total breakdown of his immune system. I feel nauseated as I watch him force the pills down his swollen throat. I moan and whine my way through the flu—I envy him his strength. The CD ends and, in the sudden silence that follows, I wonder how much time he has left—how much time I have left with him. My cell phone rings. I know it's my boss, so I go into the cavernous living room. When I return ten minutes later, Ashley seems to be sleeping. I choose another CD and tuck myself in next to him.

"Who was that?" he asks.

"My boss. He wants me to work tonight."

"What'd you tell him?" Ashley asks, braiding my hair.

"I told him it's Sunday, and I'm with my brother."

"Do you like your job?"

"No."

"But you really wanted it, didn't you?"

"How do you know?" I ask.

"Dad told me," he replies.

"How does he know?" I inquire.

"Teddy told Mom, and she told him."

Mental note: tell Teddy to stop relaying personal information to family members. "Turns out it's not really worth the effort," I explain.

"Working for a hot director who lives in New York? Why not?"

"He's a misogynist asshole, for starters."

"Most geniuses are misogynist assholes. Except me, of course," Ashley says.

"You're just an asshole," I reply.

" 'That's Mr. Asshole to you,' " he responds.

"*St. Elmo's Fire.* The job sucks all the energy out of me."

"Ah, energy that could be dedicated to . . . what? Hanging around with Jax and Jordy?"

"You're just jealous I have friends who would take a bullet for me," I tell him.

"Who are you? Kojak?"

"And for your information, my creative energy is very important to me. Being a personal assistant is not exactly my passion in life."

"Oh Jesus, now you sound like Uncle Carchie," Ashley moans.

I sit back, cross my arms and stare across the room—it's the pout I've been perfecting since I was five. Ashley should know better, even with the limited scope of our relationship.

"I was kidding, Alex. Tell me what you want to do with your life, for real."

I stare him down just to make sure he's not going to reduce this to a movie line. "I want to create children's books."

"You want to be a writer? That's great." He actually seems pleased.

"I don't just write them—I do my own drawings, too."

"You can draw? That's not fair. I can't draw."

I roll my eyes. No, but you can direct documentaries that actually make money and win awards.

"So you've been writing a story?" he asks.

"I finished one a few months ago. I can show it to you," I offer. Ashley straightens up in anticipation. "It's in my apartment. I'll get it later."

"Don't forget. Why children's books?"

I shrug. "I'm not sure. I think because they're based purely on imagination, you know? You don't have to worry about logic or reality. Suspension of disbelief is a given."

"I remember Teddy reading to you when you were little. Did you have a thing for Babar?"

I nod, conjuring the image of Teddy reading to me. For the length of a single summer, we sat on the front lawn, under the huge oak tree, and Teddy would read to me, for hours. She acted out all the voices, and wouldn't let any of our neighbors interrupt. I haven't thought about this in years; if Ashley hadn't mentioned it, I think it would've been erased by time from my memory. "Listen, Ash, I was thinking . . ."

"Yeah?" His fingers feel nice in my hair.

"What would you think about me moving in here for a while? You know, to help out?" The words are out of my mouth before I can consider the consequences; then again, we don't have time for consequences.

I feel Ashley's breath catch in his hollow chest. "I think that would be great, Alex," he whispers.

"Yeah, me, too." I lean into him, and we fall asleep in the same bed for the first time in our lives.

The sun is just starting to set when we wake up. I smoke a cigarette while Ashley calls Stella. I make him a cup of tea and pick another CD as soon as I enter the room.

"Alex, what's the craziest, most outrageous thing you've ever done?" he asks.

I don't hesitate. "Senior year of college, I gave this guy Greg a hand job during history class." I've told everyone this, so I can tell Ashley.

"I assume you were watching a film or something?" he asks, laughing.

I nod. "It was dark, but we were surrounded by a hundred students. What's your craziest thing?"

Ashley laughs, presumably at the many answers he could offer. He has lived so much more than I. My life must seem so trivial to him. "I guess it would have to be Thanksgiving, about seven years ago, when I gave Mick a blow job in the bathroom during dinner."

"I remember that guy! He was such a tool," I tell him.

"I know, but he taught me one of my favorite movie lines," he says.

"Go for it," I prod.

"You won't know it. I don't want to embarrass you," he says.

"Try me."

Ashley sucks in a huge breath. At first I think he's being annoyingly melodramatic, but then I realize he's actually short of breath. "'You're either a smoker or you're not a smoker. Pick which one you are and stick with it.'"

For the first time in my life, I wonder if I should pretend to not know something. Ashley looks so diminutive and brittle, but he would hate it if he knew I conceded. That's not what the game is about.

"*Dead Again,*" I say with pride.

"Damn, you're good."

"I know."

Ashley laughs and settles into his mound of pillows. "What's the stupidest thing you've ever done?" he asks.

I sigh. "There are so many to choose from. I suppose my shoplifting phase was the most monumentally asinine. You?"

Ashley pretends to be pensive for a moment, and then smirks. "Um, I guess it would be having unprotected sex."

The knot in my stomach tightens. "Jesus, Ashley, I'm sorry. I shouldn't . . ." I trail off, swallowed by guilt. Do the signals from my brain to my mouth even work? What kind of person would ask him that?

"Hey, I'm the one who posed the question. It's not your fault."

"It's not yours, either, you know. It just . . ." I have no vocabulary for this conversation.

Ashley finishes my thought. "Happens, I know." He looks out the window.

"Did you ever use a condom?" I've never *not* used a condom.

"Once in a while. It just didn't occur to us back then. We weren't exactly worried about getting pregnant. Speaking of the dirty deed—have you actually slept with a woman or just fooled around?"

"What do you want? Bases?" Ashley laughs at the adolescent reference, and I silently congratulate myself on a successful deflection. "Why do you keep asking about my sex life?" I ask.

"Because anytime you or anyone else looks at me, all you think about is *my* sex life and how one chance sexual encounter is going to kill me."

"I'm sorry." I don't know what to say, again. I should rescind my offer to stay with him—clearly, I can't do this. I can barely look at him without wanting to cry.

"Don't be. I think the same thing every time I look in the mirror. Actually, it wasn't a chance encounter at all. It was one of the hottest affairs I've ever had."

"You know, for sure? Who was it?" I ask.

"Tom. He was a grip on the documentary I shot in San Fran.

We spent two months together; he took off for a shoot in Africa, and we never spoke again."

"Did you call him, after you found out?" I whisper.

"Yeah," Ashley answers quietly. "I called everyone."

"And?"

"He's dead."

Ashley promises he'll nap while I go home to pack a bag. He gives me cab money but I take the subway instead—it's faster. I take the 2 to Penn Station and then cross town by way of the shuttle train. I feel like a tourist—these are not subways I normally utilize. At home, I grab my cell phone charger and children's book, write Jordy a short note of explanation, and throw some clothes into a black duffel bag I used in college. Both zippers are broken and there's a small tear in the bottom of the bag. I'm rushing but then I stop short at the door. What am I doing? For most of my life, I didn't even *like* Ashley. Now I'm going to be his nurse? I drop my bags, sit on the couch and chain-smoke, well aware of the perversity involved in loading up on nicotine before re-entering Ashley's bedroom, where death covers the room like dust. I sit and smoke and try to decipher the messages churning through my brain. This feels right, but also strange and unfamiliar, and intimidating. What if I'm cranky and claustrophobic in that capacious, rich apartment? I move into the kitchen and drink half a bottle of water. Would Ashley do this for me? Probably not. Definitely not.

I enter the living room, twirling the bottle of water. My eyes search the room, hunting for something to bring Ashley, but he wouldn't want anything I have to offer. Everything I own is old and tattered, outdated and uninteresting to someone like Ashley. Even my magazines would bore him. The word *provincial* lodges in my brain. We have so little in common—almost nothing. What will we talk about?

I realize I've forgotten to pack all my toiletries, so I march into the bathroom to retrieve my toothbrush, hairbrush and lipstick. I peek into the mirror and examine my face, imagining

Ashley's next to mine. I can't tell if we look alike, and I cannot remember anyone ever commenting on our likenesses, one way or the other. I don't think I resemble either my brother or my sister. Ashley has golden blond hair, the kind that shines by itself. Teddy's hair is as black as onyx, and equally smooth. My hair is brownish, reddish in the summer. Ashley's eyes are blue, Teddy's are blue and mine are . . . brownish. Both Ashley and Teddy inherited my father's height. I barely hit five foot five on a good day. I smile into the mirror, scrutinizing my teeth—at least they're straight, sans braces. Ashley had braces for two years. Cry me a river, Alex—you've got two best friends, an apartment downtown and a kick-ass CD collection. Get over yourself.

I walk to the front door, pick up my bags and survey the apartment for almost a full minute. I inhale, savoring the scent of my home, open the door and leave.

I hear the vomiting before I see it. Ashley is in a ball on the floor, hurling into a leather wastebasket. My throat closes, and I resist the urge to turn around and leave.

"It came out of nowhere," he says, saliva dripping onto his pajamas.

"What can I do?" I ask nervously. Is it too late to change my mind?

Ashley cringes. "Throw the can down the chute, then help me brush my teeth and change my pajamas."

I do as he asks, though I'm not good with puke. Again I wonder if I should even be here. Ashley and I have lived on two different planets for most of our lives, and now I'm going to take care of him? I retrieve a new pair of Calvin Klein pajamas from the drawer. They're so velvety, I wonder if they're cashmere; can Ashley really afford cashmere pj's? I undress my spindly brother as if he were an infant. He winces a bit when I touch him, but I think the contact of our skin hurts me more than him.

After he's dressed, he pops a Valium and invites me into bed.

"Can I ask you one last sex question?" I muse, trying to lighten the mood.

"Sure," Ashley replies.

"Are you a Top or a Bottom?"

"What do you think?" he asks, grinning.

"Top," I answer.

"'Sch-wing!'" he replies, laughing.

"*Wayne's World*," I say between belly laughs.

"OK, my turn—last sex question. Do you, um, get yourself off?" he asks, reddening.

I laugh at him. "No, Ashley. I sleep with men, I slept with a woman, I smoke pot and I spend my weekends at bars called Cock Ring and The Shaft, but I don't touch myself."

Ashley cracks up. "Are you a shower-nozzle girl?" he asks, smirking. I give up; the only way this will work is if I share my life—all of it—with Ashley.

"That's for sissies," I tell him. "I prefer high-priced machinery that requires batteries." Ashley laughs until he can't breathe, which doesn't take very long.

"Tea?" I ask. He shakes his head. We sit in silence for a while, the rhythm of his wheezing both comforting and frightening.

"What do you want your epitaph to say?" he asks suddenly.

"Ashley, don't go there," I beg.

"C'mon, we're just talking. Besides, you need to know what mine should say."

"I haven't really thought about it," I tell him.

"But if you were to die tomorrow, or next week, or next month," he says slowly, "what would be your final message to the world?"

I stare at the plush carpet. "I don't know."

"Want to know mine?"

"No." I've never thought about epitaphs before. Ashley has obviously been pondering his for a while. I swallow the urge to vomit.

" 'Get busy living, or get busy dying,' " he says hoarsely.

I laugh, even though I want to cry. "*Shawshank Redemption*. Mom and Dad will hate that. Teddy, too."

Ashley rolls his beautiful eyes. "Care, not, next. Mom still thinks it's her fault, because she named me Ashley." We laugh together.

I stare across at the park for a while, hoping Ashley will fall asleep.

He doesn't doze off; he picks lint off my ancient sweatshirt. "Jesus, Alex, don't you ever buy new clothes? I wish I could take you to Barney's," he mutters.

"So do I," I reply. "We've never gone shopping together, as adults." We share a look. We've done so few things together as adults. And now he can barely get out of bed. How did this happen to us? Why did we let it happen?

"Movie-line game—speed round, ready?" he asks, slowly sitting up in preparation.

"Ready," I answer.

"'I love the smell of napalm in the morning,'" he starts.

"*Apocalypse Now.* 'My name is Inigo Montoya. You killed my father. Prepare to die.'"

"*Princess Bride.* 'You *must* chill!'"

"*Say Anything.* 'Pity about poor Catherine; tick tock, tick tock.'"

"*Silence of the Lambs.* 'I want my two dollars!'"

"*Better Off Dead.* 'Demented and sad, but social.'"

"*The Breakfast Club.* 'I will not be ignored, Dan.'"

"*Fatal Attraction.* 'Sofa city, sweetheart.'"

"*Sixteen Candles.* 'She's my sister, she's my daughter, she's my sister!'"

"*Chinatown.* 'The greatest trick the devil ever pulled was convincing the world he didn't exist.'"

Silence. Oh my God. Ashley frowns, the wheels in his mind turning at a frenetic pace. I hold my breath.

"Give me a second," he says. "It's coming." He looks away, then back, his tired eyes fixed on me. "I have no fucking clue," he admits. He reaches out, takes my hand and kisses it. "You win."

"*The Usual Suspects,*" I whisper. Ashley nods. "Does this mean the game's over?" I ask.

"No way," he answers. "We can play for as long as you want." I stare at my brother; both of us know that's not possible. My eyes fill with tears, but then he smiles that killer smile and for an instant I forget why I'm here. Ashley winks at me and I grin at him, wiping away the two tears that trickled down my cheeks. We watch each other for a few moments.

"I'm beat," I announce, heading for the door.

"Me, too," Ashley sighs. "We'll play Star Wars Trivial Pursuit tomorrow?" he asks brightly.

"Sure thing," I answer. Ashley settles into the last bed he'll ever know. He blows me a kiss, and I blow it right back. I turn off the light, linger in the doorway for a moment, then close his door.

In the kitchen, I survey Ashley's bar. Almost every type of liquor is represented—it looks like a real bar. I smile when I see my pals Bacardi and Gray Goose. I pour myself a vodka tonic and slurp it down. I check the fridge and write a note to myself on a yellow Post-it: *Buy cranberry juice, lemons and limes.*

I finish my drink and open the linen closet—it's as big as my bathroom. I carefully transport a set of sheets from the meticulously organized closet into the guest room, which is twice the size of my bedroom downtown. The walls are sand-colored, the lush quilt is chocolate brown and a collection of antique glass vases sits on the dresser. As I make the queen-sized bed, I think about every pep talk I've ever heard in a movie. But this isn't a movie, Alex. This is real life. It's *your* life. I then switch to clichés: *You can do anything you set your mind to. It's not whether you win or lose; it's how you play the game. Mind over matter.* I laugh at my stupidity, and then marvel at Ashley's sheets again. I've never slept on such luxurious bedding, even in a hotel. I throw the pillows toward the headboard, kick off my shoes and sit on the bed, ashamed at my vacuousness. My brother is dying and I'm looking forward to sleeping on his sheets.

My stomach starts to hurt; I blame it on the vodka. An intense pain flares through me. I crumble onto the floor, then race into the bathroom, slapping my hand on the wall to turn on the light. I throw up in the toilet, one violent upheaval, and then rinse my face at the marble sink. This isn't from one glass of vodka. I clench my eyes shut, then open them and look in the mirror. When I see my reflection, I realize what made me sick: fear is etched all over my face.

Ashley died four months later. My parents and Teddy came and went—after my boss fired me for losing focus, I spent every day with him. No matter how hard I tried, though, I couldn't make up the time Ashley and I had lost.

I sold the apartment as quickly as possible, knowing I would drown in thoughts of him each time I entered it. I deposited the money from the apartment, and my inheritance—just under one million dollars after taxes—in a high-yield savings account.

Four years have passed and I still have not touched Ashley's money.

2

Sam is dead. Four years after losing my brother, I am once again forced to say good-bye, this time to my therapist, before I am prepared to do so. Sam's death did not come as much of a surprise—he was slowly ravaged by cancer—yet when I get word of his death, I can't help the swell of disbelief from rising through my body. Sam bequeathed me a cryptic message—the line "You're missing a piece of yourself" on a sheet of paper.

I saw Sam once a week for the first year, twice a week for two more years, and then once a week for another year. Sam knew me when I was a complete wreck, as opposed to the picture of mental health I am now. I adored Sam, not only because I trusted him with my psyche but also because he was a rebel, a throwback to the days I've always wished I had grown up in. Sam died a happy man, knowing he'd lived his life the way he wanted, without taking crap from anyone. He was an outdoorsy-type who refused to wear anything other than jeans unless he was at a wedding or a funeral, and he chain-smoked unfiltered Camel cigarettes. His voice was a bit creepy, so husky it sounded like his voice box was lined with tree bark.

It's just after noon when a nameless, faceless voice calls to tell me about Sam. I write the funeral information on the back of a magazine and then sit, almost frozen, staring at the cluttered kitchen table. A few minutes pass, I guess, and then I call

Jordy on her cell phone. I get her voice mail—she's in the library—so the phone must be off. I dial Jax's cell phone even though I know he's working lunch and the phone is in his locker. I suddenly feel claustrophobic, so I snatch my bag off the chair and rush into the hallway. The elevator takes too long. I use my whole body to push open the door to the stairs and practically tumble down the seven flights to the lobby. The glare of the fluorescent lights makes me squint. I shove my sunglasses on and burst out of the building. I don't remember grabbing my cell phone but it's in my hand so I call my older sister Teddy at work as I walk down Broadway.

"It's me."

"Hi, Alex. How are you?"

"Sam died."

"Oh Jesus, I'm sorry. We knew this would happen, though, right?"

"He's gone, Teddy."

"I know."

"Can I come to your office?"

Teddy sighs. "I'm on my way into a meeting."

"Can't you cancel it?"

"I wish I could, Alex. But these clients are in from Tokyo."

"Can you meet me afterward? I'll wait for you."

Teddy sighs again. "I have a lunch meeting and then a conference call and then a meeting with my accountant that I've already cancelled twice."

I turn left onto 11th Street to get away from all the people. "It's not tax season," I point out.

"I know, but I've been moving money around and I need to go over things with Gloria."

"Who?"

"My accountant."

"Oh."

"I'll call you later. Where will you be?"

I shrug, knowing she can't see me. "Wandering around."

"Where is everyone?" she asks.

She means Jax and Jordy—they're my "everyone." "I can't reach them."

"I promise I'll call you as soon as I can, as soon as I'm done with my accountant."

"OK." Good thing I live in Manhattan—I'm just another girl crying on the street.

"Try to do something productive. That always helps me when things get out of control."

My knees fold under me as we hang up. I land on a step outside the loading door of some antiques store as the sounds of the city wither away. All I hear is Teddy's voice saying *my accountant, do something productive, moving money around, my accountant.*

I don't have an accountant because I don't have any money. But I do have money, a lot of it. Ashley's money. It's just sitting in an invisible pile in some bank. Up until now, I thought the money would make me feel even worse about losing a brother I never had the chance to really talk to until it was too late. But maybe it will make me feel better. Maybe if I spend Ashley's money and buy things and hire an accountant and root my feet to the ground, I will feel better. I can be like Teddy but without the vacuous corporate job. I can pay for things and become a useful member of society. I can transfer this huge wad of money into a checking account and it will always be there—accessible twenty-four hours a day.

I peel myself off the steel step and retrace my way to my apartment. Once in my living room, it takes me fifteen minutes to find the paperwork from Ashley's lawyer. Then it takes me another five to find the name of the bank where Ashley's money has been hibernating for the last four years. It's my bank—the same bank where my paychecks live. There's a branch around the corner. I plug my cell phone into its charger and go back outside.

I meet with some woman (Linda? Leslie?) who looks sixty but is probably in her late forties. She explains that the interest on my inheritance has grown quite a bit over the years, and I might want to consider a better investment than a savings account. I tuck the scrap of paper she hands me into my back pocket, amazed at the money's ability to grow without even trying. The savings account holds over a million dollars, and as I march home I remind myself, again and again, that it's mine.

I don't know much about money, except that it feels really fucking good to have it after not having it for so long. I reach Teddy in between meetings, and she and her accountant take care of all the logistics for me. Exactly one-half of the money is put in some sort of escrow account so it will continue to grow. As a senior vice president of a worldwide investment-banking firm, Teddy knows exactly what to do—she's a whiz with numbers—and for once I don't care that she takes complete control. Teddy has been badgering me to use this money since Ashley died—it became yet another point of contention between us. We suddenly had very little to talk about, if we weren't yelling about Ashley's money, or my grieving process, or whatever else we felt like yelling about. It was while we were sitting shiva for Ashley that we drifted apart—or I drifted away.

When we were young, Teddy was my whole world. She thought of the best show-and-tell items for me to bring to school, and she helped me with all my silly school projects, like dioramas and book reports. She taught me the multiplication tables, and tutored me in long division. I was the most popular girl in third grade for a few weeks due to the colorful gems Teddy BeDazzled onto my jean jacket. When I was seven and she was twelve, she taught me to roller-skate, forward and backward. She became obnoxious while traversing puberty, but by the time I arrived at that troublesome age, she had settled into the changes and relayed all the important information to me. She offered me every book she read, so my reading level was above average for my age, and we used to cuddle in bed at night, whispering about the lives of our favorite characters. When we passed each other in the hall at school, both surrounded by chirpy, clamorous girlfriends, she winked at me. That subtle wink relayed a profusion of love, one that didn't dissipate, until Ashley died.

* * *

It's the day after Ashley's funeral. Teddy greets each and every guest at the front door, while the doorbell makes me shudder and look for the nearest escape route. She chats—with aunts, uncles, cousins, good friends, fake friends and acquaintances—about the stock market or the weather or when she and Max plan on having children. From my spot in the corner of the room, I suddenly no longer recognize my sister. I realize she's being mature and responsible, but why doesn't she break down? She shed a few tears at the cemetery, but other than that, I have yet to see her cry.

"You want a bagel?"

I look up, shaking the fog out of my head. It's Jordy.

"No, thanks."

"Alex, you have to eat."

She squeezes into the space next to me and we share the rocking chair. "You sound like my mother."

"She sent me over here, actually. She hasn't seen you ingest anything since you got here. Truthfully, neither have I. You're going to get dehydrated."

I hold up the water bottle that's been traveling with me for the past four days.

"Do you want to go for a walk?" Jordy asks.

"I can't—I'll get in trouble." I motion toward Teddy, who is refilling coffee cups.

"Who are all these people?" Jax asks, joining us in the corner.

I shrug. "Some are friends of my parents. Some are Teddy's co-workers. Ashley's friends were here yesterday. Those two over there are your parents."

Jax looks them up and down disdainfully. "When we got home last night, I heard my father say to my mother that he'd never seen so many fags in one room."

Jordy smacks him. "Shut up, Jax, for Christ's sake."

"What? Alex knows my father is an asshole. Ashley probably did, too."

I nod, watching Jim, Jax's father. As if to prove Jax's point, the door opens and half of Ashley's film crew enters—five men,

three women, six homosexuals. Teddy is upon them immediately, shaking hands, offering drinks, introducing them to my
parents. Jim says something to his wife, Ellen, and then heads
to the opposite side of the room. Once situated on the couch,
he stares at them as if they're a zoo exhibit—something for-
eign, something he can't understand, something he doesn't
want to be too close to.

Teddy approaches us. "Alexandra, do you think you could
possibly stand up and talk to people for maybe fifteen minutes?"

"No."

"Is there a reason you're acting like a five-year-old? Ashley's
friends drove out from the city. You can show them some respect."

"I thought paying a shiva call was a way for *them* to show respect," Jax says.

Teddy stares him down. "Shut up, Jax. I don't need your
help. Alexandra, would five minutes really kill you?"

Nice choice of words, Teddy. I burst into tears. Jordy wraps
an arm around my neck and I bury my head in her shoulder.

"Jesus Christ," Teddy mutters as she walks away.

After a few minutes, I decide I should splash frigid water on
my face—maybe it will freeze the tears in my eyes and prevent
them from falling. I walk toward the bathroom—stopping to
say hello to Ashley's people—and pass my father on the way.
He's in the hallway, rearranging pictures that have hung in the
same position for twenty years.

"Dad?"

He turns around. "What?"

"Are you OK?"

He smiles—a real smile. "Sure, honey. Are you?"

"No, not really." But he doesn't hear—he's on to the next
picture.

I have to wait in line for the bathroom. I decide to dash upstairs so I can use my own bathroom. Afterward, as I'm about to
descend the stairs, I hear my mother crying—the kind of crying that makes you physically ill from all the heaving and gasp-

ing—so I push her door open. She's on the bed, facedown, screaming "That goddamn disease killed my son!" and sobbing into the pillow. Ellen is stroking her back and whispering into her ear. I walk into the room but before I reach the bed, my mother looks up, her face red and puffy and tortured, and when she sees me, she breaks down all over again. I back out of the room, run downstairs, find Jax and Jordy and leave the house. We hang out in Jax's tree house for a while, until I return to the house of mourning.

When I wake up the next morning, I immediately feel differently. I wish I could talk to Ashley, as I usually do, but today I smile—today I would have something good to tell him. The haze of sudden action has burned off but, even though I feel guilty about it, Ashley's money is the first thing that enters my mind. I use a couple thousand immediately, to pay off the balances of my undergraduate loans and both my credit cards. I buy some materials for the new children's book I'm working on—something my parents consider a hobby and I think of as my calling in life. I purchase a dozen sketch pads, a sixty-four pack of colored pens and a couple reams of the expensive, thick paper I prefer. I even take Teddy to Barney's and force her to pick out a ridiculously expensive outfit—with her deep blue eyes and raven hair, the silver dress looks gorgeous on her and fills me with a sense of satisfaction that lasts for days.

I buy my Uncle Carchie a new television and have it shipped to his cabin in Saugerties, New York. Carchie shuns all technology except his audio equipment, so his television is about fifteen years old. I'm not forcing him to change his ways, but I know he's been watching more TV than usual these days. Monthly chemo treatments have devastated his once-impervious body, and he often spends an entire day on the couch, yelling and cursing at the idiots who populate daytime television. With a thirty-two-inch screen, he'll be able to see every ridiculous detail.

Carchie is my great-uncle on my mother's side, but he is not exactly a cherished member of her family. I vaguely recall an idiotic incident from decades ago in which her relatives blamed Carchie for something, but when I press for details, my mother just mumbles, "He pissed a lot of people off. That's all there is to it." Mom likes to pretend she belongs to the faction of her family that disapproves of Carchie and his lifestyle, but I know she calls him every other day, harassing him about the importance of a balanced diet and reminding him that my father's boss beat melanoma a few years ago. As a child, she adored Carchie and was devastated when her father and Carchie severed their fraternal bond. Years later, when she and my father were having problems and needed time and space in which to work out their differences, she turned to Carchie, since she was afraid to reveal her marital problems to her parents or siblings. Carchie offered to watch Ashley, Teddy and me for the remainder of the summer, and my mother was speechless (I wish I could remember *that*) with gratitude. By the time school rolled around, my parents had rediscovered their marital bliss and I had a new tutor, friend and partner in crime. Carchie was the first person to recognize and encourage my non-traditional, artistic side—he considers me his protégé. After that summer, my parents stayed in close touch with him, though we were threatened with obscenely painful punishments if we ever mentioned his name in front of any member of Mom's family. Carchie didn't mind; he had the best of both worlds as far as he was concerned—he regained the only member of his family he truly liked, he got to be a part of our lives and watch us grow up, and he never had to see "those miserable schmucks."

Finally, I take my three closest friends—Casey, Jordy and Jax—out to dinner, which winds up costing me about two thousand bucks, since Casey lives in Chicago and I fly her in to Manhattan. All three are pleased I've finally acknowledged Ashley's money. We eat at the hot-restaurant-of-the-month and, with all of us dressed up, we look like we actually belong.

I wear my favorite black pants, funky sandals and a tight, backless tank top. I've only spent a few days of spring outdoors, but my hair is already two shades lighter. The emotional avalanche brought about by Sam's death has affected my eating habits—which weren't exactly normal to begin with—so I've lost about eight pounds in the last two weeks. My stomach is flatter and my legs are leaner than usual (to be honest, I kind of like the results), though only Casey notices, since the others see me on a daily basis. My skin is on its way to being tan, and the annual flock of freckles has taken up residence on my nose and cheeks.

Casey, as usual, wears a cool vintage shirt with black pants, her tiny thighs nearly invisible. Casey somehow manages to look both adorable and pretty at the same time, her face dotted with freckles but highlighted by sparkling green eyes. Jax insists on wearing a tuxedo—well, his version of a tuxedo, which consists of black pants, the customary white shirt over a black T-shirt and black leather suspenders. Jax pulls his long, ginger-colored hair into a ponytail, and the finished product is truly a work of art. I feel eyes fall upon us every time we go out, and I revel in Jax's beauty. Jordy is the only one of us who appears in what can be considered entirely appropriate attire. Only I know, however, that her entire outfit is from Target and cost her less than fifty dollars. Still, she looks beautiful. But Jordy—with her mahogany-colored hair (recently enhanced with an indigo-colored streak), almost-lilac eyes and perfect complexion—is empirically beautiful. The streamlined, flowery sundress completes the overall picture.

We take our time at dinner, not only because we've never been in this environment before but because I want to remember how this feels, being surrounded by those who know me best. Teddy was supposed to join us but she got stuck at work again. Teddy is always at work, unless she's on her way to work, or on her way to a work meeting, or on her way home from work, where she'll spend a few hours with her husband, Max, and then go to bed in preparation for another day of work. I try not to notice her absence. Instead I focus on the mutual adoration at the table. The three of them know each other very well, having formed an affinity through me over the years.

Jax and his family moved next door to me when we were five, and we fell for one another on the spot. Jax taught me how to cook in his Easy-Bake Oven, and I introduced him to the complex simplicity of baseball, which Ashley, Teddy and I were obsessed with, compliments of our father. Twenty-three years later, Jax remains a devoted Yankees fan and I still can't bake an edible batch of cookies. Jax is known to the rest of the world as Jack, but as a child, I had trouble pronouncing that compound, multi-syllable word, so he became Jax.

My parents and Jax's parents are still close friends, which gets awkward at times, since my mother gives me weekly updates on Jax's father, who is dying of pancreatic cancer, while Jax goes for weeks without mentioning his dad. Fortunately, I have a tendency to shun family gatherings, so it isn't difficult for me to avoid seeing Jim. Our relationship has changed irrevocably, and even though I know Jim still cares about me, I can't bring myself to regard him with affection.

* * *

It's the day after Jax came out to his parents; we're home on winter break from college. Jax spent the previous night in my bed, crying and sleeping. Neither one of us expected his father to react so ferociously to Jax's confession. It snowed all night, and I'm doing my father a favor—he has a bad cold—by shoveling the driveway. Jim is shoveling his driveway, and we converge by the street, scraping our shovels over the icy pavement. Jim looks at me and smiles. I ignore him and focus on the red shovel as it stabs into the white snow.

"How's school?" he asks.

"Fine."

"Getting good grades?"

I nod.

"Making new friends?"

I nod again.

Jim stops shoveling and stands upright, leaning on his shovel. "I suppose Jack told you he's a homo."

I stop shoveling but can't look up at him. This is a man who has driven me to the roller rink countless times; he held my hand when I got stung by a bee in his backyard. He has known me since I wore a size 6X. "Jax is Jax, no matter who he sleeps with," I tell him.

"Jack has sex with men. What kind of man has sex with other men?"

"My brother."

Jim shakes his head and continues shoveling. "Jack is a homo," he says, walking up his driveway.

*   *   *

Jax sees his parents only when he absolutely has to, and I can't blame him for that, which is what I tell my mother every time she mentions Jax's absence. She's done what she can in terms of talking to Jim, but I think the (supposed) adults just try to avoid the whole issue because, by damning Jax, Jim is damning Ashley by association, and my mother can't handle that. Funny how perspectives change when it's one of your own. My mother never gave a shit about AIDS until Ashley died (not when he *got* it, just when he *died* from it), and now she dispenses information—the latest medicines, survival statistics, new research—as if she were the Surgeon General of Westchester County. Jim's only son tells him he's gay and suddenly Jax is banished to the other end of the table at Thanksgiving dinner and the two of them have barely exchanged a paragraph's worth of words since Jax came out. Jax's mother sides with Jim. I'm not sure if it's out of love or fear. There's enough passive-aggressive dysfunction in the two houses to fill the quota for the entire neighborhood.

Jordy entered my life a few years later, at sleepaway camp. We met the first day—on the bus. She was seated by a window; a knapsack and a teddy bear occupied the aisle seat.

"Is anyone sitting here?" I asked meekly. I wasn't scared, but it was the first time in a long time I had been in a situation where I didn't know anyone.

Jordy shook her head and moved her stuff. I sat down, gripping my own backpack and teddy bear. By the time the buses hit the halfway point when we stopped for lunch, we were best friends. We did not attend high school or college together but used the phone, as well as intimate, rambling letters, to stay close. Two weeks after college graduation, we moved into a perfect apartment (by New York City standards), thrilled to finally wake up and see each other every day.

Casey and I met in college, the two black sheep of a bubbly, frivolous sorority. We were both English majors, smokers and intellectual snobs. Our friendship was forged in one unforgettable week; we laughed through *Harold and Maude* and cried through *The Awakening* and recognized each other as members of the same soul tribe. Casey is a burgeoning theatrical producer in Chicago, and we are lucky if we see each other twice a year.

After dinner, we drink way too many martinis at a dark, smoky lounge and follow that up with hours of dancing at one of the biggest gay clubs in the city, a converted warehouse on the West Side. Jax took me there last year for my twenty-seventh birthday, but the thirty-dollar cover charge makes it too pricey for us to frequent. The night ends at dawn, and it is by far the best two grand I have ever spent (not that I've shelled out two thousand dollars in one lump sum before).

The following day, I'm twenty minutes late to Sam's funeral, partially due to subway delays but mostly because I leave my apartment one minute before the ceremony is to start. I was up early, but lost all sense of time as I sketched some characters for my book. I'm sure my tardiness is a sign of some deep-rooted refusal to believe that my shrink is actually dead, but since I am now without a therapist, I cannot be certain of anything.

I know I'm pushing the limits of good taste by wearing calf-high black boots in mid-May, but I just can't bear the thought of heels; they're too precarious, unarmed. I do my best New York–pace walk to the church, silently cursing myself for leaving my cigarettes on the coffee table. I am thrilled (selfish, I know) to see a few angry clouds of smoke billowing above the front door of the church. There are five people puffing away, not exactly in a group—they're standing near one another, but not too close, as if they crave the mournful company but are fearful of actually speaking. Four of the five are over forty, so I zoom in on the twenty-something, an adorable guy wearing black pants, a gray button-down shirt, a Prada leather jacket and paint-covered work boots.

"It hasn't started yet?" I ask the cutie.

"They're running late. You've got about five minutes," he answers.

"I hate when people do this to me, but . . ." Wow, nice eyes. "Can I bum a smoke? I forgot mine and I could really—"

"Not a problem." He hands me a cigarette (my brand, bonus points) and lights it with a well-used silver Zippo.

I take a deep, luscious drag. "Thank you."

He nods, his wavy, brown hair falling over green eyes. "I'm Tucker," he says, offering his hand.

"Alex." We shake. His hand feels soft but worn. The beds of his nails are rainbows of color, paint etched deep within them.

"They should let us smoke in the church, in Sam's honor," he says.

"Is it crowded in there?" I wonder aloud.

Tucker nods, tossing his hair again. "Packed. He had his practice for years and years."

"Plus he taught and supervised," I add. We stare at one another for a moment, smoke floating between us.

"Shit, I have no idea how I can deal without him," Tucker blurts out, slumping onto the step.

I'm not sure what to do or say, so I plop down next to him. "I haven't figured out a long-term solution as of yet, but I'm planning on getting completely shit-faced tonight. Feel free to join me."

Did I just ask him out?

Tucker smirks. "Only if you let me treat."

"I hardly know you. I can't let you subsidize my debauchery."

"Ooh, fifty-cent word." Tucker stands up, offers his hand and pulls me to my feet. "Don't worry about it. I'm good for it."

I can't tell if he's joking but I don't have time to ask because

we're ushered inside and suddenly I'm having trouble catching
my breath. Tucker guides me toward two empty seats just before the ceremony begins. A handful of Sam's colleagues make
speeches, seemingly smug in the knowledge that they are the
only ones who really knew Sam. It's an odd feeling to be surrounded by a few hundred people I don't know, all of us grieving the same person. We have nothing in common except our
attachment to a man who simplified and improved our lives.
Many of the men wear sunglasses inside the church, and several
women weep throughout the service. I'm a little distracted,
having never been to a non-Jewish funeral. I'm also stifling a cacophony of sneezes, thanks to aggressive allergies stimulated by
the plethora of floral arrangements. Jews don't allow floral
arrangements (I can't remember why), so at Jewish funerals I
don't run the risk of making an ass out of myself with my sneezing, which for some mysterious reason always comes in threes.

Tucker suppresses a smile when the sneezing actually starts.
After the third and what I pray to my non-existent God will be
the last, he reaches into that gorgeously expensive Prada jacket
and hands me a packet of tissues. Not a balled-up, used tissue,
but a clean, unopened pack of Kleenex tissues. I consider marrying him directly after the funeral.

When it's over, Tucker walks me to the subway station after
giving me another cigarette. We decide to meet at Finny's Place
on 23rd Street around ten o'clock tonight. I tell him I'll be with
a friend—I have plans with Jax and cannot in good conscience
cancel on a guy I have known for the majority of my life in favor
of a guy I have known for an hour. Tucker laughs and tells me
he has no problem being a third wheel.

On the subway ride home, I wonder if my friendly interac-
tion with Tucker is disrespectful to Sam. I think he'd be OK
with it, especially since Tucker and I initially bonded over a
need for nicotine. I can hear Sam laughing and realize I would
normally have a session with him tomorrow. There will be no
more sessions with Sam. Sam is dead.

ᔪᔭ

My apartment is empty when I return home, so I change into boxers and an old tank top and crawl into bed. It's late afternoon but with the blinds closed, the room is dark enough for me to hide under the covers. My eyes dart around the room, and I am astounded by the external order of my belongings. A six-foot bookshelf is meticulously organized, not in alphabetical order but in size order, with my favorite books lodged on the bottom shelf. My dresser and armoire hold drawers full of clothing, all folded neatly and arranged in a manner only I comprehend. The walls of the room are a shade of yellow— "sunflower" yellow. Jordy painted over the drab, lackluster white while I was away. She told me the color yellow is supposed to have a calming effect, so inhabiting a room with yellow walls might somehow quiet the spasmodic insurgence of my thoughts. Jordy understands the harmony of my room, so when she painted, she took great care to restore my things to their precise places.

My writing and illustration materials are housed in a smooth oak box with a bronze latch that Jax bought at a garage sale for two dollars. Blank paper and works-in-progress, like the first seven pages of my new book, are confined to my slightly damaged childhood toy box, the lid of which is now a dull, diminished black. I painted it when I was twelve, in a burst of rebellion against the pre-existing stenciled dolls. The sides are comprised of a series of parallel bars, and the lid is a solid, squeaking slab of wood. A shoe box filled with rejection letters from literary agents is wedged into a corner of the toy box. Even the framed photographs on the wall are methodically positioned, so the result is a symmetrical exhibit of those I care about most. For some reason, however, two of the frames refuse to remain aligned—they consistently tilt to one side or the other. No matter how many times I rehang them, the photos of Jordy and me reject the rigid rules of straightness.

I extricate myself from the cocoon of blankets and shuffle across the room to insert a CD into the stereo, the cool, hardwood floor launching chills through my bare feet, up my spine and across my chest, settling on my shoulders. On the way back to my bed, I suddenly get that incomprehensible, quivering feeling in my hands that ceases only when I reach behind the pine headboard and remove the tattered satchel from its hiding spot. I tuck myself into bed, release the frail drawstring and deposit the contents into my hand. I close my eyes, relishing the sensation of the smooth, sympathetic pills while detesting myself at the same time. There are twenty pills left—twelve cylindrical painkillers and eight pink sleeping pills. If I peer into the musky corners of my mind, I can visualize the other pills—all twenty-eight of them. I'm still not sure how the ones I now hold escaped notice—I assume they were furrowed into the folds of my quilt when I slipped into blissful unconsciousness—it appears that no one made the bed, which didn't need to be made, since I passed out without mussing the sheets, so no one retrieved the pills I did not get a chance to swallow. I returned home from a forty-five-day stay in the nuthouse and found almost half my stash waiting for me beneath the benevolent comfort of my cerulean quilt. Webster Ridge, my temporary home in a picturesque town in Massachusetts, was actually quite nice, though I didn't discover the serene landscape until I was granted Grounds Privileges two weeks into my stay. Visitors were not allowed until my fifth week—thirty-five days passed before I saw anyone other than patients, doctors, therapists and counselors. I was lucky enough to land a single room, so I had plenty of time alone to think, wonder and obsess about the fact that I had done exactly what I did not want to do: fail to kill myself.

I was allowed to use the phone, but I quickly realized that talking to Jax, Jordy and my family was dreadful, for me and for them. Especially Jordy. I had known she would be the one to find me, the thought of which made me dizzy and nauseated, but there just wasn't any way around it—I lived with Jordy, and there was nowhere else to take the pills but in my own bed. I didn't want to die in a park or at a random hotel room. I had planned meticulously, and chose my day based on Jordy's schedule. After I ingested my potpourri of pills, I had four-and-a-half hours, which should have been plenty of time. But Jordy's afternoon classes were cancelled because of a pipe explosion in the building. Two hours was not enough time for the pills to take me away. She found me on my bed, vomit on the floor, my suicide letters stacked neatly on my dresser. She saved my life and I hated her for it. I'm sure the image of me—her best friend, sprawled unconscious—is stained in her memory, and I'm sure she hates me for that. I didn't expect to live, though, and wasn't prepared for the avalanche of guilt that nearly paralyzed me. I felt guilty beforehand, of course, and tried my best to apologize and explain myself in the letter I wrote her. It still amazes me that Jordy missed the pills in my bed, but then again, I can't even conjure up an image of her cleaning up after my suicide attempt without curling into a ball, so I try not to think about it.

Only Sam knew about my clandestine reserve and, though he didn't exactly approve of it, he understood my need for a tangible reminder of the day I tried to kill myself. But Sam is dead, so the secret is now mine. Ashley would think I am so very weak for refusing to relinquish this link to my past, a past that is hideously bleak and scorched. It took a year for the shadows to descend, and then suddenly I was immersed in an unfathomable darkness. Regret is still the first emotion I encounter every morning, and every time I see Teddy, I glimpse the anger behind her eyes—anger at me for living a type of lifestyle that allowed me to drop everything so I could spend every second with Ashley as his life slowly skidded off into a hollow void; anger at me for not being able to withstand the aftermath, for being so weak to capitulate to depression, for trying to silence the memories by killing myself. I'm sure a part of Teddy scoffed at my reaction to Ashley's death. She probably viewed—or views—my response as incongruous; after all, it was Teddy and Ashley who had cultivated a thriving bond all their lives. I had only just begun to appreciate or understand him when he died. On family car trips—whether to a local restaurant or the New England Aquarium or the Jersey shore—Teddy always sat in the middle and balanced two conversations, one with Ashley, to her right, and one with me, to her left. I remember when I was five, six and seven, Teddy and Ashley would huddle together at meals, whispering and commiserating about secrets to which I was never privy. I was stuck talking to my parents about school or the latest episode of *Wonder Woman*. Teddy never detached from me for too long, but when she and Ashley aligned, my world felt flatter, and far lonelier. I wasn't jealous of Ashley when Teddy leaned in his direction—closeness with Ashley seemed an impossibility—for some reason, from a very young age, I stopped trying to know my older, and only, brother.

But it wasn't only about losing Ashley without ever really having him. My life became a one-way tunnel with no light, no air and no potential. I never stopped loving Jax or Jordy or Casey or my family, but in a way I did sort of stop loving in general. Every breath I took was a depressed one, and everything in my life became infused with sadness. That's all I knew, depression, and I wanted more than anything to make the hopelessness evaporate. The only way that seemed possible, though, was to make myself disappear.

I shake the pills around in my palm like dice for a moment, until disgust saturates me. Suddenly I can no longer tolerate the tiny enemies in my hand. I roll them into the satchel, lean over the headboard and banish the contraband to its dark, desolate recess. I wait for sleep but toss and turn, yearning for an impermeable shield to protect me.

I leave my apartment at a quarter to nine. The evening air is breezy and invigorating, and as I walk down Third Avenue I mentally bury the emotional explosion, and subsequent repulsion, brought about by fondling my secret supply. I envision Tucker—his cloudless complexion, searing eyes and appealing smile—but that just makes me nervous, so instead I picture Jax, rewinding the tape in my mind to display snippets of our shared life. With the exception of college, every significant memory contains an image of Jax. Even though I saw him two days ago, I suddenly long to look into his bottomless, earnest eyes, hear his thunderous, baritone laugh and disclose my every thought to him.

We made plans to meet at the bar at nine o'clock so I can fill him in on the funeral and Tucker. Jax looks great in black pants, a green rayon shirt and black shoes. His hair is down—a few loose strands dance around his eyes. I'm wearing gray capri pants, a purple tank top and black sandals. If I weren't expecting Tucker, my hair would be pulled back, away from my face, but I might need to hide behind my hair at some point tonight. Jax refuses my offer to buy him a beer, so we each get our own and head to our regular table in the garden out back. After pooling our singles to program the jukebox for the next hour, we do what we do best—talk about our lives, gossip about celebrities and fantasize about possible scenarios for our future. Three beers later, Tucker strolls in, looking even more adorable than at the funeral. His jeans fit him perfectly, in all the right places, and he now wears a black T-shirt underneath the Prada leather jacket. Seconds before he reaches our table, Jax turns to me and says, "You can have the guy if I can have the jacket." I elbow him in the ribs, knocking over his beer in the process. Tucker sees the entire exchange.

"At least you've stopped sneezing," he says to me.

"Funny. Tucker, this is Jax. Jax, this is Tucker, my funeral friend." They shake hands, and Tucker takes off his jacket, tossing it on the fourth chair.

"Can I buy you a replacement beer?" he asks Jax.

"Sure," Jax replies. Tucker takes a quick look at my half-empty beer and heads to the bar.

"You won't accept a beer from me but you'll take one from him?"

"Alex, you know how I feel about new-money people. You've read *The Great Gatsby*."

"Fuck you, Jax. I try to do something nice for you—"

Jax gives me the hand. "You know what you can do? Get a piece of Tucker and tell me all about it."

"Nice, Jax. I wonder what your boy toy would say about that."

"He wouldn't mind one bit. You know the old saying," he says, smirking.

"You can look but you can't touch?" I ask.

Jax laughs. "That only applies to breeders, babycakes." Jax and I have been calling one another *babycakes* for about five years, ever since he passed along Armistead Maupin's *Tales of the City* series to me. I read them all in the course of one week-end.

But I hate the term *breeder*. Ashley used it often during our time together, probably because he knew it annoyed me. Just because I have sex with guys doesn't mean I actually want to procreate. "So what do you queer folk say?" I ask, not sure I want to know.

"You can bump but you can't hump," he answers, entirely too pleased with himself. Tucker returns to the table with three beers and interrupts my response.

Before he sits, he holds up his bottle. "To Sam," he says. "May he feel extremely guilty for deserting us." Tucker and I touch bottles.

Jax lifts his bottle. "To my own shrink, may she live forever, and to Alex's search for 'the missing piece.' " I'm not thrilled at Jax's mention of Sam's note, but Tucker doesn't question it so I let it slide. We all take a long sip of the cold beer. Tucker sits and lights a cigarette in one fluid motion, appealing to my twisted sense of sensuality.

"So, Tucker, what's your story?" I ask. Jax looks at me and I shrug—better to be blunt than to waste my time on a guy with whom I have nothing in common.

"Well, as you know, my shrink just died. I'm twenty-six years old and just finished graduate school. I didn't particularly want the degree, since I have no plans to teach art, but I figured it would keep my father off my back. He's not too thrilled about me and 'the art thing,' as he calls it. So graduate school allowed me to keep painting, remain financially secure and avoid his wrath for another few years."

"What's up with the name?" Jax asks. I nudge him under the table and he pinches my leg in return. I'd been wondering the same thing, but I would've posed the question a bit more grace-fully.

Tucker swallows half his beer and answers. "My father is Charles Tucker Spencer. I hate the name Charles and deplore the name Charlie, so I've always been Tucker."

Jax gasps, loudly. I light a cigarette, stalling. I take too long, though, allowing Jax time to gather his far-from-diplomatic thoughts.

"Jesus Christ, your dad owns half the world. He probably owns me."

Tucker laughs. "Trust me, you'd know it if he owned you."

"So you're Charles Junior?" I ask.

Tucker shakes his head. "I prefer Charles Spencer the Second, eldest son of Charles Spencer."

"What's the difference?" I ask. Jews aren't allowed to name their children after anyone who is currently drawing breath, so I don't know about these things.

"A trailer full of kids, a bowl of cheese puffs and a job at Dairy Queen," Jax drawls.

Tucker cracks up, immediately endearing himself to Jax. "Almost, though you forgot about prenups, private planes and charity events."

I have a brief flashback to the steps of the church when Tucker told me not to worry about money. "I figured that was a pickup line," I mutter.

Tucker shakes his head. "I prefer to reveal my parentage right off the bat. A lot of people can't handle being around money. Well, it's not that they can't handle it—they just turn into people I don't want to know. So instead of being surprised and hurt six months down the road, I get it over with as soon as possible." Jax and I share a look. Tucker's points are increasing by the moment.

"And here I was worried you'd swindle my oldest friend for all she's worth," Jax exclaims, laughing. "She finally dipped into an inheritance we consider a small fortune, but it's more like grocery money for you."

"Listen, you should know that I don't have unlimited funds," Tucker begins, obviously embarrassed. "I have a trust fund I can't touch until I'm thirty and a comfortable but not lavish monthly allowance. I live alone in an overpriced apartment on East Sixth Street, and I'm currently wondering what to do with my life. I'm also looking for a summer job, preferably one that requires me to paint. And I bought that round of beers under the assumption that one of you would get the next round." Tucker smiles shyly, excuses himself and heads inside to the bathroom.

"Oh my God, Alex, I love him! I'm leaving right now so you two can talk and get married."

"You don't have to whisper, you lunatic. He's in the bathroom. You're only leaving so you don't have to buy beers."

Jax makes a big show of pulling out his wallet, sifting through the cash and placing a ten-dollar bill on the table. I laugh, in spite of myself.

"Really, I promised I'd meet Pete at The Basement. I'm sure I told you that. You probably weren't listening. You're really self-absorbed, Alex. I'm not sure we should be friends anymore." Jax gets up and begins to stroke Tucker's leather jacket.

"Eat me, you wacko. I can't believe you're going dancing without me."

"Listen, babycakes, until you get the operation that *officially* makes you a gay man, I'm afraid I'll continue to occasionally venture out without you."

Upon Tucker's return, Jax rushes inside to the bar and returns a moment later with two beers.

"Unfortunately, Little Lord Fauntleroy, I have to be in the West Village in exactly five minutes. Shit, I'm always late. It was really nice to meet you." Jax shakes Tucker's hand, throws me a kiss and walks away, tucking the Prada jacket under his shirt. Tucker laughs, whistles louder than I've ever heard anyone whistle in my life and tackles Jax from behind. Jax returns the jacket, mimes the international signal for "call me" and leaves. Tucker sits next to me, lights a cigarette for each of us and smiles.

3

The moment I step through the door of my apartment, I smell lemons. I tiptoe down the hallway—I'm lucid enough to know it's almost four in the morning. One of the good things about living in New York City is the night ends only when you want it to—I have yet to hear the words *last call* uttered by a bartender. I strip off my clothes as I walk, so by the time I enter the bathroom I'm wearing only a tank top and underwear. I methodically wash my face, brush my teeth and comb my hair without looking in the mirror. Just before I enter my bedroom, which is really half the living room divided by a fake wall (a popular and vital aspect of New York City living), I hear Jordy call my name.

"Yippee! You're up!" I dash into her room and pounce on the bed.

"Am I ever not up when you get home?" she asks.

"I know—you're such a good friend, always wondering about my rare night without you." I snuggle into her warm body, suddenly exhausted.

"Not really," she deadpans. "I'm just cursed with the worst fucking insomnia on the planet." She sighs heavily and flicks on the stereo via remote control. "So, how did your night go?"

"It was fun," I answer drowsily.

"Fun? I need a little more than that, Alex. You went out with a guy you met at your shrink's funeral, for Christ's sake. What's he like? What does he do? What's wrong with him?"

"He's really sweet and polite, and funny. Jax loves him. He's an artist—a painter, actually. He's really smart and down-to-earth, and his father is a multibillionaire."

Jordy laughs. "So he says."

"No, really. His dad is this amazing businessman who owns all these huge companies, including Spencer Publishing. Tucker doesn't have tons of money, but his father does. You've heard of him, Charles Spencer."

Jordy pops up. "Tucker's father is Charles Spencer? Holy shit, Alex, you're talking Top Five on the *Forbes* list!" She bounces up and down.

I nod into the pillow, fighting to keep my eyes open. All I want to do is pass out until noon, and now I've gotten Jordy all jacked up.

"Good thing you've got Ashley's money now. You'd probably have to sign a prenup before you marry him."

"Jesus, Jordy . . . between you and Jax . . . I'm not marrying anyone. I just met the guy twelve hours ago!"

Jordy settles back into her pillow and nudges closer to me. "Good, because he's carrying a ton of baggage."

My eyes open immediately. "What do you mean? How do you know?"

"Alex, you can find his whole life story on the Internet. If you ever read the newspaper—"

"I read the paper every day!"

"*The Post* doesn't count, sweetheart."

"Whatever. What do you know about Tucker?"

"He has a younger brother and sister, he went to a ritzy private school here in the city, he has no desire to enter the family business and his mother died when he was ten."

"How?"

"Suicide," she says.

I bury my head in the pillow. "Jesus," I mutter, turning away from Jordy to face the immaculate windowpane, through which I observe other windows, other lives. We lay in silence for a few minutes. Peter Gabriel's "In Your Eyes" reverberates through the room. "Well, that's the end of that," I finally say. "If his mother committed suicide, he's sure as hell not going to want to get involved with someone like me."

"Maybe he worked it out with Sam and understands what depression is all about. And he definitely understands grief," Jordy says. "Don't assume anything, Alex. Give it a chance." I can feel Jordy braiding my hair, her hands effortlessly twisting the tendrils into an order I can never maintain.

"You mean I should go out on a limb?"

"Out on a limb? I'd be happy if you climbed the damn tree. Did you tell him anything?"

"No. Jax told him about the inheritance and mentioned the note in passing, but Tucker didn't probe for details and I didn't volunteer any."

"Why not?"

"I don't know. I didn't want him to feel slighted, as if Sam liked me better, but who knows, maybe Tucker got a note, too. I figured I'd wait a while before explaining it."

"I think that's a good idea. Do you have plans tomorrow?"

I shut my eyes, bored with the rooftops I see through the window. "Nothing specific. I figured I'd decide what to do with the rest of my life—starting with the summer—and stare at Sam's note for a few hours."

Jordy chuckles and finishes the braid. "Want some company?"

I nod and take her hand in my own.

"Alex?" Jordy whispers.

"Hmm?"

"Never mind."

We fall asleep seconds later.

Teddy wakes me at one o'clock the next day, calling from down the street on her cell phone. She has just finished having lunch with a client and, since she was in the neighborhood, decided to stop by so I could sign some papers. I jot down a story idea that floated into my dream and answer the door in my skivvies.

"Nice, Alexandra, very mature. Good morning!" She pecks

my cheek and breezes into the living room, her four-inch heels violently attacking the hardwood floor. She's wearing a jet-black pants suit—her engagement and wedding rings sparkle in the sunbeams that push their way through the windows. I marvel at how confident, how together, she is, but then I recall she has always been like this. Teddy has always progressed forward, without any stumbles or falls. From the time she was an adolescent, whenever she encountered an obstacle, she simply figured out a way around it, whereas I was paralyzed, staring at the impediment, wondering what to do next. I remember when I was eleven, I desperately wanted to earn my Cookie Patch as a Girl Scout. The previous year, I had not sold nearly enough boxes of Girl Scout Cookies to receive the Cookie Patch. So this time, I knocked on Teddy's door. She was sixteen, and working on her precalculus homework, books and papers spread across her bedroom carpet. She listened to my request, swept her books out of the way and patted the floor next to her. She flipped the pages of her pad until she found a clean sheet of paper—she looked like Diana Prince, working in Major Steve Trevor's office on *Wonder Woman*. While I watched in awe, Teddy created a list of every house in the neighborhood and included relevant information, such as how many children lived there, which fathers were overweight and which mothers could be swayed based on what other mothers had purchased. She then dug into the recesses of her closet and yanked out her old Girl Scouts uniform (she had quit at the age of fourteen, citing the crushing pressure of uniformity, the lack of diversity and the fact that the dull green outfit simply did not flatter her complexion, all of which was probably Ashley's influence, now that I think about it). The green monstrosity still fit her, though my mother told her it was a bit "Lolita-esque," now that certain areas had finally grown. She zipped me into my green smock, took me by the hand and, consulting her list before I rang each doorbell, went about earning me my Cookie Patch. I barely had to utter a word—between her cheat sheet and her natural abilities of persuasion, I outsold myself by three hundred boxes of cookies. I was not only rewarded with the coveted Cookie

Patch, but I also won a Girl Scout Activity Pin. When I rushed into Teddy's room to show her my prizes, she wrapped her arms around my scrawny shoulders and said, "I knew you could do it, Alex. You're the best Girl Scout Scarsdale has seen in years!" When I told her it was she who really deserved the prizes, she shook her head and said, "All I did was show you how to approach the situation."

Now that we're adults, though, when Teddy approaches situations—my situations, at least—it feels like she's bullying or belittling me, the one exception being her financial expertise.

"Sit down and look these over," she says, pulling a fat file out of her Coach briefcase.

"I don't suppose you have any orange juice in that three-hundred-dollar bag?"

Teddy shoots me a look. I plop into a chair, pick up a pen and start signing.

"Alex, what on earth are you doing?" Teddy nearly shrieks.

"I'm signing the papers—isn't that what I'm supposed to do?" Where is Jordy?

"Without reading them? This is your money. You should be—"

"Teddy, even if I read each paper twice, I still won't understand. You're brilliant, you have tons of money and you wouldn't let anyone screw around with Ashley's money. I trust you."

We lock eyes for a moment and I suddenly see Teddy as a twelve-year-old on the playground, yelling at Nathan Goldstein for tripping me. She was my protector then, the barrier between me and bratty boys, catty girls and even our (sometimes) infuriating parents. Age hasn't changed our appearances all that much—I see the similarities—but gazing at Teddy, I barely recognize the soul behind her flinty eyes. She nods and I sign about ten pieces of paper. Teddy pokes around the living room for a few minutes. She skims the titles of the CDs with her long, perfectly manicured nails (not noticing the ones I pilfered from her collection) and moves on to the bookcase. She reads the back of a new short story anthology and glances over at me. I nod and she puts it in her trendy pocketbook.

"How was Sam's funeral?" she asks.

I shrug. "I met someone."

One eyebrow pops up. "At the funeral?"

I nod. "His name is Tucker. He's really cool. We went out last night."

"You actually went out unaccompanied by Jordy and Jax?" she asks.

"Jax met him briefly and Jordy was supposed to edit her dissertation. And fuck you."

"I'm kidding, Alex. I'm just thrilled you went on a date—it's been ages—and you know I adore Jax and Jordy. I just don't want you guys to end up in a millennium version of *Three's Company*."

As if on cue, the front door opens and Jordy struggles through it, hidden behind four bags of groceries.

"If that prick on the corner calls me a hot mama one more time, I'm going to have to kick his ass," she yells, dropping all four bags on the kitchen table. "Oh, hey, Teddy."

"Hi. What's wrong with being called hot?" Teddy asks.

"It's the way he says it," Jordy answers, peeling off her ancient jean jacket. She reaches into a brown bag, pulls out a quart of orange juice and tosses it to me. I smile in gratitude, Jordy winks and Teddy rolls her eyes.

"OK, Wonder Twins, I've got to get back to the office." She kisses us good-bye. "Oh, Max and I are going to stay with Carchie for Memorial Day, OK?" I nod. "We need to get out of the city. Hey, if you want to borrow the car sometime and drive up there, just give me a week's notice."

Jordy and I share a look. Why didn't we think of that? "OK, thanks. And thanks for bringing over the papers. Am I done with all this stuff now?"

Teddy heads for the door, sighing and shaking her head. "Yes. I'll send you copies of the monthly statements. You need to read them and keep them in a file. Talk to you soon." As soon as the door closes behind her, I light a cigarette.

Jordy and I spend the rest of the day on the couch. We eat chocolate chip pancakes, channel surf and compose a list of the possible meanings of Sam's note. We don't get very far; we just cannot imagine what the hell I am "missing." We sit in silence for a moment, watching the workmen on the roof of the building next door, and then proceed to think of a sexually ambiguous first name for every letter of the alphabet. Next we review and count every guy we've slept with (under six for both of us). Jordy hasn't been in a relationship in years, probably because she spends most of her time studying; she's minutes away from earning her PhD in American history. Jordy hasn't had much time for guys over the past few years—she spends her days and nights reading, studying or teaching, and her few hours of spare time with me.

We wolf down the remainder of the chocolate chips and fall asleep on the couch. I wake up an hour later, thanks to Jordy, who nonchalantly prods my stomach with her foot. Our legs are tangled together like a pretzel.

"You should buy a car," she announces.

"Why?"

"Why not? You can afford it, and you wouldn't have to rely on Teddy and Max when you want to get out of the city," she explains.

"You mean when *you* want to get out of the city."

"That, too. C'mon, you've always wanted to buy a Land Rover Discovery. You really haven't splurged on anything yet."

"Um, excuse me, I seem to remember a night not too long ago—"

"I mean material things, Alex. Something you can use for years to come. I bet it feels great to own something real. And Ashley would get a kick out of your owning a car. Just think about it, OK?"

"Sure. So why didn't you edit your dissertation last night?" I ask. Jordy always cleans when she can't concentrate.

Jordy retreats to one end of the couch and lights a cigarette. "I don't know. I just couldn't get the words right, and then I got pissed at myself."

"Do you think it's because you're almost done? Like a part of you doesn't actually want to finish?"

Jordy exhales, shaking her head. "Listen to you—your shrink is gone and suddenly you *become* one."

"Hey, not fair! I'm not therapizing you. I just know you, too well, maybe. Sometimes I feel like I'm in your head with you."

"That must be fun," she mutters.

"It is, most of the time. Nothing in there is any worse than what's in my head."

Jordy laughs. "We should offer ourselves up to the American Psychiatric Association; let them analyze dysfunction up close."

"Everyone we know is dysfunctional, Jordy. Some just hide it better." A nugget of wisdom, compliments of group therapy.

Jordy sighs, tapping out her cigarette. "Jesus, is there no end to how much our families fuck us up? Oh, I almost forgot. Some woman from work called this morning. She wants you to clean out your desk as soon as possible."

"Yeah, like my four pens and Rolodex are really bothering anyone. I think they owe me a check, actually. I'll go there to-morrow."

"At least you don't have to stress about finding a job now," Jordy points out.

"Oh sure, this week has been anything but stressful. I got fired, my shrink died—leaving me some obscure treasure map of a note that undoubtedly unlocks the key to my entire future— and I'm finally spending the money Ashley left me. Very relaxing, Jordy."

I suddenly feel nauseated and decide to go for a walk. Jordy has to shower and dress for some school-related party, so I head east across 14th Street alone. I consider popping into my old office to retrieve my personal belongings but can't bear the thought of seeing those idiots just now. I spent just under a year at that lame cable television station, and not one of my ideas was given serious consideration. No wonder they're downsizing— how far can you go with a channel about furniture? I tried to get them to air unique, publicity-driven shows, like those two obese ladies who cook, or that white-trash guy who barbeques, or that perky young woman who is the under-thirty-five version of Martha Stewart. I even came up with specific ideas, like *The*

Lesbian Lacquer Show, Retirees Go Antiquing and *Gay Men Build Beds,* all of which would fill a niche in daytime television. I polled Jax and his friends and they all agreed they'd definitely watch gorgeous, shirtless gay men sweating over a power saw. A few people at the network even agreed with me, but when my proposals made it up the ranks to the asinine producer, he nixed them all and ordered thirteen episodes of *Lola Does Window Treatments.* I have nothing against window treatments, but I do have something against Lola, namely her gravity-defying, balloon-sized breast implants. That same producer called me into his office last week and said, "Alexandra, we'll really miss your creative input around here, but I'm afraid the numbers just aren't what they should be, and you're being downsized. Don't feel bad, though. That black chick in casting and the homo in editing are also outta here." I grabbed my bag, filled it with a lifetime supply of Post-it's, paper clips and Liquid Paper, and left.

I feel a sudden vibration in my jacket (not altogether unpleasant) and it takes me a few seconds to realize it's my cell phone. Jax never tires of clandestinely reprogramming my cell phone—surprising me with the vibrate option still amuses him—so I sometimes get a little surprise in the form of three quick vibrations. Jax keeps talking about us inventing the world's first phone vibrator—with a hands-free earplug, people could actually chat and get off at the same time.

"Hello?" The number on the automatic caller ID screen isn't familiar.

"Hey, Alex, it's Tucker. What's up?"

"Did I give you this number?" I ask. I'm pretty sure I didn't.

"No, but I have my ways," he answers. An image of Tucker—those piercing green eyes, that endearing smirk—travels through my mind.

"You're not allowed to use your father's telecommunications connections."

"Lighten up. I called your apartment and Jordy gave me the number."

"Oh. OK. I was only kidding."

"Sure you were. I bet you think those E-Z Pass things are a ploy so the government can keep tabs on us," he says, laughing.

"I wouldn't be surprised, but in that case it's OK because traffic sucks balls." Oh shit, did I just say that?

Tucker cracks up. "No argument here. Listen, what are you doing tonight?"

"I was going to order some pizza and watch a *Law & Order* marathon. Why?"

"Postpone the pizza and come out to dinner with me. We can shoot some pool afterwards, if you want."

How is it that this guy has yet to lay a hand on me but somehow manages to push all my buttons?

"Does this involve me going above Fourteenth Street?" I ask.

"Nope. I know a great Italian place on Seventh Street, right off First Avenue. They even have a beautiful outdoor garden, where we can eat and smoke!" he exclaims proudly.

"You really know how to court a girl, don't you?"

Tucker chuckles. "I'll pick you up at eight?"

"Sure. Wait, don't you need my address?"

"Why, have you moved?"

"Huh?"

"I dropped you off in your lobby last night, remember? You do know who this is, don't you?"

"Very funny. I'll see you later."

I turn around and head back to my apartment. I've never gone out with the same guy two nights in a row. I immediately dial Jax's number.

"Babycakes!" he yells upon hearing my voice.

"Tucker asked me out, for tonight," I tell him.

"Alex has a boyfriend," he taunts.

"Jax, this isn't funny. This is two nights in a row."

I hear the clamor of a kitchen through the phone, and realize I've caught Jax on the break between lunch and dinner.

"I know—I can count. He's adorable. What's the problem?"

"I don't know. I'm scared."

"You're nervous; you're not scared," Jax tells me.

"No, I'm scared."

Jax sighs. "The thought of someone new actually penetrating your armor scares the bejesus out of you, doesn't it?"

"Bejesus?" I repeat.

"Shut up and answer the question."

Jax can be oddly intimidating when he chooses to be. "Yes," I reply.

"I read somewhere that you're supposed to do something that scares you at least once a week," Jax says. "So this is your thing."

"I'd rather go skydiving," I tell him.

"Alex, I'm not suggesting you become a tramp, but when is the last time you had an orgasm with someone else in the room?"

"This has nothing to do with sex, Jax."

"I know. But it does have something to do with the fact that you haven't been in a relationship since Ben, and that was seven years ago."

"Six. Thanks for your input. Talk to you later." I snap the phone shut.

* * *

It's the second week of my senior year of college, and I'm already stressed out. I have too much reading and not enough time. I'm sitting at a back table in my favorite coffee shop, injecting Diet Coke into my system so I'll stay awake until at least two a.m. Casey has just left for class, and I'm trying to make up the time we squandered talking. The table is covered with books—a southern literature anthology, Ingmar Bergman's autobiography and *Atlas Shrugged*—I'm switching every half hour.

I'm about to light a cigarette when a tall, black-haired guy walks up to my table. He's wearing battered jeans and an orange T-shirt, and he has a clean apron tied around his waist.

"What can I get you?" he asks. His voice sounds younger than he looks.

"Excuse me?"

"What'll it be—coffee, tea or me?"

I try not to crack a smile. "That's from a movie, but nice try." I light my smoke and reach toward the Bergman book.

"*Persona* blew me away, but *Wild Strawberries* is still my favorite," he says.

"What?"

"*Persona* blew me away—"

"I heard what you said. I just didn't know you're a student."

"You had me pegged as a local?" he asks, grinning.

I nod.

"No offense, but your observational skills suck. I'm Brazilian. What the hell would I be doing serving coffee in the Midwest?"

I shrug. Awkward moment.

"I'm Ben," he says, offering his hand. As we shake, he leans into me, his ebony hair inches from my face.

"If you take a look around, you'll notice that not only do you already have a beverage, but there is no waiter service in this establishment."

We lock eyes. He's right—on both counts.

"So you're either here because you love to discuss Bergman films or—"

"I'd love to talk about Bergman films on our first date," he adds, looking over his shoulder at the rapidly growing line at the front counter. "Saturday night? Dinner? Drinks? Dancing? Whatever you want. Meet me here at seven."

He starts to walk away. "Wait, you don't even know my name," I point out.

He nods. "For the next three days you're my beautiful stranger." He hands me a straw and rushes to the front counter.

Cheesy line. So why am I blushing?

We skip the dancing and do dinner and drinks, then he shows me his room.

"I don't normally do this on the first date," I say between kisses.

"I don't normally ask customers out on dates," Ben answers, kicking his shoes off.

"Just as long as you know this is very unlike me," I reiterate, pulling his shirt off and soaking up the softness of his skin.

"I'm very serious about my studies," he tells me, feverishly trying to unhook my bra.

"Me, too. I hardly ever go out. My God, you are taking *way* too long." I unhook my bra and toss it on the floor, where it joins the pile of clothes we're pulling off each other. Ben hooks my legs around his waist, and as soon as my skin hits his skin, I lose my breath.

"Do you believe in love at first sight?" he asks, traveling south to yank my jeans off.

"Oh my, no. Do you?" Am I trembling?

My jeans, and then his, land on the floor. His hands journey up my body, and it's all I can do not to explode.

"No, but I think we're experiencing lust at first sight," he says just before his mouth reappears on mine. Ben somehow manages to transfer all the heat and energy from his body into mine.

"I really hope you have—" He flicks open a drawer of his night table and extracts a box of condoms.

"God bless the ten-pack," I say, smiling. I push him onto his back, and my fingers follow Jax's advice ("Don't forget the nipples") while my tongue trails along his taut stomach.

"Do you prefer *Alex* or *Alexandra?*" he asks, his voice suddenly husky.

"*Alex*. Why?"

"Because I'm about to scream your name."

The door opens on my third try and, even though it freezes almost every day, I curse at it. (I wonder if it's abnormal to feel a strange thrill when verbally attacking inanimate objects.) Ben is reclined in his La-Z-Boy when I enter his apartment. After six months, my spine still tingles when I first see him. He's handsome—gorgeous, even—and smart, so what on earth is he doing with me?

"I got an A on that history paper you helped me with," he says without looking up from his psych textbook.

"Cool. I ran into Brian after class." No reaction. "He told me I'm ruining your senior year."

Ben looks up. I sit on the floor on the other side of the room. "He actually said that?" he asks.

"Not in those words, but that's what he meant. He said he never sees you anymore, outside of psych class and basketball."

Ben tosses the textbook onto his bed. "He's just jealous because I'm getting laid and he's not. If he had a girlfriend, he'd—" Ben stops when he sees the look on my face. "Let me rephrase that," he says, smirking. "Brian's just jealous because I am not only dating a cool, beautiful and intelligent girl, but I am also having the most fan-fucking-tastic sex of my life."

I laugh. "Nice save, Romeo."

Ben slides off the chair and peels his shirt off as he crawls across the floor. He runs a hand up my thigh—I gasp—and reaches out to kiss me.

"Do you want to be more social?" he asks, his hand creeping under my shirt.

"As long as I spend the weekdays with Casey, I don't need to see anyone but you on the weekends." I stroke his muscular back as he takes off my shoes and unbuttons my jeans. "The front door is frozen again," I tell him, my body melting into the brown carpet.

"Good," Ben says, slipping out of his jeans. "Maybe we'll get locked in."

* * *

It turns out Tucker has spent a lot of time in the loud, friendly Italian restaurant, and so the owner, as well as every waiter, dotes on him as if he were Michael Corleone. Our wine glasses are full as soon as we sit down, and the breadbasket is replaced every five minutes. Tucker introduces me to the owner, a stocky, dark-haired man who promises five-star service if and when I should return. With Santana on the stereo, good cheap wine and a wide selection of pasta dishes, I know I'll be back.

Tucker tells me about his brother, Derek, a senior at Yale, and his sister, Catherine, a freshman at Berkeley. He tracks his father's rise to success, never mentioning his mother's death. I tell him about Teddy, my parents and Carchie, never mentioning Ashley's death or Carchie's cancer. While I'm in the bathroom, I resolve to reveal Sam's note. Upon my return, I find my wineglass has been refilled, so I take a graceful gulp and try to remain composed as I explain Sam's odd bequest.

"Did Sam, by any chance, leave you anything?" I ask him.

"No, why?"

"Well, he left me something. It's nothing huge. Just a note, actually."

"Can I ask what it says?"

"Sure. It says, 'You're missing a piece of yourself.' "

Tucker frowns, takes a sip of wine and asks, "What does that mean?"

"I have no idea. I guess he was trying to tell me something." I look away, toward the bar, wishing I could talk to Sam about the note, about Tucker, about so many things.

"I know what the note means," Tucker says.

My head whips around to face him. "Really. What?"

"Well, 'the missing piece' is probably something Sam was working toward in your sessions, but then the cancer got worse and he realized he wouldn't be able to reach the conclusion with you. So his only option was to force you onto the path, on your own. All you have to do is figure out what he knew."

I laugh. "Oh, is that all?"

"Yep." Tucker raises his wineglass. "Look at it as an adventure. Here's to your journey, wherever it may lead you." We clink glasses and take a sip.

"You sound like a Hallmark card," I tell him.

Tucker shrugs with a smile. "So you want to go play some pool?"

"Sure."

Tucker doesn't let me contribute to the bill, so I pay for the cab to Finny's Place. Jordy calls en route, ranting about her boring school function. After checking with Tucker, I invite her to hang out with us. She says she's coming straight from the Soho Grand; she'll be overdressed but she'll see us in half an hour.

The bar is somewhat crowded when we arrive, but Stan the Bartender sees me and hands over two beers. Tucker racks up and breaks, and a heated game of pool follows, both of us leaning on our cues in between shots. I can't tell if Tucker is letting me win or if he's perhaps had too much to drink, but either way, we have fun and own the table. I completely forget about Jordy until she's standing right in front of me, wearing a pair of sleek, silver pants with a bright red tank top and my black slides. "Wow," I say.

"What?" Jordy looks down, as if she spilled something on herself.

"Nothing. I mean—you look great. I didn't see you before you left."

"So where's the prodigal son?" She looks around the bar, tapping her fingers on the soft green felt of the pool table.

"In the bathroom. Listen, Jordy, promise me you'll be nice, OK? He's a really sweet guy, and he just bought me dinner."

"Alex, chill out. I'm anxious to meet him, that's all." Jordy flashes me a brilliant smile just as Tucker reappears.

"Tucker, this is Jordy. Jordy, this is Tucker. I'll get us some beers." I rush to the bar.

I flag Stan and then wait for the beers. I turn to look at Tucker and Jordy. They've abandoned the pool table and are on their way out to the garden. I pay Stan and stroll outside, pausing under the threshold to observe Jordy and Tucker, who have settled at a table in the corner. It occurs to me they would make a gorgeous couple. I inhale, exhale and walk over to the table. I distribute the beers, light a cigarette and ask, "So what are you two talking about?" as I sit. I have a sudden urge to down the entire bottle of beer.

"Oh, Jordy was just wondering what political party I vote with," Tucker says, smiling.

"Jordy! You promised!"

"What? You're too polite to ask, and it's not something you want to learn six months into a relationship. What if he's a right-wing fanatic? What if he's a Luddite? You need to know these things."

"I'm sorry, Tucker. I asked her not to—"

"Not a problem. I actually agree with her, though I might've been a little more subtle."

"Yeah, well, subtlety isn't really my thing. And stop referring to me in the third person, both of you. I'm right here," Jordy says.

"For the record, Jordy and Alex, I am a Democrat. I am pro-choice. I am even a bit of a feminist. I support the federal and state hate crimes bill, support maternity and paternity leave for all employees, support same-sex marriages as well as domestic partner health benefits and am a strong believer in safe sex." He takes a sip of beer and continues. "I like dogs better than cats but have nothing against cats. I've never gotten a woman pregnant and didn't lose my virginity until I was nineteen. I was raised Catholic but am not particularly religious. I believe in the separation of Church and State, and I think the First Amendment should be protected at all costs. If I have children, I will encourage my daughter in the same manner I encourage my son. I smoke pot but go for long periods of time without it. I prefer beer to liquor, red wine over white wine and admit to enjoying a nice fat steak once a month. Anything else you want to know?"

Jordy's eyes shine with admiration. I sip my beer, trying to verbalize the swirl of thoughts in my mind. I wonder if this is a rehearsed speech, something he's been forced to learn and recite.

"Actually, I have a few questions, but they're fun to answer," I reply, handing Tucker a cigarette from his pack. He lights it and leans back in his chair.

"OK, shoot," he says.

"Which of the following movies have you not seen? *High Noon, The Godfather, Parts I* and *II, The French Connection, Annie Hall, Taxi Driver, Days of Heaven, The Silence of the Lambs, Citizen Kane* and *The Shawshank Redemption?*"

"Seen 'em all," Tucker replies.

"Favorite movie?" I ask.

"Real movie, *Apocalypse Now.* Fluff movie, *Better Off Dead.*"

"Favorite book?" I interject.

"Hmm . . . tough call. *The Thin Red Line.*"

"Least favorite book?"

Tucker smirks and answers immediately. "*A Heartbreaking Work of Staggering Genius.* That book sucks."

Jordy and I nod in agreement. "He should've called it *A Staggering Work of Exploitative Crap*," I add. Tucker cracks up.

"Favorite movie couple?"

"Bogie and Bacall, hands down."

"Favorite real-life couple?" I ask.

"Bogie and Bacall."

"Favorite short story?" I'll nail him on this one.

Tucker doesn't hesitate. " 'An Occurrence at Owl Creek Bridge,' no question." Jordy squeezes my leg under the table.

"Name a couple singers or bands you admire," I say.

Tucker takes a few sips of beer. "I'm a die-hard Zeppelin fan. I love Springsteen and The Dead. Dylan should be our poet laureate. John Mellencamp and Tom Petty can do no wrong. Harry Connick, Jr. is a world-class pianist. And since I trust neither of you will repeat this conversation to any of my friends, should I allow you to meet them, I am a closet Indigo Girls fan."

Jordy cracks up, pats Tucker on the shoulder and walks inside to the bar. Tucker shakes his head, laughing. Jordy returns a minute later and hands each of us a shot.

"It's a lemon drop," she tells Tucker. "Very sugary and easy to swallow."

"Unlike you, huh?" he replies. Jordy tilts her head back, her long hair brushing my shoulder, and allows the liquor to slide down her throat. Tucker and I do our shots.

"Watch it, Tucker, we may actually wind up as friends," Jordy says.

Tucker chuckles, stands up and heads inside to the bathroom. He pauses, turns around and returns to the table. He leans toward Jordy and says, "Too late." Jordy and I share a look as Tucker walks away.

"You're right," Jordy tells me. "There's nothing wrong with him."

"I know," I answer. Then why am I so scared?

Every time I conquer one demon, another pops up.

4

I hate waking up in the morning. I know other people feel the same way, but they usually have good reasons, like not wanting to disturb a pleasant dream or hating their jobs. I just can't bear to wake up—even a bad dream is better than my reality, which is crowded with shame and compunction and, on bad days, an utter hatred of life. On those days, I can't stand being in my own skin; I just cannot forgive myself for squandering twenty-four years with Ashley. So I often lose part of my morning, sort of frozen between sleep and wakefulness.

I don't understand my parents. It's been just under two years since Jordy found me unconscious, close to death, but aside from a couple of family therapy sessions forced upon us in the psych ward, there haven't been any other discussions. They know it had something to do with Ashley, but they've never asked for specifics and I've never offered an explanation.

Teddy and I talked about it at first. Well, not about the actual suicide attempt, or the standard emergency room visit (including but not limited to a stomach pumping and psych consult), but about what led up to the day I swallowed a fistful of pills. I told her how each day had become longer and longer, full of heavy shadows. It wasn't just the feelings of loss and shame I felt after Ashley's death, it was an overall sense of defeat, as if I'd been fighting something for twenty-four years and, after burying a brother I hardly knew, I no longer had the strength for the battle. Teddy didn't understand—she told me this—how I could torture her, and my parents, after Ashley's death. In a benevolent, gentle tone, she called me selfish and immature. She, too, loved Ashley, and would forever miss him, but she knew she had to find a way to live without our older brother, and she could not fathom why I failed to realize this as well. The difference, though, the part of the equation Teddy just could not comprehend, was that her relationship with Ashley had been satisfying, full of affection and amusement—thus she felt no regret about their shared past. I hated myself for frittering time away, for existing for years in the same house but a different domain than Ashley. Regret prowled in every corner of my mind. And I was angry at the fact that Teddy married Max while Ashley was so very sick; he didn't—couldn't—go to her wedding. How could she marry while her older brother was dying? We didn't discuss this—I knew after she told me, in a mildly condescending, wooden voice, that she would help me in any way she could—she wouldn't understand my resentment. I assumed we'd continue talking about all of these issues, but Teddy quickly became busy—with Max, with investment banking, with working dinners and dinners for work—with a life I struggle to understand. And I rarely have the energy to broach the subject with her.

Both my mother and Teddy call me often, almost every day, and ask me questions like "How do you feel?" and "Are you OK?" They never use the word *depressed* and never refer to my suicide attempt. I've purposely tried to detach myself from my parents a little, for a variety of reasons, all of which Sam condoned. Of course, not returning each and every one of my mother's messages only causes the Jewish guilt to runneth over, but I'd rather feel guilty than re-enter the dysfunctional embrace of my stone-silent family. I can confide in Jax and Jordy and Casey, and when I talk with them the conversations are devoid of blame and judgment and disdain, so I continue to turn to them. Of course, the only person who truly talked to me, who told me the truth, who never judged or blamed me for anything, was Sam.

I'm not sure why my relationship with my parents is so confusing and complex. I don't know how I would function without them, yet there are moments when I simply cannot stand them. Most of the time, though, I simply wait for them to ask: *Why?*

Teddy picked me up from Webster Ridge—she drove me back to the city; she talked and talked about nothing at all. I expected my parents to call the apartment, but they didn't. Teddy told me to call them, but I didn't. I had just spent forty-five days in a psychiatric hospital—couldn't my parents dial the fucking phone to check up on me? They called the following night, when I was hanging out with Jax and Jordy and no longer needed the safety of my parents' voices.

"Alex. Alex, wake up. Teddy's on the phone." Jordy leans over me, nudging my shoulder. I can smell toothpaste on her breath.

I swallow the morning, glance at the clock and accept the phone Jordy places in my hand. "Teddy, do you purposely call here as early as possible?"

"It's eleven thirty, Alexandra. I've been at work since eight. I could've called then," she replies smugly.

"I suppose I should be grateful you exercised some self-control. What's up?"

"Max and I are swamped at work. We've decided not to visit Carchie for Memorial Day weekend. We need access to modern machinery. Do you want the car?"

I look over at Jordy, who seems to be folding laundry—another productive morning with the dissertation.

"Jordy, do we want to go to Carchie's cabin this weekend?" She nods immediately.

"OK, Teddy, we'll take the car and the cabin." I laugh. "I sound like I'm on *The Price Is Right*."

"Don't smoke pot in my Beemer, Alexandra. I'll know,"

Teddy growls. "And make sure Carchie doesn't overexert himself."

"OK."

I click off the phone, turn over to face Jordy and realize I'm in her room. "Why am I in your bed?"

Jordy shrugs. "You fell asleep in it last night."

"We shouldn't have put up the wall—we could've saved some money."

Jordy laughs as she partners up her socks. "I did your laundry. It's on your bed."

"Thanks, Mammy. I'm going to invite Jax to the cabin."

As I dial the cordless, Jordy says, "Don't bother. He's on his way over."

"He's not working lunch today?" I wonder aloud, tossing the phone on the bed.

"He got someone to cover. Said something about earth-shattering news."

"Hmm. I hope he brings bagels. I'm starving."

Jax brings bagels, fresh coffee and a flurry of energy. He paces the living room, puffing away in between bites of a warm pumpernickel bagel.

"Jax, can you please sit your ass down? You're freaking me out!" Jordy yells.

"Wait 'till you guys hear this. I have two pieces of un-fucking-believable news. I don't know which to spill first!" Jax trips over his black shoes as he nears the couch. He kills his cigarette and takes a sip of coffee.

"Tell us in the order they happened," I offer. The hair on the back of my neck tingles.

"OK, OK, good idea. You're so pragmatic, Alex—"

"Would you shut up and tell us?" Jordy screams.

Jax pretends to be offended for about two seconds. "Pete asked me to move in with him," he says evenly. The kitchen clock ticks.

"Oh my God," I mutter.

"After six months? Jesus, Jax, what did you say?" Jordy asks.

"I told him he must be a complete nutbag and now I have to break up with him," Jax replies with a straight face.

"You did not," Jordy says.

"Of course not. But I wanted to. What is he thinking, ruining a perfectly casual relationship with this crap?" Jax lights another cigarette.

"What's the other news?" I ask. Hopefully something a little less disturbing.

"Oh! The good news! I got a voice-over gig! A national spot, thirty seconds!"

"I knew you would! Yeah, Jax!" I yell, attacking him with kisses.

"You go, girl," Jordy sings. "Your parents will be so proud!"

Jax snorts and rolls his eyes. "My mom will be psyched, but my father will now assume every voice-over actor is a faggot."

We're quiet for a moment, letting Jax's words evaporate into the air.

"You're going to ditch us as soon as you get famous, aren't you?" Jordy asks, stroking Jax's thick hair and undoing her accidental reference to Jax's father.

"Yep, gonna find me a whole new set of fag hags," he replies, eyes smiling brightly.

"What are you going to do about Pete?" I ask.

"I have no idea, babycakes. Do you think it's rude to say 'No, thank you, but I'd like to continue fucking you?'"

Jordy and I shrug. This is way out of our realm of experience—not because Jax is gay but because we've never been on the receiving end of such a terrifying invitation. I can't imagine living with anyone but Jordy. I can't even believe I lived with my parents for eighteen years.

"Want to come to Carchie's cabin over Memorial Day weekend with us?" I ask.

"Does it involve mass transportation?" Jax inquires.

"Nope, we've got Teddy's car," Jordy answers.

"Can we hit the local bars and pretend we're a threesome?" Jax asks, bouncing up and down on the couch, coffee splashing on his jeans.

"Absolutely," I reply. Jordy shakes her head, stifling a giggle.

"Can we have an *AbFab* marathon?" Jax asks, still bouncing.

"Definitely," Jordy answers. "I love watching Carchie's face when we put it on."

I lean into Jax and tuck my legs into my shirt. "Can we not talk about Carchie's cancer or Sam's note or Ashley's money?" I ask.

The clock ticks again. "I'm not sure that's healthy, babycakes. Would Sam approve?" Jax replies.

"Sam is dead," I say, pinching my leg so hard it stings. Why is physical pain so much easier to feel, and understand? I remember when I was eight, I fell in the creek behind Jax's house, hit a smoothly sharpened rock and slashed open my upper arm, above my elbow. I needed twelve stitches, but after the blood stopped gushing, I was fine. Two days later—the first day of sleepaway camp—my mother would not stop reminding me to change the dressing twice a day. I kept telling her the nurses at camp would do it for me. I was waiting for her to declare her love for me—tell me she'd miss me and everything would be great and I'd make new friends and have a terrific summer—but all she said, over and over, was "Don't forget to clean your wound."

"This is her last weekend of denial—after the holiday, she *has* to deal," Jordy announces. "OK, Alex?" Both look to me, eyes wide with sympathy, love and expectation.

"OK." I release the secret hold on my flesh.

The phone rings and rings. I'm about to hang up when I hear the familiar, rumbling voice.

"Hi, Carchie."

"Alex, I was just thinking about you."

"You know what I was just thinking?" I ask.

"How much you miss me?"

"That, and how you need to buy a cordless phone."

"No fucking way, Alex. You know how I feel about those things," Carchie grumbles.

"Yeah, but they're convenient, Carchie. You wouldn't have to get up every time the phone rings."

"The day I become so lazy that I can't walk across a room to pick up the phone is the day you shoot me, got it?"

We both know I wasn't referring to laziness, but I let it go.

"So are you coming up this weekend?" Carchie asks.

"Yeah. Do you mind if I bring a few guests?"

"I don't consider Jax and Jordy guests, Alex, more like a cabaret act."

"I invited someone else, too. A guy I'm seeing," I say slowly.

"Have your parents met him yet?"

"God no."

"How about Jax and Jordy?" he asks.

"They both like him."

"OK, he can come. What's his name?"

I take a deep breath. "Tucker."

Carchie is silent for a moment. "Sort of a pussy name, isn't it?"

"I like his name," I protest. Carchie laughs, but not the way he used to. This laugh is restrained, tired. "Do you want anything from Katz's?" I ask.

"No, thanks," he replies.

"Not even whitefish salad?" I blurt out.

"Not this time, sweetie, but thanks for asking. If I'm not here when you arrive, it means I'm kicking ass in poker."

"OK, see you Friday."

Three days later, Jordy, Jax and I are about to get in Teddy's car, which is double-parked, when I realize I forgot to pack something.

"Shit, I have to run upstairs for a second," I tell them.

"Move your ass, babycakes. If we get a ticket, Teddy will deliver a verbal thrashing we'll never forget," Jax replies. I nod, rush into the lobby, barrel into the elevator and jog down the hall into my apartment.

My stomach feels hollow as I reach behind the headboard

and seize the leather satchel. Every time I make plans to leave the city I swear to myself I will leave the satchel behind, but I can't seem to do it, no matter how short the excursion. I zip the sack into the pocket of my jacket—its heaviness makes me feel warm and safe. A shot of panic rips through my body as I realize I now have to create a reason for returning to the apartment, since I can't exactly tell Jax and Jordy I neglected to pack my warped version of a security blanket. We're already stocked up on water, Twizzlers and cigarettes, and Jordy saw me pack my sketch pad and colored pencils. I search the room with my eyes, feeling ridiculous and desperate, until my gaze falls upon the stereo. Jordy's unofficial hobby is making spectacular mixed CDs for every occasion, and I'm almost positive she's made me a driving mix—yep, here it is. Teddy is too organized to leave her CDs scattered around the car—they're all tucked neatly into a case of some sort, which she keeps in her apartment when she's not in the car. I grab another few homemade CDs, stroke the quiet bulge in my pocket and head for the door. Jordy is thrilled when I toss the CDs in her lap and immediately pops one into the car stereo.

The ride up to Carchie's cabin should take about two hours, but it takes us almost three and a half. We've left early enough to beat most of the traffic, but Jax keeps pulling over to take pictures of the "gorgeous scenery," which is really just trees. I can't blame him, though—we don't get out of the city much, and at this time of year, the Palisades Parkway is beautiful. I let Jax drive—Teddy would kill me if she knew—he's a much better driver than I and treats her car like a delicate piece of crystal.

Somewhere around Bear Mountain, I drop the bomb I've been nestling in my arms.

"Remind me to pick Tucker up at the train station tomorrow afternoon." The car is ghostly silent for almost thirty seconds.

"You invited him?" Jordy asks while Jax smirks and contains a giggle.

I turn around to face Jordy and catch my reflection in her sunglasses.

"You told me to!" Jax can no longer hold it in—his face contorts and he erupts into laughter. "So did you!" I yell at him.

"I know," he replies. "But I didn't expect you to actually do it."

"Me neither," Jordy adds.

"Well, that's just fucking great, you guys."

"Don't worry, Alex," Jax says, patting my thigh.

"It'll be fun," Jordy adds. "We'll get to know him as you get to know him. And we'll get to watch Carchie interrogate him."

"And then we can all judge him together!" Jax sings. I slap his shoulder but I know, at least on some level, that the four of us combined can topple even the most confident person.

"Come on, I think I might actually like this guy, so we have to go easy on the private jokes," I tell them. "I don't want him feeling like—"

"An outsider?" Jordy finishes for me.

"Yeah, an outsider—that's exactly the word I was searching for."

"Don't you worry, babycakes. We'll welcome him with open arms. He'll feel completely comfortable. You may not, but he will." Jax chuckles.

"Shit, I fucked this up," I say, more to myself than to them.

As soon as we roll into town, my stomach tightens. Two minutes later, the floodgates open, though it's not tears that rush their way to the surface. I throw up on the lawn of Town Hall, rinse my mouth with some bottled water and re-enter the car.

"You OK?" Jax asks.

I nod. "Must be that cream cheese from breakfast," I say.

"Yeah, must be." Jordy looks out the window.

"Carchie's not any worse, is he?" Jax asks.

"I don't think so, but I'm not sure."

"This might be too intense for you," Jordy says. Jax pulls to the side of the road.

"I agree," he responds, nodding at Jordy. "With Sam—"

"I'm capable of making my own decisions." My voice rises shakily. Jax and Jordy stare at one another as if they're my parents. I know exactly what they're thinking. "Am I going to be

judged on that one bad decision for the rest of my life?" I ask,
the pitch of my voice mimicking my uneven breaths. How
could I have screwed that up?

"It wasn't that long ago, Alex," Jax reminds me.

"Your two-year anniversary is in two months," Jordy adds.

"I promise you I'm fine, and if I stop feeling fine, I'll tell you
both right away and we can go home, OK?"

They confer by means of eye contact and then stare me
down, eyes peeled for a crack in my resolve to live a normal life.
Jax restarts the car, and we drive to the cabin in silence.

Carchie's cabin is eerily still when we arrive. We find a note
instructing us to "pick our own" for the weekend, so after we
unload the car, we head into Carchie's greenhouse to harvest
handfuls of pot. Carchie has been growing and smoking his
own pot for as long as I can remember. In a grossly strange twist
of fate, he now relies on the pot to battle the almost constant
nausea he suffers after each chemo treatment. Six months ago,
he would have sent us on a complicated, amusing scavenger
hunt to find the joints he'd rolled for us, or he would have dec-
orated the guest rooms with the pungent buds.

Laying in Carchie's bed, the tears finally overflow, flooding
my cheeks and forming a salty puddle on my neck. Although
it's quiet, the whole house seems to contain Carchie's smile, his
laugh, his touch. I curl up on the white cotton sheets, staring at
a photo of me, Carchie, Ashley and Teddy, taken that first summer, so long ago. I'm leaning into Carchie, my chubby legs
crossed, his hand casually resting on my head, as though it belonged there. Ashley is behind Carchie, his face tilted toward
the clouds. Teddy is on my other side, smiling, her mouth a
medley of teeth and metal. We're holding hands, fingers
clasped together like starfish. The lake is behind us, barely visible through the late summer dusk. I look into my own eyes—
they are wide—I seem invincible in the shadow of my uncle. I
think that was the last time I felt safe.

I can hear Jax and Jordy downstairs, putting groceries away,
blasting a Madonna CD. I should join them, help plan dinner,

or maybe take a walk on the path by the lake. But I'm comfortable here, the afternoon sun caressing my unwashed hair. I hug a pillow to my chest and watch the trees sway in the gentle Catskills wind.

I close my eyes, expecting to see a vision of Tucker in his Prada jacket, that unruly lock of hair brushing his eyebrows, but instead I see Jordy—the look on her face when I entered the car after puking on the lawn. She worries about me too much.

"Hey, you, how are you feeling?" Jordy asks from the doorway, holding a cup of tea.

Did I just will her up here? "Fine. Sorry I deserted you guys. I should've gone to the grocery store with you."

Jordy walks over, kicks off her sandals and sits on the bed, handing me the tea—Lemon Zinger, my favorite. "We do know how to fend for ourselves, Alex, even in the country. Besides, you would've been mortified," she says, smiling.

"Uh-oh, what'd he do?"

"Why do you always assume it's Jax? I'm quite capable of inventing childish, moronic games to play in public."

"Sorry, I forgot. What horror did you two inflict upon the poor schmucks in the grocery store?" I ask.

"Day Pass from the Asylum. He had multiple personalities—which he does *very* well, by the way—and I pretty much hit on anyone who looked at me—man, woman, child, cereal box, rack of lamb." She cracks up at the memory.

"Sorry I missed it." I carefully put my tea on the floor and pat the bed next to me. Jordy crawls in—her skin is cooler than mine and her breath smells of bubble gum.

"You sure you're OK? Jax and I discussed it, and we can leave whenever you want. We don't think you're ready to be here."

"He's sick, Jordy. I can't run away just because it hurts to look at him." Jordy nods, her silky hair splayed over the pillow like a fan. "But thanks for asking. And thanks for—I don't know, for everything. Why are you so good to me?"

Jordy looks at me, surprised. "You don't know?" she asks.

I shrug.

"Alex, you're my best friend. We've been friends for over half our lives. How can you not know how I feel about you? How can you . . ." She closes her eyes for a second, as if she has a head rush. "How can you not know?" she asks again.

"I do know. I just worry that I rely on you too much—that you don't go on dates or meet new people because of—"

"That's not why." She chuckles ever so slightly. "Trust me, that's not why."

"You promise you'd tell me if I were leaning too hard?" I ask.

"I promise." Jordy sits up and looks outside. "Shall we find the handsome fella and take a stroll by the lake?" I nod and we get out of bed. I envelop Jordy in a tight hug, and we go downstairs in search of Madonna's less-talented but no-less-enthusiastic singing partner.

Carchie shuffles in through the back door at around four o'clock. His orange-and-white gingham button-down shirt hangs off his shoulders, and he's wearing suspenders, which he hasn't worn since I was on training wheels. He sports a three- or four-day stubble, but his eyes still glow like the moon.

"Alex baby! It's so good to see you." He folds his spindly arms around me and kisses my forehead.

"You look good, Carchie," I lie.

"Took me a fucking day to find these suspenders," he mutters.

"Suspenders are in again, Carchie," Jax says brightly.

"You would know, Tinkerbell," Carchie answers. They shake hands, smiling at the timeworn nickname that only Carchie is allowed to use. Carchie turns to Jordy, smirking and shaking his head. "Jordy, honey, if I were thirty years younger—"

"Um, let's leave that to our imaginations, shall we?" she jokes, kissing his cheek.

"Good idea. I assume you guys have already been to the store?"

We nod.

"So break out a six-pack, light up a joint and tell me what's new."

I grab the beer and Jordy collects our cigarettes, as well as a joint. Jax settles into a kitchen chair.

"Not here, Tinkerbell. This is the country, for Christ's sake—we kibbutz on the deck."

Two hours and a pizza later, we're still talking. Carchie enjoys our ramblings about life in the city, probably because our lives are so complicated to us but so simple to him. Carchie's future is dark and demanding, as Ashley's once was. When Ashley's future ended, my present engulfed and slowly strangled me. I couldn't face each day, knowing a brother I had never taken the time to know was now dead. Gone. After Ashley died, the sky hardly ever looked blue.

I awake in the morning to find Jax fighting with the kitchen. The counter is covered in eggshells, pancake batter, toast and banana peels.

"And you call yourself a gay man?" I ask, laughing.

Jax looks up from an ugly, burning omelet. "I know—I'm a disgrace. I really wanted to surprise you guys with a gourmet breakfast, but I'm so used to serving food, I forgot how to cook it." He looks truly upset with himself.

"Don't worry about it."

"I got the coffee right. Want some?" I nod. He pours me a cup, sprinkles some sugar into the steaming blackness and hands it to me. I take a few sips and look around the airy, messy kitchen.

"What do you say we clean up and walk into town for some bagels?" I ask. Jax nods and fifteen minutes later the kitchen sparkles—we even cover up the burnt-egg smell with lemon Windex. I throw on one of Carchie's sweaters, and Jax zips into a bright blue windbreaker.

"Jordy still asleep?" he asks as we head outside.

"Yeah. I think she did some editing after we went to bed."

"And Carchie?"

"Reading the paper."

We walk in silence up the small hill that connects Carchie's private road (he put up a sign that read "Abbie Hoffman Way,"

but the town was not amused, so it officially remains Lake
Road) to the narrow street that leads to town. Our footsteps
make an even, crunching sound as they skim across the old, un-
paved road. I wonder how many times Carchie has walked
along this same ground. Are these his footprints? The sun is up,
but nowhere near its eventual pinnacle, though it already feels
warm and soothing on our faces. The smell of pine trees and
moist soil is a welcome change from the exhaust and anxiety of
the city.

"I love this," Jax says suddenly.

"What, the country?"

"That, too, but I meant us, walking in silence. I love comfortable silence."

"I know what you mean. It's so . . ."

"Comforting," Jax finishes for me, laughing. "People tend to
talk too damn much, you know? There's nothing wrong with
just shutting the fuck up for five minutes."

I nod. After a few more minutes of quiet companionship, we
arrive in town, which consists of three streets lined with artsy,
charming shops, as well as a great pizza place, a few fantastic ice
cream parlors and one mediocre deli that sells bagels. Since it's
a holiday weekend, the town is busy—bustling, in fact. Jax and I
consider ourselves professional people-watchers, so we make a
beeline for a nearby bench and settle in for some quality obser-
vation. Tremendous, towering oaks buffer the streets, and the
shade feels cool and calming. The air smells clean and familiar.
Most of my best childhood memories include this same scent—
the only colorful childhood memories I have of Ashley took
place in and around Carchie's cabin. Jax lights a cigarette for
each of us.

"We should dispose of it properly," I tell him as he hands it to
me.

"Really? I figured I'd hock a huge loogie and toss the butt
into it."

"I was just reminding you. We toss butts on the ground in the
city," I explain.

"Yeah, that's because Manhattan is one huge ashtray, except

for Gramercy Park, and that's 'cause they're smart enough to put up gates to keep the rest of us out. When I go a whole day without seeing a bottle full of piss on the sidewalk, I swear I'll stop littering."

"It is pretty disgusting sometimes, isn't it? But it also has—"

"The best food in the world? The best shopping in the world? The best dance clubs in the world? The best museums in the world? Hmm, what did I miss?" Jax asks.

"Did you say pizza?"

"I said food. That covers it all. Speaking of which . . ."

"Yeah, I'm hungry, too." The cars yield to us as we cross the street. "Jax?"

"Yes, babycakes?" He holds the door to the deli open for me.

"Would you think I was crazy if I wanted to take a break from the city for a while? Maybe get a car and drive around for part of the summer?" We enter the crowded deli (there are four people inside) and Jax hugs me from behind as we check out the bagel selection.

"I'd think you were crazier than Zelda if you *didn't* get out for a while," he replies. "Speaking of Zelda, are you planning on finding a new therapist?"

"I'm going to take a break from therapy for a while." The words sound strange as they tumble out of my mouth, even though I've been repeating this exact sentence in my mind for two weeks. Jax loosens his hold on me for a split second, and then squeezes even tighter.

"Am I invited to join you for a leg? Preferably the last weekend in June?" he asks, almost shyly.

His father's sixty-fifth birthday. "Abso-smurfly," I answer. He kisses my cheek and we order breakfast.

I think I just decided to spend the summer in a car, driving to different places with different people. It feels like my first solid decision in years.

Neither Jax nor Jordy remind me to get Tucker at the train station, but I remember on my own. While reclined on the hood of Teddy's BMW, staring up at the translucent sky, I wonder if Jax or Jordy resent the fact that I invited Tucker for part of the weekend. They both separately suggested I ask him, but I blew off the idea, leading each of them to the conclusion that I had no plans to ask Tucker to the cabin. Initially, I didn't—I wanted to spend the weekend with the three people who know me best. Laying in bed the other night, though, I tried to create a therapy session with Sam, and in my mind, I could hear him. I was actually able to step outside myself and consider another viewpoint, as long as I matched Sam's unique voice to the words I would have otherwise ignored if they'd been my own. I told myself, in Sam's voice, that it might be nice to introduce a new person to my wooded hideaway, and it would possibly even distract me from the shell of sadness I see when I look at Carchie. And I realized, as I listened to the soothing, repetitive sound of Jordy tapping away on the keyboard, that I really do like Tucker. There's something about him I trust and, while I'm drawn to the quiet, melancholy calm in him, he also makes me laugh and forget myself for a while. I can picture us in autumn, walking through Washington Square Park, holding hands.

My thoughts are suddenly carried away by the groan of the incoming train, and as I jump off the hood, I make a quick wish for a smooth, tension-free weekend. I check my appearance in the side mirror and try to force down my giddiness, which manifests in dopey grins.

Tucker bounces off the train, swinging an old knapsack over his shoulder. His eyes immediately find mine and we both smile. He patiently maneuvers around the small crowd on the platform and walks toward me without breaking eye contact. His unwavering gaze is both thrilling and disconcerting, especially when he lands in front of me.

"Hi," he says.

"Hi. How was the train ride?"

Tucker rolls his eyes. "Crowded and noisy, but fine."

I open the car door and get in as Tucker walks around to the passenger side. I can't tell if he's appraising the car or trying to remove a kink from his neck.

As soon as he sits down he says, "Nice rental. How much for the weekend?"

"Actually, it's Teddy's car."

"Right, I knew that," Tucker replies. "Investment banker, right?"

I nod.

"What does her husband do?" he asks.

"Max is a dermatologist," I tell him.

Out of the corner of my eye, it seems as if Tucker nods respectfully, but then he says, "Jobs that entail money and acne; dinner conversations with them must be fascinating."

The inherent sense to protect my sister surges almost violently through my body. The sensation flings my mind into the past, to a snowy day off from school when I was about seven. I walked into the kitchen for some cookies and wound up listening to Teddy and Ashley argue about whose turn it was to empty the dishwasher. My parents were enjoying the blizzard from the privacy of their bedroom, so interference was not on the way. Ashley said something obnoxious to Teddy—I can't remember what—and she was momentarily silenced. Both Teddy's defeat and Ashley's delight were palpable, so I screamed, "At least her friends from sixth grade are nicer than your friends are now!" Ashley and Teddy stared at me, looked at each other and cracked up into hysterical laughter. My proclamation made no sense, but they both understood the reference. A few weeks before, my mother had gone on and on about how Ashley's friends hadn't turned out the way she thought they would, and how Teddy's friends were so sweet and smart now, and she hoped they'd stay that way once they entered high school. I knew what I said didn't cut Ashley the way he had cut Teddy, but at least they were laughing, and laughing together, at that! I took my cookies into the living room. Teddy and Ashley followed, and we wound up playing Chutes and Ladders and Parcheesi for the rest of the afternoon. A few hours later, Ashley tapped two fingers on my head—his way of getting my attention—and I looked up at him. "What you did before, in the kitchen, defending Teddy—that was good. Do that, always." I nodded, then rolled the dice nonchalantly—inside, though, I could not stop smiling, and the profusion of pride propelled me for months.

I turn to Tucker and say, "We try to meet in the middle by talking about things we all care about."

I turn on the radio and try to think of something, anything, that will make me forget Tucker just insulted my sister. Only I am allowed to criticize her.

"Very pretty area," Tucker states as we roll into town. "Your uncle certainly has good taste."

"He also has cancer," I say quietly. Tucker looks at me, wipes the stray hairs out of my eyes and then returns his incisive gaze to the trees.

I exhale a huge breath I didn't even know I was holding, and wipe the slate clean in the process. I turn onto Carchie's street, then roll into the driveway.

"Ready to meet Uncle Carchie?" I ask Tucker, leading him around back to the deck.

"Sure," he replies, a blanket of false confidence wrapped around the single word. I can't decide if I admire or deplore Tucker's artificial arrogance. Then again, maybe I'd be better off if I wasn't so intimidated by the moments in life that terrify me.

Carchie is on the deck, smoking a joint, listening to an ancient Dylan bootleg. He's wearing faded army pants, a flannel shirt and the only Yankees cap he's ever owned, the rim practically devoid of material. He sits in the sun, and every time he shivers I have to control the urge to run to him, to lend him the warmth of my body.

"Carchie, this is Tucker Spencer. Tucker, meet Carchie."

Carchie gently places the lit joint in an ashtray, pushes off against the arms of his chair to stand up and offers his hand to Tucker.

"Nice to meet you," Carchie says, his eyes meeting Tucker's.

"You, too, sir," Tucker answers.

"You'll be on the next train back to the city if you use that word again," Carchie grumbles, lowering himself into the chair. Oh shit. Say something, Tucker.

"Sorry 'bout that, Carchie. You can take the boy out of prep school, but you can't take the prep school out of the boy."

Carchie reaches for the joint. "Not bad," he says, smiling. He offers the joint to Tucker, who inhales and passes it to me. Tucker cocks his head, closes his eyes for a moment and then turns to Carchie.

"This isn't Dylan at Newport, is it?"

Carchie's eyes blaze with surprise as he exhales. "Yep, taped it myself."

Tucker pulls a chair toward Carchie, sits in it and leans forward, his elbows on his knees. "No shit. I've only heard this stuff remastered on CD. Where else did you see him?"

Tucker squirms in anticipation of Carchie's answer. I completely forgot about this potential bond.

Carchie is about to answer when he leans back and looks at me. "Sit down and relax, Alex. I'm not going to hurt him, for Christ's sake."

Tucker offers me his seat and pulls up another, silently and accidentally impressing Carchie. Tucker was raised to be polite, and while Carchie understands my need for independence (at least in terms of relying only on the tried and true), I know he wants to see me taken care of, one-half of a passionate pair. It is Carchie who instilled in me both respect and passion—for art, for literature, for music, for color—and I think he worries I won't find someone with similar sensibilities. So Tucker's love for Bob Dylan is significant, at least for Carchie. Wait until he finds out Tucker is a painter.

The five of us are in Carchie's lakeside backyard, a good local radio station piping through the outdoor speakers. Carchie isn't big on modern amenities, but he insists on quality audio equipment. It's three o'clock and we've already gone through two pitchers of lemonade, but we're still sweating through our shorts.

"I'm going up to put on a bathing suit," Jordy announces.

"Oh shit!" Jax yells.

"I reminded you," I taunt, tossing an ice cube his way. Tucker is in the shade, reading a biography of one of the Rockefellers, and has yet to shed his T-shirt.

"I know, I know. I have the memory of a baby flea." He looks around, surveying the utterly private space in which we now exist. "Oh well, I've got nothing to be ashamed of," he says, pulling off his T-shirt. He turns to Tucker, as if he just remembered his presence. "You don't mind, do you?"

Tucker shakes his head. "Four years on varsity soccer—spent a lot of time in locker rooms."

"I *knew* I should have been an athlete," Jax says, tossing his shirt on a chair.

"You are not going skinny-dipping—are you?" Jordy asks, grinning. Carchie looks up from his crossword puzzle.

"Why not?" Jax replies, dropping his navy blue shorts. "It's nothing you haven't seen before in a smaller version. Carchie, you OK with this?"

Carchie shrugs his pointed shoulders. "Army."

Jax steps out of his boxers, does a quick pirouette and walks toward the weather-beaten dock.

"Damn, I wish I was your lover!" Jordy screams in a singsong voice.

"That's what they all say!" Jax yells. Carchie chuckles.

Jax shimmies along with the music and jumps in the lake, legs flailing like a gawky boy.

"That water's pretty cold," I announce. "He's got balls."

"Not anymore," Tucker says. All four of us laugh.

At dusk, we barbeque under Pisces, Orion and Cassiopeia. Of course, it takes half an hour for four city dwellers to light the barbeque, but cold beers make the situation a virtual comedy of errors. Carchie refuses to help us, concentrating instead on the last few clues in his crossword puzzle. We play bootlegs all night—The Dead, Dylan, Janis—and feast on burgers, sweet potato fries, asparagus and Rolling Rock. Jax and Tucker consume twice as much as Jordy and I. Carchie valiantly eats three-quarters of a hamburger and a handful of fries. The pot seems to curb the nausea but does nothing to stimulate his once voracious appetite. Jax finishes off his meal with a masculine belch and encourages Tucker to do the same.

"Let's play Truth," Jax says, lighting a round of cigarettes.

Jordy groans, plunges a tanned arm into the cooler and extracts frosty beer bottles for each of us.

Carchie rolls his eyes and begins the process of standing up. "I promised Alex's mother I would call her," he says. "Seems like a good time to do so." He musses Jax's hair as he leans in to kiss me. "I'll probably read in bed afterwards. See you guys in the morning."

"Uh, Carchie?"

"Yes, Alex?"

"Can you possibly refrain from—"

"You, me, Jax and Jordy are having a wonderful time," he says, smiling.

"Thanks." Carchie waves and walks inside. I turn to Tucker. "Long story," is all I say. Tucker shrugs.

"OK, Jax, you asked for it," Jordy says, taking a quick sip of beer.

"Bring it on, baby." He turns to Tucker. "You know how to play?"

Tucker nods, clearly not thrilled with Jax's game of choice.

"We can play something else if you want," I tell him.

Tucker shrugs. "Truth is fine." Liar. Who would want to play Truth with three people he's known less than a week?

"You start, Jordy," Jax instructs.

"Do you spit or swallow?" Jordy asks.

"Well, I rarely *give* head," Jax answers. "And you really shouldn't swallow these days, anyway."

"True," Jordy mumbles. She leans back, considering the stars for a moment. "Isn't it amazing how something as simple as sex always complicates our lives?"

"That's why I made up an easy rhyme about it," Jax explains. "If you spit, you'll stay fit. If you swallow, you'll be hollow." Tucker chuckles.

"You coin an expression for every occasion," I tell him.

Jax nods. "It's too bad I'm not straight—I'm quite a cunning linguist!" Jordy moans, I try not to laugh and Tucker cracks up.

"Jordy, why'd you break up with Kevin? I've always wondered," Jax counters.

"First of all, we weren't technically dating. Second, I ended it because—"

"You have to tell the truth," Jax reminds her, swigging his beer.

"He said *supposably.*"

Jax's laugh gets tangled up in his beer and spurts out his nose. "Too funny!"

Jordy smirks and turns to me. I wonder if they're not questioning Tucker out of politeness or apathy. "What's the most selfless thing you've ever done?"

"Summer of '92. I was at a Dead show with Jax and Casey and found a ticket in the grass. Instead of selling it, I 'miracled' someone—it was the greatest feeling in the world."

"You made that guy deliriously happy," Jax says. "Man, did he need a shower."

I turn to Tucker. "What do you think is the most important aspect of a good relationship?"

Tucker doesn't hesitate, not even for a second. "Honesty." He looks around the table for a moment, and then settles those turbulent eyes on me again.

"What is your worst memory?" he asks.

Watching my brother die. Waking up and realizing I'd failed to kill myself. Shit—this is why I hate playing Truth with anyone outside my immediate circle of comfort. There is no simple answer. I cannot even say "Being locked in a psych ward" and proceed with the game. That is not how I want to tell Tucker about my past. But if I don't say something that pertains to Ashley or attempted suicide, both Jax and Jordy will know I'm lying. I close my eyes and dig into my damaged soul for an answer. I just have to trust that Jax and Jordy will understand the meaning behind my lie and decline to call me on it. It's not as if it's not a bad memory.

"Hearing the news that Carchie has cancer," I answer. Jordy and Jax stare at me but remain silent. Jordy then nods, apparently agreeing with my decision to postpone the truth.

"What kind of cancer does he have?" Tucker asks.

"He had a melanoma removed from his lower back," I answer. "They got it all, but he's had a chemo treatment every month since January, just in case." Tucker nods solemnly.

"Jax, do you ever wish you weren't gay?" I ask.

"Good question," Jordy says quietly. Jax nods in agreement. Tucker opens another beer.

"No, I like who I am. But I know *other* people wish I wasn't gay, and that . . ." He drifts off and plays with a bottle cap, frowning. "I've been out for eight years. You'd think my father would've gotten over it already," he mumbles. After a few seconds, he looks up, smiles ever so slightly and points to me. "What's the best present you've ever gotten?"

My cheeks flush with the memory. "A first edition copy of *The Lion, The Witch and The Wardrobe* from Jordy."

"Tucker, if you could have sex with anyone on the planet, who would it be?" I ask.

Tucker smiles like a little boy and answers, "Angelina Jolie."

He turns to Jordy. "If you had to have sex with a woman, who would it be?" Jordy shifts in her seat while Jax pants with anticipation.

"Angelina Jolie," she answers, turning to Jax. "If *you* had to have sex with a woman, who would it be?"

Jax laughs. "Madonna, no question."

"Alex, if you had to have sex with a woman, who would it be?" he asks. A snippet of a flashback flies before my eyes. Only Casey knows about that night in college. And Ashley.

"I'd take Madonna *or* Angelina Jolie," I reply. Our laughter echoes across the silent, sleepy lake.

We move inside, driven by the thought of roasting marshmallows in the fireplace. Jordy lights a joint while Jax rambles into the garage in search of firewood. Tucker plops into Carchie's chair. Jordy and I share a look—no one except Carchie ever sits in that chair—but neither of us says a word. We hear a small crash and Jax returns moments later, holding an old cardboard box, wearing a shit-eating grin.

"Where's the firewood?" Jordy demands, handing Jax the joint.

He takes a long, smooth hit, hands the joint to me and opens the box. "Look what I found!"

None of us gets up, so Jax upturns the box on the faded beige carpet. A selection of drums, bongos and rain sticks tumble out with a small thud.

"Oh my God, I haven't seen these in years. Carchie and his friends had a drum circle once a month, way back when. And he used to shake the rain stick to lull me to sleep." I pick up the stick, the memories biting.

"Maybe you should put that stuff away," Jordy says to Jax.

"Lay off, Jordy," I say. Jax looks from me to Jordy to Tucker and then back to me, and finally sits.

He crosses his gangly legs and taps the bongos. I tilt the rain stick, letting the strangely soothing sound wash over us. Jordy reclines on the couch, watching, sharing the joint with Tucker. I grab the remote and raise the volume on the stereo a little, grinning at Jax. Slowly, tentatively, we recapture the feeling that helped define our early twenties. Jax and I found freedom and individuality during the long, sun-soaked days spent at Dead shows. We felt as if we belonged with that crowd, because not one of them fit neatly into any sort of category. We were two square pegs suddenly surrounded by thousands of square pegs, and the realization that it wasn't just us freed us. The improvisational nature of the music also changed our outlook on life, because for the first time, the mantra "Anything goes" was not only allowed, but encouraged. Responsibility, and Jerry's death, forced us to move on, but once a Deadhead, always a Deadhead. The next song begins and suddenly we are twenty-one again, on summer vacation, selling beads and braids and anything else to get from one show to another, lying to our parents for an entire month. We told them we had saved enough money to last the entire summer. The truth came out a few years ago, during a particularly peaceful Thanksgiving dinner, and too much time had passed for anyone to really care about our duplicity.

Jax's eyes are closed, but I know we see the same image—the image of our former selves, the ones who were careless but carefree, naive but happy. Now—at this moment—we let go of age and restraint, mistakes and regrets, repression and depression.

Jax taps louder, and I gain rhythmic control of the stick. We stand up, connected to the instruments in hand and reconnected to one of our favorite Dead songs.

From the other direction she was calling my eye
It could be an illusion, but I might as well try
Might as well try

She wore scarlet begonias, tucked into her curls
I knew right away she was not like other girls
Other girls

Jax is going crazy on the bongos—the floor quivers—and Jordy cackles. Tucker is in his own world, eyes closed, one foot tapping the beat.

Once in a while you get shown the light
In the strangest of places if you look at it right

Three songs later, the bootleg tape ends, and we tuck the instruments back in to the box. As I carry the box out to the garage, it occurs to me that I just, inadvertently, let Tucker see a part of me I had no intention of sharing, at least not for a long time.

The living room is empty when I return, and I circle about in confusion until Jordy beckons me into the kitchen. I find her elbow-deep in a quart of ice cream, talking to Carchie. There are peanut M&Ms scattered all over the chipped wooden table. I settle into a chair and clean the table by popping M&Ms into my mouth. Carchie pours himself a glass of water, opens a cabinet and removes a bottle of pills.

"Aren't you supposed to take those with food?" I ask. Pills, water, food—the whole process brings me back to Ashley.

Carchie swallows the pill and slams his hand on the counter. "Goddamn it, Alex. It's the first time I've forgotten, so fuck off!"

The tears descend immediately, almost instinctually.

"Oh Jesus, I'm sorry, sweetie. I'm sorry." Carchie crosses the kitchen and hugs me. "I'm just tired of being tired, Alex. You're here and it's summer and I want to hang out with you guys like I used to, but I'm either tired or nauseous or both, and I can't fucking stand it."

Why is it that so many of us are eventually reduced to a dependence on pills in order to postpone pain? "Two more treatments, Carchie," I tell him.

"And then we can have a party!" Jordy says excitedly. "We can make Jell-O shots and pot brownies and margaritas!"

Carchie and I disentangle and join Jordy at the table.

"Sounds good to me, Jordy. You're in charge," Carchie tells her.

"Where are Jax and Tucker?" I ask.

Jordy motions to her right with her head.

"They're in the pantry?" I ask, smiling.

Jordy, confused, glances at the pantry, smiles and looks to her left, through the window that overlooks the lake. She takes a gulp of water and says, "They went swimming."

I light a cigarette. Carchie reaches for a drag but I push his arm away. "If I go upstairs and pretend to be sleeping, do you think Tucker will get in bed with me?" I ask.

Jordy puts her spoon down, midway to her mouth, and lights a cigarette.

"You don't want to sleep with him?" Carchie asks.

I shake my head.

"You don't want to have sex with him or you don't want to share a bed with him?" Jordy inquires.

"Neither," I reply. "I'm just not—that's not where my head is right now."

Carchie squeezes my shoulder and Jordy nods. I can see the wheels in her mind spinning behind her eyes. "That makes perfect sense to me. Stay here. I'll take care of it."

Carchie stops her. "It's my house. *I'll* take care of it."

He strolls into the living room, through the sliding glass door and onto the deck. He whistles, and both Tucker and Jax abandon the lake and approach Carchie like two obedient Labradors. They talk for a minute or so, and then Carchie re-enters the kitchen. Through the window, I see Jax's bare ass. He prances down the dock until he reaches the end. He cannonballs into the water, laughing as he surfaces.

"What'd you say?" I ask.

"I told him that even though he's a Dylan fan, a Yankees fan and a damn good crossword puzzler, I'd appreciate the respect that goes along with being a first-time guest in my house. He knew what I meant. He's bunking with Tinkerbell in the guest room. Good night, beautiful girls." He kisses each of us on the forehead.

"'Night, Carchie. Thank you."

Jordy and I sit in silence for a few moments.

"He won't read into it, Alex. Guys aren't like that."

"He won't think it's odd that Carchie, of all people, is against fraternization?"

"First of all, this isn't sleepaway camp. Who uses that word in real life anyway? Second, even if he guesses correctly about Carchie's request, he'll think you're a perfectly normal girl who is upset about her uncle's illness."

I put my cigarette out, the bizarre words ringing in my head. "Do you think there's such a thing as *perfectly normal*?"

Jordy takes a long drag, her eyes penetrating mine. "I'm not sure," she answers. "All I know is that normal people—people who don't feel passionate about anything, people who don't read books, people who exist for years without crying—are boring, one-dimensional and usually of mediocre intelligence. I hate normal people," Jordy concludes, grinning.

"So based on the sliding scale of normalcy, you must really adore me, huh?" I ask.

Jordy puts her cigarette out and tosses the spoon in the sink. As we walk upstairs together, she links her arm through mine.

"The word *adore* doesn't even begin to cover it."

Later, alone in bed, I cry myself to sleep. I cannot help wishing I could talk to Sam about Carchie.

I wait for the clock to read 5:00 a.m. and then creep downstairs—it's been an hour and I am obviously not falling back to sleep. During the last sixty minutes, I have managed to convince myself that a fresh mug of coffee, a cigarette and the sunrise will be a splendid way to start the day.

The coffee is already made. I pour myself a cup, grab a smoke and join Carchie on the deck. In the dingy light before dawn, Carchie looks like an old man.

"Your mother's always bitching to me about how you sleep too late," he says. "What the hell are you doing up?"

I lean down and he kisses my cheek. "Don't know. Couldn't sleep."

"At what time do you think you'll start using full sentences?" he asks.

I settle into a chair, folding my legs underneath my oversized sweatshirt. "Ha ha, funny. I can't exactly tell my mother that the only way I fall asleep before three a.m. is by drinking large quantities of alcohol. What are you doing up?"

Carchie lights my cigarette for me. "I've been getting up at six lately, so I'm only an hour early."

I nod. The surface of the lake seems so still, so complete.

"I can't wait for the day when I wake up and feel fine, perfectly fine," Carchie announces.

"Not that far away," I reply.

"You know what I plan to do on that day?" he asks.

"What?"

"Visit Ashley."

Two words and I'm a speechless, shivering mass of emotion. Carchie looks me over and continues.

"I feel guilty. I haven't talked to Ashley in five months," he says.

I draw both smoke and strength from my cigarette. "You don't have to be staring at his tombstone to talk to him, you know."

Carchie nods. "Yeah, I do. I prefer to be near him." He looks across the lake, then turns back to me. "I want you to come with me, Alex."

Shit, the cigarette is gone. "No."

"Alex, it's been two years. It's time to visit him again."

A beam of sunlight hits Carchie's face as he speaks, and suddenly the lake shimmers. The sun, energized from a night of rest, appears over the horizon. I close my eyes and wish I had stayed in bed.

"I'm not ready," I finally say.

"I think you are."

"I don't care what you think."

Carchie doesn't flinch. "Yes, you do."

"The last time I was there—"

"You went home and tried to kill yourself, I know." Carchie sighs, and the silence covers us like a shroud. "You're stronger now, Alex. I see it. I wish you could see it."

I grip the lighter and cover it with my fist, pushing it into the folds of my palm. "First I'm at the grave too often, now I don't visit enough. Why don't you let me do what feels right?" It isn't until a tear splashes on my wrist that I realize I'm crying.

"Because what you feel is regret, and fear. Yes, you lost out on a valuable opportunity to be close with Ashley when you were young, but you guys were ten years apart and it just didn't happen and there is not a fucking thing you can do about it now."

My head seems to weigh fifty pounds, so I rest it on the table. I clench my eyes shut and the image of the flawless sunrise disappears. All I see is Ashley's smile, warmer and brighter than any sunrise. I feel Carchie's hands on my shoulders and his lips touch the crown of my head.

"It's time to let go," he tells me. I try to nod, but all I can do is shake my head.

∽

Jax is in the shower and Jordy's cooking an omelet for Carchie, so I recruit Tucker to help me strip the beds. I hand him two sets of clean sheets for the guest room and head into my room to make the bed. I hear Jordy and Carchie laughing in the kitchen. I love that Carchie loves both Jax and Jordy. He seems to really like Tucker, too—much more than I thought he would. I guess inviting Tucker turned out to be a good idea, after all. I grab the dirty sheets and walk into the guest room. Instead of a pile of dirty sheets and a freshly made bed, I find Tucker muttering to himself as he repeatedly flips the fitted sheet into the air, trying to lock it onto the corners of the bed.

"Oh my God, you can't be serious," I say.

Tucker looks up, his face twisted with confusion and embarrassment. "What?"

"Tell me you don't know how to make a bed."

"I don't know how to make a bed."

I drop my pile and spread the sheet across the bed, motioning to Tucker to stand back and watch. "How can you not know how to make a bed? With a fitted sheet?"

"I didn't have to do chores when I was a kid. We cleared our plates from the table and that was it."

"You went to college, didn't you? Did you sleep on the same dirty sheets for a year at a time?"

"No, I got some girl to change my sheets for me."

I look up. "Oh, so you got her to fuck you *and* make your bed for you. Very nice! I thought you said you're a feminist—I knew there was something wrong with that speech. And now?"

Tucker smirks, though I'm not sure if he's proud or ashamed. "I have a cleaning lady once a week."

I nod, pretending to be mortified. So he is the real deal—a billionaire's son who can barely take care of himself, at least when it comes to household chores.

"When you have a child, you should make your kid do weekly chores—many of them—and he or she should know how to make a bed, with hospital corners."

Tucker salutes me. "Yes, ma'am," he says, smiling.

CO

"Jax, don't speed," I order. "We've got more than a quarter of pot on us."

"And this area of New York qualifies as Smalltown, USA," Jordy adds.

Jax cracks up. "Oh my God, can you imagine? A BMW registered in Manhattan carrying a fag, a beautiful Jew, a hot shiksa and one of America's Most Eligible Bachelors, blasting Madonna. The cop wouldn't know what to shoot first, his wad or his gun!"

Jax can't stop laughing. I grab my sweatshirt, roll it up, place it on Tucker's leg and stretch out across the black leather seat. Jordy is curled in a ball on the front seat, watching the trees fly by in the morning sun. We decided to hit the road early in an effort to avoid the ugly snarl of end-of-the-holiday-weekend traffic. I know our visit invigorated Carchie spiritually, but it also wore him out physically. He would never allow us, me, to see him lounging on the couch or napping, so our premature departure will save Carchie another day of masquerading. He promised me he's been taking good care of himself, and he agreed to spend the day reading in bed. A vision of Carchie, wearing his striped pajamas, enrapt in a good book, makes me smile. Sleep creeps up on me. I'm amazingly comfortable with my head in Tucker's lap, and he smiles down at me as I kick my sandals onto the floor. I order Jax to lower the music, put my shades on and close my eyes. When I wake up, we're halfway across the George Washington Bridge.

5

She picks up on the third ring, as usual.

"Hi, Mom."

"Alex, honey, how are you?"

"I'm OK. You?"

"I'm fine. We had a nice weekend at the beach. Are you sure you're OK?"

"Yes, Mom, I'm fine," I answer as I smear peanut butter on two slices of rye bread.

"How was your weekend?"

"Fun."

"How does Carchie look?"

"Thin, but OK."

"Did you make any decisions?"

"About what?" I dump marmalade on the bread.

She sighs and pauses. "About your future? A job?"

"Actually, I'm thinking about taking the summer off, to fig-ure things out."

"Oh, Alexandra, don't tell me you need to find yourself, on top of everything else."

"No, Mom, I don't need to *find* myself. I just need—"

"So you're going to mope around the city?"

"No. I might buy a car, maybe visit Casey in Chicago, go up to the Berkshires for a while."

"I'm not thrilled about you driving cross-country alone."

"Mom, Chicago is not cross-country. And Jax is going to come along for a little while. Maybe Jordy, too, when she finishes her dissertation." I cut the sandwich unevenly in half and toss the knife into the sink.

"How is Jax? Tell him to call his parents. His father had another treatment last week."

"He's fine. He got a voice-over gig."

"Send him my love. He got a what?"

"Never mind. I have to go, Mom." I shove the jelly back into its place in the fridge.

"Go where? You don't have a job."

"I have to call my financial advisor, Mom, see how much I'm worth."

"Don't be snide, Alexandra. I just meant—"

"Yeah, I know what you meant. I'll talk to you soon. Say hi to Dad."

"OK, sweetie. I love you."

"Love you, too. Bye."

My peanut butter and jelly sandwich no longer looks appetizing, so I chug a bottle of water, spinning the cordless phone by its antenna. If Jordy were here, she'd yell and remind me how many phones I've broken. I release my grip and stare at the keypad. The little round buttons resemble pills, marching in formation. Teddy is in a meeting, Jordy is at the library, Casey is on location and Jax is working lunch. I just finished a three-hundred-page novel. I see a crinkled scrap of paper on the coffee table and dial the unmemorized number.

"Hi, Tucker. It's Alex."

"Hey, you. What's up?"

"Are you doing anything today?" I ask.

"I'm covered in paint but have no plans," he replies. I smile at the image.

"You want to come with me to the West Side?"

"You mean actually cross Broadway? Why on earth would you want to do that?"

"Fuck you. You want to come with me or not?"

Tucker laughs. I wonder if that lock of hair has fallen over his eyes yet. I also wonder if he's pissed he didn't get any over the weekend.

"Give me half an hour," he replies. "I'll meet you on Twelfth and Broadway, by The Strand."

"OK. Bye."

Did he say half an hour? I'm not even dressed. I toss the empty water bottle in the overflowing recycling bin and skip down the hall to my bedroom.

I give the cab driver an address on Tenth Avenue, not far from the Hudson River.

"Are we going to the Intrepid?" Tucker asks.

"No. The Land Rover dealership."

Tucker's eyebrows pop up. "You're buying a car?"

"Maybe. I figured I'd check out prices and stuff. I don't want to get jerked around, so we should pretend you're my husband."

"Car salesmen don't actually treat women differently, do they?" he asks.

"C'mon, Tucker, you can't be that idealistic."

"I am not idealistic. I just thought that was a stereotype from, like, 1975."

"As far as I know, it's practically a scientific fact."

Tucker chuckles to himself. "Can I call you Peaches and Honey Pie?"

The cab pulls up outside the dealership. "Whatever floats your boat. Just be really masculine, in a take-charge kind of way. Talk to him about football or the rodeo."

I pay the driver and we enter the glass-walled shrine to overpriced SUVs.

I shiver as the door closes behind us—the air conditioning is on so high I see papers fluttering gently on desks. Tucker grabs my hand just as the predatory salesman hangs up the phone and inches toward us. He's wearing cheap tan slacks, a black button-down shirt that should have been thrown out two years ago and brown pleather loafers.

"Hi, folks. My name is Seth. Can I help you with anything?"

I open my mouth to respond but Tucker beats me to it. "Yes, we're interested in a Discovery."

"Any specific ideas as to what you want?" Seth asks, practically drooling.

"Green exterior, CD player, air conditioning, automatic and absolutely no leather seats. I hate leather seats," I say as quickly as possible.

Seth looks at me as if I'm a lost child in a suburban mall. "OK, the lady has preferences. The SE over here is the best deal, but it does have leather seats," he says, pointing at a beautiful silver Land Rover.

"Can I get it without the leather?" I ask.

"Nope, sorry. If you want vinyl seats, you'll have to get the SD." He points to an equally beautiful dark blue Land Rover.

"What are the other differences?" Tucker asks.

"Well, with the SD, you lose the 220-watt stereo system with subwoofer and six-disc CD changer. You also sacrifice the Homelink system, the wood trim, the dual power sunroofs and the rear cargo cover. Oh, and the tow-hitch receiver."

I try to stop the confusion from crawling across my face, because I know that was probably Seth's intent, but I just can't help it—I have no fucking clue what he's talking about.

"What's a Homelink system?" I ask, embarrassed to inquire what the rear cargo cover actually covers.

"You program it to open your garage door, things like that," Seth replies.

"Oh, I don't have—"

"Does the SD have the four-wheel electronic traction control?" Tucker asks.

Seth nods.

"Four-wheel disc brakes? All Terrain ABS brake system? Side door impact beams?" Tucker is like a one-man Spanish Inquisition. Seth nods enthusiastically at every one of his questions.

"Could I pay to add the six-disc CD changer to the SD?" I ask.

"Sure, but you can't add the twelve speakers," Seth replies. "Are you a music aficionado?"

Tucker stares at me, waiting on my answer.

"Yeah, but—" I start.

"She probably wouldn't notice the difference," Tucker tells Seth. "Is the roof rack standard on the SD?"

Seth pats the roof rack on the blue Land Rover. "Yep, and you can upgrade to a windsurfer rack, a kayak carrier or a ski attachment."

Tucker's eyes widen and he turns to me, smiling. "The kayak carrier would be great for weekends at the cabin, hon."

Kayak? Hon? "I'm a little more concerned with the spare tire being on the outside of the car," I tell Tucker through gritted teeth.

"Oh, we can get a tire lock for that, right, Seth?"

"Absolutely. Shouldn't be a problem," Seth answers.

"In the city? The tire will be stolen the first time I park."

"Alex, sweetie, that's why you'll use the tire lock," Tucker explains, taking my hand.

"I need a cigarette. You deal with this for a minute," I tell him, although I really say it to make myself feel like less of an idiot. Tucker nods, Seth smiles condescendingly and I skulk outside.

I monitor the discussion from the sidewalk, taking quick pulls on a cigarette. Tucker has apparently done this before— he looks calm and confident, and Seth keeps smiling in a serious, respectful manner. I had no idea Tucker was an experienced car buyer, so why did I bring him? I could have called my father. He would've been thrilled to drive into the city, pick me up and take me car shopping. Yet it never even crossed my mind. Jax and Jordy are equally clueless in this situation, and I've lost touch with the few straight male friends I had in college. Tucker seemed like the perfect choice, yet I put absolutely no thought into asking him and, until this second, didn't stop to think that helping someone buy a car is not exactly a casual outing. I invited Tucker, a guy I've known for a week, to help me spend my money and make a huge commitment to the first tangible, taxable item I've ever purchased. I wonder what Sam would think about this.

I wish Ashley were here. Then again, if Ashley were alive I wouldn't have the money to buy a car. Why am I buying a car, anyway? My stomach hurts.

The frigid air wraps itself around my body as soon as I open the glass door. I browse through the selection of catalogues, grabbing a handful to show to Jordy, Jax and Teddy. Tucker creeps up behind me, puts his arm around my waist and shows me a bunch of color swatches.

"Are you sure you want a green exterior?"

"Yes," I reply immediately.

"Because black is pretty hot, and with a gray—"

"I want green. I've always wanted a green car," I tell him, trying to control the tone of my voice.

"OK, honey, green it is." Is he kidding? Seth is at his desk, on the other side of the room, punching figures into a calculator. Unless he shares the Bionic Woman's amazing sense of hearing, Seth has no idea we're even talking.

"Did you negotiate the price yet?" I ask.

Tucker nods his head. "Yep, he's working up some figures."

"Good."

"It is your money, sweetie." He laughs at the term of endearment and, taking my hand, leads me over to Seth's desk. He pulls the chair out for me and sits beside me in a matching orange, plastic chair.

"OK, folks, this is the best I can do. Keep in mind the availability—you'll be able to pick up this particular car a week from today." Seth hands Tucker a slip of paper. Tucker's demeanor reveals nothing, and he passes it to me. I try my best to mimic Tucker's poker face, but I cannot control the giggles that squirm their way up my belly, out of my mouth. I know enough about the Discovery to recognize the deal, but still—I could send a child to a state college for the same amount.

"I assume you take care of the plates, and speak to my insurance agent?" I ask.

"Yes, Mrs. Spencer, I'll have all the paperwork ready for you." I see Tucker smirk out of the corner of my eye, and the reference to marriage is hysterically funny, for about ten seconds. I can tell Tucker is immensely pleased with himself, and clearly enjoys his role.

"Actually, it's Ms. Justice," I tell Seth.

"Oh, I'm sorry. I just assumed you had the same—" I stare him down as best I can, shutting him up and punishing him for assuming anything at all.

Seth hands me some papers to fill out, and as I'm entering my address, I feel a wave of nausea hit me so hard I almost keel over in my seat. Neither of the guys notice—they are actually talking about football. I steady myself and try to make it look as if I'm casually resting my head on my hand. Jesus Christ, what the hell is going on? I inhale slowly, through my nose, and exhale through my mouth. It's only a game, Alex, relax—you're not married to Tucker. You're not married to anyone.

I slide the papers across the desk to Seth, who clips them together, inserts them in a manila file folder and hands us each a business card.

"Call me if you have any questions, and I'll see you here next week. I'll call as soon as your vehicle arrives, so you can get the bank check in order. It's been a pleasure talking with you, Mr. Spencer. And I hope your wife enjoys her new car. Maybe next time she'll buy one for you!" Seth and Tucker find this amusing. Seth shakes my hand and winks. Tucker wraps his arm around my waist again. I need to get out of here, now. I barrel across the showroom, losing Tucker in the process. He catches up at the door and holds it open for me as the final act of our performance.

We hit the sidewalk, the blazing sun dropping on our backs like a blanket. I feel light-headed for a minute—I'm uncertain if the change in temperature or the adrenaline rush is to blame. I turn the wrong way down the street and don't notice my mistake until the Hudson River flows into sight. I turn around, retrace my steps and find Tucker leaning against the translucent wall of the dealership, smoking a cigarette. "Why didn't you stop me from going the wrong way?" I ask, taking a drag of his cigarette.

Tucker shrugs. We stand in silence for a few minutes. I wonder what he's thinking. The words *I just bought a car* gush into my consciousness. The car I've always wanted. Tucker flicks his cigarette into the street and beckons me toward the corner. I just bought a car. I trail behind Tucker, a smile beginning to crack the tightness in my face.

"Holy shit!" I yell as Tucker hails a cab. "I just bought a car!"

"I thought that was the point," he replies, opening the cab door for me. He gives the driver what I assume is his address.

"It was. It's just that this is very—I don't know, grown-up. It's my first car."

"It's a very big purchase," Tucker says dryly. I'm not sure if he's being condescending, but I let it slide. "Oh, speaking of which," he continues, "I have good news! I sold two paintings. Two *big* paintings."

"Good for you! How'd that happen?"

"A friend of a friend owns a gallery in TriBeCa and offered to display them for a few weeks. The other day, some guy walked in and bought both."

"That's great. Did you make a lot of money?"

The cab driver makes a fast right onto Fifth Avenue, barely making the light. Tucker catches me as my body slides across the seat into his.

"It takes care of rent for a few months, and gives me some leeway for the summer. If I stick to a budget, I think I can skip the job thing and paint for three months." Tucker's arm tightens around my back, pulling me in for a half-hug, half-squeeze.

"Score another point for starving artists. Where are we going?"

"My place. I need a favor, so I figured I'd cushion the blow with lunch."

"I owe you one, Tucker. You just helped me buy a car." I slap the sticky, green seat. "I can't believe I just bought a car with my own money!" I scream.

Tucker covers his ears. "Jesus, Alex, turn the other way the next time you do that. Trust me, this favor makes that favor look like—it's apples and oranges, believe me."

The cab pulls up outside a five-story brownstone. Pieces of

ivy (or something green that I imagine is ivy) cling to the faded-brick façade, and a freshly painted black gate that sparkles in the sunshine separates the property from the sidewalk.

As we walk through the crimson-colored door, I ask, "You painted that gate, didn't you?"

Tucker nods. "The door, too. It used to be black. I'm one flight up, on the right. Number fourteen."

That's my lucky number. Tucker unlocks the door, and I follow him inside. There's an interesting scent to the apartment, a mixture of paint, lemon and wood. A floor-to-ceiling window on the far side of the living room allows a smiling stream of sunlight to saturate the entire space.

"Make yourself at home," he tells me. "I'll start making lunch."

I wander into the living room, which is a perfect square with a couch in the middle. One side of the room is spotless and boasts top-of-the-line stereo equipment, as well as a huge TV. Stacks of CDs and DVDs slither their way up the wall like a thick, determined snake. The far wall of the room is exposed brick—an expanse of space dedicated to what I recognize as a Jackson Pollock painting. Piles of books are everywhere, carefully assembled against the brick. I steal a look, seeing titles I recognize, as well as a collection of thick art books.

The floor-to-ceiling-window side of the room looks as if it belongs to someone else. It's chaotic, unbalanced and intoxicating. An antique wooden easel, splashed with arbitrary layers of paint, dominates one corner, surrounded by short, circular tables covered with palettes, cans of paint, paintbrushes, photographs and sketches. The opposite corner resembles a miniature storeroom. Cans of paint sit in various stages—open, full, empty. Tucker pokes his head into the living room.

"Sorry about the mess."

"This room looks like it's inhabited by a schizophrenic," I tell him.

He laughs. "When I paint I can't slow down, so things get cluttered. The kitchen and bedroom are over here," he says, motioning behind him.

I check out the kitchen, which is average for Manhattan; it's small, cramped and narrow. Tucker's kitchen has a window, so it's lighter and more spacious than most. There are half a dozen plants on the windowsill and a bouquet of landscape postcards on the fridge.

Next, I stand in the doorway to the bedroom, surveying the intimate space. Above the bed, there's a striking painting, which I assume Tucker painted. The painting is big, but not huge—it's roughly the size of a window. Somehow, it looks farther away than the wall, or maybe there's a painting within the painting. I feel like I'm looking at something through fog and spray, something elusive. There are no figures in it, just shapes, violent ones. The shapes themselves are ambiguous, and the result is calculated chaos. The painting is dark—mostly shades of red, gray and black—but tangled up in the somber hues is a lovely, lonely strand of blue. I understand why Tucker hangs it over his pillow—you could stare at the painting every day and each time it would invite a different thought.

His bed is huge—it rises at least two feet off the floor—with a beautiful, ornate oak headboard. The quilt is a deep shade of indigo, and the sheets are pale blue. There aren't any stray socks or boxers lying around. Against one wall, there is a desk, with an expensive laptop computer on top of it. Tucker's Prada jacket hangs unevenly from a chair. A cherry wood dresser and a few shelves are the only other accoutrements. Some choice books, a few framed photographs and some funky-looking pottery lines the shelves.

I head back into the living room, hoping to find the meaning of Tucker's life by further scrutinizing his belongings. Tucker is still banging away in the kitchen, but he must have turned on the stereo because Bruce Springsteen is moaning about Rosalita. I sit on the couch and look at photos. On one table, alongside a lamp, there are photos of a cute, college-aged boy who looks like a younger, happier version of Tucker, as well as a picture of an attractive, fair-haired girl, her arm wrapped around an older man I recognize as Charles Spencer.

They smile for the camera—both exude some sort of inner light. I turn back to the other photo—this boy has it, too.

Tucker meanders into the living room, wiping his hands on his jeans. "That's Derek, and the other one is Catherine and my father." He sits next to me on the couch, reaches out to the other end table and hands me a framed photo.

"That's my mom," he says.

I cautiously hold the frame and gaze at the photo. The woman pictured is thirty, maybe thirty-five, with blonde hair, salient green eyes and a demonstrative smile. "She's beautiful," I tell Tucker.

He nods. "She was a painter, before she met my father. She taught me to paint. She gave me that easel for my eighth birth-day. I used to stand on a pile of phone books and we would paint together."

I take another look at the easel—it seems fragile, almost im-practical. As I turn back to Tucker, I notice another easel in the corner, leaning against the wall. It's huge, and even though it's folded up, I can tell it's stronger, more modern and functional.

"Do you use that other easel for bigger pieces?" I ask.

"I never use that one," Tucker answers curtly.

"Why do you have it?"

Tucker shrugs. "My father bought it for me. I tried it once, but it didn't feel right."

We sit in silence for a minute or so, both peering into the frame.

"She's dead," Tucker says, almost whispering. "She killed herself when I was ten."

"I know. I mean, I heard about it—" Jesus, Alex, you really are an idiot.

"It's OK," Tucker says, touching my arm. "I mean, it's not OK, but I understand—part of my life is in the public domain."

"And you're fine with that?"

"No choice," he says, shrugging. "Are you fine with that?"

"Do I need to be?" Tucker takes the frame from me, gently placing it on the table. Springsteen wails about the Badlands.

My scalp tingles and my stomach drops into the apartment below us.

"If you, well, if we—" He pushes the hair out of my face and rests his hand on the back of my neck. His emerald eyes bore into my own, and suddenly his lips are on mine. We meld together, and even though the kiss lasts only half a minute, I know I won't be frightened of the next one. My favorite part is actually not the kiss itself, but rather how Tucker's hands grace the back of my head, holding me, keeping me stable.

"I'm fine with that," I say, after the kiss ends. Tucker smiles, takes my hand and leads me to the kitchen table, where lunch awaits.

Jordy isn't home when I arrive at the apartment, so I call Jax and Casey to tell them about Tucker's favor—he asked me to accompany him tomorrow night to his father's fifty-eighth birthday party, which is being held at the swanky Le Cirque 2000. Both ask what I plan to wear, which makes me realize I don't have a clue. After Casey describes a nightmare scenario in which I show up at the party way over-, or under-, dressed, I dial Tucker's number.

"You calling to complain about lunch?" he asks, chuckling.

"No, the grilled cheese was sublime. I need specific clothing directions."

"The word *formal* isn't specific enough?"

"No. *Formal* as in a wedding, or *formal* as in business attire?"

"I don't know. Just wear something appropriate," he tells me.

"That's what I'm *trying* to do, Tucker. *Appropriate* as in sexy or sophisticated?"

"Both. Sexy is good, as long as nothing dangles too low or slits too high."

I visualize the perfect combination hanging in Teddy's closet. "Gotcha."

"I'll be at your apartment around seven-ish, OK?"

"OK. Jesus, I can't believe I'm doing this."

"I know—you rock."

The next day, I pick up Teddy's dress from her doorman, then sit around my apartment, trying to melt the cold shoulder Jordy has pushed in my direction. Instead of being thrilled that I followed up on her idea to buy a Discovery, Jordy is pissed I didn't invite her to the dealership. Since nail salons give me a headache, I use the excuse of wanting a manicure to force Jordy to permit me into her space.

"I can't believe you bought a car without me," she finally says, filing my nails.

"You weren't here! I feel like you're never here," I reply.

"Excuse me for trying to finish my dissertation before I turn thirty. I need it to get a good teaching job." Jordy concentrates on my nails—the dusty remnants twirl between our heads.

"Jordy, you know as much as I do about buying a car, which is next to nothing. Tucker knew how to talk to the guy, how to get the best price. And he was around. It's not a big deal. All I did was pick my preferences and sign some papers." Jordy releases my left hand and grabs the right, the nail file skipping around the edge of each nail.

"Uh-huh," Jordy mumbles.

"Come on, don't be mad. Want to come with me to pick it up next week? That's the fun part, anyway." Jordy pauses but still evades eye contact. I yank my right hand out of her grip and, using both hands, physically turn her head to face me. "You're being ridiculous, Jordy. I'm sorry I didn't wait for you, but I promise, you didn't miss anything. We'll pick it up together and go for a ride, OK?"

Jordy's eyes flicker for a few seconds, and then something in them softens, almost dissolves. She nods, clutches my right hand and continues filing.

"So this thing with Tucker looks promising, huh?" Jordy asks.

"I guess so."

"He's sweet, he's not a corporate asshole and you said he's a good kisser. What seems to be the problem?"

"There isn't one—that's the problem. He's too good to be true." It feels good to verbalize a thought that entered my mind after Tucker and I first hung out.

"Give it time—his baggage will eventually come tumbling out of the overhead compartment."

"Thanks, Jordy."

"It's true. Look, you haven't exactly revealed your life story to him, much less the summary version of the last two years, so why should you expect him to expose his internal debris to you?"

"You're right. I just—"

"Do you like his personality?"

"Yeah."

"Do you enjoy being with him?"

"Yeah."

"Are you attracted to him?"

"Yeah, but—"

"But what?"

"My mind is more attracted to him than my body is," I explain, finally understanding the gnawing feeling I've had for days.

Jordy looks up for a moment, somehow staring at me without really looking at me. "Hmm," she mumbles, her gaze returning to my hands. "I wonder what that's all about."

"You're going to help me get dressed tonight, aren't you?" I ask.

Jordy shakes her head. "Can't. I have to meet my advisor."

"At six o'clock on a Thursday night? Are you dating him?"

"It's a her. And no. I just need help with this section. I thought Teddy was coming over for moral support."

"She is, but I want you here, too."

"Sorry. Take a picture. And don't eat anything with spinach in it," Jordy warns.

"Why not?"

"Because I won't be there to check your teeth."

"I wish you were coming with me—I'd feel much better about the whole thing."

"Yes, well, we can't go everywhere together."

At six o'clock, I get dressed, alone. No phone call from Teddy. Usually she calls to cancel—she must have completely forgotten about me. I do my eyes the way she taught me, pack my too-small evening bag and rush down to the lobby so my doorman can zip me up (nice to know the enormous tips we're forced to give at Christmas are good for something). I need to talk to Jax but he's working dinner. I take a shot of vodka, then hate myself for crossing another line—I've already crossed too many for a twenty-eight-year-old. I shove the shot glass away and wander around the apartment, astonished at all the crap Jordy and I have accumulated. We're both suckers for pretty vases and bottles, so our living room looks a bit like an antiques shop. The remains of Ashley's apartment, crammed into two huge boxes, sit in the same corner they've occupied since he died. There are picture frames sprinkled all over the shelves. The walls are covered as well, with framed museum-exhibit posters and a variety of Ansel Adams photographs. Jordy loves his pictures, and her favorite hangs over the kitchen table—it's a monstrous iceberg, surrounded by a seemingly endless, serene landscape of untouched water and snow. The ice has a bluish tone to it, and the sun illuminates the background so the tip of the iceberg almost glows.

Pacing is making me more uptight, but I'm afraid to sit down—I don't want to wrinkle my outfit. I'm wearing a two-tone silver dress with spaghetti straps and black Manolo Blahnik heels—everything except my underwear belongs to Teddy. I'm thrilled when the buzzer goes off.

"OK, send him up," I tell the speaker in the wall.

Should I wait in the doorway? Pretend I was watching TV? Tucker knocks, making my questions irrelevant.

I sneak a quick peek in the mirror, take a deep breath and open the door. At first, all I see are a dozen yellow roses, then Tucker's face comes into focus. He's adjusting his bowtie, which is crooked, but the rest of his tuxedo is perfect.

"You look beautiful," he says, kissing my cheek. I don't think I've been this dressed up since Teddy's wedding—can that be? It seems so long ago, but if I blink, it seems only a few moments have passed since we were all together, posing for pictures. All of us except Ashley. He was still alive, barely. Merely reminiscing about Teddy's wedding causes me to clench my teeth. I literally have to shake off the anger and remind myself to talk to Tucker.

"Nice tux," I reply as he walks in. "Do you own or rent?"

Tucker narrows his eyes, as if I just asked him the most bizarre question. "Own."

I put the flowers in a vase and help him fix the bowtie. It isn't until I reach for my bag that I notice his shoes. "Tucker, you can't wear work boots with a tux."

"I hate tuxedo shoes—they're so dorky."

"Won't your father be pissed if you wear paint-covered boots?"

Tucker shrugs.

"That's why you're wearing them, to annoy him?"

"Are you channeling Sam?"

"Psych 101. Don't you have black boots, or shoes, besides tux shoes?"

"Yeah."

"You're wearing those. We'll have the cab stop by your apartment."

By the time we hail a cab, make the pit stop and drive back uptown, we're twenty minutes late. Tucker's sister and brother are outside the restaurant when we pull up.

"You're late," Derek says.

"Dad's got that look in his eye," Catherine adds.

"It was my fault," I tell them. "Zipper problems." If nothing else, clinical depression taught me how to lie, about anything.

Tucker takes my hand and squeezes it. Introductions are made.

"We're already late, may as well smoke a butt," Tucker announces.

Neither Derek nor Catherine lights up, but they stay with us, chatting with Tucker. Derek is handsome in a clean-cut, boyish way. He and Tucker look alike, but Tucker is rougher around the edges. I can tell just by looking at Derek he will one day run his father's business. Catherine is about to be beautiful. She is tall and slender, around five foot eight, though in heels she stands shoulder to shoulder with Tucker. She has long, shiny blonde hair, pulled back in a round, crystal barrette. Catherine looks painfully similar to her mother, and I wonder how the men in her family deal with that.

The restaurant is lavish but classy, and very crowded. Some of the faces look familiar—not because I know them but because I've seen their pictures in the "Style" or "Business" section of the *New York Times.* I recognize many of the dresses from fashion magazines. The abundance of Dolce & Gabbana, Valentino and Stella McCartney dresses is staggering, and it dawns on me that each dress costs more than my monthly rent. Having learned all about diamonds (by osmosis, not active desire) when Max proposed to Teddy, I find myself gawking at the women's hands, my eyes drawn to the oversized, flawless diamond rings they display as casually as I wear my sterling silver jewelry. Within the first five minutes, I spot two canary diamonds, one yellow diamond and a quarter-size pink diamond. My palms leak and my nerves quiver for a drink, now. Tucker grabs us each a glass of champagne from a passing waiter. Then he indicates his father, who is holding court at the far end of the restaurant. Sip it slowly, I warn myself.

"You ready to meet my father?" he asks.

"No, but let's get it over with." Suddenly my teeth start chattering, and I resist the urge to dash into the street, hail a cab and track down Jordy.

I take a small gulp of what I recognize as good champagne and snatch a napkin off a table so I can shake with a dry hand. And suddenly we're here: face-to-face with Tucker's billionaire, world-famous father. His dark hair is thinning, but his gray eyes are luminous and friendly. His tuxedo is perfect, and his skin glows with the energy of good food, good wine and good taste. He seems solid, powerful.

"This is Alex. Alex, this is my father, Charles Spencer."

"Nice to meet you. What is your full name?" he asks, shaking my hand. Tucker steps to the side, helping himself to more champagne.

"Alexandra Justice. But I prefer Alex, Mr. Spencer."

"And I prefer Charles," he tells me. Tucker's eyes become saucers for a moment.

"What do you do, Alex?"

"I was recently downsized from The Furniture Channel, but—"

"They'll be out of business in a month," he says. "I'm sorry, I interrupted you."

"That's OK. What I really want to do is write children's books."

"Another artist," he mutters, shaking his head. "Tough business."

"I know."

"Have you written any?"

"Three. I do my own illustrations, too. But I can't get an agent."

"Interesting." He glances at the dance floor and extends his hand. He still wears his wedding ring. "Care to dance?"

"Sure."

Tucker's father taps Tucker on the shoulder. "I'm going to dance with your date, yes?"

Tucker shrugs, drains his champagne and heads for the bar. I try to make eye contact, but he quickly becomes just another black jacket in the crowd. Tucker's father leads me to the dance floor and we join the floating couples. It occurs to me that I haven't danced with my own father in years, over a decade. Even the pleasant piano music cannot prevent these thoughts from infiltrating the concrete wall around my heart. I try to shove the feelings away, knowing Sam would hate this blatant repression. I sway with Mr. Spencer, recalling my boycott of the dance floor at Teddy's wedding. As her wedding day loomed closer and it was obvious to my family that Ashley would not—could not—attend, I assumed Teddy would postpone. When she didn't, I asked my father, usually my unquestioning ally, to intervene. Clearly, Teddy had been swept away by the pleasure of planning her wedding, or by the notion of her Big Day. Ashley could barely sit up, and even if he could, there was no way he could be exposed to so many people, so many germs. His body could barely tolerate the pneumonia he had once again caught and was trying to conquer—to introduce him to an uncontrollable, unhygienic environment would be beyond careless. My father, instead of forcing Teddy to utilize her wedding insurance and postpone the celebration, reprimanded me for butting into my sister's life and second-guessing her. He snapped at me—in a tone I'd rarely heard or felt growing up—and said that since it wasn't my wedding day, I should shut up and smile. When I relayed the exchange to Ashley, he took my hand, grinned and said, "Don't worry about it, Alex. Just take lots of pictures for me." So in addition to acting as Teddy's maid of honor, I became the unofficial photographer—I snapped picture after picture, except during the ceremony—and swore to myself I would not dance, not even with Jax, whose family was, of course, present. The next morning, I paid a fortune to have the pictures developed immediately, and Jax and I played bitchy red-carpet hosts, regaling Ashley with who wore what, who shouldn't have worn what, who had too much to drink, who we caught smoking out on the terrace and who danced like a gorilla defending its territory. Ashley laughed—his chest whistling—and scrutinized each photo, but it wasn't enough for me. My brother—Teddy's brother—should have been at her wedding. She should have waited for him to recover from the pneumonia.

I look away from Mr. Spencer, not wanting Tucker's father to perceive my weakness, my anger or my guilt, and suddenly comprehend why the piano music has so swiftly seeped into my spirit. "Oh my God, that's Harry Connick, Jr.!" I almost yell.

"Indeed. Tucker enjoys his music." I was under the impression this father-son relationship is antagonistic, yet here's Mr. Spencer, ordering up Harry Connick, Jr. for Tucker's enjoyment.

"You're a wonderful dancer," Mr. Spencer tells me.

"Thank you."

"There's something about you, the way you carry yourself—it reminds me of my wife. You don't look like her, but somehow there is a similarity. I suppose Tucker has already told you this."

I shake my head, embarrassed and touched at the same time. "Where do you live, Alex?"

"New York City, by way of Westchester County. And you?"

"New York City, London, Martha's Vineyard and East Hampton, by way of Pennsylvania."

"Philadelphia?" I ask, picturing a blueblood, Main Line family.

He laughs. "Allentown. My father was a steelworker."

"Wow. He must be really proud."

"He was. He died many years ago."

"I'm sorry. At least he got to see you succeed."

"He did. I bought him a house after I made my first million. He died knowing one son became a businessman and the other a heart surgeon, though I suspect he was more impressed by my brother, the doctor."

I laugh. "Was he Jewish?"

Tucker's father tilts his head back and laughs—a great, big head-turning laugh. "No, but I see your point. So what are your plans?"

"I'm traveling over the summer. Then I'm going to find an agent if it kills me and try to sell my books."

"Are they any good?" he asks.

My feet stop moving momentarily. I see the sincerity in his eyes, and can't help thinking that my own parents have never read my stories, or even asked about them. Teddy flipped through my first and said it was "cute," though she couldn't understand why I no longer aspired to be a television producer, which was all I had talked about through most of college. When I told her the producers I knew were either overworked and underappreciated or overpaid, pompous morons, Teddy snapped "Welcome to the real world!" and shoved the book into my chest. Ashley read the same story—the only one I had written before he died—and showed it to every visitor who entered his room. I thrust these thoughts away, knowing they will revisit me during a sleepless night in the near future. I rally every bit of confidence I can find within me and, as my feet resume the pattern set by the music, reply, "Yes, my books are good."

"Get my address from Tucker and send them to me."

I silently beg my stomach to stop doing flips. "Everyone knows your address, Mr. Spencer. The building has your name on it."

"I meant my home address. And call me Charles, Alexandra."

"Touché. Thank you for taking the time—"

"Nonsense." The song ends. Everyone applauds. Harry takes a bow. Charles squeezes my shoulder before he walks toward a gaggle of guests.

Before dinner, Catherine and Derek make a brief toast. Tucker doesn't say a word, but he presents his father with a painting. The artwork is fantastic—it's a portrait of Charles Spencer standing in front of the Spencer Building on Sixth Avenue. His headquarters looming behind him, he looks huge but also terribly alone, like a stubborn, solitary pine tree surviving in a burned-out forest. Someone takes a picture, and the four Spencers huddle together, smiling like a normal, happy, motherless family.

Tucker avoids most of the other guests. We eat dinner (Tucker eats; I push the bizarre-looking food around on the plate) with Derek and Catherine, then the two of us escape into the cool, vibrant air to smoke a cigarette. Tucker leans against a rotund, rust-colored flowerpot, brooding, and I stare at the starless sky, not wanting to interrupt his thoughts. I'm also not sure I'm equipped to deal with his family issues—I'm barely equipped to deal with my own. Actually, some would argue I'm not *at all* equipped to deal with my own.

When we re-enter the restaurant, Derek asks me to dance. His heated gaze is flooded with arrogance; Derek's desire to be his father's son is overwhelming and leaves a bad taste in my mouth. He tries to get to know me, but I cannot help feeling as if he is grilling me.

"So Tucker tells me you just got fired."

I nod.

"Looking for a job?" Derek asks.

"Actually, no. I'm taking the summer off."

Derek laughs, as if he is so beyond the notion of taking time off. "Are you independently wealthy?"

I nod again. "Actually, yes." I can't believe I just categorized myself as independently wealthy. The money lives and breathes, alternately pleasing and persecuting me.

"So are you and Tucker dating?" he asks.

"I don't know. We're hanging out."

"He doesn't date, or hang out, much. Did you know that?"

I feel like a fourth grader. "We haven't really discussed it."

I'm relieved when the song ends and Tucker supplants Derek by taking my free hand and placing it on his shoulder.

"Pretty cool to be dancing to Harry Connick, Jr., no?" I ask.

Tucker nods, smiles and pulls me close. His hair smells like summer and his arm feels like a fortress around my waist. His cheek is silky and soft against my own, and I suddenly realize this is the first time since we've met that I've seen him clean-shaven. It annoys me that it took me over an hour to notice such an obvious change in Tucker's appearance. When the song ends, Tucker checks his watch.

"You ready to go?"

"Whenever you are," I tell him. If this was my family, I would have at least another hour of face time, but I'm not about to impose upon Tucker the ins and outs of the Justice Family's expected behavior.

"Let's exploit the bar for half an hour, then leave."

We drink an unhealthy amount of alcohol in thirty minutes and top it off with two shots of tequila. I run into Catherine in the bathroom. She gives me a hearty hug good-bye. Derek and Charles are sitting at a table, engrossed in conversation, so Tucker and I join them for a few minutes, reflecting on the success of the party. Charles surprises all of us by standing up and wrapping his arms around me. He slips me his card, shakes hands with Tucker and thanks us for coming. Tucker grabs my hand and leads me out of the restaurant. I can barely keep up with him as he races toward the door.

Without thinking, I give the cab driver my address, then immediately regret it. We're both drunk, though at least now

Tucker is smiling and seems to have clawed his way out of his familial trench. It's after midnight and I realize, as we walk through the lobby, I am not at all prepared for this scenario; I'm not ready to sleep with Tucker tonight, and I am inexplicably worried about Jordy's presence in the apartment.

As Tucker veers into the bathroom, I find a note from Jordy, explaining she will be at the library until the wee hours. Relief, as well as disappointment, swells my senses. Thankfully, Jax has left a loud and boisterous message on the machine, which Tucker hears as he ambles into the living room.

"I hope you had fun with the rich people! Come dancing! We're at Oblivion!"

I kick off the uncomfortable heels and turn to Tucker, trying to mask my eagerness to move us out of the apartment as soon as possible. "Want to go dancing?" I ask, assuming he knows Oblivion is a gay nightclub.

"Dancing?"

"Oblivion is the best gay club in the city," I tell him. Tucker just stares, and I realize that statement was probably not the shrewdest way to convince him. "There's a really great crowd, and they play amazing music. We can dance for hours and no one but you will be the least bit interested in me." This seems to pique his curiosity, so I go in for the kill. "Watching gay men get it on is a real turn-on for me."

"OK, let's go," he says. I make a mental note to brag to Jax and Jordy about the wily way in which I lured a straight man into a gay club.

"We need to do something about your outfit. Take off your jacket." I survey Tucker after he shrugs out of the ebony jacket—I can't help but notice it is Gucci—but he still looks like a billionaire's son.

"I don't suppose you're wearing a wife-beater under your shirt?"

"A what?"

"A guinea tee." Tucker shrugs, clueless. "You know, a sleeveless undershirt."

"Oh. No. T-shirt, sorry."

"I may have one of Jax's around here somewhere. Ditch the dress shirt. I'll be right back. Oh, unzip me." Tucker's hands tremble as he starts to unzip me, and I get the chills as his fingers travel down my back, tracing the path of my tired spine.

In my room, I slither out of the dress, then search through my drawers for one of Jax's undershirts, finding one among my pajamas. I choose a pair of funky black pants and a cotton, lilac tank top. I change, reapply some eye shadow and return to the living room. Tucker is staring at the Ansel Adams iceberg, slowly swinging the dress shirt to a rhythm only he hears.

"Here, put this on."

Tucker turns away as he sheds his white T-shirt. I'm sure he was shirtless at one point at Carchie's cabin, but I can't recall really looking at him. I sneak a peek as he changes into Jax's undershirt. His arms are smooth, muscular. Nice shoulders, strong back.

"I see you checking me out," he says.

"Yeah, well, people know me at this club. I have a reputation to uphold."

He turns around and approaches me. "Now what?"

I put the suspenders back in place. "Voila."

He examines himself in the hallway mirror. "Now I look gay?" he asks.

"No," I answer. "Now you look cool."

Oblivion is only a few blocks away. We cut through Union Square Park and walk west.

"You're not nervous, are you?" I ask.

"Should I be?"

"Well, you'll be one of maybe five straight guys in Oblivion, surrounded by thousands of gay men."

Tucker shrugs. "If anything, it's you who should be nervous," he jokes.

I take his hand as we cross the street.

∽

Oblivion, as usual, is packed. I escort Tucker to the front of the line, feeling the typical pang of guilt as Jason, the bouncer, waves me through the thick glass doors.

"Hey, Alex, where's your other half?" he asks as I pay the cover for both of us.

"At the library, working on her dissertation."

"Jesus Christ, I've been on three different soaps in the time it's taken her to get that damn PhD." Jason is one of those guys straight women refer to as a waste. He's breathtakingly gorgeous with a perfect body, plus he's sweet, funny, smart and gay. "This guy with you?" he asks, surprised, pointing to Tucker. I nod. Jason's brow scrunches as he pulls the blood-red curtain back for us. I take Tucker's hand and lead him into Oblivion.

I know exactly where to find Jax, but I want to wait a few minutes so Tucker can acclimate. Places like Oblivion can be very intimidating to the uninitiated, especially those of the straight variety. Not everyone's heart skips a beat when they encounter a vast, two-tiered universe brimming with sweaty, shirtless gay men. The music is so loud you can feel it pumping through the floor, into your feet and up through your body. The club is dark, but the strobe lights, floor lights and spotlights create fleeting flashes of brightness, highlighting the glistening pecs and burnished biceps of the dancers. There are some, but not many, women in Oblivion. The club's management is pretty strict when it comes to their clientele—they won't admit a group of straight guys unless they're accompanied by a gay regular, and they don't grant too many women access. All of this is done to ensure a safe and sensual vibe within one of the city's biggest and most popular gay nightclubs. My moral conscience knows the sexist door policy is wrong, but I really despise sharing the dance floor with loud, gum-snapping girls who decide a gay nightclub is a great idea for a bachelorette party. Morals have no place in Oblivion, anyway.

Tucker absorbs the atmosphere while I order drinks. The bar is covered in cold, silver steel, with a shirtless, sculpted bartender behind it. When I turn around to hand Tucker a drink, he's looking right at me.

"You OK?" I ask. He takes the drink, and I wonder if this was a good idea.

"This place is fucking huge," he half-yells. I nod. "The rent's gotta be twenty grand a month!" I shrug, having never thought about it.

I sidle up to him so I can talk directly in his ear. "I should warn you about something."

"What's that?"

"The bathroom," I answer, pausing for a sip, or twelve, of my gin and tonic.

"Oh, yeah, I know." He nods, as if unbothered by the idea.

"You do?"

"There's no girls' bathroom, right? So I have to hold the door for you?"

I laugh, nearly dropping my drink—what a cutie. "Well, yes, but that's not what I'm—" Shit, am I really going to explain this to him? "You might see more than you want to see in there." Leave it, Alex. He's not a child.

"Oh, OK. Want to find Jax?"

We locate Jax, leaning against a railing on the second floor, surveying the chasm of sexuality below him. His hair is slick with sweat, his pupils are huge and he's with Pete, the guy who asked him to move in. I lean against one of the marble columns, my flushed body trying to absorb the coolness of the marble.

"Hey! How was the big night?" he asks, kissing me full on the lips for a moment too long. It never fails to amaze me how even the gayest of men are still, inherently, men, and how in the middle of Oblivion, a veritable temple to gay sex, Jax finds it necessary to remind Tucker of our intimate bond.

"It went well—my father loves her," Tucker replies.

Jax swallows the rest of his beer. "Yeah, my dad used to adore her, until she became my fag hag. Or I became a fag. I can't remember which came first."

I need to dance, now. I down the rest of my drink. I know Jax instantly regrets his minidrama, but I also know he's too far gone on alcohol and whatever else when he refers, flippantly, to his dying father. He'll dance all night—dangerously close to the edge—go home with someone for hours of safe sex (Ashley's death scared Jax into an almost religious commitment to condoms) and then wake up angry, tortured and guilt-ridden. At least I tried to end my cycle of self-destruction. Jax and I often discuss our theory that we smoke too much pot and drink too much alcohol because of the guilt and shame that flows through us like a lucid force—they are emblems of all that is wrong with us—but then we decide that for the most part, the recreational abuse of our bodies is harmless. Maybe not harmless, but not harmful—at least not consistently harmful, anyway. We could be inflicting a lot more harm.

I dance with Tucker, and eventually Jax, for hours. The dance floor is crammed with men, but most of them respect the notion of personal space, so there is very little bumping (although there is a lot of humping) among the dancers. Tucker handles himself really well—not only among the throng of sexy, experienced club goers but as a dancer in general. He seems loose and relaxed, which to me is a sign of innate comfort with his body and sexuality.

Dawn bursts through the skyline as we leave the club. The streets barely hum, and a golden hue loiters over the east side of the city. Tucker and I stroll silently through Union Square Park, sharing an ice-cold bottle of water. As we wait for the light at 14th Street, Tucker turns and kisses me—a slow, lingering kiss. Then he takes my hand and leads me across the street to my apartment.

He kisses me again in the lobby of my building. I hate kissing in front of the doormen—they're like catty high school girls, and this doorman will tell another, and he'll tell another, and eventually my super will hear about it, and for the next week, they'll all shoot me that knowing glance when I enter or exit the building.

"Thanks for getting me through my father's party," Tucker

says after the kiss. I'm leaning on him—my hands grip his bare biceps, my thighs rest on his—and when I stare into his tired, gleaming green eyes, I almost fall in, willing him to catch me.

"He seems like a good guy."

Tucker's face goes completely blank for a second. I reach out and pull him toward me, craving the strength in his kisses. When the elevator doors open, we move as a unit, and it isn't until the doors close that I remember to hit the button for my floor.

I lead Tucker through the door of my apartment, down the hall and into my room without turning on a light. He flicks on the bedside lamp in my room, but I turn it off. He's drunkenly dealing with his shoes and doesn't notice. I grab a benign CD and slide it into the stereo, in case Jordy isn't fast asleep by now. While my fingers fumble to unlace my own shoes, Tucker's hands dance along my back, gracefully tapping a tempo that encourages my mind to shut down. I give in to the darkness.

We kiss for about thirty minutes, until I turn over and pretend to sleep. Tucker sinks into the bed, his naked torso impressing a mold upon the mattress. As I sit up to reach for something with which to tie my hair back, Tucker reaches out and touches my shoulder.

"What are you doing next week?" he asks.

"Besides picking up my new car, nothing." I relax into my pillow.

"Want to drive me to D.C.?"

"As in Washington, D.C.?"

"Is there another?"

I throw a fake punch to Tucker's gut. He flinches and then drapes his arm across me, resting his hand on the back of my neck.

"My best friend, Scott, lives down there. We've been friends forever; we even went to the same college. I haven't seen him all year, and his girlfriend just dumped him. I really hate the train," he says, grinning. Dawn's ray of light peeks into my room. It feels odd to be talking to Tucker, not Jordy, at this hour.

"And here's an unemployed girl with a new car who won't mind driving four hours to visit someone she's never met."

Tucker certainly seems sure of himself, at least in relation to me. I wish I could borrow some of his confidence.

He laughs. "My thoughts exactly. You'll like him. Come on. Three days in our nation's capital? It'll be great!" Tucker's arm travels down my back and comes to a rest near my thigh. His eyes fall shut, and I wonder if he's asleep.

"OK, let's go," I tell him. Tucker smiles and wraps his arms around the pillow. I wait a few seconds to make sure he's fallen asleep, pull on a T-shirt and tiptoe out of my bedroom. Jordy's door is shut, and I struggle to recall if it was closed when I piloted Tucker into my bedroom.

It isn't until ten minutes later, while I'm smoking a cigarette in my kitchen, staring at the iceberg photograph, that I realize the implications of those three words. Two nights, three days equals constant togetherness, a seemingly endless exchange of conversation and a new level of physical proximity. No comic relief from Jax, and no opportunities to seek shelter in Jordy's sunny, inviting eyes.

6

I create a dozen plausible lies to tell Tucker in order to back out of the D.C. trip, but as the weekend creeps closer, I actually begin to look forward to it. The usual things still freak me out—seeing Tucker as soon as I wake up, not having any solitary moments, meeting his friend—but the thought of driving to a city I've rarely visited, in my new car, makes me tingle with excitement. My only forays outside the city since Ashley's death have been to Carchie's cabin and Webster Ridge.

Random images of my pricey prison jut into my mind as I pack for D.C. I still remember every detail of the walk from my room to my therapist's office, and I can still smell the commercial cleansers that were swabbed on every surface each morning. The stench of ammonium mixed with fake lemon made my throat tighten. I catch myself gritting my teeth as the memories surge back into my mind. My shoulders sag as I recall that Jordy was not the only one who read the suicide letter I wrote to her. During my first team meeting in the psych ward of the hospital, I realized every psychiatrist, intern and social worker in the room had read my letter, private thoughts that were intended only for Jordy. The letter followed me to the expensive enclave in Massachusetts as well—what began as a privileged confession to the person I loved most in the world became fodder that perfect strangers (highly trained medical professionals, but perfect strangers nonetheless) utilized to harvest my exhausted mind.

The doctors in the psych ward prescribed medication, and the doctors at Webster Ridge continued dispensing the pills throughout my stay. Actually, the pills remained a part of my life far longer than the critical care—I didn't go off antidepressants until last summer. Sam and I had previously discussed meds as a way to disconnect my depression, but I didn't recognize the power of pills to lighten the darkness, so I refused to take medication. In the psych ward, however, you don't have much choice, and by that time, I really didn't care one way or the other. All I could think about, night and day, was that I had failed at yet another effort to exercise some control over my life. The only medication I was eager to swallow was sleeping pills, and the overnight nurse would deliver the goods each evening at ten o'clock. I sketched or wrote in my journal— keeping one eye on the clock and the other on my rambling, miserable outpourings. (They took away my watch, my jewelry, my makeup and my colored pencils—apparently all these were considered dangerous. How do you kill yourself with a four-dollar colored pencil?) I tossed the sleeping pill down my throat as soon as the nurse handed it to me, desperate for dreamless sleep. I can still envision the terribly bright rooms and hear the shuffling footsteps of the other patients—people who couldn't find reality even if they wanted to.

I dropped everything but the antidepressants when I arrived at Webster Ridge, though if I bitched long and loudly enough, I would occasionally score a sleeping pill. I told the nurses that if they wanted me lucid and aware during the endless hours of therapy (individual therapy, group therapy, art therapy, dance therapy) during the day, they would have to assist me in getting to sleep at night. It astounded me that after ten months of consistent insomnia and a level of exhaustion I never imagined possible, I still could not fall asleep. I've had spates of insomnia since returning to life, and each time it terrifies me, since it not only reminds me of that horrendous period of time but also makes me wonder if another black cloud is approaching.

And that's what worries me about Tucker. Well, not about Tucker, but about our potential relationship. If I am to live a normal life, acting like a normal person (whatever that is) along the way, then at some point I am going to have to tell him about my twenty-sixth year, and all that led up to it. This is frightening enough. That his mother killed herself only makes matters worse because, in all honesty, I don't blame her. I understand her need for escape. Tucker, however, may not ever comprehend that, and though I sympathize with him—growing up without a mother is something one never recovers from—I cannot condemn his mother for her choice.

As I fight with the zipper on my overnight bag, I decide not to tell Tucker this weekend about the past two years of my life. I won't speak of my dead brother or my attempt to join him. I will participate in conversations, of course, but I will not volunteer information. This weekend, Tucker will see only the surface of me.

Jordy camps out in the library all week, obsessively editing her dissertation. Jax works a few double shifts at the restaurant so he'll have two free days to tape his voice-over commercial next week. Tucker is trying to finish a painting before we leave, so when Teddy calls me at five o'clock and asks if I want to go out to dinner with her, I accept the rare invite. I know she's only taking me to dinner because she feels guilty for standing me up the night of the party, but it's still dinner with my sister.

We meet at our favorite Mexican place—an airy, multi-colored restaurant in the Village. I arrive first—I pick a table outside so I can smoke—and order a margarita, Teddy's favorite, and a glass of sangria for myself. I haven't yet told her about the trip to D.C. with Tucker, and the thought of doing so makes my throat constrict. Since Ashley's death, I am less concerned about my mother's approval, but involuntarily seek Teddy's approval, despite my bitterness. Although Sam and I discussed my relationship with Teddy on a weekly basis, I still cannot fully fathom what happened to us. I know what the tight ball of anger within me is all about, but I don't understand why she started treating me with such impatience and disdain. And yet all I want is to hear her praise me, compliment me, salute my efforts to bounce back into life. I suppose I'm trying to re-capture our childhood roles—I was the youngest, and since Ashley essentially ignored me, I sought non-parental validation from Teddy, my smart, cool, big sister—but those roles become skewed when one sibling slowly, suddenly disappears. Teddy and I have been off-balance since the day we buried Ashley.

She flutters to the table fifteen minutes late. I put my book away. We order food and I take a few quick sips of my drink, an-noyed that I'm actually nervous to share news with her.

"Tucker and I are going away for the weekend," I blurt out as quickly as possible.

"Where?"

"D.C. To visit a friend of his."

"You're driving your new car, I presume?"

I nod.

"And I assume all the paperwork and insurance will be taken care of beforehand?"

"Yes, Teddy. Even I know not to drive without insurance."

Teddy doesn't react. Instead, she waves daintily at the curl of smoke I've spiraled in her direction. "So you're just going to take off, driving wherever you feel like going?"

"No, I'm going with Tucker this weekend and coming back to the city. Then Jordy and I are going to spend a week in the Berkshires. What's the big deal?"

"You're running away, Alexandra. I thought finally accepting Ashley's money would help you settle down."

"Who says I want to settle down? I don't want your life, Teddy. I don't know why you can't understand that."

"That's fine, Alexandra, but find some sort of life. Don't run away with the first guy you've dated in years."

"I'm not running away! And I thought you were happy I'm dating Tucker."

"Dating, sure, not traveling with him. Does he know what you're recovering from?"

"No." She makes it sound like I've had a bad case of the flu and need to warn everyone who travels into my personal space.

"That's just great, Alexandra—travel alone with a guy who has no idea you spent time in a psych ward—very intelligent. Does he even know about Ashley?"

"Everyone has issues, Teddy. We don't all spill our guts over the first cocktail." I'm no longer hungry; actually, I'm fighting the urge to throw up.

"You can't forgive yourself for throwing away all those years with Ashley who, by the way, didn't exactly go out of his way to know you for most of your life. You were clinically depressed for over a year. And you tried to kill yourself, Alexandra. These are *not* issues. An issue is middle-child syndrome or low self-esteem, not attempted suicide!"

"Why is it that every time I see you, you find it necessary to remind me of that choice, and of how inherently weak I must be to have made that decision?"

"I wish I didn't have to remind you, but you seem to think you're going to coast through the rest of your life without dealing with it."

"Without dealing with it? Are you fucking crazy? What do you think I did in the hospital? Do you think I was baking and knitting at Webster Ridge? I was analyzing everything in my life, Teddy, until my heart wanted to annihilate my brain for the agony it caused. I turned my internal life upside down, for hours upon hours, every day for forty-five days, Teddy. And when I was alone, *all* I did was think about you, and Mom and Dad, and my friends, and I hated myself for scaring you but at the same time, I also hated myself for not taking enough pills, for surviving. So don't tell me I'm not dealing with what happened—that's just bullshit. If you honestly think I'm the type of person who could coast through life, then our relationship has finally fallen over the precipice."

At some point during my rant, the waitress must have dropped off our food. My empanada looks like a bloated turtle, and I know there's no way I can eat it. Teddy will then comment on my eating habits, or lack thereof, and the cycle will begin again. When was it that she started aiming disapproval at me? Was it when I was fired from my job and moved in with Ashley?

Or was it when I started to write and design children's books? I struggle to recall when I stopped calling Teddy every day, when we ceased sharing the minutiae of our daily lives. All through my high school and college years, Teddy was my external moral compass, the voice of reason on which I relied—she took my calls at all hours of the day and night; she listened and made suggestions as I read her ten-page papers over the phone; she hosted me (and my friends) in her Upper East Side apartment when we were home from school and bored in the suburbs; she guided me through my first job search after I graduated college. Teddy imparted every piece of real-world knowledge to me that she possessed, and made my life infinitely easier in the process. We used to finish each other's sentences but now, every time we talk, it feels as if there's an impenetrable obstruction between us. I stare at Teddy, exhausted and exasperated.

"What is that supposed to mean, *the precipice?*" she asks.

I look down at the turtle and decide I can no longer sit here. This is one of the moments Sam and I worked on so diligently—though I may feel guilty about it later, I have to remove myself from this situation. I can feel the rage begin to brew, and if I continue talking to Teddy, this fury will transform into feelings of futility, which I will then repress. No matter what I do or say, I cannot convince Teddy I am OK—that I am able to navigate my own life, however meaningless she may find it—and so nothing will change. I will wind up feeling small, sorrowful and unbalanced, and I do not want these labels following me to D.C. I want to leave this restaurant feeling as stable as when I walked in.

I grab my bag, down the rest of my sangria and stand up. "It means we're in the fucking abyss, Teddy. And I'm so tired of this abusive cycle that I don't have the energy to rescue us. I'm going to D.C. with Tucker, whether you like it or not. I tried to commit suicide, and I'm still not over Ashley's death. Deal with it."

I walk out of the restaurant, the hyperkinetic noises of the West Village filling my head. By the time I reach Washington

Square Park, I am starving and slightly buzzed. I stroll up Sixth Avenue until I hit my favorite pizza place in the city.

I practically inhale the pizza and then retrace my steps, heading east. As I meander through Washington Square Park, it occurs to me that maybe Teddy's domineering concern is forgivable, since at least she verbalizes her fears, as opposed to my parents, who slap me with silence. It's really a no-win situation—Teddy wants to run my life and my parents hardly express any interest in it. No wonder I feel helpless without Jordy.

I leave a message on my parents' answering machine, explaining the weekend jaunt to D.C. I tell them I'll call from the road but I know I won't. These days, it's easier for me not to call them at all than to call and keep wondering what they're thinking. My relationship with them seems to have been altered irrevocably, twice—since Ashley died and since I tried to kill myself. When I was a child, I was their baby; this was a role I rejected, and fought to grow out of, despite their blanketing overprotection. Often, it was Teddy who succeeded in convincing our parents to loosen their grip on me, to let me fall and fail on my own. I think my mother feared what would happen to her when I found independence; after all, she had gone from Vassar to Scarsdale, from college girl to wife and mother, with no pauses in between. I guess she wanted to postpone my flight as long as possible, so she wrapped her arms around me and held on. My father was the same way until I was twelve, and Ashley came out to us. Although I couldn't compute the equation—I was too young to recognize it—Ashley's honesty caused a ripple effect, one that shook us up for years to come. My father worked longer hours; my mother doubted her mothering skills; Ashley visited less and less (certainly he put two and two together); and Teddy became a surrogate Everything to me. By the time my parents stopped questioning themselves and accepted—embraced—their gay son, I was finishing high school. They had inadvertently let me go too early—released me into the arms of my older sister—and though I was relieved that our family dynamic had returned, my life was about to begin and it was time for me to explore, without parental supervision. When I graduated college, my mother began treating me like a child again, even though I was living in the city and supporting myself. And then, when I needed her most, all I felt was silence. It's as if she views me through a fun-house mirror and thus sees me through broken, refracted light. After Ashley died, my mother somehow managed to pretend I was fine, to *not* see that her third child, her baby, was gravitating toward my dead brother.

I spend the evening finishing a few sketches and starting an outline for another story. The phone sits mutely by my side. Shortly after midnight, I fall asleep in Jordy's bed.

The phone wakes me at nine o'clock the next morning. I screen the call—assuming it's Teddy—but it's Jordy, calling from the library to report she completely forgot about our plan to pick up the car.

"I'm knee-deep in revisions, Alex. Otherwise I'd come home right now."

"It's OK," I reassure her.

"Are you sure?"

"Yeah. It's no big deal."

"I'm sorry, sweetie. Can Jax go with you?" She sounds really upset, so I perk up in order to assuage her guilt.

"I'll call him. It's really OK, Jordy. You'll be in the car with me next week."

"I cannot wait to get out of the city, out of this fucking library," she rants.

"You and me and the Berkshires, sweetie pie." I can see Jordy smile as I say it.

"I'll see you later. I'll be home by ten," she promises.

"OK, bye."

"Bye. And, Alex, I'm sorry."

"Don't be. Get back to work."

I dial Jax's number as soon as I hang up, fully aware that I will wake him up. But I want to make sure he can come with me to pick up the car—it's too monumental a moment for me to go alone, and something tells me Tucker will not share in my enthusiasm. Jax screens the call, so I sit up in bed and scream his name until he picks up the phone.

"What?" he growls into the phone.

"Hi, babycakes," I say sweetly.

"What's wrong?" he demands.

"Nothing."

"Then why are you calling me so early? I thought our shared love of sleep was the foundation of our friendship."

"Are you working lunch?" I ask.

"Hmm . . . what day is it?"

"Jesus, Jax, even I can keep track of the days. It's Thursday."

"First of all, fuck you. Second of all, I'm not working lunch."

"So you don't need to be at work until five-ish, right?"

"Alex, please tell me you did not wake me up simply to in-quire about the restaurant's staff schedule."

I forgot how pissy Jax gets about his sleep. "I'm wondering if you want to come with me to pick up the Discovery," I say as pleasantly as possible.

"Ooh! New-car day!" he yells, undergoing a personality change within five seconds. "What time?"

"I'm supposed to be there at two o'clock," I tell him.

"I'll pick you up at one thirty, dahling."

"OK. Don't fall back asleep, Jax."

"Bye, babycakes."

Jax and I stroll, arm in arm, into the Land Rover dealership at exactly two o'clock. I hand smarmy Seth a cashier's check, sign some papers and accept two sets of keys. Seth does a dou-ble take at Jax and then looks at me.

"Where's Mr. Spencer?" he asks. His brows are furrowed so deeply into his face they look as if they're going to fall off, and he's staring at Jax as if he's a serial killer.

"Oh, he has an appointment with his proctologist," Jax an-swers.

"He told me to send you his regards," I add.

As the mortification spreads across Seth's face, Jax and I rush to the rear exit.

"Jax, you are evil and you're definitely going to hell."

He takes my hand. "I'll save you a seat, babycakes."

We're still laughing as I drive out of the dealership in my Discovery.

"Yum! New-car smell, or truck smell, whatever," I say.

"Oh my God, Alex, this is a beautiful car!" Jax yells, stroking the immaculate black dashboard.

"I know."

"I'm in love with this car! Seriously, I think I'm getting a hard-on."

I pull out of the lot and head across town. "You are truly insane."

Jax pretends his finger is a pen and writes in the air. "Note to self—discuss Land Rover–influenced boner in therapy."

"Where should we go?" I ask.

"Want to drive over the Brooklyn Bridge?"

"Too much traffic."

"Want to drive up Madison Avenue?"

"Too much traffic."

"Want to drop me off at my apartment?"

"Sure."

After Jax and I say good-bye, I park my new car (my new car!) in the garage next to my building. I've got a few hours to myself before Jordy gets home, so I finish packing and write yet another draft of a letter to send out to literary agents. I almost call Teddy, but I talk myself out of it, using Sam's voice, of course. I shouldn't always be the one calling a truce between us. I can't remember if Jordy and I are supposed to eat dinner together, so I eat a handful of pretzels to curb the impatient hunger pangs. I'm about to start getting dressed when Jordy calls.

"You are not going to believe this," Jordy says.

The pretzels turn to stone in my stomach. "What?"

"I ran into my advisor in the library, and her dinner date cancelled on her and she wants me to practice defending my dissertation," Jordy explains breathlessly.

"Jordy, you have plans tonight."

"I know, but Alex, this will be an extra practice session for me. She's not doing this *instead* of the original practice session—she's doing it *in addition* to the original. I can't not take her up on it—I need the practice."

"How long is it going to take?"

Jordy sighs. "A couple of hours."

"I can't wait up for you—I'm waking up at seven o'clock tomorrow."

"I know. I'm sorry, Alex. I really wanted to hang out before you left."

"I'm sure you did," I reply.

"What does that mean?"

"If you really want to hang out, then come home." The tone of my voice surprises me, as does my violent grip on the telephone.

"Alex, this is my dissertation we're talking about here. I've been working on this for years. It could get published. It could get me a really good job."

"Uh-huh," I answer. I can feel Jordy pacing.

"Alex, chill out. I'll see you in two days."

"Yeah, if you're not too busy." I hang up on Jordy for the first time.

I chain-smoke, channel surf and mope all night.

Tucker throws a knapsack on the backseat and practically jumps into the passenger seat. It never ceases to amaze me how guys can pack so lightly, and without any stress at all. My bag overflows and holds enough clothes for a week. I've also brought along a knapsack full of books, pens and sketch paper, and enough medical supplies for a small army.

"Nice ride," he says, checking out the car.

"I know—I love it."

It takes us about twenty minutes to get out of the city. As soon as we hit the New Jersey Turnpike, Tucker reaches for his bag, rummages through it and pulls out a CD.

"I brought a CD for you," he says.

"Cool, thanks."

Tucker slides in the CD and turns up the volume. As soon as

I hear the opening bars of music, the back of my neck starts to sweat and my breakfast does a 360 in the pit of my stomach.

"I heard this song on the radio the other day and thought of you," he adds. Peter Gabriel's "In Your Eyes" blasts from the speakers.

He couldn't have known Jordy and I have obsessively loved this song since it was released. He's not trying to push his way into my life—he just didn't know this is my song with Jordy. I wipe my palms on my shorts. Don't look at him, Alex.

> *In your eyes*
> *The light the heat*
> *In your eyes*
> *I am complete*

I hate that I left the city on bad terms with Jordy. We so rarely argue that I'm not sure how to fix things between us. I'm also a little surprised at myself for getting so upset—it was definitely an overreaction that happened so quickly I couldn't regain control. Sam would say, "To hell with control. Why'd you over-react?" I shrug, as if he's in the car with me.

The song finally ends and an insignificant tune starts. Tucker rambles on about some new idea for a painting, and I feel my shoulders relax—my heartbeat returns to normal.

The drive to D.C. is not exactly a scenic one, but the fresh air is invigorating as it whips through the car. We stop once to pee, and Tucker buys an overabundance of snacks, none of which I'll eat. We listen to a handful of CDs and pass Camden Yards around two o'clock. Tucker reads the directions to me and we find his friend's house without getting lost or yelling at each other.

"Where am I parking?" I ask.

"Scott said there's a garage next to the Watergate. There, right across the street," he points out. I glance at Tucker. "I fig-ured you'd be uncomfortable parking your new car on the street," he adds.

We leave the car in the garage and walk across the street to a row of houses that resemble brownstones, without the brown stone. The sidewalk slopes downward, and the only sound we hear is our own footsteps. Each house is a different color, all shades of pastel—yellow, orange, pink, green.

"It looks like a box of rainbow sorbet," I tell Tucker.

He laughs and points to the orange one. "This is Scott, number 1814."

I take a deep breath and follow Tucker up three steps. I wish my bag wasn't so big. Tucker rings the bell and someone immediately dashes to the door. Tucker can't stop grinning. I stand behind him, waiting and watching. The door opens and a wiry, red-haired guy covered in freckles attacks Tucker with a bear hug.

"Tucker! It's great to see you, man," Scott says.

"You, too, Scottie," Tucker replies.

They shake hands and touch each other's heads in some strange form of greeting. I forgot how straight guys act with one another. Scott is taller than me, but short for a guy. He's almost an identical twin to my image of Huckleberry Finn. He has a sly but infectious smile. Tucker turns and beckons me up the steps.

"Scott, this is Alex. Alex, this is Scott."

We shake hands. "Nice to meet you. Thanks for driving my buddy down here," Scott says. He takes my bag and we follow him inside. The entrance to the house looks like it's supposed to be a room—a living room or den or something—but there's nothing in it except a half-dozen bikes, piles of newspapers and bags of beer bottles. The house smells like a cross between wet carpet and stale beer. Scott leads us into the living room, which is much smaller than the first room but also much neater. There is a prehistoric couch against one wall and a brown futon against the other. I silently pray that the futon is not where we are sleeping. Two yellow Formica tables stand in front of the couch, both littered with ashtrays, newspapers and video-game joysticks. The kitchen is a long rectangle, not unlike Tucker's kitchen, but a hell of a lot messier. A quick glance at the once-white shag carpet tells me I won't be traipsing around barefoot in this place.

Scott runs upstairs with our bags and heads into the kitchen upon his return. "My jackass roommate is out of town, so you guys can sleep in his bed." I unconsciously frown, wondering what has gone on in that bed. "Don't worry," Scott continues. "I changed the sheets myself."

He steps into the living room and hands us each a beer. I glance at the clock above the TV—it's not even four. Tucker and Scott toast and suck back their beers. I take a tiny sip and put the bottle on a table.

"Can I use your bathroom?" I ask.

"Sure. Upstairs, first door on your left. I cleaned that, too," Scott offers. I nod and walk upstairs. I peek in the bedrooms. One is light and airy, with a freshly made bed and a poster of Jimi Hendrix on one wall. The other is smaller, with a sloped ceiling and the messiest closet I've ever seen. The bathroom is small but neat, with stacks of *Playboy* next to the toilet. I flip through one as I pee, wondering how on earth these superficial, plastic women can actually turn guys on. After I wash my hands, I steal a look in the medicine cabinet. The only thing that stands out is a box of condoms with one lonely condom in it. Jax forced me to accept a handful from his collection, but I purposely left them at home. Things inevitably change after sex, and I want Tucker and me to ride this phase out a little longer.

We eat dinner in a huge restaurant on the harbor, overlooking the Potomac River. Tucker and Scott devour lobsters, and I have filet mignon with onions and mushrooms. We empty three bottles of wine by the time the check arrives. Tucker won't let either of us pay, which pisses me off. We walk up a hill into Georgetown and spend the next four hours barhopping. Tucker keeps an arm or hand on me at all times, and I feel his eyes follow me on each of my trips to the bathroom. Scott seems to know every bartender in town, and half the general population, as well. He goes out of his way to introduce me to everyone, and he asks a lot of questions about my life. It's Scott who notices when I start yawning, and five minutes later, we're in a cab.

"I'm sorry I'm such a wimp tonight," I announce as we enter Scott's house.

"It's after one—some people consider that a late night," Scott replies.

Tucker laughs. "Not Alex and her crew. Their nights end when the sun rises."

Scott closes and locks the door behind me. "She spent half the day driving, locked in a car with the likes of you, so I don't blame her for needing sleep." He winks at me and I smile in return. "Tomorrow we'll do the monuments."

"Oh man, not again. How many times can you see those fucking monuments?" Tucker complains.

Scott turns to me. "Alex, have you seen the monuments?"

"Not since I was a kid."

Scott punches Tucker in the shoulder. Tucker almost falls over. Instead, he drops himself onto the couch.

"See, Alex hasn't seen the monuments. She'll appreciate my tour," Scott says.

Scott and I stare at Tucker for a moment or so, watching his eyes flirt with closure. "The Washington and Lincoln monuments?" I ask.

Scott nods. "And the Vietnam Wall, plus a bonus, semisecret monument. They're all right down the block." He motions with his head, smirking at Tucker, who is now passed out. "I can drag him upstairs if you want," Scott offers.

I shake my head and look at Tucker—his chin has landed on his chest and his body is limp. I remove his shoes, swing his legs onto the couch and cover him with a ratty blanket. I'm not drunk, but I'm pretty sure I drank enough to drift into a careless sleep, which I'm looking forward to now that sex isn't an issue. I follow Scott upstairs. He hands me a towel and offers me use of the bathroom.

"Let me know if you need anything," he says.

"Thanks. Good night."

The house is quiet when I wake up at nine, so I shower and

dress before descending the stairs. Tucker is awake, though he's still on the couch. I can't help laughing at him—he's got hangover written all over his pasty face. As soon as I sit down, Scott scampers through the front door. He's wearing shorts, a sweat-soaked T-shirt and serious running sneakers. He hands us each a cup of coffee and heads for the kitchen. He rummages around for a minute and then returns with a plate of bagels, as well as cream cheese and butter. Scott goes for the butter, while I spread a thin layer of cream cheese on a bagel. Tucker sighs. Scott takes one look at him and tosses him a bagel. Tucker rolls his eyes.

"Eat it," Scott demands.

"You eat it," Tucker replies.

"Tucker, don't be an ass. You know you'll feel better if you eat it," I tell him.

Scott chuckles. "She's right. And I won't give you any aspirin unless you eat it."

Tucker groans and takes a bite of the bagel. Scott and I chat while Tucker concentrates on eating. After he's finished, Scott doles out three Advil. I fiddle around with Sony PlayStation while the two of them shower and get dressed. They lumber downstairs just as I'm mastering baseball.

We spend the day walking around Dupont Circle. Tucker tries to buy me something in every other store, but I refuse all his offers. We all pay for our own lunch. Tucker suddenly insists on seeing the White House. We sit in the park across the street for a few hours, ruminating on all the fabulous and evil people who have visited 1600 Pennsylvania Avenue.

I take a nap when we get home, partially because I'm tired, but mostly to give Tucker and Scott some time alone. I wake up to the smell of garlic mixed with pot—Scott is cooking dinner for us. We get good and high, eat dinner and laugh at every-thing. Tucker and I wash the dishes, and Scott packs another bowl. After we smoke another round, Scott walks out the front door and returns a second later.

"OK, kids, time to go."

"Where?" I ask.

Tucker rolls his eyes and sighs, exaggerating both. "Scott's addicted to the damn monuments."

"Tucker, what is your problem?"

"Dude, how many times can a person stare at the same statue?"

Scott's about to answer but I cut him off. "Tucker?"

"Yes?"

"If you use the word *dude* one more time, you're walking home."

Scott laughs hysterically as he walks toward the door. "You found yourself a real firecracker, Tuck. Let's go."

I offer Tucker my hand, wondering if I embarrassed him. His lips curl upward and he grabs my hand. Scott locks up behind us, scales the steps in one jump and hugs us both. He leads the way to the monuments.

We stroll into the darkness as Scott explains the origins of each monument. He could be bullshitting, since I doubt anyone would question what year the Washington Monument was erected, but the tone of his voice reveals his zeal for the monuments. We pass the Vietnam Wall on the way to visit Abe Lincoln, and its dim, potent loneliness gives me the chills. Scott orates a short history of the Lincoln Memorial, and we read pieces of Lincoln's speeches from the walls. It's a warm night, but underneath Lincoln's marble home, the air is cool and thin.

"Holy shit," Tucker suddenly mutters.

"What?" I ask, immediately imagining a mugging-in-progress across the mall.

"Look at that moon," Tucker replies.

I race down the stairs and remind myself to hit the brakes before I near the reflecting pool. The moon glistens almost directly overhead—the reflecting pool is doing its job and then some. The whole area glows with a shimmery stillness, and the rectangle of water mirrors the elliptical moon's reflection.

"Scott, I need your keys," Tucker says.

Scott tosses his keys to Tucker. "Dare I ask why?"

"I have to sketch this. I'll be right back."

Tucker turns and starts to run toward Scott's house. "We'll be at the Wall!" Scott yells. Tucker waves.

Scott leads me to the Vietnam Wall, which is similarly desolate but a bit more illuminated. We're quiet for a while, as we both walk its length. Scott reads the names, but I'm more interested in the items left behind by visitors—a six-pack of beer, a solitary rose, a photograph of a child, a Xeroxed college degree—a seemingly random collection but I know each article means something to both the person who left it and the veteran for whom it was left. Even though they're stowed away in boxes, every item Ashley ever gave me is of tantamount importance; I will never throw any one of them away. I seem to attach too much value to inanimate, sentimental objects. I've even kept my suicide letters. None of the addressees have ever read them, and I have no intention of sharing them with anyone—I haven't even read them since I got out of Webster Ridge—yet I can't bring myself to throw them out or shred them or burn them.

I'm halfway through my second lap when I suddenly collapse in tears. Scott sits next to me.

"Did you know someone who died in Vietnam?" he asks.

"No," I say through sniffles. "It just seems like these people didn't want to die, and they did. There are people in the world that actually deserve to die, or want to die, yet all these soldiers . . ." I can't even finish, not that I know how to articulate my thoughts anyway.

Scott nods. "Total fucking waste. My uncles fought in the war. My father is diabetic, so he couldn't enlist."

"Did your uncles come back?" I ask.

"Yeah. One lost a leg and the other lost his mind."

More tears parachute from my eyes. Scott sighs and squeezes my leg.

Tucker runs by, whistling. We wave.

"He's in love with you," Scott announces.

I resist the urge to cry all over again. "How do you know?"

"I know him like I know myself. I've never seen him look at a woman the way he looks at you."

"Maybe he just thinks I'm a freak," I suggest, half-hoping it's true.

Scott shakes his head. "No. He wants to be with you."

"So why'd your girlfriend break up with you?" I ask.

Scott grins, acknowledging my not-so-sly subject change. "She decided I'm not the marrying kind." As he says the words, Scott's face seems to tremble a tiny bit.

"Are you?"

"We were together for two years and had just started to talk about marriage. I knew I wanted to marry her, but I wanted to do it right—when I had money for a ring, a honeymoon, a nice apartment, all that. So I started saving half of every paycheck. I didn't tell her—I figured when I had close to enough, I'd take her to Manhattan to pick out a ring. I saved for six months, and didn't buy a single CD or video game or anything for myself. You've been in my house, so you know I'm not very neat, but I'm organized when it counts and I don't give a shit about that shit hole, so why bother making it sparkle?"

Scott pauses, takes a deep breath and continues. "I have a good job and I make good money, and if I stay with this firm, I'll make *really* good money in a few years. Pam knew that. But she decided that because my house is messy and I play video games and I hadn't brought up the idea of marriage again, I'm clearly not marriage material. So she dumped me."

"Did you tell her about the money you'd saved?"

Scott plays with his shoelaces, and he reminds me of a little boy. "Nah. I realized we didn't really know each other that well. If she could judge me and my future based on such superficial evidence, then she's not the woman I want to end up with, anyway."

"Good point." I tap Scott's knee. "I'm sorry you had to go through that."

He looks at the sky and shakes his head, as if he's flinging away the pain. "So, are you the marrying type?"

I light a cigarette. "This isn't really fair, you know, because anything I say is going to find its way to Tucker."

"I would only repeat the good things, Alex."

"Right. Well, I kind of like the idea of marriage—hanging out with your favorite person forever—but I just cannot picture myself married."

"Married to Tucker?" Scott asks.

"Married to anyone. I can't visualize it, you know? I try to, but I just cannot *see* a man, nor can I see pulling away from my friends and retreating into a marital bubble."

Scott nods. "You're in luck, because I think Tucker's got a handful of his own marriage issues."

"Like what?"

"Somehow marriage gets all wrapped up in his mother's death. I assume you—"

I nod and Scott continues.

"I'm not too clear on it, since Tucker doesn't talk about it much. But in his mind, there's a definite link between his parents' marriage and his mother's suicide."

"He blames his father, doesn't he?"

Scott nods. "Are you a shrink?" he asks.

I laugh. "No, but I've spent enough time on the couch to figure that one out pretty quickly."

"Tucker's world crumbled when his mother died. I mean, any kid would be devastated, but the way I remember it, Tucker never recovered—he's never been the same."

I wonder if Jax or Jordy would describe me this way. I'm certain I've changed since Ashley's death, and I *know* I was a different person during the black year that led up to my suicide attempt. I couldn't stand to be awake, much less interact with people, and it showed in everything I did, or didn't do. I stopped seeing movies once a week and quit my weekend walks with Teddy; I even lost my craving to dance at Oblivion. I spoke only if spoken to, and spent every evening in my bedroom, alone. No one could reach me, and that's the way I wanted it. But afterward, I emerged from Webster Ridge much like the person I was before, I think— fragile, definitely, but no longer broken. Jax and Jordy were anxious to restore the strained relationships, my parents were not, and thus I gravitated toward the part of my world that has always been easier to maintain.

We share a peaceful silence for a few minutes and then Scott stands up. I grab his outstretched hand and he pulls me to my feet. He smiles shyly and I hug him, trapping all our words between us. We stroll toward Tucker, who is busy sketching the lustrous moon.

After he's done, Scott takes us to the Einstein Memorial, which is hidden behind a circle of shrubs. The statue of Einstein, sitting, is huge—over eight feet tall. All three of us sit in his lap, and Scott and Tucker take turns telling stories from their crazy college days. It makes me miss Casey, but for the most part, it's entertaining and even interesting, because I hear about a side of Tucker that doesn't emerge in the city. I guess there are parts of both of us that are, at first glance, invisible to the eye.

Tucker is wide awake, which means I'm actually going to have to tell him that I don't want to have sex with him. We hang out with Scott in the living room for a while, until he goes to bed. We drag ourselves upstairs shortly afterward.

Tucker and I kiss as we undress one another to the waist. As his fingers find my jeans, I refind my voice. "Tucker?"

He looks up at me, his face flushed. "Yeah?"

"I don't think I'm ready for this step," I tell him. Very original, Alex.

Tucker stares at me for a moment, looking either right into me or right through me—I can't tell. "Oh, OK."

An apology lodges itself on the tip of my tongue, but fuck that, why should I apologize for not wanting to have sex with him yet? I swallow it as Tucker's lips land on mine. We kiss and uncover each other's bodies for a while longer, until we're both too tired. Tucker pulls me close and falls asleep. It takes me twenty minutes to get out of his hold and fall asleep in my own space. Right before I drift off, I picture Jordy at her computer. I wonder if she's still mad at me.

We're on the road by eleven the next morning. It's an ugly day—the sky is gunmetal gray and mad clouds dart across it.

Tucker is quiet, which is fine with me—I'm trying to figure out what to say to Jordy and how to fix things between us as quickly as possible.

As we hit New Jersey, Tucker starts talking. He doesn't ask too many questions, and it's not all that hard to steer the conversation away from my life when I need to. Tucker will pretty much discuss anything except his father, which is so textbook it's kind of funny. Not that I should talk. Tucker would probably get out of the car and hitch a ride home if he knew what I'm not telling him.

It's only been two days but my heart still skips when the Manhattan skyline comes into view. No matter where I go or how long I've been gone, I'm always relieved to re-enter New York City. It's as if the granite, skyscrapers and concrete echo the barricade I've built around myself, so returning to the city makes me feel safe and right again. I drop Tucker off at his apartment and sit in traffic for half an hour. I pass the time by taking deep breaths.

7

The apartment is empty when I get home. It takes me a few minutes to find Jordy's note on the coffee table, which is covered with index cards, gum wrappers and overflowing ashtrays.

Welcome home. At the library—will be home for dinner.

That's friendly, right? She's obviously been working really hard—there are half a dozen dirty coffee cups in the sink, and the garbage begs to be taken out. I dump my bag on my bed, clean the living room and call my mother. She doesn't say anything about my fight with Teddy, so I don't, either. She spends our entire brief conversation asking if I'm OK, which so irritates me that by the time I finally curtail the conversation, I am actually no longer OK. I spend the next fifteen minutes debating with myself whether I should take a shower before going out for groceries or if I should shower right before I cook dinner. I finally decide I'm being a jackass and head down the street to the grocery store.

The panorama of the store, the streets and the crowd is familiar and comforting but also aggravating—I miss the contained quiet of my car. I unpack the groceries, smoke a cigarette and take a shower. In the steamed heat of the bathroom, I amend my plan to make chili—it's too hot and I don't have the patience. Pasta with chicken and green peppers will be just as nice. Jordy probably hasn't eaten a home-cooked meal in days. Nor have I gone three whole days without talking to Jordy since . . . Actually, I have no recollection of ever going this long without some sort of verbal contact.

I check on the sauce as I get dressed, which takes longer than usual because I can't decide what to wear to eat dinner in my own kitchen. I finally settle on tan capris and a black tank top. I add a minimal amount of makeup to my face and two cloves of garlic to the sauce. I crank up the volume so Nina Simone's voice slides across every wall as I blow-dry my hair. I pull it back into a low ponytail, boil water for the pasta and collapse on the couch, embarrassed at how tired I am after completing a few menial tasks. In an effort to ward off sleep, I stare at the Saturday crossword puzzle, knowing I'm just faking it—I can never accomplish much beyond Wednesday's puzzle. I'm about to dial Jax's cell phone when the door opens. Jordy enters. She stays expressionless as she drops her bulbous bag of books, crosses the living room and lands in my lap. We hug and giggle as if we're thirteen, reuniting after a month-long absence.

As we eat, I tell Jordy about the weekend in D.C. and she absorbs every word of it. She tells me about the changes she's made to her dissertation, and while I'm opening a second bottle of wine, she clears the plates and stands next to me in the kitchen. "I'm sorry," she says.

"I'm sorry, too. I was selfish and immature," I tell her.

Jordy shrugs. "I could've handled it better. I'm glad you had a good time with Tucker. Did you sleep with him?"

I feel Jordy's entire body tense up and then relax when I shake my head. "I actually used the words *I don't think I'm ready for this step,* can you believe it? I couldn't think of anything else to say."

"So what? It's true, isn't it?" she asks as she walks toward the kitchen table.

"Yeah, but I felt like Molly Ringwald in some eighties flick. I should've offered something a bit more creative."

Jordy places the last of the dirty dishes in the sink. "Like what?"

I wash as she dries. "I don't know. Something witty or charming."

"You've been seeing him for what—three, four weeks? You're under no obligation to fuck him just because you went out of town together."

"Speaking of which, when are we leaving?"

"I think I should be good to go by Friday afternoon."

"Great—just in time for rush hour."

Jordy elbows me in the gut, tosses the towel on the counter and refills our wine glasses.

"Want to pop in a movie?" she asks.

I nod, knowing I'll fall asleep halfway through whatever we watch.

Jordy is gone when I wake up in the morning—at the library, no doubt. I can't drag myself out of bed and since it's still too early to call Jax or Casey, I call Teddy at work. I have no idea what I'm going to say to her, but I don't want to be surprised by a phone call from her later in the week. At least this way I'm prepared, though I have no idea for what.

Teddy's secretary patches me through. "Alex?" I can tell she's shocked I've called.

"Hi."

"How was D.C.?" she asks. I can picture her rifling through paperwork at her massive mahogany desk.

"Good. We hung out at the monuments. Remember when Mom and Dad took us there? Ashley thought the reflecting pool was—"

"A kiddie pool. I remember. I can't believe *you* remember that; you were four."

"Five." I recall other pieces of our family trip to D.C., too, now that I think about it. Ashley had just turned fifteen, and he was starting to be funny instead of surly and obnoxious. He was also really smart, and both he and my dad narrated facts and

trivia as we meandered our way through the marble monuments, the Supreme Court and the Smithsonian. My mother
was overwhelmed by the city's stature, or lack thereof. "I just
can't understand why all the buildings are so short," she re-
peated day after day. Finally, we found out that no building in
Washington, D.C. is allowed to be taller than the Capitol building. We all thought this rule a bit unfair, and not very democra-
tic. We had planned to mention it during our White House
tour, but once we were inside, walking the carpeted halls, even
Ashley's bravado was lost. I remember Teddy and I held hands
and pretended to be the First Daughters as we strolled from
room to room.

Now, though, Teddy and I share the silence. I hear Sam's
voice—urging me not to apologize, at least not first.

"I'm sorry for making you run out of the restaurant," Teddy
says.

"You mean you're sorry for yelling at me, which pissed me
off so much that I *chose* to run out of the restaurant?" I ask.

Teddy sighs. "OK, yes, I'm sorry for yelling at you. I would
really like to fix things between us, Alex. I hate fighting with
you. I hate that you don't like me anymore, and I hate that I
don't confide in you anymore. Remember when I used to tell
you everything?"

"Like when you called me at three in the morning, freaking
out because your date had passed out, fully clothed, in your
bathtub?" I laugh, and I hear Teddy giggle.

"Oh God. Drew was his name. Couldn't hold his liquor."

"I'll say!" We both laugh.

"See?" Teddy says. "Don't you miss that? Don't you want it to
be like it used to be between us?"

"I don't want to fight anymore, either, Teddy. I don't like
being yelled at, and believe it or not, I'm not a huge fan of
yelling at other people, especially you."

"So let's repair the damage," she suggests.

I want to say *it's not that easy* but instead I ask, "How do you
propose we go about it?"

"Therapy."

"What?"

"Therapy," she says again, her voice steadier than I've heard it in a while.

"Teddy, you've never been in therapy and I'm currently on hiatus from therapy."

"So?"

"So you can't just expect me to sign up for sessions with you. This isn't couples therapy—there's no sisters therapy."

"There's family therapy," she replies. Has she been watching *Dr. Phil?*

I sigh, regretting I called her in the first place. "How many times did I ask you to come see Sam with me?" This is beside the point, I know, but I need a tangent.

"I'm ready now," she answers.

"Good for you, Teddy, really. I'm glad you've thought about this and I appreciate that you're willing to go out of your comfort zone, but I'm not just going to walk into some family therapist's office because *you're* finally ready. I can't go to therapy with you without having my own therapist, and my therapist is dead."

Now it's Teddy's turn to sigh. I know she's mentally belittling the whole process—probably the whole field of psychology—as well as the notion that I need a support system in place before she rips my heart out once a week in front of a totally new therapist, someone who is not Sam.

"So get your own therapist," Teddy says.

"First of all, it's not that easy. Second of all, I told you I'm taking the summer off—I don't want to find someone right now."

"So you're willing to put our relationship on the back burner for the rest of the summer just because you don't feel like shopping for a new therapist?"

What the fuck was I thinking, calling her?

"Teddy, listen to me, listen to the words. It's not that I don't *feel* like shopping for a new therapist—it's not laziness or lack of motivation or whatever else—I don't *want* to go to therapy. I need to take a few months off. And if I remember correctly, I asked you to come with me to see Sam the day after Ashley died, so don't imply I'm the one who doesn't want to deal with our problems."

Teddy is quiet, for maybe twenty seconds. "It's amazing you can remember *anything* correctly, with all the pot and alcohol you ingest."

So we're back here. Sorry, Sam, I did my best—at least I called her. I breathe into the phone for a few seconds, my memory transfixed on how we used to be—how it felt to have a big sister I adored and an older brother I hardly knew. Ashley is gone, Teddy is here, and the roles have reversed. It's Ashley who knows me, and he's been dead for years. I open my mouth to respond but there's nothing I can say so I hang up the phone.

I'm a knot of energy for the rest of the week. I'm not sure if it's anger that propels me or sheer boredom. I see two movies, meander through the Whitney Museum and the Museum of Natural History, take Jax shopping in SoHo—he lets me buy him a fabulous pair of shoes—and start and finish three more illustrations for my newest book. I wake up at ten on Friday morning (without the alarm clock!). I confirm our motel room in Williamstown as soon as I get out of bed and then pack so the rest of the day is mine. I don't do much, but I'm relaxed, knowing I've done all the important stuff. I talk to Carchie for almost an hour, mostly about his last two treatments and last night's poker game. Then I straighten up the apartment and choose CDs for the car ride. Jordy calls at three.

"Hi," she says. She drags out the word for about five syllables—something's wrong.

"What?"

"I just caught myself plagiarizing."

"Good thing you caught it."

"I am so immersed in this fucking paper—and so tired and bored and burned out—that I accidentally copied, verbatim, someone else's sentence."

"But you caught it," I tell her again.

"No, Alex, you're missing the point. I have to go through the entire thing, to make sure I haven't done it anywhere else."

The phone feels heavy in my palm. "When do you plan on doing this?"

"My defense is in two weeks. I have to do it this weekend. I am so, so sorry."

I inhale a huge breath and exhale it into Jordy's ear. My jaw hurts and I can't find my lighter.

"Alex, I can't go away for five days knowing my dissertation might contain pieces of plagiarism. I have to hand it in before the defense."

"Yeah, I know. What if we leave on Sunday?"

Jordy sighs. "I'm not rushing through it just so we can go to the Berkshires. It's not like either of us hasn't been there twenty times."

"So now you don't like going to Williamstown anymore? You should've told me you wanted to go somewhere else," I tell her.

"I don't. You're missing the point again."

"What if I buy you a laptop? You can do your work up there."

Jordy sighs. "Thanks, Alex, but it's just too complicated to start moving all my stuff."

"Why? Everything's on your flash drive. Throw a couple books in the car, and we're all set."

"Alex, don't do this."

"What? I'm trying to help."

"But you're not. And you're making me feel guilty."

"You should feel guilty, Jordy."

"What the fuck is your problem? I cancel plans for a completely legitimate reason and it's the crime of the century?"

"This isn't dinner plans, Jordy. This is a week in Williamstown—we have reservations, we have tickets, we have *plans*. You got mad because I didn't invite you to come with me when I bought the car, then you cancelled on me to pick up the car, and cancelled again before I left for D.C. Not to mention I've barely seen you since the weekend at Carchie's. You can't understand why I'm pissed?"

"Yes, Alex, I realize I've been a little distracted lately. But I thought you understood that it's only because I'm finishing the most important part of grad school, and I want it to be perfect, because it's going to earn me a fucking PhD! So I assumed— wrongly, as it turns out—that you would put aside your selfish need to come first in my life for a little while and be supportive and helpful. But you're bored, and obsessing about Tucker and Sam and Carchie and Ashley and everything else you can't control, and you're insecure and scared, so I should drop everything I've worked for in order to hold your hand while we wander around the same New England towns we've visited since we were kids. I understand *that* perfectly," Jordy says. I can tell she wants to scream but she's in a library so she can't.

"This has nothing to do with Tucker. This is about you and me and our friendship and priorities and loyalty—"

"Alex, I think you should reconsider taking a break from therapy."

"What?" My ears feel like they're on fire.

"If you are actually questioning my priorities and my loyalty and what our friendship means to me, you really are crazy. You're a total fucking lunatic. I'm the one who found you, re-member?"

I sit down exactly where I am, hitting the floor with a thud. "Good luck on your defense, Jordy. I think we should not speak to each other for a while."

"Finally, we agree on something."

We hang up on each other at the same time.

I can't go alone. The idea of having no company—no dis-tractions—makes my head hurt. I'm pretty sure I wouldn't be calling Tucker right now if I didn't know his number by heart. But I do, and I am, and he enthusiastically agrees to fill in for Jordy and accompany me to Williamstown, under the condi-tion he can bring his easel and paints and get some work done. I'm fine with that—I'll need time away from him anyway. Of course I really want Jax to come with me, but I know he's busy with work and the voice-over taping. While I'm waiting for

Tucker to get ready, I leave a message for Jax. I do my best to prevent hysterics but toward the end of my summary my voice slouches and a few rogue tears droop down my cheeks.

It's a perfect June day—sunny and warm with no humidity—and we're driving north on the Taconic Parkway. I love feeling this sturdy, stable truck under me as I accelerate in and out of the turns. Tucker is next to me, wearing deliciously worn-in jeans, a Polo T-shirt and Converse sneakers. His face is clean-shaven and his hair is freshly cut.

"There's someone I want to visit while I'm up here," Tucker suddenly says.

"You know someone who lives in Williamstown?"

"Lenox, actually."

"Cool." I wonder why he's just telling me now, thirty minutes from our destination, but I don't prod for information, mostly because I don't want him to ever pull information out of me. I can't help thinking this car ride is so different from the one I would've taken with Jordy. There's a static of some sort in the car. With Jordy, there's never any vapor in the air, nothing weighing it down. Right now I'm still angry enough that I can't call her, yet I know I will—eventually—because, well, she's my best friend.

"Alex?"

"Huh?"

"You OK?"

"Yeah, sure."

"You might want to loosen your grip on the steering wheel. I can see every vein in your hand."

Does he have to be so fucking observant?

"Have you figured out Sam's note yet?" he asks.

I've never been so grateful to see the exit. I fumble for the button and lower the window, then raise the volume so the Stones are loud enough to impede conversation.

"Alex?"

"What?"

"Sam's note—any ideas?"

"No. None."

I fly down Route 7, counting the seconds until we can get out of the car and breathe different air.

"You'll figure it out eventually," Tucker says. He taps his fingers on his knee in time to the music and smiles at me.

My whole life can be summed up in the word *eventually*.

The Corner Motel is a two-tiered, off-white building that makes me want to take a nap when I look at it. It sits on a small hill overlooking not only Route 7 but also the peaks of the Berkshire Mountains. In the morning—the real morning, not my ten o'clock, city version of the morning—a delicious dampness covers the whole area. It starts in the mountains and creeps across the fields, the roads, the lakes and the streams—it travels as far as it can before the sun rises and burns it off. When I was at sleepaway camp, we used to go to breakfast in sweats and a sweatshirt—maybe even a jacket—and by the time we'd eaten our well-balanced meal and were ready to walk back to our bunks, the sun was roaring through the evergreens and we would have to make the first of many clothing changes of the day. Now, as adults, we never set an alarm, but somehow—when we're up here visiting—Jordy and I manage to get up at dawn, crawl out of bed, bundle up and take up positions in the white plastic chairs on the balcony of the motel, where we watch the weather change for the next three hours. I wonder if Tucker will want to do that tomorrow morning.

We check in, and of course Tucker hits it off with the owner. He knows her name is Shelley within five minutes. I've been staying here once a summer for the last five years and I always forget her name as soon as we drive back to the city. He's so damn nice—what is he doing with me? Would he still want me if he knew I allowed my best friend to find me on the edge of death?

Shelley gives us room 9, which is on the second floor, right in the middle. Perfect sunrise seats. Tucker gets annoyed when I won't let him carry my stuff upstairs but I don't really care—

I'm not a society doyenne who waits for doors to be opened. He's got the key, so I let him speed ahead of me. I walk slowly, waiting for Charlie. I'm about to call his name when I see him peek around the other end of the building.

"Hey, Charlie, come here." I can't believe I remember the name of the motel's cat but not the owner. Charlie strolls over and I squat down to pet him. He's huge—probably fifteen pounds—and every shade of brown from amber to chocolate. Tucker sticks his head out the door, no doubt wondering where the hell I am.

"Who's this?" he asks, sitting down next to us.

"This is Charlie. Isn't he adorable?"

Tucker nods. "He's fat."

"He's not fat. It's all muscle."

Tucker laughs. The lock of hair hangs over his eyes, and he suddenly looks relaxed, peaceful. His skin is appealingly smooth. I kind of want to make out with him right now.

"We hang out every summer. He has a tendency to wander into the rooms."

"I'm starving," Tucker tells me. "Go put your stuff down and let's hit The Den."

I look up at Tucker. "You know—"

"I know more than you think I know," he says, smiling.

I hope not.

"You want to drive?" I ask, tossing Tucker the keys before he answers.

"Sure."

"Don't pretend you're all blasé about it. You've been dying to drive this car since I ordered it."

Tucker laughs. "I wouldn't say *dying*, but it is a pretty fucking cool car."

Tucker takes off toward Vermont. Route 7 is the kind of road that a lot of people don't like driving on—it's narrow with terrible twists—but I love it. I'm surrounded by verdant fields one minute and stopped at a traffic light in a Norman Rockwell town a minute later. There are hills and dips and curves. I insert a U2 CD, and Tucker nods into the rhythm. The silence is just getting comfortable when he speaks.

"I spoke to my father today—to tell him I was coming up here with you."

There are so many shades of green out my window.

"He mentioned he never got your books."

"I wasn't sure if he was serious. I meant to call and ask him."

Tucker shakes his head. "He wouldn't have offered to help if he didn't want to."

"OK. I'll drop them off next week." I peek behind Tucker's shades. "Has he helped you? With your paintings, I mean?"

"I've never asked and he's never offered. Have you ever had the mac and cheese at The Den?"

Christ, he has no subject-changing skills whatsoever. No idea how to deflect, probably. Is it a hetero-guy thing or a Tucker thing?

We discuss food for the rest of the ride, so by the time we get there, we're both ravenous. There's a huge line, of course— I've never waltzed into this place and sat right down. Sometimes the line falls outside the double doors and drips down the exterior stairs, and yet people wait—I wait. The Den is an old-fashioned diner housed in a long, rectangular structure that resembles an old railroad car. A chipped yellow counter stretches from one end to the other, and there are about six booths on either side of the entrance, all of them with smooth red banquettes. There is a huge, colorful jukebox just inside the front door that looks like it would be a gold mine of musical possibilities but is always out of order. The walls are covered with blackboards announcing daily specials, weekly specials and house favorites, in addition to the four-page menu. The waitresses are orange—their skin is wrinkled, but not from laugh lines. They're all locals, and I have a feeling very few of them have been to New York City more than once. They have names like Shirley and Flora and Belle, and they probably hate people like me, so I always leave them a huge tip, so at least they'll think *some* city folk are good people.

Tucker and I peruse the local free weeklies while we wait but I don't want to get too involved in the reading material because I'm busy keeping a vigilant watch on the line. We're fourth, but the first twosome—we might skip ahead of the line if two seats at the counter open up. Tucker reads me my horoscope but I hate those fairy tales so I dig a pen out of my bag and suggest we try the crossword puzzle. Tucker grabs the pen and jumps in, answering questions on his own. I lose interest and watch our fellow customers-to-be, most of whom fall into the category of "burly." If Jordy were here, we'd be guessing what each person was going to order—bacon would be mentioned several times in a row.

"What's a seven-letter word that means to try unsuccessfully?" Tucker asks.

I lean over his shoulder and count the empty boxes. "Attempt."

"Thank you," he replies, furiously scratching in the answer. "Where are we?"

"Third, but I think second is moments away."

Sure enough, a haggard waitress beckons to a group of five and they file through the magic doors.

"What's an arty vampire movie starring Susan Sarandon? Nine letters?"

"*The Hunger.*"

"Alex, you are fucking brilliant." I wouldn't necessarily go that far, but it's always nice to hear the words *you* and *brilliant* in the same sentence.

"One more and we're in," I tell Tucker, slapping his thigh to get his attention.

He shoves the pen and the puzzle in my bag and bounces in the line. "Do you know what you're going to get?"

"No, but I know I'm going to order a cinnamon donut to eat while I'm deciding. And you should order a blueberry muffin—we'll share."

"Why?"

Because that's what Jordy and I do. "Because."

We score a booth. Tucker orders milk; I order coffee and a

cinnamon donut. We finger the worn, dog-eared menus until the drinks are delivered, then pore over our options in silence.

Our waitress, Betty, was probably really pretty at one point, until she stopped caring.

"I'd like the macaroni and cheese, please," Tucker says.

"I'll have a tomato, Swiss and mushroom omelet, please. Rye toast."

Tucker hands her the menus. "And we'll share an order of fries, well done." He smiles big for Betty before she walks away.

"How'd you know I'd eat fries?" I ask.

Tucker smiles. "Please, I've been here with my sister. I know you food-obsessive types sometimes need help pigging out."

"That's twice you've surprised me today."

"Yeah? Consider it payback."

"For what?"

"Almost everything you do surprises me," he answers.

"What are you talking about?"

"I saw you before you saw me at Sam's funeral, and I never once for a second thought you'd talk to me. Then you tell me about this crazy message Sam left you, and I immediately think you'll go on some sort of vision quest to figure it out, but you hardly mention it. I have no idea how you feel about me after the first few times we hung out, then you invite me to your uncle's cabin with your two best friends, yet we don't kiss once the whole weekend. Then you ask me to help you buy a car. You don't want to have sex while we're in D.C., and then you make me your last-minute replacement for Jordy on a trip up here. The average guy would've walked away weeks ago, Alex."

Out of the corner of my eye, I see the food coming. "But you, Charles Tucker Spencer Junior the Second, are not the average guy."

Tucker laughs and puts his napkin in his lap. "You know that if we were anywhere but The Den, we would talk about this over our food, right?"

"But we are at The Den," I reply. "So we're going to shut up and eat."

On the way up the stairs at the motel, it suddenly occurs to me to ask, "Hey, Tucker, when were you up here with your sister?"

Tucker looks back at me as he hits the landing. "What?"

"You said you'd eaten at The Den with Catherine. When?"

We walk toward the room. The late afternoon shadows have fallen like a giant, dark veil over the mountains.

"We come up here once a year, usually at the end of October."

"To visit the person who lives up here?"

Tucker fiddles with the lock. "Yep. Well, sort of. I wouldn't say she really lives here—rests, is more like it."

Something tells me not to follow him into the room. "What?"

Tucker turns to face me just before he crosses the threshold. "My mother is buried here. In Lenox."

8

I can't even smoke my cigarette because some sort of shivering attack has seized my entire body. The meal I so thoroughly enjoyed an hour earlier is burning a hole in my stomach. Tucker is asleep in the room. I'm on the balcony watching the sun shrink behind the mountains. As fucked up as I may be, I would never do this to someone—it's harsh and selfish and childish—and it seems so unlike Tucker, not that I *really* know him. My mind wanders through a possible list of excuses, but I know it's a waste of time because there's no way I can rationally explain why I would rather endure Chinese water torture than accompany him to his mother's grave. And then there's the part of me that's honored he wants me next to him when he visits his dead mother. But the fear wins—I'm scared because there's simply no way around it. I have to tell him I tried to kill myself, which also means discussing Ashley's death. Between Sam, Tucker's mother and my brother, our relationship seems haunted by death. And as much as I've tried to eject the thought from my mind, I cannot forget that I remind Tucker's father of his wife. What will happen when Tucker finds out I'm even more like his mother than he thinks? I wrap my arms around my knees. It takes me three shaky cigarettes to ease the fear.

I go inside the room, brush my teeth and curl up next to

Tucker. He breathes easily—sleep seems to come to him so naturally. I don't have a plan and I don't want one—all I can do is hope Tucker understands—but I have a feeling my disclosure is going to change us.

It's dark when I wake up. Tucker is in the shower, so I turn on the TV and watch a rerun of *Law & Order*. Tucker's skin glistens and he smells like lemon soap when he re-enters the room. I shed my clothes and leave them in a pile on top of my bag. I can't imagine Tucker would poke around in my stuff, but I'm toting around the satchel of pills, so it's important for me to shield my bag. I don't make eye contact with him but I feel his stare as I stroll into the bathroom. While I'm in the shower, I think about Jordy—a flash of her sitting in the library, surrounded by papers and books, rushes through my mind. I try to wash the resentment and rejection away but it's still there as I wrap the small, rough towel around my body. I regret not bringing clothes into the bathroom. I grab a hand towel, wrap it around my head and, holding on to the towel, which barely covers my body, walk into the room. Tucker now wears khaki cargo pants, a black T-shirt and a brand new pair of black Kenneth Cole shoes. His Prada jacket is slung on the coatrack.

"What are you in the mood to eat?" he asks.

"There's a place down the road with the best chicken parm on the planet," I answer as I choose an outfit from my bag, which is, of course, crammed full of clothes I won't need.

"Do they have lobster?"

"Yep."

"Cool. I'm in the mood for lobster. And a good Merlot—something from the seventies, maybe."

He's craving red wine from a specific year?

Tucker channel surfs while I get dressed in the bathroom. I put on black pants (Jordy's), a pale blue T-shirt, a black button-down shirt (Jordy's) and black sandals. I apply some eye makeup, blow-dry my hair and then sit on the closed toilet for a few minutes, trying to control the compulsion to call Jordy. I could call Jax but I'm sure he's working dinner. I've picked two fights, sort of, with Jordy within two weeks—what is wrong with me?

"Alex, you almost done? I'm starving."

I open the door and almost bump into Tucker.

"Look what I brought," he sings as he pulls a thick joint out of his pocket.

"You are the wind beneath my wings," I say, smiling with relief. Tucker hands me the car keys and I kiss him on the mouth, leaving all thoughts of Jordy in the bathroom.

"Now this is good wine," Tucker says, sighing.

I laugh for no reason. We're sitting at a square table on the restaurant's deck. The sky is indigo and the stars are so close I could touch them. Billie Holiday's voice soars above our heads and, I have to admit, the 1978 Merlot is pretty damn good.

Over salad, Tucker tells me about adventures he shared with Scott while in high school, and I evoke some of the more hilarious Jax-related memories from my childhood over the main course. It feels odd—but also pleasant—to be on the cusp of familiarity with someone new. Since I know Scott, and Tucker knows Jax, the tales we exchange are actually funny and there's no need for polite laughter. A swell of confidence rolls through me as I look across the table—I trust Tucker, I like Tucker, I want to be able to share things with Tucker.

Tucker pours us the last of the wine, lights a cigarette and asks, "So aren't you curious about Sam's letter?"

"Of course I am."

"It seems like you're not being very proactive in trying to solve the big mystery."

"I think about 'the missing piece' all the time."

"And you can't imagine anything he might have meant?"

I shake my head. "Not a fucking thing."

Tucker smiles. "Maybe he meant me."

I laugh. "Sam was a great therapist, but even he had no way of knowing I'd bum a cigarette off you at his funeral."

"No, but maybe he knew we'd find each other that day."

I laugh again. "You're not serious, are you?"

"No, but if I were you I'd be doing everything and anything to figure it out."

I take a drag of his cigarette. "I'm working on it."

We split the tab and, while Tucker is in the men's room, I stare at his empty chair. I know I have to relinquish control but I also know I need to feel safe and protected when I tell him about my past, about my dead brother. The wine and pot have brought my defenses down a notch; I'll tell Tucker about Ashley—about everything—in the motel room.

It's after one when we pull into the parking lot of the motel. We sit on the balcony for half an hour, smoking the rest of the joint and searching for constellations. I shouldn't have smoked more—the increased high has rendered me inarticulate. I'd like total control of my words when I explain my past. Tucker wraps his jacket around my shoulders but I shrug it off and then unbutton my shirt. The motel is silent—except for the chorus of crickets—as I pull my T-shirt over my head. Tucker smiles, stands up and offers me his hand. We both crack up as we realize we're re-enacting a moment from the day we met at Sam's funeral. Tucker has my shirts and his jacket in one hand and me in the other. He closes and locks the door behind me. I yank the maroon bedspread off and leave it hanging from the end of the bed. Tucker removes his shoes and then slips my sandals off my feet. I sit on the bed and motion for him to turn off the light. He seems unsure, so I shake my head to discourage the notion of leaving the light on. He flips the switch with one finger and joins me on the bed. Our lips meet before our bodies merge.

Tucker's hands have already taken their first journey across my body when I pull away from him.

"Do you have condoms?"

Tucker nods and runs his hand through my hair. "Of course."

I find his lips and bury myself within his touch. A few minutes later, as Tucker reaches into his bag, he says, "I can take care of you, Alex. Let me take care of you."

I don't reply. It's pretty dark in the room—a lone candle

flickers on the dresser—so Tucker can't see my body language, my lack of response. When Tucker rolls over to face me, I wrap my arms around his neck, savoring the tangible closeness. I stare into his green eyes—they're so incredibly alluring, even in the semidarkness—and look for something, anything, that will help me relax. I lock his arms around my back and immerse myself in his openness. Tucker's hands are less steady than I thought they would be—or my body is not responding to his touch. Every few minutes something he does feels fantastic, but I find myself focusing on other things—a trip to Chicago to visit Casey, illustrations for my book—and I eventually lose track of Tucker's progress, until it's over.

Afterward, when we're lying in bed—the sheets nearly perfect—Tucker tickles my back and I finally relax. I close my eyes and treasure the warmth of his body, the sweetness of his breath.

I watch the sunrise alone, folded into Tucker's sweatshirt, thinking about Jordy. I used my cell phone as an alarm clock and brought it with me onto the balcony. I check my messages and find one from Jax—he tells me to call him whenever I want. It's only seven thirty but he said whenever I want, so I dial, wincing while I wait for the ringing phone to disturb his sleep.

"Jax! Jax! Wake up!" I'm doing the whisper-yell thing.

He must be on alert for my voice because he picks up after only a few seconds.

"Hey, babycakes," he says, his voice hoarse from the morning.

"Hi."

Jax takes a deep breath, no doubt trying to wake himself up. I hear him roll over and can picture him cuddling under his purple quilt. "I miss you. How's the trip so far?"

I put my feet up on the railing, glance at the closed door of the motel room and sip the mediocre coffee I got from the motel office. "I had sex with Tucker last night."

"I thought I felt the earth move!" Jax laughs.

"It so did *not* move."

"Oh. Shit—must've been the subway. It didn't move at all, not even a little?"

"It was enjoyable and sweet and comfortable, I guess."

"Yikes. I knew there had to be something wrong with him. But he's so cute. Maybe he's gay."

"Shut up, Jax. You think everyone is gay."

"And I'm very rarely wrong, babycakes. Remember Jordy's cousin Billy? I nailed *that* one on the head within five minutes."

"Yeah, and then you nailed *him* five days later."

"I ran into him at Oblivion. What was I supposed to do? Not fuck him because he's related to Jordy?"

We laugh. I miss him.

"Have you spoken to Jordy?" he asks.

"No. Have you?"

"Yeah. She called me yesterday on my way to the restaurant. We met up at midnight for a quick drink."

"Oh."

"Don't you want to know what we talked about?"

"No."

"Liar, liar, pants on fire! Everything we discussed was on the record, so I can tell you. She wants me to."

I light a cigarette. "OK, what?"

"She's pissed, Alex, but she'll get over it. And I hate to say this, because you're my oldest friend and I can't live without you and all that, but she's right—you were selfish and your reaction was way over the top. Have you been watching soap operas since you got fired?"

"Fuck you."

"Don't you think she wants to go away with you? This is her dissertation, Alex—it's her entire life right now. And you and I and everyone else have to understand that. She's almost done, and you left her hanging when she needs you most."

"I know."

"You do?"

"I didn't while we were yelling at each other but now I do. I feel like a bad friend. I am a bad friend."

"You're not a bad friend, Alex. You just acted like one for five minutes. You're a fantastic friend, and Jordy knows that. You do know she loves you more than anything on this planet, right?"

"Yeah."

Jax pauses for a moment, inhales, exhales and continues. "Really—do you know *how* much she loves you?"

"Yeah," I say again.

Jax sighs. "So call her, apologize and have fun with Tucker. You fucked Ben twelve ways 'till Sunday. Try to teach Tucker a thing or two in the sack."

What if it's not Tucker?

"How'd the taping go?"

"It was great. The producer really likes me—she's going to put in a good word for me on her next gig. Oh, Teddy and Max came into the restaurant. Are we sure Max is straight? 'Cause he's got fabulous taste in clothes."

"Teddy dresses him," I reply. "What'd she say?"

"Nothing. I wasn't her waiter. I brought them a round of free drinks, we chitchatted and that was it."

"She didn't say anything about me?"

"No, she never does that, Alex. Never has, never will. She did suggest I call my parents. Apparently my father's been pretty sick."

"Yeah—the chemo and radiation make him sicker than the cancer does. When's the last time you called home?"

Jax thinks for a moment. "I don't know. A month ago, maybe." We're both quiet for almost a minute. "Do you think he's going to die?" Jax asks.

I sigh. Sam, Carchie, Jim. Ashley. What's the point of letting people in? "I don't know. Probably."

I hear Jax light a cigarette. "I guess I should call him. But if he hangs up on me again . . ."

"Wait until I get home. I'll call with you."

"OK. Thanks, babycakes."

"Thanks for telling me about Jordy."

"Call her. She's pretty much always in the library but leave her a message declaring your remorse and undying love."

"Thanks, Jax. I don't need you to write a script for me."

"Will you call me in a few days? And remind me not to work dinner the day you get home. I'll have my voice-over check by then, and we can go out and get loaded with our new money."

"Sure thing, Jay Gatsby."

"I didn't say I would buy *you* drinks—we'll each buy our own. It's not nouveau riche if we don't show off."

I hear the bathroom door close in the room. "I have to go, Jax. I'll call you the day after tomorrow. I love you."

"Love you, too, babycakes. Use a condom!"

"Bye."

While I shower and dress, Tucker takes the Discovery and picks up muffins and coffee at The Den. I drink my third cup of coffee as I get ready, and a fourth with Tucker on the balcony as we watch the weather change yet again. It's not the caffeine I covet so much as the warmth of the hot liquid—I've been cold for the last twelve hours. I want to know what our plan is but I don't want to say something asinine, like, "So after we visit your mother's grave, do you want to walk around Lenox or see a movie?" I wish I could call Jordy, apologize for being a brat and then ask her how the fuck I'm supposed to tell Tucker everything, but the timing is all wrong—Jordy is definitely in the library, cell phone off. And besides, Tucker is right next to me, and he's not going anywhere. I should tell him now.

The sun inches across the parking lot as I finish my muffin and light a cigarette. Tucker leans against the railing, the muscles in his body untroubled. A flicker of him naked, his skin against mine, scurries through my mind. I blink and lose it.

Tucker turns to face me and says, "You want to see a movie after the cemetery?"

"Get off my wavelength."

"What?"

"I was just thinking that."

Tucker smiles, leans down and kisses me. "Last night was great." He takes my empty coffee cup and walks into the room.

I let Tucker drive again, since I have no idea where we're going. I slide in a Melissa Etheridge CD and close my tired eyes behind my sunglasses. Suddenly, I start sneezing and can't stop. I close the windows but it only gets worse. After about ten sneezes, I look in the back of the Discovery and see a bouquet of flowers. He must have picked it up when he bought breakfast. I'm about to complain about Tucker's insensitivity to my allergies when I realize the flowers are for his mother's grave. I lower the windows and sneeze into the wind.

"Sorry," Tucker says. "I forgot about your allergies."

"That's OK. I should've taken an antihistamine. I forgot you'd want to put flowers on the grave."

"What do you mean? What else would you put on a grave?"

"Jews do rocks."

"Rocks?" Tucker's face is caught between amusement and surprise.

"Rocks. Jews aren't allowed to put flowers on a tombstone."

"Why not?"

Tucker slows as we approach a traffic circle. He takes a road I'm not familiar with. "I forget why."

Tucker shakes his head. "Seems like something you should know about your own religion."

"Yeah, well, I'm not very religious."

"Do you believe in God?"

Tell him now, Alex. "No."

Tucker doesn't process my answer because he's busy making a right turn onto River Avenue and I see grass—lots and lots of grass—spotted with tombstones. He turns into the entrance of the cemetery and slowly drives up the hill to the parking lot. I reach for my bottle of water and drink half of it as he parks. I pop two Advil and wash them down with more water. I push my sunglasses as close to my eyes as possible and pull my hair out of the ponytail so it shields my face. Tucker pats my hand and turns Melissa off. He smoothes his jeans and checks to make sure his shoes are tied.

"Ready?" he asks.

No. "Tucker, I have to—"

He doesn't hear me. He's out of the car, opening the back

door to retrieve the flowers. I missed my chance. I'll have to tell him at dinner.

Tucker leads the way up a narrow brick path. I untie my sweatshirt from my waist and put it on. The sun rages through the colossal evergreens but I'm cold. I concentrate on the scenery in order to stop my mind from rehashing the moment I just let slip away. Now that we're in the fresh air, I've stopped sneezing, but my head pulsates, matching my footsteps. Tucker's back is perfectly straight and his stride is even, resolute. At the end of the path, he pauses, his eyes skimming the horizon of tombstones. He takes my hand and turns us to the right, but then he stops short.

"Jesus Christ, Alex, your hand is freezing."

He drops my hand, hands me the bouquet of flowers and zips my sweatshirt. His hair is still slightly wet. "Tucker, I have to tell you something." Everything.

"OK, let me just find her first. I always think I know exactly where I'm going but then I lose her."

He takes my hand again and we walk past rows and rows of tombstones. I focus on Tucker's shoulder to avoid seeing Ashley's coffin being lowered into the ground. I can control my vision but not my auditory memories, and all I hear is the dirt as it falls upon the simple pine coffin. First my father shovels on a pile of freshly upturned dirt, then my mother, then Teddy and then me. We stand shoulder to shoulder afterward, to form a receiving line of grief. Jordy and Jax stand behind me. Jax keeps a hand on my back at all times—I'm not sure if it is so I will feel his support or if he is literally supporting me. My lips are so parched the salty tears that slide down my face make them sting. I don't bother to wipe away the tears so Jordy keeps dabbing a tissue on my face. I really want to take care of my mother, but she bursts into tears every time I go near her. My father is never more than five feet from Jim, and Teddy is busy with the caterers, the lawyers and the burial. Silence is the prevailing noise in our house.

∽

"Here we are," I hear Tucker say. He releases my hand and places the flowers on his mother's grave. The tombstone is huge, almost waist-high, gray marble. It says:

Elizabeth Spencer
Beloved Wife, Mother,
Daughter and Sister.

No dates. Terribly unoriginal epitaph, Ashley would think, especially for the wife of a mogul.

The area around the tombstone is immaculate. The grass is shorn, practically every blade is the same length—the violet and red flowers are blooming, the tombstone is spotless and shiny—year-round maintenance, obviously.

"Sit," Tucker says.

I sit down, but I face him, not her. "Are you sure you don't want to be alone?" I ask.

"Maybe in a little while."

I stare at Tucker as he stares at her. After a minute or so, he says, "I wish you could have met her. You would have really liked her, and she would have loved you."

I can't do this. I thought I could but I can't. How can I be in a cemetery but not with Ashley? I stand up and walk away from Tucker, who surprisingly doesn't question me.

I stagger over to a bush and kneel down, searching for a rock. I can't find one the right size—they're either too small or too big—and when I finally locate one, I have to force myself to stand up. It would be so much easier if I could just stay where I am.

Tucker stares at me, his head cocked to the side, as I approach. His legs are now crossed and he looks comfortable. I stand next to his mother's tombstone, place the rock on top of it and stroke the cold, indifferent marble. The texture of the granite invokes a soundless explosion in my mind, and I am suddenly a witness to my own history, my past. I am twenty-six years old—frozen—kneeling at Ashley's grave. I am unable to leave the cemetery, leave Ashley, for more than two days at a time. Today is different, though—today is the last time I will be here, until next week, when they bury me next to my older brother after I commit suicide.

"Alex?" I hear Tucker, and it takes me a few seconds to return to the present—the past always seems to tempt me. Tucker stands next to me, his arm on my shoulder.

I pull my hand away from the tombstone. "What?"

"What's wrong? Why are you crying?"

Shit—I am crying. I can feel my wet eyelashes sticking to my face. The warmth of my tears and the chill of my skin cause some sort of chemical reaction and I realize I might throw up. I grab the bottle of water and swallow as much as I can as quickly as I can.

"Alex, are you all right?"

I let my legs crumple under me—I land on the grass, facing his mother's grave.

"Tucker, I have to tell you something. I meant to tell you last night, and this morning, but . . ." I open my mouth to continue but the words disappear. I take a small, slow sip of water, inhale through my nose, exhale out of my mouth and grab hold of the grass. This is so selfish. "I tried to kill myself."

Tucker's eyes glimmer for a split second. "What? When?"

"July twentieth, two years ago."

"How?"

"Pills."

"Why?"

The big question, such a trite answer. "Clinical depression."

Tucker nods and then shakes his head—as if he knows exactly what I'm talking about.

"Was your mother depressed?" I ask.

Tucker nods. "It was under control, but she went off her meds without telling anyone. She thought her art was suffering because she was on such an even keel. She wanted her moods back. She created two amazing paintings and then swallowed a bottle of Valium."

I nod to show Tucker my sympathy but also because I empathize with his mother about the loss of mood swings while on meds.

"It wasn't only the depression," I tell him. I take another gulp of air. "My older brother died two years before, and I just couldn't live with his death. Or without him."

I expect Tucker to stand up or walk away or at least appear shocked and appalled that it's been a month and this is the first he's hearing of my dead brother. Instead, he sits next to me— so close our legs touch—and asks, "How did he die?"

"AIDS."

"Was he—"

"Yes." I shrug. "He was ten when I was born and I was twenty-four when he died, and the only real time we spent together was during the last four months of his life. Once the depression took over, all I could focus on was the time I *didn't* spend with him. I should've been grateful for those four months." I can't believe I just said that out loud.

Tucker's shoulders slouch a bit, and his eyes are glassy. He turns to look at his mother's tombstone. I dry my face with the sleeve of my sweatshirt, then recline and watch the sky. The clouds have been banished and there's nothing but blue—the clearest and most magnificent blue I have ever seen. I close my eyes and think of my room in the city. I imagine Jordy at my closet, picking out an outfit to wear to Oblivion. I'm already dressed— wearing her clothes, of course. We're laughing and singing, and Jax yells at us to hurry up. Jordy and I ignore him and spend five minutes debating between the red or the black tank top, fully aware that no one at Oblivion will notice Jordy's outfit but me. By the time we emerge from the closet, Jax is half-cocked and immersed in some nature show on the Discovery Channel. We all do a shot and then charge into the night, not to return until dawn.

"Alex?"

I sit up. Tucker is sprawled on his stomach now. His body faces his mother but his head is turned toward me.

"Yeah?"

"Are you still on meds?"

"No."

"Why not?"

"I was on them for over a year after . . . after . . . it. Sam and I decided I was ready to move on—unregulated—so I weaned myself off the pills, and now I don't need them anymore."

Tucker nods and smiles. "It'd be fine, you know, even if you were on meds. I understand depression, and I'll be here for you. I know all the warning signs."

I drink the rest of my water, unzip my sweatshirt and wipe the sweat off the back of my neck. "I'm not depressed anymore," I tell him, staring above his head at the seemingly never-ending rows of tombstones. From my perspective, they look like pills sticking out of the grass. Then again, they also look like cookies, as if this is the place where Keebler rejects are exiled.

"Well, either way, this won't change anything. I really care about you, and I want to be with you, and I'm glad you told me."

I am, too. I think. "I didn't mean to tell you here. I tried to explain earlier—"

Tucker leans in, kisses me on the cheek and stretches out on the grass, his fingertips dancing across the base of his mother's grave. "Don't worry about it. It's fitting, in a way."

My sunglasses keep sliding off my nose because I'm looking down at him. I push them back over my eyes. I get the chills and shrug into my sweatshirt. I remove the car keys from Tucker's pocket and stand up.

"I'll meet you in the car," I tell him.

Tucker nods and smiles, his face a patchwork of emotions. As I'm walking away, Tucker calls to me. I turn around.

"What was your brother's name?" he asks.

I'm about twenty feet from him. I take off my sunglasses and look directly into his eyes for the first time today.

"Ashley."

We decide to skip the movie and drive around town instead. We buy water and snacks at a store in Lenox. There's some sort of kite-flying demonstration at the park, so I drive us to Tanglewood, where I know we'll have peace and quiet and our own space. Since Tucker is almost as organized as Teddy, he had the foresight to throw a blanket in the car this morning. We spread the blanket on the pristine grass, slip Tucker's canvas and paints under our now-unnecessary sweatshirts and eat chips and pretzels while we listen to the Boston Pops rehearse for their evening performance.

"Have you been here before?" I ask.

Tucker squints into the sun, munching on some sort of ridiculously fattening potato chips. "I think so, when I was really young. We used to come up here every August. My grand-parents—my mother's parents—lived up here."

"She grew up in Lenox?"

Tucker nods. "Went to boarding schools, of course, but she spent every summer here."

"Do they still live here?" Shit, what if they're dead, too?

"No. They sold the house after she killed herself."

Can't he say *after she died*? It's as if he likes saying the words.

"Why do you love it up here so much?" he asks.

I close the bag of pretzels and light a cigarette, careful to ash in the assigned water bottle.

"I went to sleepaway camp here. Ten years as a camper, three years as a counselor. That's how Jordy and I met. When I was a kid, all my best friends were camp friends, except Jax. I counted down the school days to camp. June, July and August saved me, every year."

Tucker chomps away. "What'd you do at sleepaway camp?"

"What do you mean?"

"What did you do every day? I've never been to camp."

"Not even day camp, when you were little?"

Tucker shakes his head. I laugh—I started day camp when I was four and sleepaway camp when I was six—remembering it's mostly Jews who send their kids away for an entire summer, to everyone's benefit.

"We played softball and tether ball and tennis and elimina-tion and capture the flag. We performed in talent shows and concerts, and went on day trips and overnight trips. I learned to water ski and wind surf, and passed the Basic Rescue water test when I was older. We sang in the morning after cleanup and went on raids at night. We listened to tapes that were passed down by the older kids, and we fell in love with a different person every day."

I stop, because if I don't shut up right now, I'll go on and on and then get either really excited or really sad, knowing this utopia from my youth is minutes away, and soon I'll need to talk to Jordy, whose cell phone seems to be perpetually off.

"You realize I don't know what half those words even mean."

"Like what?"

"Tether ball. What is that? Or capture the flag?"

"You've never played capture the flag?"

Tucker shakes his head.

I laugh. "You would fucking *love* capture the flag."

"So let's play."

I laugh. "Okay, go round up about forty people." I motion to the other picnickers. "All of them are WASPs like you who didn't go to sleepaway camp, so I'll just have to teach you all how to play."

Tucker cracks up, looks around and strokes my leg. "Do you mind if I go sit over there, by the bluff, to paint for a while?"

I look where he's pointing. Jordy and I have sat there so many times, staring at the mountains, which materialize as if they are so deceivingly nearby, talking for hours. "Go ahead."

He squats down and gathers his supplies in his arms. Then he kisses me—the kind of kiss I usually make fun of other people for sharing in public. My stomach tightens, and the backs of my knees get sweaty. He waves as he strolls away.

I watch him for a moment, wondering how long he'll be in my life. It seems like he wants to stay, if I let him, but I think he wants a bigger role than I'm ready to cast. I find my cell phone as soon as he's out of sight. I light another cigarette and dial Jordy.

"Hi, it's me. I've been trying to reach you for twenty-four hours but you're never home and your cell phone is always off. I really want to talk to you but I know you're crazy-busy, so I'm just going to talk to your voice mail. I'm really sorry, Jordy. I acted like a total imbecile and I didn't mean anything I said. I know your dissertation is the most important thing in your life right now, and I respect that. I just miss you and now that I have the Discovery, I want to go places with you, take you places. But we can do that when you're all done. I hope your revisions are going well. You wouldn't believe what's going on up here—you are going to fucking freak out when I tell you! I'll be home Tuesday afternoon. I have my cell but according to Tucker, calls don't always come through because of the mountains. Call me if you can—even if it's only for a minute. I miss you and love you."

I sleep for three hours when we get back to the motel. Tucker sits on the balcony, painting. He wakes me up at five o'clock and we have sex. It's a little better but not really—I still can't have an orgasm, and I don't even do a good job of faking it. It's as if I'm here, in the room with him, but at the same time, I'm not here. I feel his touch but it doesn't penetrate my skin—it stays on the surface. He suggests we shower together but I pretend I want to watch the news and tell him to go first. While he's in the bathroom, I turn my phone on and check my messages. Jordy called fifteen minutes ago—while I was screwing Tucker. "You are always the most important thing in my life," she tells my voice mail. I smile, pull on a T-shirt and sweats and choose my outfit for dinner.

Tucker and I wait for an hour to eat at Home. He wants lobster again, and I love their salad bar. We wait at the bar, and by the time we're seated, I need way more than greens in my stomach. Tucker orders a bottle of wine and we eat and drink and then just eat. He cuts himself off before dessert, so I finish the wine. We're just a little bit louder and more animated than the couples at the surrounding tables, but this makes sense—we're New Yorkers. I let Tucker pay for the entire meal, mostly because I'm drunk and not in the mood to argue with him about money. When we leave the restaurant, it's midnight, and I force Tucker to walk a straight line to prove he's fine to drive. We clod up the stairs of the motel, strip the clothes off one another, have sex and pass out.

I wake up first, bundle myself in a heavy sweater and sneak out to the balcony. I call Jax—to remind him I'm coming home tomorrow—and sketch a few illustrations. Tucker is still asleep when I get out of the shower, so I run a clean paintbrush over his naked stomach to wake him up. He covers his morning wood and disappears into the bathroom. I watch TV while Tucker gets ready. He wears a satisfied smirk on his face that confuses me until I remember I went down on him last night. Jax wears the same grin the morning after he gets head. Gay, straight—guys are essentially all the same when it comes to sex.

Tucker and I spend the morning at the outlet stores, which at first seems like a bad idea because I assume he'll be a bad shopper, but he brings along a book, so anytime I spend more than five minutes in a store, he finds a little nook somewhere, leans against the wall and reads. I buy Jordy a funky crimson lamp for her desk, and I get Jax a bunch of shirts from the Gap. I consider buying Teddy a pair of silk pajamas but I'm sure she already has a pair, so I put them back. Tucker doesn't buy anything for anyone. We make a last minute decision to see a movie, and marvel at the fact that they actually charge matinee prices for an afternoon movie. I buy the tickets ($4.50!), and Tucker buys a bag of popcorn for himself and a pack of Twizzlers for me. It's seven o'clock when we emerge from the darkness but neither of us is hungry, so we go back to the motel room and watch TV all night. I wake up at three—Tucker's arms are wrapped around me like a vise, and the TV is still on. I slip out of his grip, turn off the TV and stand on the balcony smoking a cigarette. I'm glad tomorrow is Tuesday. One more day—or night—with Tucker might be too much. I feel good about our conversation at the cemetery, and having sex with him definitely brought us closer, but the ground beneath my feet is starting to quiver.

We pull into the city around five. Tucker takes a cab from my apartment so he doesn't have to listen to me whine about the traffic the next time we talk. I call Jax as soon as I get upstairs, and he promises to swing by the library to forcibly remove Jordy from her paper cocoon.

I dump my bag on my bed, stow away my satchel and stare at the empty space above my headboard, trying to figure out what the hell happened to the *New York Is Book Country* poster that's hung there for the last two years. I find it in the living room, the glass almost completely shattered. Maybe Jax really did feel the earth move—could there have been an earthquake in New York City?

"The upstairs neighbor's bookcase fell over. One of mine broke, too."

I turn around and see Jordy at the front door. I glide across the living room floor and wrap my arms around her. She kisses my cheek and hugs me back.

"I'm sorry," I say.

"Apology accepted. How was the trip?"

I pull away and fall into Jordy's gaze. "Oh, we need drinks. And Jax. Where is he?"

"Getting club soda, lemons and limes."

"Always thinking, my Jax."

"Always thinking of you," Jordy adds.

I nod and take her hand. We walk into the kitchen to start preparing dinner.

A half hour later, the chicken Marsala is cooking on the stove, Ella Fitzgerald's voice curls out of the stereo and Jordy, Jax and I sit at the kitchen table over a round of Frescos. We take turns relaying the past week to one another. While Jordy and Jax argue about the best way to make a Cosmopolitan, I smile to myself. I hand them their presents, refill their glasses and revel in this intimate, gentle stability.

9

I wake up around eleven o'clock. I'm actually in my own bed, with Jax. He's curled into a ball next to me, his arms wrapped around a spare pillow. His face is completely relaxed, and he looks about twelve years old. I retuck the quilt into him and quietly leave the room. While I'm brushing my teeth, I poke my head into Jordy's room but I know she's at the library—time is not on her side and she probably shouldn't have taken the night off to catch up with Jax and me. I walk through the living room, letting my feet linger on the sun-soaked spots of hardwood floor. Jordy has, of course, turned the coffeemaker on, so I fill a mug with coffee and wander through the apartment. The first thing I notice is a pile of bills on the hall table. I grab them, pull my checkbook out of my messenger bag and fumble through drawers in search of a calculator. I find it in the top desk drawer. I drop onto the area rug in the living room and pay each bill—in full—for the first time in my life. I know I should wait for Jordy's share, but I can almost hear Sam propelling me, telling me to take control. This is what I want to do; it's just money, of course, but I owe this—and so much more—to Jordy.

I'm chomping on Cheerios when the phone rings. I don't move from my perch on the floor, so the machine picks up.

"Alex, hey, it's Tucker. It's almost noon on Wednesday. Just wondering what you're doing today. I'm going to paint for a few hours but I was thinking maybe we could catch a movie later. Or shoot pool. Or something. Give me a call. I had a great time in the Berkshires; I'm so glad you asked me to join you. Bye."

I finish reading the *New York Times*, fill in a few of the more obvious clues in the crossword puzzle and find the phone hidden under a pile of magazines.

It rings twice before she picks up. "Hi, Casey."

"Hi, darlin'. How are you?"

"Good. What's up in Chicago?"

"Busy as hell—I have a meeting in two minutes—but I think this next show may actually make some money, so I shouldn't complain. Tell me about D.C."

"I think you'd rather hear about the Berkshires."

"You and Jordy, stoned, wandering around a quaint New England town? I bet I can guess what you ate at that diner place you love."

"I was with Tucker, not Jordy."

"Ooh, juicy! How'd it go?"

"I'll tell you in person."

I hear an intercom buzz in Casey's office. "Shit, Alex, that's my meeting. When are you driving here?"

"How's the week after next? Can you take a few days off?"

"Absolutely—I've got tons of vacation days coming to me. Are you serious?"

I laugh. It's seems like forever since I talked to Casey in person. "Have car, will travel."

"Excellent. Talk to you soon."

"Bye."

At one o'clock, Jax shuffles out of my bedroom. I hand him a cup of coffee and steer clear for the next twenty minutes. I could really go for a bagel but my hips feel heavy so I reject the idea. The only problem with spending time in the Berkshires is the total lack of non-fat or low-fat food options. I should fast for a day to force the butter and whole milk out of my system.

"Morning," Jax says suddenly. He's reclined on the big green chair in the living room, his bare feet hanging on to the matching ottoman.

"More like afternoon," I reply.

Jax shakes his head. "I'm going to pretend you didn't just say that."

We share a look—a guilty one—knowing we both need to call our mothers.

"Are you working tonight?" I ask.

Jax nods. "Want to come in for dessert?"

"No way. I have to shed all the extra weight I picked up in Williamstown."

Jax looks me up and down. "You look the same. Stop being a neurotic New York Jew. You're a hottie—work it."

I laugh. Jax's cell phone rings and he dashes into the bedroom to pick it up. He's gone for about five minutes, during which I stare at the Ansel Adams iceberg photograph while my head hangs, upside down, off the arm of the couch. I'm just about to make myself completely nauseous when Jax skips back into the living room.

"Good news, babycakes."

"You don't have to work dinner, and you want to see a movie with me?"

"Better."

"Your dealer finally got us some 'shrooms."

Jax sits on the chair and crosses his legs ever so primly. "Better."

"You were nominated for the Mr. Oblivion contest."

Jax rolls his eyes. "Please, I said good news, not impossible news."

"Can you just tell me already? I'm seeing stars over here."

Jax gets up, pulls me to a sitting position and kneels in front of me, holding my hands.

"Is this the part where you tell me you're gay?" I ask.

"Do you want to know my good news or not, you snooty, cynical, elitist bitch?"

"Don't call me cynical."

"I got another voice-over gig. National spot, sixty seconds, mucho *dinero*."

I pull my hands out of his and wrap my arms around his neck. "You are *so* on your way to being famous, Jax."

"Anonymously famous," he corrects.

"That's the best kind. When do you tape it?"

"Oh! This is the best part. Once I sign the contract, I'm committed to them and they're committed to me."

"Oh my God, like a marriage."

"Without the sex or the cuddling or the resentment. Are you listening? This has to do with you."

I snap to attention on the couch. Jax shakes his head. "You really are a self-absorbed, immature JAP."

"Don't call me a JAP."

"So as I was saying before you interrupted me for the eight millionth time in our friendship, once I sign the contract, it's all good to go. But we don't tape for a few weeks, so we can go somewhere in the Discovery!"

I purposely reign in my reaction just to see what Jax will do, but he's too busy ransacking the kitchen for a calendar to notice. He finds one—on the fridge—and runs back into the living room.

"How 'bout we leave on Friday?" he asks.

"You needed a calendar to choose Friday?"

"You needed a book to find your G-spot."

My mouth falls open. "I was twelve, you jerk."

Jax shrugs and smirks. We're at a standoff, separated by the couch. Jax slowly strolls over and sits in the middle, fingering the calendar. I sit next to him. We're both trying really hard not to crack up. Finally I lose it, and then he does, too.

Jax shrugs. "So where do you want to go?"

I lean back on the arm of the couch, my legs resting on Jax's lap. "How many days can you take off from the restaurant?"

Jax stares at the ceiling. "Without pissing them off? Five."

"So we need to stay sort of local. How 'bout Staten Island?"

Jax slaps my shins. "Come on, I never get to go anywhere. Let's go somewhere pretty, with water—the ocean!"

"Maine?"

"The whole fucking state smells like lobster. And it's too far away."

"The Jersey shore?"

"I'm a gay man, for Christ's sake, not a varsity football player."

"OK, OK. Why don't you come up with something, then?"

Jax stares at the ceiling again. I can almost see his brain wrap itself around an idea, volley it back and forth for a moment and then approve it. Jax turns to me.

"It's close, it's got beaches, it's got hotties and it's *the* place to be this time of year."

I shrug.

"Oh, Alex, babycakes, you are hopeless—the Hamptons!"

It's perfect. Jax is perfect—in my world, at least.

The reservation gods are on our side and we get a room in Southampton—at a cutesy inn a few blocks from town. It looks nice online, and we really can't be picky, since we're making reservations two days in advance. Later, I play phone tag with Tucker—though I'm not sure if screening all his calls counts as phone tag. I kill time while Jordy edits her dissertation and Jax works at the restaurant. I finish the first draft of a book and make tiny improvements to the illustrations of three others. I wrap these in tissue paper and insert them into a padded envelope addressed to Tucker's father. I'm supposed to drop it off in person, but that has *awkward situation* written all over it, so I drop the envelope in a mailbox instead.

There's a slow but steady drizzle dripping on the windshield of the Discovery as we head east on the Long Island Expressway. Jax is hardly contained by his seat belt and, judging from the luggage on the backseat, you'd think we were going away for five weeks instead of five days.

Jax extinguishes his cigarette in his new favorite toy, a fold-up travel ashtray, and pulls out my CD holder. "What'cha in the mood for? Indigo Girls?"

"OK."

"Or Melissa Etheridge?"

"OK."

"Come on, Alex, decide. What do you want to hear?"

"I don't care, Jax. I love both."

"So do I. Should we flip a coin?"

"We're twenty-eight years old—we should be able to make a simple musical choice without resorting to fate."

Jax looks at me, looks out the window and then looks down at the CD holder in his lap. He flips a page. "How 'bout Peter Gabriel?"

I laugh. "Excellent choice."

He slips in the CD and turns up the volume. We sit in silence for a while, our mouths alternating between cigarettes and bubble gum. I'm just about to ask Jax something when I hear the beginning of "In Your Eyes." No matter what I'm doing or who I'm with, I always have to stop and sing along with this song. Jordy and I do a fantastic harmony.

> *Love I get so lost, sometimes*
> *Days pass and this emptiness fills my heart*
> *When I want to run away*
> *I drive off in my car*

The music washes over me, rinsing my skin with the years of affection I've shared with Jordy. I can't wait for her to be done with her dissertation so I can drive us somewhere—anywhere— and be with her as she relaxes for the first time in ages.

"This song always makes me think of you and Jordy," Jax says suddenly.

"That's because it's our song."

Jax nods. "Did I know that? I don't think I knew that."

"You probably did, somewhere in the recesses of your muddled memory."

"It's just so . . . you."

"We've loved it since we were kids," I remind him.

Jax gives me the hand and whispers, "Let's just listen."

We pull into the parking lot of the inn around one o'clock. We're both starving and have to pee. I check us in, careful not to let Jax see the room rates—I told him it cost fifty dollars less than it actually does. The inn is not exactly cute—more like stately, or refined. There's a monstrous church across the tree-lined street, and the town of Southampton is a block away.

"Great, I can go to confession if I get bored," Jax says, pointing at the church.

"I don't recall seeing any temples on the way in."

Jax laughs. "This is Gatsby-land, Alex!"

He hands me one bag and throws the other three over his shoulder.

"Yeah, but this is Long Island—home to Great Neck, Syosset, Roslyn . . ."

"All in Nassau County, babycakes. Out here, you're just another shyster. You may as well be in the diamond business. I bet there's one temple out here, and it's in whichever town Spielberg lives."

We lock the car and walk toward the manicured pathway. "You Goyim are always sticking it to the Jews."

Jax holds the door open for me and follows me inside. "What do you expect? You killed Christ."

We laugh and walk upstairs, pointing out the luscious floral bouquets and antique furniture.

Our room is maroon. The carpet, the bedspread, the flowers and even the chairs are all maroon. There's another vase of fresh flowers, a phone in the bathroom and a basket of cookies and crackers on the dresser.

"We are way out of our league here, babycakes," Jax says, pouncing on the bed.

"This is Nick Carraway's worst nightmare," I reply.

Jax reties the shoelaces on his ridiculously worn-in sneakers. "Let's go eat—I'm starving."

We wander through town, which takes about fifteen minutes—we are both in awe of and intimidated by Southampton's
retail options. Most of the restaurants appear too fancy for us,
both spiritually and literally—we're not dressed appropriately.
We wind up in a restaurant called Isabella's and sit outside in a
small but pretty garden. We drink our beers in silence, waiting
for the sustenance of Hamptons-priced hamburgers to reinvigorate us. When the food arrives, we each plow through half the
serving before uttering a word.

"What do you want to do tonight?" Jax asks.

I shrug. "I could do anything."

Jax washes the last of his hamburger down with the last of his
Heineken. "You know what I'm in the mood for?"

I don't know why I know but I do. "Dancing."

"You are one witchy woman, Alex," he says. "Do you think
there's anywhere decent to dance out here?"

I shrug. "There must be someplace—it's summer," I answer.
"We should find one of those places the locals hate because of
the traffic and drunken behavior."

"Whoa." Jax gives me the hand again. "We are *not* going to
one of those nasty clubs."

"Duh, I was kidding! Do you really think I'd let us walk into a
place like that? We can ask the concierge if there's a gay club
around."

Jax signals the waitress for another round of beers. "We
should ask the concierge if there's a gay *Jewish* club around."

"You're just jealous of the Jews. We don't have to confess our
sins out loud to anyone. Plus we're much healthier—we starve
ourselves one day a year and we avoid all bread products one
week a year."

"You really do have food issues, don't you?"

I shrug. "I'm a Jewish girl raised in the New York suburbs."

The concierge gives us directions to a dance club in East
Hampton. After a long nap and a snack, we pop Madonna into
the CD player and drive east. It takes us almost half an hour to
arrive at the club, which vaguely resembles a barn, at least from

the outside. A beautiful gay man checks our IDs, which thrills Jax. The guy winks at Jax, and we walk through the gate into what can only be described as a cement garden. On our left is a classy but Hamptons-esque restaurant, and to our right is the club, which vibrates with a heavy bass. The pathway is lined with huge potted Rose of Sharon trees—their perfect pink buds a constant reminder that gays are safe here—and six-foot heating lamps warm the area. There are men everywhere—I might be the only woman here—and I feel completely comfortable and secure. Jax takes my hand and leads me through the glass double doors into the club. It's a pretty substantial space, though it seems tiny compared to Oblivion. Men are dancing, men are waiting at the bar and men are chatting at small, chest-high tables, but men are not making out, nor are they grinding, shirtless, on the dance floor.

Jax turns to me as we approach the bar. "Would it be cliché to go for the 'Toto, we're not in Kansas anymore' comment?"

I nod and gesture for him to squeeze into the space just vacated by an overly tanned man in too-tight jeans.

"Two Frescos, please," Jax tells the dark-haired bartender. He turns around, eyebrows raised—I'm not sure if he's impressed by the handsome bartender or put off by the price of our cocktails.

We take our drinks and lean against a wall near the dance floor, surveying this supposedly trendy crowd. Jax laughs.

"What?"

"Look at us."

"I know. If Jordy could see us now!"

"If our parents could see us now!" Jax adds.

We nod and slip into silence. The music vaults off us and back into the crowd.

"You know who would fucking love this scenario?" I ask.

Jax sips his drink and shrugs.

"Ashley."

I take a long, slow sip of my drink and picture Ashley. Most of my images of him are from those last four months, when he weighed less than I did and couldn't even walk as far as the bathroom. I toss those images away and retrieve older, cleaner ones. I envision him swimming in the lake in Carchie's backyard, his long, agile legs cutting seamlessly through the water.

"He'd bust a gut if he could see us here," I tell Jax.

Jax finishes his drink and dips his hand into his pocket. "I brought us a little party favor," he says, handing me a pill.

"Hi, self-absorbed, nice to meet you!" I offer him my hand to shake.

"Huh?"

"Jax, we can't both do Ecstasy. Someone has to drive back to the inn, and Teddy would not be pleased to get a phone call from the Southampton Police."

Jax laughs. "Man, *she* needs to drop some E. I bet it would lighten her up. Maybe she'd be the old Teddy again. Remember when we were in high school and she used to smoke us up in the tree house?"

I nod.

"Remember that time your parents went away for the weekend and she and her best friend from college showed us how to make pot brownies?"

I nod again. I want to smile at the memory but I'm afraid if I move too many muscles, I might wind up crying from the memory. I wonder where that lively woman went—was it Ashley's death that caused her to disappear, or did Teddy merely lock her away when she felt it was time?

Jax continues plucking memories from his mind. "Remember that time you, me and Teddy got thrown out of Tower Diner? What'd we do? I can't remember."

I laugh, this memory is too funny to make me sad. "We kept playing the same song over and over on the jukebox. When they asked us to stop, Teddy invoked our First Amendment rights."

Jax cracks up; he literally bends over in laughter. "Right, right. Indigo Girls, right? 'Galileo.'"

I nod. "They wouldn't even let us finish our cheese fries. My parents still boycott that place."

"Your parents are cool like that."

I shrug. "I'm not taking this," I tell him, handing him the pill.

Jax looks around the club. "Do you mind if I do?"

"Go ahead. How often do you get to roll in a gay club in East Hampton?" Jax is about to pop the pill when I grab his wrist. "But do *not* leave the premises, and do not tell anyone where you're staying. Pretend you're a migrant worker."

Jax swallows the magic pill and pulls me onto the dance floor.

Four hours, five bottles of water and two packs of gum later, we close the club. We're both drenched, and I'm starving. I smile on the way to the car, remembering the basket of treats in the room. Jax dances with an invisible partner toward the car. I glance upward and almost fall over—I've never seen so many stars. The sky is dotted with them, bright white winks in the smiling universe. I check my watch and unlock the Discovery.

"Well, I didn't think it could be done, but we've managed to uphold our tradition of dancing until five o'clock in the morning. Not bad for our first trip to the East End, huh?"

Jax searches through the Madonna CD as I back out of the gravel parking lot. He's looking for "Nothing Really Matters." When he finds it, he cranks up the volume, and the rhythm steers us all the way back to Southampton.

The room stays pleasantly dark, so we both sleep until noon. I call Jordy while Jax showers, and he grills the concierge over the phone while I shower. We decide to start our Saturday in the Hamptons by pretending to go antiquing in Hampton Bays, which apparently has several stores perfectly suited to our phony pursuit.

Old Montauk Highway, the original main thoroughfare that connects the towns comprising the Hamptons and was supposed to be a better route than the newer one, is jammed with vehicles—mostly luxury cars—and it takes us over twenty minutes to actually get anywhere. I'm finally pressing the gas pedal when Jax yelps and points out the window.

"Turn here!" he orders, gesturing frantically at an upcoming traffic light.

"Why?" I ask.

"It's a college. Turn right, turn right!"

I turn right and then left, pulling into the parking lot. "Jax, what are we doing?"

"I miss college. Let's walk around and see what's it like. Can you imagine going to school in the Hamptons?"

I park and we get out of the Discovery. We walk toward the smallest building we see. The grass is a perfect shade of green, dimpled with tall evergreen trees. The air is still and light, and there aren't any people around. It's hot, but we're both wearing shorts and T-shirts and, without the hazy cloud of pollution-induced vapors hanging over our bodies as it does in the city, the heat doesn't bother either one of us.

"Look how cute the library is," Jax announces. "Let's go in."

"Are we allowed?"

Jax narrows his eyes at me. "First of all, since when do you ask 'Are we allowed?' and second of all, we look like students. We got ID'd last night, remember?"

Jax leads the way up the wooden stairs and into the library. A blast of cool air hits us, followed by the delicious, unmistakable smell of books. There's a dark-haired man behind the counter reading Faulkner's *As I Lay Dying* but otherwise the library is empty. Jax silently signals me to follow him, and I immediately see his plan: magazines. We settle at a round table and take turns reading magazines—*Rolling Stone, Esquire, OUT, Vanity Fair.* No one pays attention to us, and we lose ourselves in the glossy monthlies.

Jax stops to rub his neck. "I'm hungry."

"You're always hungry. All you do is eat and pee and sleep and fuck. You're like a caveman."

Jax laughs. "Do you think there were gay cavemen?"

I swat his leg with *OUT.* "Let's go eat."

Jax nods and we stroll toward the door. "Tie your shoelace, dopey." As Jax bends down to fix his laces, I scan the announcements and flyers and advertisements on the rectangular bulletin board—lots of rooms for rent, babysitting jobs available and garage sales. I smile at the suburban-ness of it all—I'd forgotten what it's like to live in a town rather than a city.

Jax's head pops up, and he examines the flyers. "What's Quogue? It sounds like a rash, or some sort of mouth herpes." Jax steps back and does his best whispering-Jewish-mother imitation. "Did you hear about Flo? She picked up a bad case of Quogue from that Irish Catholic she was dating." He laughs at himself.

"Quogue is a town, you lunatic." I check my watch—it's almost three o'clock. "Come on."

We accidentally drive right through Hampton Bays, so we wind up driving west for a while, experiencing the towns of the Hamptons through the car window. Somehow, this suits us both. We stop for a sandwich at a deli in Quogue, and Jax takes a picture of the town's welcome sign. After buying Slurpees at a 7-Eleven, we drive east again, heading for our room in Southampton.

Jax convinces me to stop at a video store on the way back to the inn—to look for DVDs on sale. We wind up losing ourselves for half an hour, meandering up and down the aisles, pointing out amazing and agonizing movies. I start to wonder if it's cool or pathetic that between both of us, we've seen almost every movie in the store. I find Jax in the documentary section. His shoulders are hunched over, and his sunglasses are about to fall off his head. He looks up as I approach and hides a videotape behind his back.

"You buying me a present?" I ask.

Jax's eyes shift from left to right, and he bites his lip. "Um, no. But we're having such a good day, I didn't want you to see this."

His arm slowly unravels from behind his back, and he reveals the tape. It's the last documentary Ashley filmed—the one about Paris in the 1920s.

Jax places the tape in my hand and walks away. I lean against a blue wall, staring at Ashley's name in the credits. This film did really well—it won a lot of awards—and probably paid for my Discovery, the trip to D.C., the room at the inn. I squint my eyes and Ashley's name—written in white—turns into a diamond-shaped fractal of light. When I open my eyes, the letters are back to normal. I wish I could get back to normal—or is this normal?

"Alex. Alex."

I hear Jax but I can't seem to open my eyes. I want to stay in this dream. I want to stay asleep.

Jax is tapping my arm. "I'm starving. I have to eat right now. Can I take the Discovery?"

I point to the keys. "Get me a big bottle of water." I hear the door close.

I can't re-enter my dream. I'm awake. I can't even remember the dream now. The air in the room is cold and stagnant—I open the window to let some salty sea air in. I smoke a cigarette, leaning out the window so I can see the sapphire sky, which is dotted with countless stars. My smoke drifts into the atmosphere, joining the blue whiteness that hangs over the town.

Jax is back when I get out of the shower. He's sprawled on the bed, surrounded by candy bars—many, many candy bars.

"I couldn't bring myself to order a greasy, disgusting hamburger from McDonald's, so I bought a buffet of candy instead." He's also sipping another Slurpee.

I sprinkle water on Jax as I comb out my hair, and he covers the candy protectively.

"Good choice—consuming ten chocolate bars is *much* healthier."

"First of all, not everything is chocolate." He holds up a bag of Twizzlers. "Second, at least I'm familiar with the ingredients."

I pull on a pair of sweats and a tank top and join Jax under the faded maroon quilt.

"The sugar stuff is for me, right?"

Jax nods. "Yes, babycakes."

"What do you want to—"

"Shh, shh." Jax points at the TV. "Commercial's over."

Someone on the screen seems vaguely familiar. "What are you watching?"

Jax raises the volume. "*Batman.*"

The TV series. Adam West at his best—his only.

"*Batman*? Since when are you into superheroes?"

"Trust me. Watching as an adult is totally different than watching as a kid. The homoeroticism between Batman and Robin can barely be contained in the TV set."

I bite off both ends of a Twizzler and stick it in my drink, just like Jordy and I used to do in camp. "You sense homoeroticism in everything."

"I'm serious, Alex. You like gay porn—I swear, twenty minutes of *Batman* and we'll both be horny."

I laugh and burrow into Jax's warm body.

In the morning, we eat real food. After a breakfast of omelets and orange juice, we walk through a lush park in Southampton, watching the locals and weekenders stare one another down disdainfully. We settle under an elm tree. I rest my head on Jax's stomach, and we watch clouds drift by, feeling small and irrelevant. My cell phone rings—it's my mother.

"Hi, Mom."

"Where have you been, Alexandra? No one ever picks up the phone at your apartment. I even called Jax's apartment but he's not home."

"He's with me—we're in the Hamptons. I left you a message."

"That was three days ago."

I sit up and see stars for a few seconds. "We're still here."

My mother sighs. "It'd be nice if you could call your parents now and then."

"Mom, I left—" Forget it. It's not worth the aggravation. "I'm sorry. What's new?"

She sighs again, making the tiny phone in my hand feel like it weighs ten pounds. "Jim is not doing well."

I glance at Jax. His eyes are closed, and his arms and legs are extended away from his body. He looks dead. "What does that mean?"

"It means he's sick, Alexandra. What do you think it means?"

I don't say anything.

"Can you convince Jax to call home?"

"Mom, you know how I feel—"

"Yes, I know how you feel about Jim, and about Jax. But he's dying, Alex, and I don't want any of us flooded with guilt because we didn't do everything possible to reconnect Jim and Jax. They're family."

"I'll mention it to him."

"And speaking of family, do you have any plans to reconcile with Teddy?"

"Not at the moment, but I'm sure I will eventually."

She sighs for a third time. "Oh, Alexandra, you shouldn't waste time—you'll only regret it."

"I know all about wasting time, remember?"

"I didn't mean to bring Ashley into this. I just want you and Teddy to get along. You used to be so close."

Jax sits up and lights us each a cigarette. "I've got to go, Mom."

"You'll tell Jax?"

"Yeah, I promise. I'll talk to you soon."

I toss the cell phone into my bag. Jax sits up and hands me a cigarette.

"What'd the lovely-but-passive-aggressive Mrs. Justice have to say?"

"Your dad's really sick, Jax. She wants me to persuade you to call him."

Jax crosses his legs and takes a sip of water. "You were on the debate team in high school—convince me to call a man who thinks my 'chosen lifestyle' is vile, who hasn't looked me in the eye in eight years and who has all but ruined my relationship with my mother." He looks at his watch. "You have two minutes—go."

I inhale, exhale and speak only one word: "Ashley."

"What about Ashley? My father thought the same about him—you know that, right?"

"That's not what I mean, Jax. Once he dies, you'll never be able to say another word to him. I'm not sure it will save your relationship—it probably won't—but maybe if you talk to him one last time, even if you yell at him, it might be enough to save *you*."

Jax nods and smokes his cigarette. Silence surrounds us. He drops the cigarette butt into an empty soda can and reaches into his pocket for his cell phone. I kiss him and walk toward town.

I'm standing in front of a crowded shop, debating whether or not to consume ice cream calories, when my phone rings. When I see Teddy's name pop up, I panic and shove the phone back into my bag. Then I change my mind.

"Hi, Teddy." I try to sound singsongy and jocular.

"Hi, Alex."

"What'cha doing?" I sing.

"We may not hang out much anymore, but I know that's not your real voice. Do you have a minute to talk?"

Damn—so much for lighthearted. I sit on a green bench and ask, "About what?"

"I can't sleep. I can't stop thinking about you and me, and Ashley."

"Welcome to my world," I reply.

"He wouldn't be happy to know you and I aren't close, that we keep fighting."

"No, he wouldn't," I agree. He wasn't happy wasting away in his bed while you got married, I think to myself. I envision him then—the smallest movement took Herculean effort—and the anger swells through me like a swirling tempest. I verbalize what has remained locked in my mind for so many years.

"He wasn't happy wasting away in his bed while you got married, either."

I hear what sounds like a gulp of air. "Is that what you think, Alex?"

"What I know, Teddy, not what I think."

"You know nothing," she mutters.

"I know what I saw."

"No, you don't." Her voice breaks—is she crying? "You really think I would do that to my brother?"

Before I can answer, she hangs up.

Jax is leaning against the tree when I return fifteen minutes later. He's standing perfectly straight, staring at the sky.

"The chemo's not working. The radiation's not working, either. The cancer has spread from his pancreas to his spleen. And all three are making him incredibly ill."

We stand there for a while, inches apart.

"Jax?"

"What?"

"Let's go see them."

"I can go alone."

"No, you can't, and neither can I. But we both need to go."

Jax laughs lightly. "It is his birthday. Field trip to Scarsdale?"

I nod and take his hand. We walk back to the inn, pack, check out and drive to Westchester.

The only sound in the car is Van Morrison's voice. We're minutes from home—we've just passed our high school. I'm trying to think of a pep talk for Jax but nothing seems appropriate—I can't help him with this one. He stares out the window, his left leg bouncing up and down out of time to the music. A minute from home, we both instinctively reach for the box of Tic Tacs in the glove compartment. He pours four into his mouth and two into my hand. I bite the Tic Tacs right away and inhale sharply as the mint dissolves across my tongue. I turn down our street—our childhood emerges before us, oppressing the atmosphere. I turn into my parents' driveway.

Jax grabs his knapsack—but not his overnight bag—and walks around the truck to open my door. I stay seated. He leans on the open door and we look at each other, then at the houses we grew up in.

"It's weird, huh?" he asks.

I nod. "I haven't been home for any reason except Thanksgiving in years."

"Me, too. I think the last time was for Ashley's funeral."

I choke back a gasp. That was four years ago.

I slide off the seat and my knees almost buckle under me. The driveway feels uneven. Jax grabs my elbow and leans into me until I steady myself. "This is *so* an episode of *Oprah*," I tell him.

Jax laughs. "Your cell phone on?"

"Yeah. Is yours?"

Jax nods and squeezes my hand for a second. He looks at my parents' house. "Keep in touch." He turns and walks toward his parents' house.

I close the car door quietly and scuffle to the front door of my parents' house. I turn to my left and see Jax lingering on his parents' doorstep, looking at me. I close my eyes and see us as children, teenagers, high school seniors. I can't remember ever planning it, but somehow Jax and I have always paused in this very spot, staring at each other across the lawns, infusing strength into our weak smiles.

10

The house is immaculate, as usual. I lean my messenger bag against the door of the hall closet and walk into the kitchen. It looks like a museum exhibit—there's not even a coffee cup in the sink. It smells differently than I remember. The house used to contain an aroma of clean laundry and hot chocolate and rosemary. Now its scent is Earl Gray tea, lemon floor cleanser and spearmint gum. I open the fridge, hoping to find some juice, but there's only bottled water. I take one, unscrew the cap and drink half of it while I ponder what I'm going to say—or not say—to my parents.

The phone rings. I know it's Jax's mom, informing my mother that their children have returned, of their own volition. Barely two minutes pass before I hear my mother's tired footsteps drag up the basement stairs. The door opens—it still creaks—and I'm in the kitchen with my mother.

"Alex! It's so good to see you!" She pulls me into a hug, then quickly releases me. "What are you doing here?"

"You told me to bring Jax home, so I did."

"I asked you to talk to him. I didn't know you'd physically drive him home. It's good that you did, though—Jim is so sick, I doubt he'll live through the summer. I think he's finally ready to accept Jax."

What about you, Mom? Will you accept me, suicide attempt

notwithstanding? "Why? Because he's dying? It's all so cliché it makes me sick."

My mother gestures for me to sit at the kitchen table. "You can't know how Jim feels—you're not a parent."

"No, but you are. You didn't treat Ashley like shit for eight years when he came out."

"Watch your language. This isn't your kitchen."

I mouth an apology.

"Your father and I did have some trouble accepting Ashley's sexuality. You were too young to remember."

"Did you ever ask him to leave the dinner table?"

My mother shakes her head.

"Jim felt the same way about Ashley as he does about Jax."

My mother nods, her fingers wrapped around the sapphire bracelet on her left wrist—a fiftieth birthday present from Ashley, Teddy and me. I bought the card.

"How can you stay friends with him? How can you eat at the same table with him when you know he thinks your son was repugnant?"

She unfurls her fingers and stares at the bracelet. "Because losing people is hard. It's exhausting."

She looks at me and I nod. Her eyes burn through me, and I burst into tears. She slides her chair next to mine, wraps her arms around my back and hugs me. She holds me tighter than she's ever held me before.

My father isn't here; he's on his way home from work. I make my way upstairs, vaguely comforted by the noises emanating from the kitchen—the sounds of a family dinner being prepared. My hands start to shake as soon as I reach the second floor, but for the first time in years, I don't allow the fear to smother me. I've climbed the stairs for only one reason—to enter Ashley's childhood bedroom. I pause at the closed door. Memories overtake me so violently, I get lightheaded—I rest my head on the threshold and clench my eyes closed. I see Ashley on the day of his high school graduation. He's standing in the middle of the floor, the black gown slung over his shoulder, surveying his room, which is already half-packed because he's attending a month-long acting workshop before he starts college in September. I'm spying on him—crouched in the doorway—my head craned around his black desk. He sees me and motions for me to come in, which he never does. I spring to my feet—the untied laces on my Adidas sneakers slowing me down—and enter Ashley's bedroom.

"Do you want these?" He points to a stack of records—none of which I like—and I nod.

"How 'bout these? Want these?" He holds out a pile of old sweatshirts and T-shirts that won't fit me for years. I nod again.

"OK, last one—and don't tell Teddy. Do you want this?" He reaches to a shelf above his bed and hands me a baseball—signed by Ron Guidry and Thurman Munson. My mouth falls open, and Ashley laughs.

"I can't bring it with me—it'll get stolen or I'll lose it. It should be appreciated, not forgotten in an empty room. But *do not* tell Teddy—she's always wanted it, and she'll get mad at me, OK?" I nod.

"And don't *ever* sell it, understand? Unless you're a whore in the street and you have no money for food. You promise?"

I don't know what a whore is but I promise anyway. Ashley helps me carry my loot to my room down the hall. He lingers in the doorway for a minute.

"Are you going to miss me, Alex?"

I'm busy showing my new sweatshirts to my stuffed animals. "What?"

"Do you think you'll miss me when I go to college?"

I turn to the door and look at my big brother. I hardly see him and we live in the same house. "Yes."

Ashley looks around my room. His gaze lands on my face. "Liar."

I giggle and fondle my new records. Ashley laughs—his eyes cloudy—and walks back to his room.

I open the door to my dead brother's room, slowly at first and then very quickly. The room looks huge, probably because

there's nothing in it except two towers of boxes in the far corner. The air feels dry and heavy. I leave the door open and
enter the room, trying to picture where the furniture was,
where Ashley once lived. There are tiny holes in the walls from
his posters, and the windowpanes are still speckled with stickers
of Ashley's favorite bands, circa the 1970s. I run my hand across
some of the boxes—the cardboard is soft and misshapen. I take
a deep breath, wondering if any of Ashley's scent remains. The
room has no odor at all—it looks and smells and tastes like an
empty room.

I hear my father enter the house just as my cell phone rings.
It's Jax.

"Hi."

"Tree house—five minutes," is all he says.

I start to say "OK," but he's already hung up. I run downstairs and literally bump into my father. He looks thinner—his
hair is sprinkled with gray, and the lines around his eyes are
deeper, more pronounced. His tie is loosened and he's holding
his shoes.

"Hey, sweetie," he says, kissing my cheek.

"Hi, Dad. I'll be right back."

I dash out the back door, walk across the backyard—past the
old swing set and my mother's garden—and cross into Jax's
backyard. I see his feet disappear into the tree house just as I
reach the ladder, which is carved into the tree itself. I pause for
a minute, remembering the last time Jax and I hid out in the
tree house—after Ashley's funeral. The limos had just dropped
us off—his family, my family, Jordy, Max, Carchie—and cars
began arriving before we even opened the front door. Everyone was holding overflowing trays of food—cold cuts, cookies,
cheese and crackers—and the thought of eating made my
stomach shrivel. There was a line to get into the house so I ran
around to the backyard and threw up in the bushes. It hurt to
vomit because I hadn't eaten anything in days and my stomach
muscles were already sore from crying. Jax was the only one
who saw me run away. He rubbed my neck until I stopped dry
heaving and led me to the tree house. He sneaked into his

house for water and we sat—huddled together on the old, dusty throw cushions—for over an hour.

I climb the ladder and crawl into the tree house. Jax has spread a few towels on the weathered wood planks. He rolls a bottle of water at me and waves a pack of cigarettes.

"Want?"

I shake my head. He lights one, exhaling a plume of smoke out the small circular window to his right. He slides back so he's leaning against the wall. I do the same. We stretch out our legs so our feet are touching.

"Remember when this space seemed huge? We used to fit half the neighborhood in here," I say.

Jax nods. "It's ironic."

"What is?"

"My father was so fucking thrilled he had a son. He was so excited to teach me all the things he knew—how to throw a football, how to knock someone out with one punch, how to talk to girls—and I never wanted to learn any of it. He built me this tree house after he saw my face on Christmas morning when I opened the Lite-Brite your parents bought for me. I lost interest in the lights pretty quickly, but I've always loved this tree house. I got my first blow job in this tree house. And I can't count all the times we used to hang out in here—plotting our lives, our plans for the future."

I nod. "What happened in there?"

Jax sighs and takes a gulp of water. "They were both really happy to see me. He looks awful, Alex—he's dying. I think we're coming over for dinner, so you should prepare yourself— he looks a little like Ashley did toward the end. Anyway, he's living in the study so he doesn't have to deal with the stairs, so I walk in there and wake him up and he just keeps smiling. We shake hands—which we haven't done in years—and I tell him about the voice-over gigs and he actually listens and makes eye contact. Then I guess I was talking with my hands too much, or maybe it was because I crossed my legs. I don't know. Something made him see the word *gay* in big red letters on my forehead and suddenly he looked out the window, drank his tea and didn't say another word to me."

The walls of the tree house close in on us for a second. I've been friends with Jax for twenty-three years, and I have no idea what to say to him right now. The guilt is starting to seep down from my brain, traveling in a straight line to my chest.

"Let's go back to the city," Jax says, about to cry.

"Jax, this could be the last time you see your father."

Jax stomps his foot and the tree house shudders under the pressure. "Alex, this isn't you and Ashley recapturing your lost youth before he died. This man doesn't want me in his house."

"But dinner's at my house," I reply, just barely concealing a grin. Jax smiles.

"If you really want to go home, I'll take you, but I think we should stay—you should stay. Give him one last chance," I tell him.

"He doesn't deserve it."

I lean forward. "I know, but you do."

Jax surrenders to his tears and I crawl across the floor to hug him.

I know dinner is going to suck when my mother asks me to change my clothes. If she wants our outer appearances to cloak our inner turbulence, we're all in trouble. After leaving Jax in the tree house, I hang out with my dad for ten minutes—he asks about the Discovery, the lease on my apartment and the progress of Jordy's dissertation—and then retreat to my old room for a nap. I don't get any sleep, though, because I'm busy fantasizing about a movie-of-the-week ending for Jax and Jim— one where Jim realizes he's losing his only son for no other reason than his own fear and ignorance, and in the middle of dinner Jax and Jim hug, we all cry and that's that. Peace returns.

At some point, I drift off, and wake up to find my mother sitting on the edge of the bed, staring at me. I roll over and face the wall.

"Do you know how long it's been since I've seen you sleep?" she asks.

"You're always bitching about how I sleep too much."

"Yes, but that's just because I don't want you sleeping through life. But to actually watch you sleep, it brings me back—"

"To the good old days when all three of us were here and life was pretty?" I'm not sure I could say this if I were facing her.

"No."

"To the days before your son died and your daughter tried to kill herself?"

"Sort of."

The bitterness in me is waning, or she's a lot stronger than I give her credit for. "What then?"

"To the days when you smiled for no reason, when you loved me and your father in the most uncomplicated way, when Teddy was your hero, when you and Jax played in the snow and then curled up in our bed for a nap, when you . . . when you . . ."

I turn over to look at her. In a way, it feels like I haven't seen her for a long time. "What?"

She brushes the hair out of my face and rests her palm on my forehead. "When you were happy."

Even my father feels the tension. There's nowhere for him to slink off to, no way to escape the downpour. He offers me a drink as soon as I walk downstairs. I'm wearing black pants and a black tank top with Jordy's black slides. My mother is wearing black, too. My father's red shirt is the only burst of color in our kitchen. He drinks scotch, I drink vodka and club soda and my mother sips white wine. The front door opens and Jax's parents walk in, followed by Jax, who looks so angry and indignant I want to grab him, throw him in the car and drive us away. Jax has shaved, and his hair is pulled away from his face into a low ponytail that rests on his neck. Jim is most definitely dying—a slow, burning death. He's lost more than twenty pounds since I saw him last, and he uses a cane to support himself. His eyes are blanks, and the only skin that remains on his face clings desperately to his cheekbones. His knees are knobs and his elbows protrude starkly from his arms. My mother ushers him into a chair in the living room, and my father places a glass of bourbon in his hand. Jax's mother, Ellen, stays in the kitchen. She hugs me and kisses my cheek.

"It's so good to see you, Alex. It's been too long."

I nod. I promised my mother I would help keep things on an even keel.

"How are you?" I ask her.

She leans against the kitchen counter, her hands fingering the buttons on her black blouse. Her nail polish is chipped and her lipstick is unevenly applied. "Fine, considering. Thank you for bringing Jax home."

I look at Jax, who's sitting at the kitchen table, staring at our fathers in the living room. I pass him my drink and he sips it, the ice cubes falling against his lips.

"So how are things in the city? Your mother told me you got fired."

I turn back to Ellen. "Yeah—I was downsized. But now I have more time to work on my children's books, so it worked out."

I see my mother glance at me and then Ellen. "I sent three of them to the CEO of Spencer Publishing," I continue. My mother turns away from the stove and looks at me.

"Do you think that's a good idea?" she asks. Jax gets up and stands next to me.

"Why not?" I answer.

"Because of the rejection." She turns back to the stove and stirs something.

"You mean the *possibility* of rejection?" Sam would love this response.

My mother nods but doesn't say anything. Ellen is staring at Jax.

"She actually knows the CEO of Spencer Publishing," Jax says.

"How?" Ellen asks.

My mother turns around again, waiting.

"I'm dating his son."

A last burst of light enters the kitchen as the sun deserts the skyline behind our house. My mother puts the spoon down, wipes her hands on a towel and walks over to Jax and me. Ellen smiles for the first time since entering the house. "Really? You're dating someone?" she asks.

"Yeah, I am." All eyes are on me. "His name is Tucker. He's a painter."

"But his father owns a publishing company?" my mother asks.

"He owns way more than a publishing company. He owns TV stations, film studios, radio stations, newspapers—"

"OK, Jax, they get the point." He knows my mother too well—she's already picturing the wedding.

"He's not Jewish," I tell the wedding planners.

"But he is the son of a billionaire," Jax adds. "He's a nice guy. Cute, too."

The balloon deflates. Ellen sinks back against the counter; her hands collapse to her hips. My mother stares at me—she wants more information on Tucker, but she hides within the tense silence brought about by Jax's accidental use of the word "cute," and returns to the stove. Jax finishes my drink, dissolving any hopes I still harbor for a happy ending to this dinner. I mix another cocktail, swallowing the inflation of guilt that gradually moves toward my gut.

My mother serves salmon with rosemary potatoes and asparagus. It's been years since I've eaten anything but her Thanksgiving food, and I would really like to enjoy this meal but my stomach is not cooperating. I'm sitting between my mother and Jim—diagonally across from Jax. He's eating everything in sight and drinking glass after glass of water. I can't look at Jim during dinner because all I see is Ashley—the slow rise of the fork to his mouth, that same wince when he swallows, the lethargy of the whole process. The man is already a ghost. I watch as Ellen cuts his salmon and potatoes into tiny bits. I try my best not to stare at the wall above my father's head, where it's impossible not to notice the outline of time. A framed watercolor hangs on the wall, but it's smaller than what hung there for most of my life—a family photo, all five of us, before AIDS took Ashley, before depression claimed me, before our family splintered into disparate pieces. The outline of years is visible—it's the frame of a colorful but bland painting. The conversation is ridiculous, as there are so many verboten topics between the two families that we're forced to discuss the current water shortage and the mileage of my new car.

"Jax and I saw Ashley's last documentary at a video store in the Hamptons."

"Yeah, it was actually a rental. Pretty cool," Jax says.

Jim swallows a tiny piece of salmon and says, "The one about Paris in the twenties?"

"Yes," Jax answers. Does this count as them having a conversation?

"That was his best one. I loved that film," Jim says.

I look at my mother, whose plate is covered with untouched food, and then at Jax. I close my eyes for a second, remembering my promise. I see Sam, sitting in the brown leather chair in his spare but comfortable office. I glance at the evidence left behind when my mother took down the family photo a few months after Ashley died.

"You do know it was written, directed and produced by a gay man, don't you?" I ask.

An abrupt silence covers the table. Jax shakes his head, frowning at my attempt to force the issue. My mother's face loses color—her disappointment fills me, not with fear but with a flame of anger.

"He's my oldest friend," I tell her, as if it's just us at the table.

My mother's entire body tenses up, then she curls her back against the chair, as if she's waiting for the onslaught. My father gets up, leaves the room and returns a minute later with an ice bucket and three bottles—bourbon, scotch and vodka. He passes me the vodka, and we share a small, sad smile. "Defend me, Dad," I want to yell—these are values you instilled in me, for Christ's sake. When did you become so meek and tired? When Ashley died, I realize.

"Did you hear the movie theater in town might turn into a multiplex?" my mother asks no one.

Jax is staring at his father while spearing potatoes and shoving them into his mouth.

"No," I answer.

"Yes, apparently the stores on either side are closing and they're thinking of—"

"No!" I yell. "Do not change the subject, and do not pretend I didn't say what I said."

"Alexandra, this isn't the time—"

"This *is* the time, Mom. He's dying—we all know that. If this isn't dealt with, Jax is going to be fucked up forever. Excuse me, I meant *screwed* up forever."

Jax smirks behind a full glass of vodka and club soda.

"If what isn't dealt with?" Ellen asks.

"Your son is gay, and your husband hates him for it. And you've completely abandoned him. Don't you think you should talk about it before Jim dies?"

Jax looks at her. Ellen's eyes fill with tears and for a second I think maybe they'll hug and Ellen will act like his mother again. But she slowly turns away from Jax to face Jim, whose unseeing eyes are on Jax.

"Jack?"

Jax, his eyes on fire, stares at his father. "Yeah, Dad?"

"Do you have something to say? Is Alexandra making any sense to you right now?"

"Well, yes. I think we have things to talk about, don't you?"

"We're thinking of taking a cruise to Alaska next summer," my mother says.

"I've heard the landscape is just stunning," Ellen says.

"Mom?" Jax says.

"What?"

"Get your head out of the goddamn sand!" Ellen doesn't get

it. I crack up—holding my hand over my mouth—which doesn't help matters.

Jim looks at Jax, takes a sip of bourbon and rests his fork and knife horizontally across his plate. "You're my biological son," he says, his eyes and voice muted. My mother is frozen, and my father looks like he might throw up. I wonder if they're thinking about Ashley. I can't stop my mind from speculating what would happen if the second of their three children came out. Would they love me, regardless, as they did Ashley? Is it different for a girl? Would it be just another source of disappointment for them from their youngest daughter, who can't seem to live a seamless life?

Jax nods.

"Do you have any plans to alter your chosen lifestyle?" Jim asks.

Jax's jaw tightens and he closes his eyes. My mother reaches out to me and slowly slides the knife out of my hand, which I hadn't even realized I'd been holding.

Jax opens his eyes and looks at his parents. "It is not a choice."

"I think it is," Jim replies. Ellen closes her fingertips around his.

"According to recent research, they're pretty sure it is not a choice at all," my father says. I smile at him. Under the table, my mother takes his hand. "Keep going, Dad," I almost yell.

"Are you actually so ignorant you think I'd *want* to do something that makes my parents hate me? That forces me onto the periphery of society? That marginalizes me and puts my life in danger in certain places in the world? Why would I *want* to do that?"

"So don't do it," Ellen says, her voice tremulous and unsure. Jim leans in close to Ellen; their arms now touch.

Jax tilts his head. He seems to be looking above my father's head—at the spot where the family photo no longer hangs. He then looks from Jim to Ellen, back to Jim. His shoulders are firm and his hands are steady. "I have to."

"Why, goddamn it, why?" Jim asks him. "Why can't you just

marry a nice woman and have children and pay your mortgage and rake leaves in the fall and replace the gutters in the spring, like a normal person?"

My mother takes my fork away. Jax's chest rises and falls. He looks at me, and I wonder if he might hit his father, or break something. His eyes betray his sadness, but only I see it. He raises his right arm and yanks the rubber band out of his hair. He unsettles the ponytail, shaking his head from left to right.

He looks back at Jim. "I *am* normal. I *am* gay. And I *am* your son."

Jim sits back in his seat and sighs—exhaustion flutters from his eyelids. He's still holding Ellen's hand—it seems like an extension of his body. He shakes his head. "No, you're not."

Jax untucks his shirt, shrugs it off his shoulders a bit and stands up. He looks at me, takes a deep breath and returns his gaze to his father. There is a clarity in his eyes I cannot ever recall seeing.

"This is *your* problem, Dad, not mine. If you change your mind and would like to tell me you love me for who I am, you know where to find me. The next time I see you, you'll be dead. I'll do my best to take care of Mom, but she's been pretty shitty to me since I came out, so I can't guarantee I'll be there for her." If it were me saying this to my parents, I'd be trembling and crying, but Jax is poised—his body is perfectly still and his voice completely stable.

My mother gasps and I can see my father's grip on her hand constrict. Jim shrinks further into his chair—Jax looms over the dining room table like the spiral of a tornado. My thoughts have no shape, but my body is suddenly filled with an uncertain dread. The only thought I can contain in my mind for more than a minute is, for the second time in a month, I have been a lousy friend—I should never have brought Jax home, much less convinced him to stay after he saw his father this afternoon. I wish I could call Sam and confess my guilt. Jax isn't me and Jim isn't Ashley—why did I connect the two? Ashley and I loved each other, before the last four months, though it was in a distant, detached way. There was nothing wrong with our relationship—we just didn't have one. But there is something wrong with the relationship that just unraveled in front of me—it's been there for years—and I should have known better than to push for a reconciliation that is, on a certain level, none of my business. I know Jax will forgive me, but I wonder if this incident will leap out of life and onto the long list of things for which I cannot forgive myself.

Jax and I are in the car within five minutes. My parents hug me in the driveway; I tell them I'll call tomorrow. We drive back to the city in silence—no music, no words. I drop Jax off at his apartment and we both cry when we hug. Jax's arms feel strong around my back, and his breathing is unbroken. The wall of guilt within me has finally collapsed, and I'm utterly depleted by the time I park the car and enter my apartment, dragging my bags behind me. Jordy is asleep in her bed, encircled by books and papers. I change into sweats and a T-shirt, and creep into bed with her. I listen to her breathing, close my eyes and think of Jax—the expression on his face when he finally conquered his father's shame, and the internal light that transformed from a lackluster spark to a pulsating flare of belief in himself.

11

I call Jax every few hours for seven days in a row. I leave messages on his answering machine, on his cell phone and at the restaurant. On the eighth day, he finally tells me to stop—he knows he's loved and appreciates my concern but he's fine. Jordy calls him twice a day for the next four days, until he leaves us a message threatening to call the phone company to cancel our service.

Jordy is done—well, she's not done but she's *about* to be done. She submitted her dissertation while Jax and I were in the Hamptons, and now she's counting down the days—ten— until her defense. She can't sit still, can hardly eat and is lighting one cigarette off the end of another. She keeps dyeing and redyeing the stripe in her hair. It's been blue for months, but now it keeps changing—candy-apple red to kelly green and back to blue again. She winds the stripe around her fingers as she stares out the window or at the TV. To distract her, we walk around a different neighborhood every day. SoHo is crooked and colorful and uneven; TriBeCa is wide and dark, with strange smells and trendy restaurants; Chinatown is demanding and unfamiliar and economical; the East Village is placid and musical at once, with Polish restaurants and Jewish delis and gay bars; and the Lower East Side is vibrant, with long forgotten neighborhoods and new sex-toy stores and the dissonance of language on every corner. We schedule our departure so we run into the mailman on the way out—but I don't get a letter (rejection or otherwise) from Tucker's father or anyone he may have sent my books to. We clean the apartment so it sparkles and smells like a combination of evergreen and lemon trees. We've just finished reorganizing our CDs when the doorman buzzes.

"Who stops by at noon on a Wednesday?" Jordy asks, walking toward the intercom.

I shrug. "Jax is working a double and I'm still not talking to Teddy."

"Hello?" she asks the wall, holding down the button.

"Tucker is here to see Alex," the doorman's voice reports.

Jordy turns to look at me. I shrug again. I haven't spoken to Tucker since we returned from the Berkshires—we've been playing a wicked game of phone tag.

"Send him up." Jordy opens the door a few inches and sits on the couch.

Tucker appears in the doorway a minute later, holding a bouquet of daisies and a bottle of wine. He looks a little embarrassed, which makes him look cuter than usual.

"I have painter's block," he announces, closing the door behind him. "Anyone up for a liquid lunch? It's a 1972." He holds up the bottle.

Jordy smiles and gestures for Tucker to sit on the couch. She takes the flowers from him, walks into the kitchen and re-enters the living room with three wine glasses.

"I love you artists," she says, handing us each a glass. "You turn your suffering into a celebration."

Tucker opens the bottle of wine without looking at it, fills our glasses and looks at me; I suddenly feel terrible for not making more of an effort to see or speak to him.

"I went on a trip with Jax," I tell him, hoping it will serve as enough of an explanation.

"Have fun?" he asks.

I nod.

"Good." He holds up his glass for a toast. "To drinking Merlot at noon on a Wednesday—life can't be all bad."

Jordy clinks glasses with him. Tucker leans over to touch his glass to mine. "Good to see you, Alex."

I take a sip of wine. "You, too."

Jordy retreats to her room after we finish the bottle. Tucker and I don't move from our seats for the next few hours. We switch to margaritas, and play backgammon and Mastermind.

"I sold a painting."

"Congratulations," I say, kissing him. His skin smells familiar and tempting.

"But now I'm blocked—I got nothing. I think I need a change of scenery."

"Want to drive to Chicago with me?" The words are out of my mouth before I can stop them.

Tucker turns to me—to answer—but I turn my head around before he can say anything.

"Wait—let me think for a second—that just fell out and I want to make sure I think about this in a vaguely mature manner," I add.

Tucker cracks up. "My oh my, wouldn't Sam be proud."

I give him the finger without looking at him. Do I want Tucker with me when I visit Casey? As I drive halfway across the country? This will be our third trip together—even I can't deny the evolution of our relationship. I turn around.

"I'm staying with Casey, so I'll have to check with her, but I think she'll be fine with it."

Tucker grins—he looks as if he just won the biggest prize at the ring toss.

"How long are you staying in Chicago?"

I shrug. "I'm figuring a week for the whole trip, including driving there and back. I want to be here when Jordy walks out of her dissertation defense."

"Are you going to let me split expenses with you?" he asks.

"Hell yeah," I reply. "Gas, food, lodging, all of it."

Tucker laughs. "OK, I'm in." He stands up and swings his

arms in what I assume is some sort of dance. "I'm going to Chicago with Alex," he sings.

Jordy walks into the living room just as Tucker is celebrating my invitation. "What's he doing?" she asks. Either she's really tired or her voice has a sharp edge to it.

"I invited him to Chicago," I reply.

Jordy looks sideways at Tucker. She rolls her eyes and lights a cigarette.

I have three bags. Tucker has one. He shakes his head and laughs to himself as he gets in the car. He tucks a CD case under his feet, slides Gucci sunglasses on his face and says, "Take me away, Calgon."

I drive across the George Washington Bridge and pick up Route 78 in New Jersey. The Dave Matthews Band is pumping through the car, and it suddenly dawns on me that I'm driving my dream car almost eight hundred miles to see Casey. And I'm bringing Tucker. Ashley would be pleased.

"What should we do?" Tucker asks.

"About what?" I reply.

"With all this time. We could play Twenty Questions, or I'm Going on a Picnic. Oh, how 'bout movie lines? I say a line from a popular movie, and you have to—"

"I know how to play. I don't want to play that game. Or any game," I announce coarsely.

We're only in New Jersey—it's not too late to turn back. I can fake a stomachache. Or appendicitis.

"OK. No need to freak out."

Yes, there is. It's been four years and I still can't trade movie lines with anyone else. At Webster Ridge, they told me it would take a while for me to able to play the game that, for most of my life, was the only bond I shared with Ashley, but this is ridiculous. Tucker—a guy I'm dating, a guy I'm sleeping with, a guy I theoretically care about—innocently mentions the game, and I hate him for it. I should've waited for Jordy and driven to Chicago with her.

I light a cigarette, plug my cell phone into the lighter and turn up the music. I know I should say something to settle the discord in the car, but I'm just not in the mood. I want Tucker to *know* what he's allowed to say or mention or reference. I want him to read my mind.

"You're extremely non-confrontational, do you know that?" Tucker suddenly asks.

I nod.

"You should work on that in therapy," he instructs.

"I'm not in therapy at the moment."

Tucker's entire upper body swerves around to face me. I switch to the left lane.

"Why the fuck not?"

"I'm taking time off."

"Alex, you tried to kill yourself. You're susceptible to depression."

It's too bad Teddy's married—I could set her up with Tucker and they could write songs about my suicide attempt and depressive phases. "That was two years ago. And I plan to find a therapist, just not now. After the summer, maybe."

Tucker shakes his head and lowers the music. "Two years is not that long ago. I'm sure you still have issues to work out. Are you telling me you're *never* depressed anymore?"

I shove my cigarette into the ashtray, thrust my foot on the gas pedal and ignore Tucker.

"What about 'the missing piece' search?" he asks.

"What about it?"

"Gotten anywhere on that?"

"No, Tucker, I haven't. I got sidetracked when my oldest friend walked away from his homophobic family in front of me at my mother's dining room table. But I'm back on track now, thanks to your reminder."

Tucker sighs, lights a cigarette and looks out the window for a minute. "I'm sorry, Alex. I'm just trying to know you, to understand you. And to help you."

"I have no problem with the knowing or the understanding, Tucker. But in the help department, I have Jax and Casey and Jordy, and they're all I need, at least for now. OK?"

Tucker clenches his jaw and then nods. "OK." He exhales a
thin string of smoke out the window. Silence hovers in the car
for almost twenty minutes.

I block Tucker from my peripheral vision and force myself to
relax. An image of my youth darts into my mind, and I am surrounded by the deep, chirping sounds of bullfrogs, the crunching of sneakers as they traverse the rock-covered paths that
wind their way through the camp and the reverberation of muf-
fled laughter that knows it's after lights-out but cannot help itself from giggling and sputtering into a pillow. The last time
Jordy and I returned to camp was a few months after Ashley
died.

We're sitting, cross-legged, on a chipped green picnic table
in the section of camp that juts farthest out into Lake Jester.
The waterfront is to our left, placid now that all the campers
have gone to bed. We spent the day wandering around, laughing and crying as the memories pounded into us. We ate
lunch—vegetable soup, grilled cheese sandwiches and chocolate pudding—with the camp director, and he asked about our
lives and commented on how well we turned out, considering
how rebellious we were as children and teenagers. We played
tennis for a while, made beaded bracelets in crafts and put-
tered around the ceramics bunk. Mostly, though, we walked—
letting our feet lead us on a journey we had taken so many
times before. And now it's almost ten o'clock, and we should
really leave but neither of us wants to travel beyond the front
gates, because if we do, this microcosm will dissolve.

"I just can't get over how naïve we were," I tell Jordy. She's
wrapped in a tattered sweatshirt. Her legs unravel from beneath her, and she swings them under the table.

"What do you mean?"

"The whole group thing. We actually thought the ten of us
would be friends forever. We believed that the power of friendship could overcome all obstacles."

"*Naïve* is the wrong word. We were innocent—we had no reason not to be." Without speaking, Jordy and I change positions so we're both facing the water. I lean into her and she plays with my hair while we listen to the sound of the lake hitting into the shore.

Jordy rests her chin on my shoulder and, without warning, my memory falls and all I can see or think about is Ashley. I'm crying—the way a child cries—gasping for breath. My face is covered in salty streaks and I can't inhale anything but the ash from these infernal memories. My tissues ball up into a pile of wetness within seconds. A fresh supply of tears plummets from my eyes, and my nose drips a steady stream toward my lips. Jordy jumps off the table and hugs me, rocking me back and forth for a few minutes. When we break apart, she half-smiles at me and then, using the sleeve of her sweatshirt, wipes my nose and cheeks. A thought gallops through my mind—it feels heavy and sinewy—but I can't grab hold of it quickly enough, and I lose it. And all I am left with is awareness: I had a brother, and now he is dead.

* * *

Tucker finally quells the silence. "Isn't New Jersey lovely? I just adore the putrid stench that lingers in the air. What do you think it is that reeks? Garbage? Pollution?"

"Years and years and layers and layers of hairspray," I answer.

Tucker laughs. I turn the music up again and exhale.

We sit in stillness for over half an hour. The scenery isn't all that interesting—asphalt and minimal foliage—but we let the music drift between us and remain within ourselves—until I finally remember to ask Tucker the question I've been meaning to ask since he walked into the apartment holding the wine and flowers.

"Has your dad said anything about my books?"

"I haven't spoken to him in a while."

"What's *a while*?"

Tucker shrugs. "A few weeks—since before the Berkshires."

"Oh."

Tucker flips through his CD holder, knowing the Dave Matthews CD is going to end after this song. "You sent him some books, right?"

"Yeah, three. But I haven't heard anything, from him or anyone else. I assume he's really busy, though, right?"

"Yeah, but it seems out of character for him. Derek tells me he always follows up on favors. I can call him when I get home."

"No, don't. I should probably call. Yeah, I'll call when we get back."

Tucker shrugs and holds up an Elton John CD. "OK?"

I nod my approval and we submit to the music once again.

We're not planning on stopping until we hit Cleveland—we both want to visit the Rock and Roll Hall of Fame. Beyond that, we have no plans. The air around us is clean again, and every time I look over at Tucker, I feel like hugging him. His semiconstant need to be acknowledged as someone who cares about me is annoying yet endearing at the same time.

I pick up Route 76 near Harrisburg, and we take it all the way through Pennsylvania into Ohio, where it becomes the Ohio Turnpike. The landscape is still monotonous, and I start to wonder if it would've been worth it to drive miles out of my way just to improve our surroundings. I look over at Tucker, about to ask him this, but he's sleeping. I know he's going to be very unhappy when he wakes up, thinking he deserted me—he'll be disappointed in himself as a road tripper and my "boyfriend." Although I refuse to use that term in reference to him, I have to admit that he is, essentially, my boyfriend.

Tucker wakes up as we pull into Cleveland. First we argue about getting gas—Tucker insists on pumping—and then we debate staying at Motel 6 versus The Comfort Inn as he fills the tank. We decide on Motel 6, mostly because we like the lurid undertones to the name. Tucker heads toward the check-in counter as soon as we enter.

"I'll check us in," I say, holding my messenger bag. Tucker is holding two of my bags and his own, striding ahead of me toward the counter.

"Nah, I'll do it. You go to the ladies' room."

I follow him to the counter. "Tucker, I don't know what your female friends are like but, in my circle, the women are just as competent as the men."

"What's your point, Alex?" He rests the bags at his feet and rifles through his wallet at the same time, as if he's competing for the Best Multitasker Award.

"My point is, you have this antiquated idea in your head that the man carries the bags, the man fills out the forms, the man holds the key, the man orders the wine and so on."

The blonde, blue-eyed and bushy-tailed motel clerk steps back, observing our argument.

"You don't know shit about wine."

I pull my wallet out of my bag, hand over a credit card and nod to the clerk. "Not the point, Tucker."

He leans on the counter as I fill out the registration form. "What *is* the point?"

I hand the form to the clerk. "I did manage to exist before you entered my life—I do my own laundry, I cook my own meals, I carry my own bags, I interact with strangers in strange places and I can even change a tire, though it takes me about five hours. Don't treat me the way you treat your sister—it won't work."

"Why would you even want to deal with checking in?" Tucker fiddles with a pen, accidentally breaking it.

The clerk laughs. "Let me guess," she says to us. "You folks are from New York."

I nod. She giggles and turns around to get our key. Tucker rolls his eyes at me and I laugh.

"I understand you were raised this way, but I wasn't, and I hate the way you coddle me," I tell him. His eyes dip at the corners and now I feel guilty.

"Can I open a door for you every now and then?" he asks, approaching me with open arms.

I fall into his hug. "You most certainly can."

All I want to do is sleep, but after Tucker finishes moaning about the scratchy towels, small shower and cheap TV, he seduces me with sweetness and we have sex that feels like wading through mud. I'm so tired—I keep trying to picture the Rock and Roll Hall of Fame while we have sex—so I'm miles away from having an orgasm. Tucker, of course, thinks it's his short-coming—it takes me a few minutes to convince him otherwise, and then I roll over and close my eyes. I realize within seconds sleep is now out of the question—my mind is turning over and over like a Ferris wheel, trying to ascertain whether it actually is tiredness, or perhaps boredom, that stopped me from really feeling Tucker's touch. Finally, at some point, I fall asleep.

We eat breakfast at IHOP (Tucker complains about the cheesy décor and weak coffee) and are among the first tourists to line up outside the Rock and Roll Hall of Fame. I can't de-cide if the museum is a funky, modern building or a wannabe funky, modern building. It's rounded, with layers of floors, each curling into the other, seven stories high. The air inside smells of history, of glory, of pain—my life seems tiny and in-consequential as I look at memorabilia from the music indus-try's most famous and infamous artists. Tucker takes my hand as soon as we walk in and presses me toward anything related to Bob Dylan. He doesn't want to split up; I have to persuade him to even let go of my hand. We spend fifteen minutes staring at Janis Joplin's car and then scan the walls covered with gold and platinum records. I buy Carchie a Bob Dylan print, even though he'll scoff, knowing it's a reprint, multiplied thousands of times. Tucker and I head into another exhibit to examine the ple-thora of clothes—everything from Elvis' cape to Liberace's boas. Four hours later, we emerge, tired but invigorated. We linger outside, smoking a cigarette and staring up at the mu-seum. Tucker talks, but I tune him out—I'm staring at the façade of the museum, thinking how sometimes the outer shell of something does not even come close to revealing what lies within.

"Let's go eat," Tucker suggests.

"We ate a few hours ago." It's just past noon.

"I'm in the mood for ice cream. You want ice cream?"

I put my cigarette out in an ashtray full of sand. I've always wondered where the sand comes from. Is it beach sand? Do they manufacture sand especially for ashtrays?

"No."

"How can you not want ice cream? It's a beautiful summer day."

Tucker looks, and acts, like a little boy so much of the time. He had a fun morning and now he wants to top it off with ice cream.

"If you want ice cream, we'll get ice cream," I tell him.

Tucker takes my hand and we walk toward the car. He swings our arms, his smile so wide it's about to fall off his face. I unlock the car with the remote control and watch as Tucker climbs in, careful not to bump the door on the car parked alongside mine. He quickly stoops to grab his CD holder and rifles through it, obviously searching for something. He finds what he's looking for, slides in a CD and looks to his left—for me. When he realizes I'm not in the car, he panics—looks right, then left again—and jumps out of the car. I can almost feel him exhale when he sees me. I smile to prevent him from speaking.

"I'm right here."

Tucker smiles and lets out a forceful sigh. I get in the car and pull out of the parking lot.

"Scott burned a CD for me," Tucker says, pointing to the radio.

The first song is a live version of Zeppelin's "Ramble On." Tucker strums his leg as I propel us toward an ice cream place. The song seems to continue for hours, and I'm about to tell Tucker my body cannot take another minute of Zeppelin when it ends and, after the requisite four seconds, "Walking in Memphis" begins. My hand can't reach the dial fast enough to turn up the volume.

"I *love* this song," I yell above the music.

Tucker just smiles as he mouths the words. We sing the entire song aloud, more to ourselves than to each other. When it ends and "Sympathy for the Devil" starts, I readjust the volume.

"That is one of the best driving songs," Tucker says.

"Don't you love good driving songs?"

Tucker nods and lights a cigarette. "Yeah. I'm going to make you a driving CD."

"I just—"

"What?" he asks.

"I just love music so much," I blurt out. "It sounds ridiculous, but I don't think I could live without music."

Tucker exhales onto the end of his cigarette, making the tip glow like a tiny beacon. "I know exactly what you mean. Music makes life—"

"Bearable," I say.

"I was going to say *better*."

Tucker orders a double cone, mint chocolate chip and chocolate ice cream with rainbow sprinkles, or jimmies, as they're called here. As he eats, I remember how happy ice cream used to make Ashley—when the ice cream truck rolled through the neighborhood, the bell ringing loud enough to annoy every mother on the block, Ashley used to fly into the house, his sneakers barely skimming the floor, and yell, "Ice cream man!" Each word was infused with at least three syllables, and Teddy and I would drop whatever we were doing and meet Ashley in the foyer, the three of us a united force against my mother, who had served us dinner, with dessert, less than an hour before. She always gave in, handing us each a few dollars to spend on bubble gum or a pack of Fun Dip, along with a Sno-Cone or Push-Up Pop. We always ate our treats on the front porch, watching the wisteria tree sway in the descending darkness. We talked about the Yankees or flipped baseball cards, dissecting the season as if we were baseball analysts, which, of course, we were. Ashley always had to try everyone else's ice cream treat, even Jax's, to "make sure it's all right." Teddy and I usually shared, switching treats in the middle so there was more to enjoy.

Right now, though, here in Cleveland, I have no desire for ice cream. "Want some?" Tucker pushes his cone in my direction.

"No, thanks."

"What do you want to do now?"

I shrug.

Tucker looks around, his tongue flicking ice cream into his mouth. I suddenly want to throw his ice cream cone on the ground.

"Do you mind if I drop you off at the motel?" I ask.

Tucker stares at me, chocolate ice cream dripping over his hand.

"I just need some space—it has nothing to do with you," I say.

He wipes the corners of his mouth with the back of his hand. "No problem."

I drive around Cleveland for a while, listening to "In Your Eyes" over and over. I call Jax and Jordy but neither answers. I'm about to dial Teddy's number but I stop myself—if it doesn't go well, I'll be alone, in the Midwest, and I don't trust myself to deal with the outcome if it's not good. Tucker is useless in this situation; he is so blissfully unaware of his own issues—with his father, with his dead mother—yet he truly believes he so clearly understands me now that he knows I tried to end my own life. I have a feeling Sam would no longer condone our relationship—dysfunction lurks above us like a profuse, stubborn fog.

The sun has begun its calculated journey toward the horizon when I pull into the parking lot of the motel. I need a nap, some food and a change of scenery. I also need solitude—an impossibility—and a long talk with Teddy. I need to find out what she was talking about before she hung up on me.

I'm still thinking about Teddy when I turn the key in the door. I need to speak to her—I'll call her when we stop in Toledo, or maybe I'll wait until Chicago. I push the door open with my knee and enter the room. The darkness surprises me at first, enveloping my entire body. I stand in the threshold—a tentative trepidation fills me.

"Tucker?"

"I'm here."

"Why are the blinds closed?" I ask, pulling the cord. Light rushes into the room and Tucker is revealed to me, sitting on the bed. My satchel rests on his knee. The pills are splayed on the ugly, beige bedspread. My mind reels but I literally can't say a word. Tucker looks up at me, his forehead a map of lines. I suck in a colossal breath and find my voice.

"You went through my stuff?"

"That is *so* not the point, Alex."

"If this were a court of law, that would be inadmissible as evidence," I say, pointing to my pills, my satchel, my secret.

"This isn't a court of law, Alex. It's a relationship, for Christ's sake."

"And that gives you the right to violate my privacy?"

"I was looking for Advil. Are you going to tell me what this is all about?"

"It's hard to explain."

"Keep it simple, Alex," he says, the condescension dripping from his voice like wet cement. "Why the fuck are you walking around with enough pills to kill a small town? What, you have a bad day on the road, you check into a Motel 6 and kill yourself?"

"No."

"Why then?"

"I hardly ever think about taking them. It's more of a—sort of like a security blanket, or a touchstone. It reminds me."

Tucker shakes his head, staring at the pills.

"Sam knew—he said it's fine."

"Well, Sam is dead and I'm not, and I think it's pretty fucking morbid, not to mention stupid. No wonder you're still so fucked up."

I prop myself against the door. "What the hell is that supposed to mean?"

Tucker leans back on his hands—the veins in his forearms pulsing—and the lock of hair falls against his forehead. His eyes manifest an unformulated fear. Of me, or the pills? "It means you shouldn't take time off from therapy. It means you need to make new friends. It means you need someone to watch out for you. And you should probably decipher 'the missing piece' thing—or are you planning on carrying around Sam's note, the mystery unsolved, for the rest of your life?"

"Don't psychoanalyze me, Tucker. You're the last person who should be telling me how to live."

"Meaning?"

"You can't look at your father without gritting your teeth. You hate him, but it's her you should hate. You just refuse to accept the fact that you're angry at your perfect, dead mother."

Tucker springs from the bed like a metal coil. For a split second, he looks as if he might hit me. His eyes are enormous and the muscles in his legs are strained. I clutch the door. Tucker turns around and slams his foot against the cheap, wooden dresser. Then he kicks his knapsack across the room. It lands near the bathroom door—the thud echoes throughout the room, accentuating the growing volume between us.

"I don't hate my mother, Alex. I hate him."

"Why? It wasn't his fault."

Tucker looks at me. "He knew she was depressed."

"What should he have done, Tucker? Stopped living his life so he could stay home and watch her?"

"He should have paid more attention. He should have insisted she stay on meds."

"Maybe that would've worked, but maybe not. Trust me on this, Tucker. When you want to die, you'll do anything—find any way—to kill yourself. It doesn't matter who you'll leave behind; when opening your eyes every morning becomes a miserable task instead of a natural instinct, the people you love suddenly matter less. She loved you—and your father and Derek and Catherine—but the love couldn't save her, and neither could your father. And you can't save me, so stop trying. I'm in a pretty good place compared to two years ago."

"Don't you want more than that? Don't you want to be whole again?"

I laugh, which makes Tucker clench his jaw and close his eyes for a moment. His hands curl into fists and he breathes through his nose—the air forces his nostrils to flare. "Who do you know that's whole? Some voids are not meant to be filled, Tucker. They're supposed to stay empty, to remind you of what you've lost, whom you've lost."

"That is one fucked-up way of life, Alex. I don't want to live like that."

"You are living like that! You've built an internal shrine to your mother. You've canonized her and punished your father, and until you forgive him, you're going to waste so much energy hating him. You're blaming the wrong person, Tucker. Didn't Sam teach you anything?"

"What'd he teach you? How to obsess about your dead brother? How to carry around an arsenal of pills, just in case life gets too tough and you want to torture your family by committing suicide? How to avoid a relationship by disappearing for weeks at a time? How to push everyone except Jax and Jordy out of your life so you won't actually have to love anyone? You're so fucking blind you can't even recognize when someone's in love with you. You're boxing yourself in, Alex, and soon no one will want to make the effort to know you."

"Fuck you, Tucker."

"Have a nice drive to Chicago, Alex. I'm sorry I won't be able to meet Casey. I was *so* looking forward to hanging out with another one of your emotional bodyguards."

Tucker throws his stuff together, slapping my clothes and bags out of his way. "Where are you going?" I ask.

"I'm taking a cab to the airport, and then I'm taking a plane back to the city. I've spent enough time on your dysfunctional planet, Alex. I'm going home."

"*My* dysfunctional planet? You're the fucking mayor of dysfunction! At least I acknowledge that I'm fucked up, Tucker. You pretend you're perfectly fine, but really you're so pissed off at the world—and your mother—that you can't even deal with it."

"It's *you* I can't deal with!" he yells as he pushes past me and out the door.

I slam the door so hard the walls quiver. I meticulously retrieve each pill and place it into the satchel. I let the satchel rest in my hand a moment, and then hurl it across the room at the closed door.

12

An hour evaporates. I pace the motel room, muttering clever responses to Tucker's accusations. I wash my face, smoke a cigarette and call Casey.

"Hey, Alex. Where are you?"

"I'm in a Motel 6 in Cleveland. Tucker and I got in a fight and he left."

"Where'd he go?"

"To catch a plane back to New York."

"What happened?"

I sigh—Casey doesn't know about the pills, so how can I relay the argument? "It's a long story."

I can hear Casey breathing. I finger the fringed edges of my shorts.

"You OK to drive?" she asks.

I sigh again. "I think so, but I need to regroup. Can we postpone my visit?"

"Are you sure? It might help you take your mind—"

"Wherever I go, my mind will follow."

"True. Drive carefully. Call me if you need me."

"I promise I'll visit, Casey, after I solve Sam's note and figure out what to do about Tucker. Things will be calmer then. I hope."

I glance at the clock—it's almost eight—and realize I haven't eaten since breakfast. I find a pack of Twizzlers in the car and, as I'm about to close the passenger door, notice that Tucker left his CD holder behind. I eject the CD from the stereo, carefully replace it in the holder and throw the whole thing in the back of the Discovery before returning to the room.

I stare at the grubby yellow walls of the motel room and rewind the fight with Tucker in my mind. I call Jordy—she's not in the apartment and I get her voice mail on the cell phone. I leave a message and then pack my bag. The motel room suddenly seems huge—like a murky, empty cavern—and as I'm laying out my clothes for tomorrow, the tears careen down my cheeks like bumper cars. I cave in on myself, crying over things that are beyond me, and also those that I should be able to control. A vague hunger has trailed behind me for years.

I wake up at six—half an hour before the wake-up call—and I'm out the door by seven. I check my cell phone—no message from Jordy. I'm wearing gray cargo shorts, a black tank top and sneakers. I can pull my hair back now that Tucker is gone. I walk half a block to buy a cup of coffee at Perkins, which seems to be the Midwestern version of Denny's, and force myself to purchase a plain bagel. It looks pathetic—not only because of the shrink-wrap clinging to it but also because, for some reason, no one outside the Tri-State area seems capable of properly baking a bagel. The aged, animated waitress is stunned that I don't want either cream cheese or butter.

I pick up Route 80 and mindlessly drive east. I'm suddenly quite aware of my New York license plate and the trance music emanating from the car. I fit the headset into my right ear and try to call Jordy again, but her cell phone is off. It's way too early to call Jax, even though I want to hear about the voice-over taping. I'm about to dial when the cell phone rings. It's my mother.

"Hi, Alex," she says. Her voice shoots upward, an attempt at a casual tone, but I know she's calling for a reason.

"Hi, Mom. How are you?" Maybe if I don't ask what's wrong,

she won't tell. It'd be nice if the whole world could function as the United States military does.

"I'm fine, but Jim's taken a turn for the worse. Ellen and I checked him in to the hospital last night."

I squint at the road, trying not to remember the time Jim taught Jax and me to bowl—we were seven—and then took us to Arthur Treacher's for fish and chips.

"Alex?"

"Yeah, I'm here."

"Are you using the headset? It's very dangerous—"

"Yes, Mom, I know."

"Do you think I should call Jax?" she asks.

"No."

"Why not? His father is very ill—"

"Mom, the only phone call Jax wants to get is the one telling him his father is dead."

I hear a quick intake of breath; she's crying. My eyes immediately tear up, and the sky—the day—is no longer unclouded. "Mom, there's nothing you can do. You've tried. You have to let this go. It's none of our business."

"But I've known Jax his whole life. I love him like a son."

The tears escape. "I love you, Mom—you know that, right?"

She gasps for air, and more tears tumble down my face.

"You haven't said that—unprompted—in a long time."

I wipe the tears away with my bare shoulder. "I know. I'm sorry. I just—I just sometimes get—"

"Lost?" she asks.

I smile, picturing the way her eyes flow into mine.

"Yeah," I reply.

"I love you, Alex. I'll see you when you get back?"

"Yeah—maybe I'll drive up and we'll get salads from Enrico's."

My mother laughs. "Enrico's closed two years ago."

I stare at the bumper of the car in front of me.

"We could go to the mall and buy winter coats," she suggests.

I hate buying winter coats in the summer. "Sounds good."

"Drive carefully. Don't speed."

"I'm OK, Mom. You're going to have to trust me to take care of myself."

"I know. I'm trying."

I smile. It suddenly occurs to me that I love my mother—and all her inevitable imperfections—more than I realized. We are inextricably, irrevocably and, sometimes, involuntarily linked. "I'll talk to you in a few days. Bye."

I shut the phone and toss it on the empty passenger seat. I reach for a cigarette but change my mind. I let my shoulders relax and allow the music to flood my senses—it feels as if the layered rhythm is less encumbered than before.

I drive and drive, focusing on the road and the music, blocking out thoughts of Tucker, of Sam's note, of Jordy's eyes. I'm in no hurry to get back to the city—confrontation awaits on all sides. There aren't many cars on the road so I fly, keeping an eye on the speedometer to avoid the legendary Pennsylvania speeding ticket. My body demands water—I can't seem to quench my thirst—so I'm impelled to stop every few hours. I grab a few brochures at a rest stop outside Harrisburg and flip through them while I smoke a cigarette in the sun. It's hot—I don't know the exact temperature but it's got to be around eighty-five degrees—sweat seeps from my skin. I buy another four bottles of Poland Spring and get in the car. I glance at the tourist brochures one more time, and as I'm pulling onto Route 80, I decide to detour to Cooperstown, New York—home of the Baseball Hall of Fame. My father took me, Ashley and Teddy there once, when I was six. I remember eating pizza afterward, but I can't picture the actual museum. My restlessness eases now that I have a destination, and I smile as I scan the directions and realize I can visit Carchie on the way back to the city.

I cruise through the rest of Pennsylvania and into New Jersey. I close the windows and put on the air-conditioning. I surprise myself by letting my thoughts now linger on Tucker. Although I tense up at the thought of his angry words, I'm not really upset at having lost my boyfriend. I guess the fact that I considered him my friend and not my boyfriend was the problem all along.

I pick up Route 287 in northern New Jersey and switch to the New York State Thruway in Rockland County, in Suffern. I laugh out loud at the name, and wish Jax were with me so we could spend some time examining the repercussions of living in a town called Suffern. "Hey, babycakes, I wonder how many people are sufferin' in Suffern," he'd say. Route 87 takes me north, through New York, and as I pass Woodstock, I decide to call Carchie to tell him I'll be stopping by later in the day.

"Alex, it's excellent to hear your voice," he says as soon as I greet him.

"How are you?"

"Eh—not great. This last round of chemo was a fucking killer. I've been puking for three days. But I've got two more days to get over it, because me and my buddies are going to Lake George on Friday to go fishing for a week."

"Are you sure—?"

"Alex, you know how you hate it when your mother—?"

"Got it, Carchie. Sorry."

"'Love means never having to say you're sorry.' I read that somewhere."

I laugh. "You didn't read that somewhere—it's from the movie *Love Story*."

Carchie laughs a tired laugh. "*Love Story* was a book first. Maybe I read the book."

"You so did not read *Love Story*! You just quoted a line from one of the sappiest movies of all time!"

Carchie laughs for a good thirty seconds—it sounds like he hasn't laughed in a while—and then takes a deep breath. "You know who would find this fucking hysterical?" he says.

"I know."

I tell Carchie my plans to see him later and he's thrilled, though he warns me he can't venture more than two feet from his puke bucket. When I hang up and ruminate on the movie-line exchange, I can hear Sam's voice as clearly as if he were sitting next to me in the Discovery: "It's about fucking time, Alex."

Cooperstown is possibly the most adorable town I've ever seen. Every shop is quaint and every resident is affable. The town's economy clearly revolves around the Hall of Fame, and thus the tourists are treated with respect and appreciation. I pay the entrance fee and throw in another ten bucks as a donation. The astonishment I felt while entering the Rock and Roll Hall of Fame flickers out of my memory as I walk through the doors of the Baseball Hall of Fame. I feel like a ten year-old, dwarfed by the images of the players I grew up idolizing. I convince myself to bypass the large gift shop—saving it for later— and inch my way along the wall of the first exhibit. There are life-size photos everywhere, as well as plaques and display cases full of bats, baseballs, gloves and uniforms. I have no desire to be a professional athlete—much less a baseball player—but I still feel some sort of inspiration as I gaze at the achievements of these near-perfect players who excelled at the perfect sport. I wander through the museum for hours. I sit in front of some of the exhibits, staring up at the images of my childhood, Teddy's childhood, Ashley's childhood and my father's childhood. I smile in spite of myself as I realize that two things— baseball and Ashley's premature death—bond my family.

I buy Carchie a Brooklyn Dodgers cap even though I know he'll never wear it because it's a reproduction. I get a full-size Yankees flag for my dad—he'll hang it in the front yard and my mother will absolutely freak out. I buy Jax a poster of the 1977 Yankees team, and I get Teddy a signed, limited-edition Catfish Hunter baseball card. I'll save it for her birthday—hopefully we'll be speaking by then. I throw in a handful of postcards, shaking my head at my own obsession with consumption—I'm less than four hours away from the city and it seems ridiculous to send my friends postcards. I hop down the steps and quickly leave the building before I purchase anything else or take another tour of the exhibits. It's two o'clock and I'm starving. I cross the street with a throng of loud, happy tourists and sneak into the pizza place ahead of them. I realize I smoke a lot of pot, but I'm almost positive this place looks exactly as it did when I was a kid. I order a slice and a diet root beer, then pop into the Apothecary next door for some stamps. While waiting for my pizza, I write postcards to Jax, Jordy, Teddy and my parents. The pizza is surprisingly good, and I treat myself to another slice, knowing I have a few hours of driving ahead of me. Jordy calls just as I'm throwing out the grease-stained paper plates.

"Where are you?" she asks.

"Cooperstown."

"You're at the Baseball Hall of Fame?"

"Just left—it's amazing. I could walk through it once a week."

"Why aren't you in Chicago?"

I sigh. "Long story."

"Synopsis, please."

I walk outside, light a cigarette and sit on the steps. "Tucker and I had a fight. He left me in Cleveland, and I wasn't in the mood to go to Chicago, so I just got in the car and drove east. And now I'm here, or I was here. I'm about to leave."

"To come home?" she asks, her voice hopeful.

"I'm going to stop by Carchie's—it's on the way, and he doesn't sound too good. I should be home by midnight."

"All right."

"You OK? Ready for tomorrow?"

Jordy exhales a long breath into the phone. "I guess so. I just want this whole thing to be over. What are we going to do to celebrate?"

"Whatever you want."

"I'll mull it over while I'm staring mindlessly at the TV tonight. I can't wait to see you—it feels like forever."

"I know. I'll see you later. I'll call from the bridge."

"OK. Bye."

I stroll in and out of some stores, looking for a congratulations present for Jordy. My pulse speeds up when I glance at my watch and notice it's after three o'clock—I don't want to get stuck in traffic, and I need to get to Carchie's before he's too tired. I toss my bag of baseball goodies in the back of the car, slide in a Dead CD and pick up Route 87, this time heading south. I know I'm in a picturesque region of New York, but the concrete walls and lifeless, barely green grass that line the New York State Thruway obscure the natural beauty of the surrounding area. I check my watch every ten minutes, but it isn't until my third inspection that I glimpse the date—July fifteenth. My two-year anniversary is five days away. Last year I kept track of the days as soon as July unraveled. My stomach crumples and I can feel my hair fuse to the back of my neck. I try taking deep, yogalike breaths; I try smoking a cigarette, and then another; I try listening to "In Your Eyes." Nothing works.

* * *

The walls are a heinous white-yellow. I can't decide if they were once yellow and have faded over the years, or if they were once white and the insane aura has built up over time, staining the walls. The space is an elongated rectangle with rooms on either side. There is a TV mounted on one end of the room, high against the wall—almost touching the ceiling—protected, I assume, from violent outbursts by its viewing audience. To the left of the TV is a double door—*the* double door—that leads to the hallway, the elevator, the lobby, the street, the world. On the opposite end is a lounge littered with abrasive, soiled couches.

I see only one bedroom—mine—and I see way too much of it, since I spend twenty hours a day trapped within it. There is a corner-less desk, which I cover with used paper cups, as I've decided to abandon all semblance of cleanliness. There is a night table, which I blanket in gum wrappers; there are dozens of them, since smoking is illegal in New York State hospitals. And then there is the bed. I know, after sitting on it for only five minutes, that I will never forget this bed. Both the pillow and the mattress are constructed from a heavy rubber, and the bed itself is nailed to the floor. A sleeping bag on the cold, dingy tile would probably be more comfortable and receptive than this bed. The room itself only adds to my depression, which I find slightly funny. I leave my dreary cell for only one of four reasons: to line up at the Medication Window, to call Sam, to attend mandatory therapy sessions or to sit with Jordy and Jax when they visit. I stare at books, sleep or gaze at the grimy ceiling, wondering how and why I've landed here. I do not look in the glassless mirror. The face there is shrouded in defeat, in depression and in the worst sin of all: survival.

* * *

The end of the CD spins me back to the present, and the dryness in my throat dwindles away as I pull into Carchie's driveway. I leave my stuff in the car, walk around to the back of the house and enter the living room through the sliding glass door. I slap my hand over my mouth so Carchie won't hear me gasp—he looks like Ashley did, like Jim does. He's asleep on the couch—the TV is on mute—and even his bare feet somehow look smaller. I stare at him for a few seconds—trying not to look at the orange plastic bucket placed on the floor next to his head—until the tears sprint down my face. I can't move and I can't stop crying. Carchie wakes up, stares at me and smiles. It takes him thirty seconds to rise from the couch and enclose me in a hug.

"I'm sorry," I say.

"For what?"

"I came here to take care of you, and I can't even keep it together for the first five minutes."

Carchie laughs. "I look like shit, I know. Sometimes it makes me cry, too. It's OK, Alex. You can do this. It's not the same—this is temporary."

I wipe my tears on his shoulder. "Hopefully." I shouldn't have said that.

Carchie nods. "Hopefully."

He squeezes me one more time and then releases me from his feeble grip. "This is life, Alex—we take turns caring for one another."

I nod. "I have presents."

"For me?"

"Yeah."

"Well, go get them." Carchie smiles and leans against the couch as I slip through the sliding glass door.

I walk outside, lean against my car and then crouch down for a minute. The street is silent—all I hear is the rustling of the trees and the sound of my own sadness scraping inside me. I slowly inhale the clean air. I stand up, wipe the remnants of tears from my face and smooth my crinkled clothes. I grab Carchie's presents and my stuff and, balancing all the bags on one arm, open the front door.

"This is a do-over!" I announce as I march down the hall. I sneak a quick intake of breath and turn into the living room. "Your favorite niece has arrived." I plop next to Carchie on the couch, delivering a kiss to his cheek in the process.

Carchie looks around the living room and even leans toward the sliding door, craning his shrunken neck to peer outside. "Where is she?" he asks, smiling.

I smack his thigh, cringing at how easy it is to feel his bone. "Now you're not getting any presents."

Carchie grabs hold of the arm of the couch, swings back and forth for a moment and then gets up. "Aw shit, no stupid T-shirts from Buttfuck, USA?"

"Where are you going?"

Carchie hesitates. "To get us a joint. You want a drink?"

"I'd love a glass of ice water."

Carchie nods. "So would I. Make us some, would you, baby?"

I know before he turns the corner I'm not going back to the city tonight.

Carchie and I smoke a joint on the deck, watching the birds skitter across the lake and listening to a Dead bootleg. He swears he's been eating well and drinking enough water, but nothing stays in his system for more than half an hour. It's been this bad before, he tells me, but not for this long. His oncologist says it's because this last treatment was the harshest. Carchie speaks to him every day, asking about the upcoming fishing trip to Lake George. Dr. Spock, as Carchie calls him (apparently his ears are slightly larger than average), isn't sure Carchie will be well enough to travel, much less fish—he has to keep food and water down for at least a day if he is to receive his doctor's blessing to join his friends for their annual fishing retreat.

"What have you been eating?" I ask.

Carchie shrugs. "The usual—bologna sandwiches, fried eggs, vanilla ice cream. Mrs. Barnes, Jake's widow from down the street, makes me meatloaf sometimes. I tried to eat a slice of pizza last week, but that didn't work out so well."

I laugh, spitting smoke into Carchie's face. "No wonder you're puking. I would puke from all that crap and I don't even have cancer."

Carchie's eyes widen. I can tell he's shocked (but thrilled) by my flippant comment. "What do you mean?"

"Your stomach is weak, Carchie. You need to eat bland, gentle foods, not bologna, for Christ's sake. I bet it's not even fresh bologna—it's Oscar Mayer in a package, isn't it?"

Carchie nods. "Been eating it half my life."

I shake my head and stand up. "What are you putting in the eggs?"

"Not much—onion, salt, a little oregano. Sometimes I have cheddar cheese and red peppers, too."

Carchie hands me the joint and I wave it away. I turn toward the door.

"Where are you going?"

"I have to call Jordy."

"To tell her I'm eating packaged bologna?"

I laugh. "No, to tell her I'm staying here until you stop puking."

Carchie's breath catches in his concave chest. He starts to say something but changes his mind. I smile and walk into the living room to use the phone.

Either Carchie's become a better liar or he actually likes the Dylan print and Brooklyn Dodgers hat. He shuffles up and down the front hallway—wearing the hat—testing wall space. I sift through the refrigerator, throwing out almost half its contents. We eat dry pasta for dinner, with Carchie complaining, "How am I supposed to eat this without butter?" Then Carchie reads the paper while I compose a detailed grocery list for tomorrow. At around ten o'clock, he heads for the stairs, toting his orange bucket.

"Good night, Alex. Thanks for dinner."

"You're welcome."

"You sure you have enough clothes? I can give you money to buy stuff in town."

"I'm fine, Carchie. I'll do laundry tomorrow and refill the fridge."

Carchie leans into the banister. "Is Jordy disappointed you won't be there?"

"A little, but she wouldn't have it any other way. You know how she feels about you."

Carchie smiles. "Big crush, I know. I thought the torch would've gone out by now."

I laugh. "Good night, Carchie," I say, almost singing the words.

" 'Night."

I wake up early, do a few loads of laundry, toast a dry bagel for Carchie and call Jordy.

"How's he doing?"

"I slept pretty hard, but I don't think he got up to puke during the night."

"That's because he has you taking care of him. How are you?"

I sigh. "Strangely enough, fine. He's healthier than Ashley was when I first moved in. I think a lot of it is him being here alone, bored and feeling sorry for himself. And eating garbage three times a day didn't help his stomach."

"It's good that you're doing this, especially now."

Neither one of us says anything for a minute—we listen to each other breathe.

"Amazing it's been two years already, isn't it?" she asks.

I can picture Jordy, her hair falling in waves down her back. I light a cigarette and hear Jordy light one, too. "How are you—nervous?"

Jordy exhales. "I've sort of arrived at this Zen state—very calm, very rational. I do miss you, though. Is it obnoxious to say I wish you could come with me?"

"No—I wish I could be there, before and after the defense. But he wants to go fishing so badly, and I'm pretty sure that a few days of my cooking and company will help him."

"I'm sure it will. I'm glad you're staying with him, Alex. I'm proud of you."

"Thanks. I'll talk to you later?"

"Yeah. I'll call you after I'm done. Send Carchie my love."

"I will. Oh, has Tucker called?"

"No."

I leave Carchie snoring in a chair on the deck, his newspapers flapping in the wind, and drive into town to the grocery store. I buy a variety of nutritious foods, trying to satiate Carchie's taste for appealing food with the need to repair his stomach. I throw in a pack of Silly Putty and a few fishing magazines to cushion the fact that I'm going to force him to ingest apple juice, Saltines and oatmeal. I load the back of the Discovery with grocery bags, return to Carchie's house—he's still sleeping—and fill his cabinets and refrigerator. I place his Yankees cap on his head to shade him from the sun, and go upstairs to call Jax.

"Hey, babycakes, where the hell are you?"

"At Carchie's."

"How is he?"

"Skinny and sick to his stomach, but all right, I think. I'm going to stay here for a while."

Jax pauses—I bet he's pacing. "How long are you going to stay?"

"I'm not sure."

"Will you be there on the twentieth?"

"Probably."

"It's sort of poetic, in an odd way. Full circle, you know."

"Yeah, I know. Hey, how was the voice-over recording?"

"Great. The people were really cool and they paid me on the spot—a big fat check that takes care of rent for a few months. I'm thinking of investing some of the money—should I call Teddy?"

"Oh my God, Jax—you know what it'll mean if we both have investments?"

He laughs. "What?"

"We're adults."

Jax and I share an affectionate silence for a few moments. He breaks it with his resonant laugh. "I can't think of anything funny to say to that."

"Me, neither. I miss you, babycakes."

"I miss you, too. We'll hang when you get home."

I stay at Carchie's for four days. We read to each other, rent movies and look at old photos. Carchie eats everything I cook for him, with a minimal amount of moaning and groaning. He throws up a few times during the first few days, but as the week progresses, he's able to keep food down for longer periods of time. By day three, he's not throwing up at all, and he's drinking six glasses of water a day. He calls Dr. Spock to report his weight gain—five pounds—and to brag about his niece, who cooks him boring but healthy meals. Dr. Spock tells him to enjoy Lake George. Carchie hugs me and disappears into the basement for half an hour. I recline on a chaise lounge on the deck—my eyelids are falling just as he reappears, holding something behind his back.

"There's no way I can thank you, of course, but here."

He hands me a dusty green champagne bottle.

"I bought it years ago for some special occasion that turned out to be not so special. Then I lost it, found it and lost it again. I just ransacked the basement looking for it. I want you to have it, to drink with Jordy."

I get up and hug Carchie, secretly smiling because he feels more substantial and more alive than when I got here. "Thank you."

"No, baby, thank you. I'll bring you something back from Lake George."

I laugh and settle into my sunny spot again. "Oh good, a stupid T-shirt from Buttfuck, USA."

Carchie cracks up and sits next to me. He pulls a pencil from behind his ear and examines his crossword puzzle, which is missing only two answers. "That's my girl."

I leave Carchie's at around two o'clock. He holds my face in his hands and says, "I couldn't love you more if you were my own daughter." He reminds me that I got through a second July twentieth. He's certain the historic day will get less painful as I move through life. We hold hands and walk toward the Discovery.

"This is the perfect car for you, Alex. I'm glad you bought it."

I nod. "Have a good time fishing, Carchie. Take it easy, and don't ruin all my work by eating crap all week."

Carchie laughs. "I'm sure the boys will make fun of me, but I promise to avoid butter and grease and all the good things in life."

"And eat salad and fruit and protein."

Carchie pushes me toward the open car door. "Now you sound like your mother. How is it that I never got married, yet I'm surrounded by women who take care of me?"

"That's what you get for being a Jewish bachelor."

Carchie laughs. "If I were in Florida, I'd be getting laid left and right."

"Yeah, but you'd be in Florida."

"Good point. Now go home and celebrate with Jordy. I'll talk to you when I get back next week."

I lean out the window to kiss him.

"Thank you, Alex."

"You're welcome, Carchie."

I stop the car at the corner, unable to turn the steering wheel. I smell Jordy. It's impossible, I know, because she hasn't even been in the Discovery yet. It takes me half a minute to realize I'm wearing her shirt. I fold my neck into the cotton blackness and inhale—Jordy's essence floats through the car. I turn right, slide in an Alanis CD and slowly roll through town. As soon as I merge onto the Thruway, I push the gas pedal and coast back to the city.

13

There are hardly any cars on the Palisades Parkway, and even the George Washington Bridge looks like a skeleton. It's as if the planets have aligned and paved a clear path for me to reach the city effortlessly. I park the car and climb the parking-garage ramp to the street. The air feels thick in my chest, and sweat springs to the surface of my skin—August in Manhattan. I turn down Broadway and walk south, wanting to smile at everyone who passes me. By the time I reach Tucker's apartment, my tank top sticks to my back and strands of hair are glued against my neck.

It occurs to me that I have no idea if Tucker is home, but I intentionally didn't call before walking over. I press his buzzer and wait a few seconds. It buzzes back.

"Hello?"

"It's Alex."

He buzzes me in.

The front door is half-open—I slide through it and walk into Tucker's living room. He's painting—his mother's easel looks as if it wants to collapse under the weight of the canvas.

Tucker glances at me and nods toward the kitchen. "Help yourself to a drink or whatever," he says.

I move to the kitchen and take a bottle of water out of the

fridge. I walk back into the living room and lean against the couch, a few feet away from Tucker.

"I'm not in love with you," I tell him.

Tucker nods. "You're in love with someone else."

"What? No, I'm not."

"Yes, you are."

"I barely know any other straight guys." I place the bottle of water in front of the photo of his mother.

Tucker shakes his head. "Forget it." He turns and looks at me for a moment, then squeezes some paint onto a palette.

"I'm sorry, Tucker."

"It's not your fault."

"I want you in my life, and I want to be a part of yours." I say this even though I know it seldom works.

Tucker continues to paint. I walk over to the front door.

"Bye."

Tucker turns around and we stare at one another across the sunny living room. I wish I could fall in love with him.

"The 'missing piece' is right in front of you."

I sigh. "It's not you, Tucker."

He sighs and shakes his head. "I didn't say it's me." He turns around and picks up a paintbrush.

"Bye," I say again. He holds up a hand. I walk out and close the door behind me.

I take a cab home, descend the ramp to the garage, unload my bags and drag it all upstairs. I'm tired, but the thought of seeing Jordy washes away my desire to nap. I enter the apartment, my heart beating at the thought of hearing Jordy yell, "Alex! You're home!" I spoke to her only briefly yesterday—she was exhilarated to have completed her dissertation defense, which she said went really well—and Jax was picking her up in a cab and taking her to dinner. I turn the key in the lock, open the door and toss my bags into the hallway. The apartment is silent, and immaculate. The cracked glass on my *New York Is Book Country* poster glares at me from across the living room, but I ignore it and rush over to the kitchen table, then the coffee table, looking for a note from Jordy, but I don't find one. I hook the handles of my overnight bag, messenger bag and shopping bags through my arms and tow them down the hall. I'm just about to start unpacking when I notice what's hanging above my bed. Jordy has covered the cracked, empty space with the Ansel Adams poster of the iceberg, the one that used to hang in the kitchen—her favorite photograph. I forget about my bags and stare at the framed photo. My legs fold under me and I sink onto the bed, Peter Gabriel's lyrics playing in my mind.

> *In your eyes*
> *The light the heat*
> *In your eyes*
> *I am complete*

The front door opens and closes. Jordy has no idea I'm home—I left no evidence in the living room and she probably assumes I'm sitting in traffic. I quietly walk down the hallway and lean against the cool, smooth wall of the threshold, watching her. My whole body is trembling. Jordy is by the window, flipping through the mail, her face tense and annoyed. The frown vanishes as her gaze falls upon a new piece of mail. She holds up the postcard from me and when she smiles, I feel weightless.

"Hi," I say, walking toward the window.

Jordy jumps for a split second. "Oh my God, Alex, hi!"

She glides across the living room to hug me. Everything about the hug is old and familiar—the scent of Jordy's hair, her arms wrapped tightly around my body, her cheek against mine—yet also new and changed.

"Why are you early?" she asks.

Somewhere I know the answer to her question, but I can think of only one thing—the only thing that matters at this moment.

"How long?" I ask.

"What?"

"How long?" Jordy stares at me—disbelief overshadows her face. She backs away and retreats to the window. "Jordy, how long have you . . . felt . . . known?"

We are at opposite ends of the living room, yet I've never felt closer to her.

Jordy looks out the window for a second, then turns to me. "A long time," she answers. We stare at each other and Jordy's eyes fill with tears. "How did you figure it out?"

I smile and shrug as Jordy crosses the living room toward me. "I saw the iceberg photograph and thought of us, and it just sort of melted into my mind, or my heart—I don't know. It just popped into place. Like the—"

" 'Missing piece.' "

" 'The missing piece.' You knew all along, didn't you?"

Jordy nods.

"You knew before Sam died, and after he died—his note. Why didn't you ever tell me?"

Jordy sits on the couch and tries to light a cigarette. She can't get the shaking lighter to the cigarette quickly enough. I sit next to her, take it and light it for her. She takes a drag and hands it to me. I pull deeply on it and exhale.

Jordy sighs. "I wanted to tell you—a thousand times—but I couldn't. You had to get here on your own."

I nod. "So you've just been waiting for me? What if I didn't realize?"

"I've been waiting—but I didn't stop living. I figured if you never realized, then it wasn't meant to be. I've been sleeping with guys every now and then, but there's always been something missing."

I nod. "I know what you mean."

Jordy starts to turn away from me. "You need to be alone—you need to think about this for more than five minutes. I can stay with—"

I grab her hand. "Stay with me." I slide my hand into hers and we sit on the couch—in silence—sharing cigarette after cigarette.

Twenty minutes later, Jordy turns to me.

"Are you sure you're ready for this?" she asks.

"Yes."

"But there's a reason it took you this long to figure it out, Alex. Obviously you weren't able to handle it."

"I am now."

"This is going to change your life, if you want it to."

I nod. "Yours, too."

Jordy reaches for a cigarette but the pack is empty. "We need—" She starts to get up but I pull her back onto the couch.

"We need more than cigarettes," I say, my hand on her shoulder.

Jordy's eyes fill with tears, though she's smiling. "You have no idea how long I've waited—"

I place my hand on the back of her neck, and she relaxes into me. "I'm sorry for taking so long."

Jordy shakes her head. "In a way it was good, because it forced me to check and double-check my feelings."

"And?"

A lone tear travels down Jordy's cheek. "I'm in love with you, Alex. I've been in love with you for a long time."

Jordy tilts her head down so I can't see her face. Without thinking about it, my left hand pulls her chin up so we're eye to eye. Our faces are so close, I can feel her jagged breathing. My right hand still rests on the nape of her neck. I pull her face toward mine until our lips—gentle, uncertain—meet. Neither of us pulls away—after a few minutes, we just sort of fall back against the couch, exhausted and invigorated.

"Do you have any plans for the next few days?" I ask.

"No, why?"

"I owe you a ride in the Discovery."

Jordy smiles. "Where are we going?"

I get up and pull her with me down the hallway. "The only place that could possibly host this party," I reply.

"Carchie's cabin," Jordy says without a tinge of surprise. "But aren't you sick of driving?"

"Carchie's cabin," I repeat.

We're both smiling as we enter our rooms to pack.

After Jordy gushes about the Discovery, we're quiet for most of the trip up to the cabin. We exchange glances and smiles but no words. I'm not scared—shaky, maybe, but not scared. Not of Jordy, anyway. This will change everything. The snapshot of my future has been irrevocably altered—I no longer see a blurry, faceless man and two children. I see Jordy. And rather than frightening me, it's reassuring. A sudden rush of respect and love for Jax overcomes me. He chose this freedom over his father's conditional love. I feel as if I am now living on the edge of a cliff, constantly wondering if I'll fall over into the abyss. At the same time, though, I feel a safety I haven't felt before. I feel OK—my skin fits. It's like I've made a decision without having made a decision at all. Images of my parents and Teddy blink in and out of my mind, but for the first time in my life, I am able to shut these thoughts off—to push my family's opinion of my life away, at least for now.

I want to be angry at Sam but at the same time, I know he couldn't possibly have told me. Not only did I need to arrive at this place on my own, but I probably wouldn't have believed him, anyway. I almost laugh out loud, partly from embarrassment, when I remember Tucker's words from this afternoon: "You're in love with someone else." Even he knew. No wonder I couldn't force myself to fall in love with him. As I pull off at Carchie's exit, I realize this all-consuming fear I've been fighting for so many years isn't just a fear of commitment, a fear of opening myself up or getting hurt or getting lost. It's a fear of living my life without Jordy. Not just having Jordy around— somewhere near me—but having Jordy by my side. That's what's always felt comfortable, felt right. In my mind, I turn back time, to the way Jordy has looked at me for the past few years—those intense looks, the stares I interpreted as a sadness of some sort. The haze has cleared, and I realize it wasn't sadness—it was longing. *Jordy is the missing piece.*

We pull into Carchie's driveway around seven o'clock. I turn off the ignition, but neither of us moves.

"Alex?"

I turn to look at her. "Yeah?"

"I'm not sure I'll know what to do. I mean, I've thought about this a hundred times, but in reality, I'm not—"

"Let's just go inside. I haven't eaten since this morning. Let's just do what we'd normally do"

Jordy nods and smiles. We get out of the car and walk around the back to the sliding glass door. It's unlocked—as it always is—and I can tell by the dent, or lack of, in the couch that Carchie has been gone for hours. I wonder if he knows about Jordy and me.

We have a pack of cigarettes and a lot of dope. We're sitting on the deck, a roof of stars over our heads. We both changed into sweats before the sun made its grand finale, knowing this familiar chill would enter the air as soon as the orange fire exited the sky. The remains of a salad and chicken parm are on the table, but we've abandoned dinner and are each stretched across a chaise lounge. The Merlot is floating through my body—the stars are a bit too bright—and tucked within an old red sweatshirt, staring at the sky and listening to Jordy relay her dissertation defense, I am as warm as I have ever been.

Jordy and I have now been together—alone—for six hours, and talked about everything except the one thing we really need to discuss. Most of the reason we're chatting about everything else is because we haven't seen each other or talked for more than ten minutes in over two weeks. But it's more than that. We're both chain-smoking—the green ceramic ashtray has already been dumped twice—and Jordy is twirling her streak of blue hair around and around her right index finger. All our supplies are within reach, clustered on a small, white, square table—cigarettes, a lighter, a half-smoked joint and a box of white Tic Tacs. I'm listening to Jordy talk, but at the same time, a single question echoes through my mind: *What happens next?* I have found the "missing piece" Sam wanted me to find, and there is not a doubt in my mind that I am in love with Jordy. Now, I want the edginess to go away so we can ride this wave and fully enjoy it.

"Let's go inside," I say, interrupting her.

"OK."

Jordy collects our cluster while I carry the dirty dishes into the kitchen. She sifts through her CD case, pulls out a CD and walks upstairs without saying a word. I smile, eased by a current of confidence.

Jordy and I meet in the bathroom. We go about our usual routine as if this is any other night. As we're brushing our teeth, Jordy says, "Jax knows."

I spit a mouthful of toothpaste into the sink, look at Jordy through the mirror and ask, "You guys have talked about this?"

Jordy spits, looks up and answers, "No."

"So how do you know he knows?"

"I just know."

I laugh. "You haven't even kissed a girl yet and already you have gaydar."

Jordy cracks up, rinses off her toothbrush and dries her mouth on a red hand towel. "For your information, I kissed Danielle Palomino freshman year of college."

I replace my toothbrush in its holder, wipe my mouth on the back of the towel and lean against the sink. "You're shitting me."

Jordy shakes her head. "I shit you not."

"Why didn't you ever tell me?"

Jordy shrugs. "To tell you the truth, I have no idea." She turns around and walks into the hall. I follow her.

"I had sex with Monica Fitzgerald sophomore year of college." I'm telling her to come clean, but also because a part of me senses that Jordy needs to know I've been with a woman. She needs to turn this over to me, and I have to accept the responsibility.

Jordy stops walking but doesn't turn to face me. "And you never told me?"

"It was a one-time thing, and it totally confused me until I eventually buried it and—" Jordy turns around and looks at me. "No, I never told you," I admit.

Jordy smiles, I smile and we both laugh. I turn off the hall light and Jordy follows me into the bedroom. I light four candles while Jordy puts a CD in the small silver stereo. A lush, velvety voice I've never heard slinks into the room. Jordy sits on the end of the bed. I peel my socks off, pull the comforter back and slide between the cool sheets and the gray comforter. Jordy does the same.

My mind wants to ask Jordy about the music, but my body doesn't want my mind interfering with words. While I'm battling these disparate urges, Jordy rolls over and faces me. Her hair, now in a ponytail, rests on her shoulder, which peeks out from beneath the comforter. It's cool in the room—the windows are wide open, welcoming the Catskill breeze into the room. Jordy takes deep breaths and closes her eyes for seconds at a time.

"Do you think Jax will be all right when his father dies?" she asks, her eyes open again.

"At first he'll fall apart, and then he'll be all right."

We're quiet for a few minutes. The wind and the music are the only sounds in the room.

"This is weird," Jordy says.

I inch over to her—our breath gets tangled up. "Are you sure about this?"

Jordy nods. "Yes. I'm just—"

"There's no reason to be nervous." I take her hand and string her fingers through mine.

"I know, but I am, anyway."

I squeeze her hand, smile and stare at the ceiling. Silence curls through the bed, and I close my eyes.

Jordy releases my hand. "Alex?"

"Yeah?"

"Kiss me."

I open my eyes. I take a deep breath, prop myself up on my elbows and, as if there's a magnetic pull, my lips find hers. The apprehension in my body vanishes as our lips open. Jordy's body trembles as I touch her face, her shoulders, her arms. My heart relaxes as I feel everything I did not feel with Tucker, feel everything that has been missing with every guy I have ever slept with. Jordy and I kiss exactly the same way—the sensation of her tongue on mine puts my mind, and my body, completely at ease. We do nothing but kiss for a while, until I'm sure Jordy's nervousness dissipates. I pull away for a second and look at her.

"Wow," Jordy says, smiling. "Nobody's ever kissed me like that."

I shrug and smirk. Jordy laughs and pulls me into her. She wraps her arms around my neck and we kiss again. I undress her, and then she watches as I pull off my own clothes. I don't really know what I'm doing, but it feels like I do. Jordy follows my lead, and I feel a jolt when our bare skin touches. Remarkably, it doesn't feel at all strange to explore Jordy's naked body. In fact, it feels right—totally and completely right.

I've never understood why people make love with their eyes open, until now. It feels as if my body has finally awakened. I cannot stop looking at Jordy. I don't ever want to stop looking at Jordy. There is so much to see, and it feels so good to finally *see* her.

I've never truly enjoyed spooning with anyone—I just never felt comfortable in my nakedness or the other person's nearness—but now I am spooned around Jordy, my right hand entwined in her left hand, and it seems as if the earth has stopped spinning on its axis. We are both naked, covered by a pale purple sheet, and it feels as if we are enmeshed on a silky, secret cloud. Softness is everywhere.

I had assumed Jordy was asleep, but she suddenly starts to hum, and then she sings, in an airy, tranquil voice: "I feel so light, this is all I want to feel tonight, I feel so light, tonight and the rest of my life." When Jordy exhales, her body curves into mine.

"What's that?" I ask.

"Hmm?" Jordy answers. I can't see her face but I bet her eyes are closed.

"The song, those lyrics. Is it from the CD you put on earlier?"

"Yes. It's called 'Tonight and the Rest of My Life.' I'll play the song again for you later—it's really beautiful."

"Those lyrics are so . . ." I drift off as I stare at Jordy's shoulder for a moment, searching. "Perfect," I finally say. Jordy squeezes my hand and we fall asleep.

During the night, we take turns waking each other up to have sex. Then we fall asleep for about an hour, and the sequence begins again. By the time the sun invades our quilted cocoon, we're both grinning like idiots, and we immediately start kissing. I've never kissed anyone in the morning without first sneaking out of bed to brush my teeth. Jordy has one hand in my disheveled hair and one hand on my back; my hands frame her face while we kiss. My cell phone rings.

"C'mon, let it ring," Jordy says.

I unravel the sheet and walk naked across the cool hardwood floor. "No one knows where I am—I should get it."

I kneel on the floor and pull the phone out of my messenger bag. As soon as I see the display, I know what's happened.

"Hi, Mom."

"Jim is dead."

I don't breathe.

"Alex?"

"I'm here."

"Ellen is on the phone with Jax right now. I expect he'll be calling you any minute. Where are you?"

I look up at Jordy. She's propped on a pillow, watching me. "I'm at Carchie's cabin with Jordy."

"I thought you were going back to the city when he went fishing."

"I did. And then I—Mom, is this important right now?" My skin is flushed and itchy.

"No. What's the plan?"

My gaze falls from Jordy to the open window. I can't remember the last time my mother asked me what the plan is.

"We'll drive into the city, pick up Jax and bring him to Scarsdale. We'll stay with him, and you and Dad and Ellen, until all the arrangements are made. Then we'll go back to the city, sleep there and drive out for the wake. Jax can stay with me or Ellen or wherever he wants. Call Teddy and tell her to clear her afternoons for the rest of the week. Have Dad order two limos for the funeral. Am I forgetting anything?"

My mom is crying. "No, you're not forgetting anything. Thank you for—"

The phone beeps. "Mom, Jax is calling. Let me go."

My mother inhales, trying to control her tears. "Call me when you leave the city."

"I will. I love you." I don't wait for her to answer—I click over to Jax. "Hi, babycakes."

"He's dead."

My eyes fill. Jordy notices, gets out of bed and wraps the purple sheet around me. She puts on a T-shirt and sits next to me.

"I know."

"My mother thinks he died around seven a.m. He had been in the hospital until the other day."

"He died at home, Jax. That's good."

Jax takes a deep breath. "Yeah, I know."

I hear him light a cigarette.

"Where are you?"

"I'm at Carchie's cabin, with Jordy. We'll pick you up in about two and a half hours."

"OK. Thanks."

"I'm going to help you through this, Jax. I promise."

He breathes deeply again. "I know."

"I'll see you soon, babycakes."

Jordy packs our stuff while I call Mrs. Barnes to find out where Carchie and the boys stay in Lake George. I leave him a message about Jim, take a quick shower and call Teddy.

"Hi," she says.

"Hi." I try to remember when we last spoke, but I can't. It doesn't matter.

"You're taking Jax to Scarsdale, right?"

"Yeah. I don't want to sleep at Mom and Dad's house, but I'll drive out every day to be with him."

"I'll go with you."

"You're going to take three full days off from work?"

Teddy sighs. "Yes. It's Jax."

"We have to watch Mom—this is going to bring her back to Ashley."

Teddy sniffs, then blows her nose. "It's going to bring us all back to Ashley. We'll have to look out for each other. You get my back, and I'll get yours."

I laugh at Teddy's rare colloquialism. She laughs, too.

"Max and I are leaving in a few minutes. I'll meet you in Scarsdale."

"See you later."

"Alex?"

"Yeah?"

"Drive carefully."

"You, too."

I hang up the phone, wipe the tears from my cheeks and walk downstairs. Jordy is waiting in the living room.

"I want to come with you and Jax to Scarsdale," she tells me.

"You don't have to come today—you can go tomorrow."

"I know. I want to."

"Jax will appreciate that," I say.

I smile, pick up my bags and retrieve the car keys from the cluttered coffee table.

Jordy brushes the hair off my face and kisses me softly on the lips. "I want to support Jax, but let's not lose what happened last night."

My arms go limp and I burst into tears. I sit on the floor, weeping.

"Jesus, Alex, I'm sorry. I didn't mean—of course Jax comes first right now. I just meant we—"

I shake my head but cannot articulate my thoughts.

"Don't cry, Alex. We're going to be crying for the rest of the week."

I use the bottom of my T-shirt to dry my face. "I'm not crying for Jax, or for Jim. I'm crying for us—for last night."

Jordy sits next to me, totally confused.

"Forget it. I can't explain," I tell her. I start to stand up, but Jordy yanks me back to the terracotta tile.

"You mean happy tears?" she asks.

I cry and nod at Jordy. She laughs.

"Oh, all right, you can cry happy tears. Happy tears are good."

I laugh, she laughs, and soon we are breathing easily, in synch. After a few minutes, we stand up. I kiss Jordy and my eyes fill with tears again.

"Shit, here come the waterworks," Jordy says.

I'm laughing and crying at the same time. "'Laughter through tears is my favorite emotion,'" I tell her.

Jordy's eyes widen for a split second. She smiles and hugs me. "*Steel Magnolias,*" she whispers into my hair.

We drive onto the Thruway just before ten o'clock. My body is tired—exhausted—but my mind has never been more awake.

14

Jax calls as we're crossing the George Washington Bridge. Jordy answers, since I'm not wearing my earpiece.

"I'm so sorry about your dad," she tells him. She's quiet for a few minutes, nodding and looking at me. She covers the mouthpiece and hands me the phone.

"He's hysterical. He doesn't have anything to wear to the funeral. He's practically hyperventilating."

I take the phone, hook up the earpiece and switch lanes so I can merge onto the Harlem River Drive.

"Hi."

"I don't have a tie." Jax is crying as hard as I've ever heard him cry.

"What do you mean? You wear a tie at work."

"I wear a silver tie for work. *All* my ties are silver, Alex. I can't wear a silver tie to my father's funeral." He sounds like a boy, gasping for breath.

"What about the tie you wore to Teddy's wedding?"

"That was a bow tie!" he cries. "I don't own a single conservative tie. What kind of a man doesn't own a simple, conventional tie?"

A gay man, I want to reply, but I know Jax is well aware of the answer.

"I can stop at Bloomingdale's and buy you a tie, babycakes."
He's so upset I'd rip a tie off someone's neck at this point.

"There's no time! My mother is probably weeping on the
kitchen floor. I have to get to Scarsdale."

"Jax, slow down—take a few breaths. My mother is with your
mother, so don't worry about that. I'll have a plain, black tie
when I pick you up, I promise. Just pack a bag, drink some
water and I'll be there as soon as I can."

Jax inhales and exhales directly into the phone. "OK,
thanks."

I hang up and look at Jordy. "I'm going to drop you off at the
apartment. Fill up my messenger bag with anything you think
we, or Jax, might need. I'll pick you up and then we'll pick up
Jax."

"Where are you going?" Jordy asks.

I steer the Discovery onto the FDR, which is—for once—not
jammed with bumper-to-bumper traffic. "I have to pick up a
conservative tie for Jax."

Jordy looks out the window, drawing an invisible map in her
head. She looks at me—her eyebrows crinkled in thought—
and tries to picture a store that does not exist.

"Tucker's apartment. I'm going to borrow a tie from
Tucker," I explain.

Jordy nods and then smiles. "Jax is lucky to have you as a
friend."

I lower my window and light a cigarette. "I'm lucky to have
him. I'm lucky to have both of you, actually."

Jordy takes a drag off my cigarette. "We're all lucky we found
each other." She hands me the cigarette. "Do you want me to
come with you?"

I shake my head. I have to break the silence by myself. "No."

Jordy nods and touches my hand.

It's noon when I drop Jordy off at the apartment. I call
Tucker as I drive down Broadway. When he answers his phone
and realizes it's me, his greeting sounds more like a question.

"I need a huge favor. I know I'm probably the last person you want to help, but it's not for me—it's for Jax."

Tucker doesn't say anything. I envision him—standing in front of his mother's easel, paintbrush in hand—nodding and waiting for me to continue.

"Jax's father died this morning, and he doesn't own a conservative tie. Do you have a simple black tie he can borrow for the funeral?"

Tucker sighs. I know that even if his eyes flame with anger toward me, he'll still want to help Jax.

"Sure, I have a ton of black ties. You want me to drop one off at your place?"

"Actually, I'm in the car right now. I was hoping I could swing by and pick it up."

"No problem. I'm here. I'll have it waiting for you."

"Thanks. I'll be there in a few minutes."

Tucker opens the door, and I have to fight the impulse to hug him. He smiles sadly and I realize how badly I want to remain friends with him.

"Hi," he says.

I smile. "Hey."

"Please give Jax my condolences."

I nod. We stand in the doorway for a minute, the gash in our relationship obvious to both of us.

"Come in," Tucker says.

I cross the threshold, my eyes on him.

"You all right?" he asks.

I nod and then shake my head.

"Come here, Alex." Tucker wraps his arms around me and we hug. It was this—the safety of his embrace—which I mistook for romantic love.

I don't want to tell Tucker too much—not yet, anyway—but he deserves some sort of explanation.

"You were right," I tell him.

He pulls away a bit but his face stays close to mine. "About what?"

I take a breath. His eyes are so generous. "I am in love with someone else."

Tucker's face knits together in surprise for a moment, but then he smiles. He nods and walks over to the couch. I follow. He holds up three black ties—all traditional and conservative and perfect.

"What's the difference between them?" I ask.

Tucker smirks and flips the ties over so I can see the labels. "Nothing, except the brand names."

I laugh. "What are my options?"

"Gucci, Armani or Versace. I think Jax will like the Versace the best."

I wait for the lump in my throat to dissolve and then say, "I think you're right."

"I'll get you a tie box so it doesn't get wrinkled."

Tucker strides across the living room to his bedroom. I move toward the window to see Tucker's new painting but stop short when I see his mother's easel—folded up—leaning against the wall. It's been replaced by the sturdy, functional easel his father gave him.

"Here you go," Tucker says as he re-enters the living room.

I turn around and point to his mother's rickety, wooden easel.

"Yeah, a piece I really liked was ruined when it fell off. I figured it was time," he says quietly.

I nod and smile. "You should tell your dad you're using the easel he gave you."

"I did. He loves your books, by the way. So does the agent he sent them to. Someone should be calling you soon about representation."

"Really? That's amazing!" I store the information, knowing this week will not be about celebrations. I walk up to him and put my hand out. He places the tie box in it. "Thank you."

"You're welcome."

"Not just for the tie, Tucker."

He nods. "I know."

We hug and he kisses my cheek.

"Will you call me with the funeral information?"

"Sure."

We walk to the front door together. Tucker opens it and rests his hand on my lower back for a moment. "Keep in touch."

"You, too," I reply.

I run down the stairs, jump into my car and speed back to the apartment.

Later, Jordy gets in the car and flips through my CD case while we sit in traffic.

"What should I put on?" she asks.

"Something neutral. Something none of us love, so—"

"We won't associate it with Jim's death for the rest of our lives." She flicks through the CD case a few times and then stores it under the seat. "There's nothing bland in here. Radio?"

I nod. Jordy chooses a station and lowers the volume. The traffic clears and I pull up to Jax's apartment. He's waiting for us, leaning against the brick wall of his building, a cigarette in his mouth. He's wearing a white button-down shirt, black pants and black shoes. His hair is damp and his face is still slightly red from shaving. I pull up in front of a fire hydrant, flick on the hazard lights and get out of the car. Jax is in my arms before I reach the sidewalk.

"I am so sorry, babycakes," I tell him.

Jax gives me a squeeze and pulls away. "I'm sorry you have to deal with this," he replies.

"What do you mean?" I see Jordy exit the car, waiting for us.

"This is going to be a fucking nightmare, Alex."

"Maybe not."

Jax picks up his bag and kisses me. "Oh, it will be. And I hate that you have to see it. I hate that I have to see it. But I've already called my shrink—she's on standby."

"At least you're prepared."

Jax steps back for a moment and looks me up and down. "What's up?"

"What do you mean?"

"What's changed? You look different," he says.

"I don't know what you're talking—" Oh, yes I do. He can't *see* it, can he?

"C'mon, let's go."

Jax shifts his bag from one shoulder to the other. "There is definitely something different about you," he says, pointing.

I can't help but smile. "Later, Jax. Get in the car, or else it'll take us three hours to get there."

Jax throws his bag in the back of the Discovery and curls himself into Jordy's arms. They argue for a minute about the front seat—both want the other to sit in it—until Jordy wins. Jax gets in next to me and Jordy sits in the back. I head across town to the West Side Highway. By the time we hit the Henry Hudson Parkway, an odd stillness has entered the car. The three of us are used to constant chatter and endless taunts— today we're placid and restrained. Jordy is stretched across the backseat—her head leans on my messenger bag and her eyes relax on my profile. Jax sits upright, his fingers wrapped around a lighter, his jaw tight. Some classic rock song plays on the radio, but the volume is so low I can't identify it.

After we cross the Hudson, Jax suddenly says, "The wake starts tomorrow. The funeral is on Saturday—final viewing at ten, burial at eleven. Your father reserved two limos, Teddy ordered flowers and food, and your mother is helping my mother pick out a suit for him to wear."

"Nobody can call my family inefficient," I reply.

Jax nods. "There's nothing left for me to do."

"You have to figure out how you're going to make peace with your father before they lower him into the ground," Jordy says.

I smile at Jordy through the rearview mirror. Jax relaxes his posture and lights a cigarette.

Ellen's living room is cluttered with sadness by the time we arrive. I sit between Jax and Jordy on the love seat, my mother and father share the couch and Ellen slumps in a wooden rocking chair. I know as soon as I see Teddy that she's in the zone— she wants to confirm all the wake and funeral plans; she wants to make sure there will be enough food; she wants to make Ellen feel better. I'm disappointed but not surprised. Sam told me a long time ago the worst part of therapy is that, despite my own contemplation and growth, the chances of other people ever changing are slim to none, so resolving certain issues with them would be nearly impossible. The look in Teddy's eyes proves Sam's point. Then again, Ellen, and even my mother, seem broken, so it's good Teddy is here to take care of all the arrangements. She motions to me, so I cross the living room and follow her through the kitchen and out the back door to the patio. Jax's tree house beckons to me—I know it's a safe haven and Teddy won't be comfortable up there—but I ignore it. Teddy takes my hand and gently pulls me onto the soft grass with her.

"Are you OK?" she asks. "I mean, about Jim."

I nod. "My heart hurts when I think about Jax, and even Mom, but truthfully?" I lean in and whisper, "Jim was a bigoted homophobe. I may have known him all my life, but I can't say I'm sad he's dead. If Ashley doesn't get to live in this world, there's no way Jim should get to, either."

Teddy nods, then stares at our house. "We need to talk about what you said, about my wedding."

"Teddy, I've tried really hard to get past it, but I just can't. I can't forgive you for marrying Max without Ashley." There, I said it.

Teddy turns and looks at me. Her eyes are swimming in sadness and disappointment. "Do you really think so little of me?"

"I didn't, ever! But then you didn't change your wedding date, even though he had pneumonia again. You went ahead with all your plans while our brother was dying!" My chest heaves and I grab handfuls of grass to steady myself.

"Alexandra."

I'm on my hands and knees, my neck slack, my shoulders shaking. My tears feel like pebbles—they roll down my cheeks and land in the grass.

"Alexandra," Teddy says again. Her voice quivers just slightly. She grabs my shoulders and I force myself to look at her. "Have you been angry about this since Ashley died? Since my wedding?"

I nod and crumple onto my heels. Teddy sucks in some air and stands up. She pulls her hair away from her face, then she looks at her hands for a minute and says, "You were close with him for like five minutes—he and I were close our entire lives! Do you really believe I'd want to leave him all alone on my wedding day?"

"I couldn't believe it, but you did!" I yell.

"Alex, why didn't you ask me about it? We shared everything—why didn't you say something?" She sits down, hard, next to me.

"What was I going to say, Teddy? 'How can you be so callous?' 'Cancel your wedding until Ashley recovers, or dies?' I thought he was the whole reason you got wedding insurance!"

"He was!" she yells. I automatically cower, and she lowers her voice. "Alex, Ashley *wanted* me to get married on that day! He wouldn't let me cancel, or postpone. He begged me not to change any plans. I wouldn't listen at first, but he kept insisting. We talked about it all the time, Alex. Finally, he made me promise—he said he'd never forgive me if I didn't marry Max on that day."

I shake my head, thoroughly confused. If Ashley was fine with Teddy getting married without him—if he's the one who told her to do it—why have I been angry all these years? Of course Ashley and Teddy would discuss something as significant as his presence at her wedding, and of course Teddy would do as Ashley asked—he was her big brother! They'd had a stable, dependable relationship all their lives. Actually, Teddy had had it all—and then Ashley died, I almost died and her family splintered apart into sharp, dangerous slivers.

I touch Teddy's knee—there is frustration imprinted all over her face. "I'm sorry, Teddy. I know it sounds trite, but I thought you had wronged Ashley, and I turned it into—"

"Let's forget about it, OK? Let's put our relationship back together, starting now. Can we try to do that?"

I nod and sniffle. Teddy wipes the tears off my cheeks. "I miss you," I squeak, fresh tears falling. Teddy pulls me to my feet, and we hug, tighter than we have in a long time. She takes my hand and smiles what used to be our secret smile, the one that meant we were allies, secret-sharers. I don't know what it means anymore, but I do know she's trying, and I have to find a way to help her understand me. I must remember that it is love that drives Teddy to protect me. I look in her eyes and time disappears—we're kids again, and she is my hero, my role model and my all-knowing older sister. Teddy blinks, and she is now the fallible, hard-working older sibling who can't quite grasp the person her little sister has become. These two images of Teddy are so very different, but she is still Teddy.

When we re-enter the living room, everyone stares up at us—no one is talking; no one is doing anything. Jordy stares at me, her eyes a question, and I answer with a nod and a smile.

"Who wants a drink?" Teddy asks the quiet mourners.

Everyone except Max answers, "Me."

Teddy gestures for me to help her in the kitchen. We don't bother asking who wants what—we're family, and we know the others' drink preferences by heart.

Teddy gathers the bottles of alcohol while I line up the glasses. She adds ice while I cut slivers of lemons and limes. She pours the liquor and I add the mixers. We're done in five minutes. As we line up the glasses on a black slate tray, Teddy says, "I've started seeing a therapist."

I keep my eyes on the drinks. "Really?"

"Really."

"How'd you—"

"A colleague recommended her. I didn't like her at first, but I think it was because I expected her to ask me questions, and she didn't."

"They don't start asking questions until much later," I tell her. I should be reveling in the fact that I know more about this than Teddy.

"Yeah, that's what she told me. Anyway, she's very pleasant, very professional. She might even be cool, if I met her in another context."

"How many sessions have you had?"

"Three. The first one was a double."

Teddy in a double therapy session? "Wow." I can't think of anything else to say.

"I thought you'd want to know."

I slide the tray off the counter and into my arms. Teddy looks at me and I nod. "Thanks for telling me."

Teddy pushes the stray hairs away from my face. "Alex, I'm—"

"I know."

We share a secret smile, and this time I know exactly what it means. Teddy grabs some napkins and follows me into the living room.

Carchie arrives an hour later. He smells of fir trees and campfires, and I know it must have hurt for him to leave the fishing trip, since he earned it with so much physical pain. He hated Jim, but he loves Jax, and it is for Jax that he left his friends in Lake George. Carchie makes his way around the living room, saving Jax and me for last. He gives me a quick hug and kiss, and then encircles Jax in a long hug.

"How you doing, Tinkerbell?"

Jax shrugs. "All right, I guess."

Carchie reaches into his shirt pocket and slyly hands Jax a thick joint. "What doesn't kill us makes us want to smoke pot," he whispers.

Jax slides the joint into his pocket. "Thanks, Carchie."

"Light that up next week, when you're feeling better. It'll remind you how to laugh," Carchie whispers and pats Jax's shoulder.

The doorbell rings. "Thanks for coming, Carchie. I'm sorry you had to cut your fishing trip short."

"Eh, it was just a bunch of men sitting around shirtless in a boat. You would've liked it, Tinkerbell."

Jax smiles and crosses the living room to greet the incoming guests.

This is my second non-Jewish funeral in six months, and—I have to say—at least the Jews get the dead-body part over with as quickly as possible. You're in the ground within a day or two, and we don't feel the need to sit around drinking any and all liquor in sight while we wait for the burial, surrounded by bright, pungent floral arrangements. On the other hand, we do mourn for a week after the funeral, and it's impossible to check your teeth for poppy seeds because every mirror in the house is covered with a black shroud. The most striking similarity between the two is, of course, the food. Food, and the consumption of it, is the first thing to go when I'm depressed, or even the least bit sad, so I just can't understand the abundance of platters that arrive on an hourly basis. While it's refreshing not to share a living room with whitefish salad or gefilte fish (neither of which are appetizing when fresh, never mind after a few hours), the scents of the sandwiches and mounds of cheese and piles of cookies don't meld together very well. By the afternoon session of day two of the wake, Teddy and I have come up with a nearly flawless plan to air out Ellen's living room. Teddy distracts a certain population of the living room while I open the windows and lower the shades, so by the time the old ladies in attendance start complaining about how cold they are, most of the stench has evaporated and we can actually breathe without wanting to throw up. Once Ellen (who, understandably, wants all the mourners to be comfortable) closes the windows, it's my turn to distract the shrinking elderly women while Teddy takes care of the windows. Jordy watches from across the room, trying not to laugh.

"You guys are great together," she says after I've returned from yet another conspiratorial window-opening session.

"What do you mean?"

"It's like you both know what the other is going to do before she does it. It's kind of cool to watch. I bet you guys were hilarious when you were toddlers."

I nod and smile, watching Teddy tend to Ellen. Teddy has run this entire show, except when Jax has the energy—or the desire—to take care of things. He either eats and drinks and smokes everything in sight while staring at family photos on the wall, or he's dizzy from dehydration and nicotine withdrawal and hiding out in the tree house. He's been quiet on the car rides back and forth from the city and Scarsdale. Neither Jordy nor I can get him to tell us where he is, what he's thinking.

My parents have been spending almost every minute with Ellen, which kind of pisses me off because neither Ellen nor Jim supported them in a similar manner when Ashley died. Well, I guess Ellen did, but it always seemed to me that she was checking her watch, wondering when she could leave. I suppose that was Jim's influence, but what kind of a woman cheats her best friend of shoulder support during a time like that? It's a fucking miracle these two dysfunctional people gave birth to a beautiful boy like Jax.

"Maybe we should tell Jax about us," Jordy whispers in my ear.

"What? Why?" I pull her into the hallway.

"It might cheer him up. He hasn't smiled in days."

"Jordy, his father died. It's not exactly a smiley time in his life." I pull her into the guest room. "And considering the guest of honor at the funeral, I don't think now is the best time to celebrate a gay coupling."

"It's the perfect time! Jax will love it—it's a big 'fuck you' to his homophobic father."

I want a cigarette, right now. "OK, well, that may be true, but how 'bout this—I'm not ready to tell anyone yet."

Jordy's eyes widen. "Not even Jax?"

I've never heard those words before, and they sting. "I'm just not—"

"You regret it, don't you?"

I take her hand. "God, no, not at all. I just, I can't say it out loud yet."

Jordy nods and is about to say something but my mother stumbles into the room.

"Oh, here you are, Alex. I need you in the kitchen, if you don't mind."

She turns and fixes her hair in the mirror. Jordy mouths, "Is she drunk?" I nod.

"Actually, Mom, I'm in the middle of a conversation with Jordy. Can it wait?"

My mother turns around. Sorrow seeps out of her eyes—all she sees is Ashley's funeral. No wonder she's drunk—she doesn't have the vocabulary to deal with this any other way.

"Please, you and Jordy are always in the middle of a conversation. I just need you for a few minutes. You have forever to talk to Jordy."

Jordy smiles—the sweetest, sexiest smile I have ever seen. I want to kiss her, but my mother is waiting for me, leaning against the door.

"I'm right behind you, Mom."

I follow her through the living room, which is even more crowded now, and into the kitchen. The Bowling Wives are huddled around the fridge, trying to figure out how to squeeze in yet another elongated sandwich platter. My mother rolls her eyes. She motions for me to join her outside and makes sure I've securely shut the door behind me. When she turns around to face me, there's a look in her eyes I have never seen before. It takes a few seconds, but then it registers—it's desperation.

"I need a cigarette, sweetie."

If there were a chair nearby, I would fall into it. "You haven't smoked in twenty-five years."

"I know, but I really want a cigarette. Can I have one?"

Jesus, where is Teddy when I need her? I pull a pack out of my back pocket and hand her one. "I guess so."

She waves at me to hurry up and light it. The clouds stop moving as I light the cigarette hanging out of my mother's mouth. She takes a deep drag, exhales and grabs onto me.

"Whoa," she mutters.

"Light-headed?" I don't know whether to laugh or cry.

She nods and takes another drag.

"Mom." She's staring at the sky. "Mom?"

"What, honey?"

"Talk to me."

She shakes her head.

"Mom, talk to me, for Christ's sake. I just gave you a cigarette! We're way beyond our usual mother-daughter parameters here."

She doesn't move.

"Mom!"

She wheels around to face me, her eyes flooded with fear.

"What?"

"Talk to me!" I sound like a petulant child.

"Why? You never talk to me. You never tell me one goddamn thing you're thinking, so why should I tell you?" she hisses. "You don't trust me—why should I trust you?"

Screw the chair—I sit on the grass. Wherever Sam is, he must be loving this confrontation.

"It has nothing to do with trust. Of course I trust you—you're my mother."

"So why don't you ever tell me anything? Why didn't you tell me how depressed you were? Why didn't you tell me the reason you tried to kill yourself? Why didn't—"

"OK, OK, I get the point."

I take a deep breath, then light my own cigarette. My mother spreads her cardigan beneath her and sits across from me on the soft grass. Tears fall from her eyes but she's composed now, steady.

"I didn't tell you because you never asked."

My mother shakes her head. She rolls the cigarette between her thumb and forefinger, the way they do it in 1950s movies. "I didn't ask because I was waiting for you to tell me. I didn't want to push."

"I was in a fucking psych ward, and then an institution!"

"I know. I didn't want to disappoint you, Alex. I was so scared of saying or doing something wrong that I didn't say or do anything at all. I was terrified of losing you. I knew I wouldn't survive if I lost another—"

The composure melts away and she hunches over, her shoulders trembling with the force of her tears. I take her cigarette, wipe it out on the grass and hold her hand while she cries for the son she lost and the daughter she almost lost.

After a few minutes, she looks up at me and says, "I miss him, Alex. I miss my Ashley."

"That's the first time I've heard you say that."

"Really? I think it every day, as soon as I wake up."

"I picture him in my mind every night before I fall asleep. It's probably why I have trouble sleeping, but I do it anyway."

My mother looks at my hand, then at me. "I wish I'd known that all these years."

"We need to start saying things out loud, Mom."

She pulls a tissue out of her front pocket and wipes her eyes. "I know, baby, I know."

We sit outside, talking about Ashley, for half an hour. Jax joins us for the last few minutes, and he breaks down when my mother hugs him. The three of us re-enter the house together.

A while later, I rescue Carchie from a gaggle of geriatric aunts, and we seek refuge in a corner of the living room.

"You feeling all right, Alex?"

I nod and shrug.

"Listen, I hate to do this to you, but you're the only one I can trust. I want you to promise me—"

I sigh. "You better specify your directions on paper, in case I get stonewalled."

Carchie smiles. "How'd you know what I was going to say?"

"I know you, Carchie. You sure you want to leave me in charge?"

"Absolutely."

"You want a party, don't you?"

Carchie laughs quietly. "Not quite, but I sure as hell don't want a room full of people pigging out and talking about everything but me. Once I'm in the family plot, I'd like one day of shiva, but only for your family and my buddies. No lox, no whitefish, nothing that makes a room smell like a dirty armpit. My pals are salt of the earth—feed them roast beef, turkey, that kind of stuff. And none of these useless cookie trays—get a Carvel ice cream cake, the kind with the little chocolate crunchies. Load up the stereo and don't let the music stop. I've already added it to my will, but I need you to make it happen. Can you do that for me, Alex?"

I sniffle, shake a tear free and nod. "I can definitely do that for you, Carchie."

He brings my hand to his lips and kisses it. "You are my favorite person on this earth, you know that, right?"

I squeeze his hand.

It's raining the next morning. I can't help but remember the day we buried Ashley; it was sunny and slightly breezy, a perfect day. Jordy and I spend ten minutes gathering every umbrella in the apartment, even though I'm sure Teddy will show up with five huge black umbrellas. I'm wearing what used to be my interview outfit—a black DKNY suit I bought off the rack at Marshall's after college graduation. Jordy wears a black pantsuit and the diamond studs her grandmother left her. We pick Jax up at eight o'clock in the morning. He's wearing a black suit with Tucker's Versace tie. His hair is tied back and he's clean-shaven—he hasn't had facial hair all week. We drive to Scarsdale without the radio, without conversation. We get lost in the town we grew up in because neither Jax nor I have ever been to the funeral home. We have to park far away from the building because we're so late.

As I reach behind me to dole out umbrellas, Jax says, "I can't go in yet. Can we sit here for a while?"

I nod. "How long do you need, babycakes?"

"A cigarette."

I lower the windows a few inches and we all light up. Jordy's hand brushes my shoulder as she reaches over the front seat to light my smoke. I get the chills.

"Do you guys believe in hell?" Jax asks.

"Jews don't believe in hell," I reply.

"I know Jews don't believe in hell—but do *you* believe in hell?"

Jordy leans between the front seats. "To believe in hell, you have to believe in heaven, and I just can't imagine a heaven, so no."

"I think the spirit leaves the body and goes somewhere, but I don't believe in hell," I answer.

"Do you think he's in pain?" Jax asks quietly, staring out the window.

"No," Jordy and I reply at the same time.

Jax turns to look at us. "Are you just saying that because you want me to feel better?"

Jordy shakes her head and says, "No."

"When Ashley died, I didn't think for one second that he was in pain. In fact, the one positive thought I had was that he was finally *not* in agony. Death frees us, Jax, from pain, from guilt, from everything."

Jax nods and crushes his cigarette out in the ashtray. "I didn't like him—I might have even hated him—but I don't want him to be in pain."

I touch Jax's knee. "I know."

Jordy exhales the last drag of her cigarette unevenly and throws the butt into the ashtray. I put it out for her. I know without seeing her that she's crying. I lower the window, let the rain extinguish my cigarette, then toss it into the ashtray.

Jax turns to face me. "I'm ready now."

We get out of the car, open our umbrellas and walk through the puddles toward the funeral home.

All I see are flowers—they're everywhere. I've got a pocketful of tissues and two backup allergy pills, so I just smile at the Goyim (as my mother would say) traditions and lean our umbrellas against the wall with the others. Carchie is wandering through the crowd—annoyed, no doubt, at the pomp and circumstance dedicated to a man who couldn't find it within his heart to love his gay son. Teddy isn't here yet, but my parents are; they're standing, alone, against the far wall of the foyer. Jordy heads into the bathroom, Jax hugs his mother and I join my parents.

"Hi."

"I know this is inappropriate, but you look really good," my mother says to me.

My father nods and kisses my cheek. "Very pretty."

"I assume you'll be joining us for the final viewing?" my mom asks.

"Jax asked me to go in with him, but isn't it for immediate family?"

"Technically, but I guess the definition of immediate family has changed over the years," my father replies.

"We've been friends with Ellen and Jim for over twenty-two years—I'd say that qualifies as family," my mother adds.

"What do I do?"

"You hold Jax's hand and help him say good-bye to a father who loved him very much," my father explains.

"A father who once loved him very much," I correct.

My mother shakes her head. "Jim never stopped loving him, Alex. He just lost sight of that love when Jax came out."

"Did you lose sight of your love for Ashley when he came out?" I ask, knowing the answer.

"No, of course not," she replies.

"So what does that mean—that you and Dad are better people than Ellen and Jim?"

My father leans into the conversation. "Not better people. Better parents." He takes my mother's hand, and she takes mine. We walk into the room where Jim's body is laid out, surrounded by Ellen, Jax and a handful of aunts and uncles. My parents bookend Ellen, and I curve my arm through Jax's. He's not crying, but he looks so sad. We stand here, in a circle of grief, for about five minutes. Then we leave so Ellen and Jax can have time with Jim. I reunite with my parents in the hallway, and my mother takes my hand again. Carchie joins us as we walk toward the chapel, where Jordy is standing by the door, waiting for me. I take her hand and we enter, a string of mourners draped in black.

Teddy and Max are already seated—they must have arrived too late for the final viewing. Max is on the end, his arm around Teddy. He's wearing a beautiful black suit—it fits as if it were made for him. Teddy wears a black dress with no jewelry except a watch, and her hands fiddle with the buttons on the sweater she's brought in case she gets cold. Carchie sits next to Teddy, my father next to Carchie, my mother next to him, then me, then Jordy. We're two rows behind Jax—I can see his ponytail and sloped shoulders. I have an overwhelming desire to hug him, but the minister is on his way up the aisle and it would be terribly improper to pop out of my seat at this point. I turn around—everyone is seated, eyes on the pulpit. The minister is halfway up the aisle. I try to shake this need to check in with Jax, but I just know he's flailing, standing up there next to his mother and an aunt he sees once a year, two feet away from the coffin that holds his father's dead body.

Fuck it. I'm up and out of the pew before my mother can form the words to reprimand me. I see the minister approaching just as I wrap my arms around Jax. His body slumps into mine a little bit, but his knees are steady and his hands are neither cold nor sweaty. Maybe it's me who's flailing.

"What'cha doin', Alex?" he whispers.

"I need to hug you."

"Always a pleasure," he says, kissing my lips as we end the hug.

"Are you OK?" I ask.

"Yeah. Sort of. For now. Are you OK, babycakes?"

"Except for the occasional flashback to Ashley's funeral, I'm fine."

Jax squeezes my hand. "Distilling yet another atrocious situation with humor—some might say we're not accomplishing anything in therapy."

"I'm two rows behind you."

"Ride with me to the cemetery?" he asks.

I nod, return to my seat and replace my hand in Jordy's.

I miss much of the ceremony because I'm stuck in my head. I try to focus on Jim but it's pointless—the tears explode from my eyes and drop like bombs of ice down my cheeks. I cry for

Jax, for the loss of a father he couldn't reach. I cry for Jim, and his willful refusal to accept his son. Although Jim knew Jax as a child, he never really knew him as an adult, and I'm certain he would have been proud to see that his son had evolved into a warm, wonderful man.

I cry for Ashley, my intelligent, talented brother whose life concluded before it should have, and for my parents, who had to bury their firstborn, their only son. I cry for the silence that has haunted our family since the day we watched Ashley's coffin lowered into the fertile earth. I am finally in a position to put an end to the immobility that has paralyzed my family, and it is my intention to do so, in honor of both Sam and Ashley.

I cry for Jordy, too, and the terrifying but exhilarating journey we are about to begin. I dread the prospect of telling my parents and Teddy—I know they won't hate me, but I'm not sure they'll jump for joy, either—so I've decided to wait a while. This is mine, finally, and I want to enjoy it, privately. I feel a bit stupid that Jordy and Sam knew for so long, while my mind was so clouded I could hardly see beneath the surface.

I cry, too, for the inevitable ways in which my life will now change. I am a minority, I am different and I will even have to fight for certain rights. But my atmosphere is no longer blurred, so how can anything else matter?

I cry for Sam—I cry the tears I wouldn't let myself release when he died. I miss him. I'm ashamed to admit it, but sometimes I miss him more than Ashley. Most of my feelings in regard to Ashley are all tied up in a messy bundle of guilt and regret, about what could have been, not what actually was.

And I cry for Tucker, for the friendship I may have inadvertently sacrificed, as well as the deep-rooted pain and anger he holds toward his mother. I hope he can eventually forgive me for wanting to die as his mother did, and consider my survival a testament to my courage.

I cry for Teddy, and the relationship we shared as children that is now lost. At the same time, though, I think Teddy and I can, as adults, create a new bond—one based on friendship and affection and a shared history.

I cry for Carchie, for the cancer that might take his life within the next few years. I cannot bear to think of life without his presence, but I know I am now resilient enough—much to Carchie's credit—to go on without him.

The minister ends his eulogy, and everyone stands. Jax and my father and two other men walk silently to the coffin and, as if they have rehearsed their actions, take positions at the four corners of the casket. In one seamless movement, they lift it and walk down the aisle of the chapel. Jax looks strong and, somehow, proud as he helps carry his father's casket out of the funeral home. I release my mother's hand but hold tight to Jordy's as we file outside. The rain has stopped but it left a cutting gray chill to the air. The clouds move aimlessly, overlapping one another so the sun has no chance to show itself. As we walk down the steps, I see Tucker standing by the curb. He smiles at me as he waits for Jax to load the coffin into the hearse. I smile back and watch as he shakes hands with, and then hugs, Jax. Tucker waves at me before walking toward a waiting car.

Jordy and I split up for the ride to the cemetery. She goes with Teddy, Max, Carchie and my father, while I ride with Jax, Ellen and my mother.

Ellen rests her head on my mother's shoulder as the driver steers the car out of the parking lot. Their arms are linked. I take Jax's hand and weave his fingers through mine. We are silent for the thirty-minute drive to the cemetery. We are four people bound by history, by love, by family and now—for the second time—by death.

15

Jax and I both return to life-altering messages on our answering machines. His is from a voice-over agent who wants to represent him and has already lined up two one-minute radio ads. Mine is from Charles Spencer, asking me to call him at home. When I do, he seems rushed and distracted but tells me to meet him at one o'clock at Daniel, the venerable restaurant on the Upper East Side, for lunch tomorrow. It isn't until I hang up that I realize I'm missing a crucial piece of information—does Mr. Spencer know Tucker and I broke up?

I do three loads of laundry, pay bills and clean the bathroom—all without a single cigarette break. I open a bottle of wine (Tucker taught me red wine needs to breathe before it's served) and pour myself half a glass. I sit on the couch, turn on the five o'clock news and light a cigarette. As I suck back the smoke, I analyze the anchorwoman: nice shirt, bad blazer, terrible brooch. The cigarette feels heavy between my fingers and the smoke crowds my lungs. I put it out in the ashtray, rearrange the pillows and curl up on the couch.

"Hey, baby," Jordy whispers into my eyes.

"Hi." I open my eyes and smile at the same time. "What time is it?"

"Seven."

"You're late," I say, sitting up. The sun has started its downward dip—summer's almost over.

Jordy stands up and extracts a bottle of Diet Coke from her bag. "I know. The subway ride from Queens took forever. And it was packed. I hope if they hire me, they give me a midday class. The Queens College campus is really nice, by the way."

Jordy sits and lights a cigarette.

"How'd the interview go?" I ask, sliding closer to her.

"Good, I think. I met with two people, both really nice. They're apparently pretty desperate for professors, since school starts in two weeks and they're still interviewing. They both read the first fifty pages of my dissertation and didn't laugh in my face, so maybe they'll hire me."

"When's the Hunter College interview?"

"I meet with the Chair tomorrow at one o'clock."

"I'll be having lunch with Tucker's father tomorrow at one."

"What?"

"Yeah, about my books."

"Does he know—?"

I shrug. "I have no idea."

I walk to the kitchen, pour Jordy a glass of wine and top off my glass. She turns on the stereo, and Billie Holiday's gossamer voice breezes through the living room. I stir the sauce and boil water for pasta.

"Smells good," Jordy says as she enters the kitchen.

"Me or the sauce?" I slide the glass of wine across the counter to her.

Jordy meets me at the stove and wraps her arms around me from behind, sinking her chin into the space between my shoulder and neck.

"You smell good; the sauce smells great."

She breathes into my hair. I place my hands on top of hers. We eat dinner—pasta with sun-dried tomatoes, mushrooms and asparagus—half an hour later. We compute the lowest possible salary Jordy needs to earn in order to live in the manner to which student loans have accustomed her. I offer to pay rent for a while, but Jordy nixes the idea with an exaggerated roll of her eyes. We estimate her cost of living—with rent, utilities and minimal shopping—and figure out that she'll need to teach at least four classes.

"OK, enough math." Jordy slides out of her chair and approaches the stereo, which has been quiet for about ten minutes. She places another CD on the rotating disc-changer, turns up the volume and begins to clear the table. I wash dishes; Jordy dries.

"Cigarette?" she asks when we're done.

I nod. We sit on the couch—our legs touching—and Jordy lights two cigarettes. I take a drag, but instead of the satisfying postmeal inhalation, my chest constricts and my tongue rejects the taste. I put it out.

"I think I want to quit smoking."

Jordy laughs. "As if this summer hasn't been hard enough, Alex. Jesus, give yourself a break."

"It's not just a whim. I don't like the taste anymore."

"So switch brands."

"I've been smoking for too many years. It's a waste of money, it's bad for my skin and it stinks up my clothes. It's time."

Jordy shrugs. "OK, so quit."

I take her hand. "Want to quit with me?"

Jordy closes her eyes for a second, then opens them. "I knew you were going to ask me that."

"Come on. It'll be so much easier if we do it together."

"Yeah, we can get fat together."

"No way. We'll chew gum or toothpicks or pens. We'll use the patch, so we can kick the actual habit before the addiction."

"You sound like a commercial."

"I remember this stuff from when Teddy quit. And she didn't gain a pound. Although she did meet Max right after she finished the patch."

"Ah! So that's your motivation—you want to drop an addiction and gain a husband," Jordy says, laughing.

"Yeah, that's exactly why I want to quit smoking. You busted me."

We stare at one another, smiling and giggling on the couch

as we have so many times in the past. But our stares are more concentrated, our breath accelerates and the short distance between our lips seems way too far. Jordy and I kiss—we make out like teenagers, actually—and our bodies pick up the rhythm of the jazz CD. The sounds tumble over one another, and the pace of the music stimulates me.

I pull away from Jordy, take a long swig from a bottle of water and stand up.

"Bedroom?" I ask her.

Jordy stands. "We've only had sex ten times and already you've lost all sense of seduction."

I grab her hand, push her up against the speaker and kiss her. When I pull away, her eyes are still closed; she holds on to my waist and leans heavily on the speaker. A sheepish smile spreads across her face as she opens her eyes.

"You were saying?" I ask.

Jordy laughs and leads me down the hallway to her bedroom.

"'Maverick, take me to bed or lose me forever,'" I chant.

"*Top Gun*," she answers.

I wake up at 10:45 a.m., five minutes before the alarm blares. I put on a T-shirt, brush my teeth and saunter into the kitchen, smiling as my thoughts return to last night. I load the coffee-pot, marveling that I am wide awake despite only four hours of sleep. I shove a handful of cereal into my mouth and head back to the bathroom to shower. The water clears my head, and I focus on having lunch with Mr. Spencer. I assume he has good news about the agent, but I'm worried about the strings that may be attached. He read my books and sent them out because I was Tucker's girlfriend. Now I'm just a regular citizen, not a potential daughter-in-law.

Jordy stumbles into the shower while I'm towel-drying my hair at the sink. I drape her towel over the shower-curtain rod and place her robe on the closed toilet seat. I know she's concentrating on her interview, so I blow-dry my hair in my room, which of course gets me all sweaty. I take off my robe and stand, in my bra and underwear, in front of my closet, wondering what one wears to a business meeting with an ex-boyfriend's billionaire father. Should I go for the mature, fashion-conscious look, which would consist mostly of clothes borrowed from, and not yet returned to, Teddy? Or do I go for the downtown chic look, with bare arms and lots of cool bracelets?

Jordy enters my room wearing a charcoal gray business suit with a black shirt. Her hair is all over the place. I know she's going to pull it into a low ponytail while she rides the elevator to the lobby. But she's interviewing for academia. I just want an agent.

"What should I wear?" I ask her.

Jordy scans my closet as she slips into a pair of my black heels. "Wear the long lavender skirt, the fitted white button-down and Teddy's silver Gucci slides."

Funky, classy *and* fashionable! Anyone who can dress me in five seconds flat for an awkward, unknown entity such as lunch with Tucker's father deserves my eternal devotion.

"Thanks."

"No problem. How do I look?"

I scan her and smile. "Like a dorky, studious professor."

"Good. I have to go. I'll see you later. Good luck with Tucker's dad."

She rushes down the hallway and out of sight before I can wish her good luck, or kiss her good-bye. I step into the gauzy skirt and am about to button the shirt when Jordy flies back into my bedroom and kisses me on the lips.

"Good luck," I tell her.

Jordy winks, smiles and disappears down the hall again. I hear the front door open and close.

The restaurant is crowded but quiet when I enter, ten minutes late. Mr. Spencer is already seated. He skims *The Wall Street Journal* and savors a scotch. I stand next to the table, sliding my feet in and out of Teddy's shoes, which are a little too big.

"I am so sorry I'm late, Mr. Spencer. I couldn't decide between the subway or a cab, and of course I just missed a train and had to wait and—"

"It's fine, it's fine. It gave me some time to decompress. Sit, please." He motions to the seat across from him. "And I thought we had settled the matter of our names. You're Alex and I'm Charles." He smiles and gives a slight nod to a waiter standing across the room.

"Can I get you a drink?" the waiter asks me. He's tall with blond hair, and I can almost see his biceps through his white shirt—no doubt a struggling model or actor.

"I'll have a glass of pinot grigio." The waiter nods and walks away.

"How are you?" Charles asks me.

"I'm fine. How are you?"

"Fine, thanks. Tucker told me about your friend's father—I am sorry."

I nod.

"He also told me you and he are no longer seeing each other."

I nod again. I haven't planned anything to say, and my throat is now dry and itchy.

"I was very sorry to hear that," Charles continues, seemingly nonplussed by my stupid silence. "I think you are good for him, in many ways. Then again, I recognize that it is not your job to fix my son."

"Funny you should use that word," I say, finally finding my voice. "One of our problems was that Tucker wanted to fix me."

The waiter places a glass of wine directly above my knife. "Would you like to hear our specials?" he inquires.

Charles orders the salmon special and I order garlic and rosemary chicken. As soon as the waiter departs, Charles picks up the conversation right where we left it.

"I presume you are referring to your struggles with depression?" Charles asks.

I take a sip of wine, and then another.

Charles smiles and touches my hand. "I assure you, I will keep all this information to myself—I am well aware it is none of my business. And I am not smiling because it is funny; it is not. I smile because for the first time in many, many years,

Tucker is confiding in me. Alex, by breaking my son's heart, you have inadvertently returned him to me."

I take another sip of wine. "Well, I'm glad something good came of our fight and breakup."

"I am sure you are aware of this, but he has never truly gotten over the death of his mother. Until you came along, I don't think he ever considered forgiving her—he views suicide as the ultimate insult to loved ones. But you made him question that."

I nod.

"When my wife killed herself, Tucker was too young to have the kind of friendships you seem to have with your friends. He really only had Scott, and although Scott is now a terrific young man, it is difficult for one ten-year-old to support another ten-year-old."

Charles pauses, perhaps wondering if he should continue.

"There is nothing quite as painful as losing the mother of your children. And despite what Tucker has always thought, I do suffer from guilt and regret. I know, rationally, that her suicide was not my fault, nor was there anything I could do, beyond what I was doing, to prevent it. But there are days when I wonder—maybe she would be alive if I had stayed home that day, or if I had locked up her pills."

Charles swallows his scotch and adjusts his tie.

"She would have done it another day, and found another way."

"You think so?" he asks. At this moment, he looks so much like Tucker.

"Absolutely. I've tried to explain to Tucker that no matter how much she loved him, or you, or Derek and Catherine, at a certain point, that love isn't enough. It doesn't counterbalance the pain. It's a terrible place to be, when your desire to die outweighs your desire to live."

My wine glass is empty. So is Charles' scotch glass. He motions to the waiter and both are refilled just before a server delivers our food, offers fresh pepper and disappears. I wonder if Jax is able to make himself nearly invisible while working at the restaurant.

"Do you think there's any chance for a reconciliation?" Charles asks.

I smile. If the *New York Post* ran a photo of this business-world titan as he appears right now, stocks would tumble—his eyes are wide and hopeful, and something tells me that if I say yes, the word will make him happier than any business acquisition or bank account balance.

"No," I reply. Charles swallows his disappointment along with a piece of salmon. "I love Tucker," I continue. "And I really, really want him in my life."

"As a friend," Charles adds.

I nod. "I had sort of a revelation a few weeks ago." I trust this man, and I admire and respect him, but I cannot tell him before I tell my own parents. "I'm in love with someone else."

Charles nods. "I hope it doesn't sound condescending to state that I want what's best for you. I think I told you when we first met; there is something about you that reminds me of my wife. You fill a room the way she did, and your presence comforts me the way hers did. You are, perhaps, what she could have been, if—"

His eyes are so crisp behind their watery screen. I blink tears away so they won't fall. What a turn my life has taken—here I am, bonding with Charles Spencer.

"Did we just become friends?" I ask.

He laughs. "Yes, I believe we are now friends. And as your friend, I advise you to try the caramel ice cream for dessert—it is extraordinary."

The waiter reappears and Charles orders two bowls of caramel ice cream and two cups of coffee. Over dessert, we chat about the Yankees' pitching staff, and discuss the team's chances of winning the World Series. As Charles walks me to Lexington Avenue, he tells me about his friend, the literary agent. When we reach the subway station, he offers me his hand. I skip the handshake in favor of a hug, and he smiles.

"Thank you for lunch, and thank you for sending my books to your friend."

Charles steps back and tightens his tie. "I hope to see you soon, Alex. Good luck with your books."

I smile back at him. "Thank you." He turns, crosses the street and hails a cab.

I walk to 59th Street, take the R train downtown, get out at 57th Street and walk a few blocks to Jax's restaurant. I assume he's working lunch, since his phone is off. I hope to catch him before he goes either home or on his break. I haven't seen him in a few days, and I can't tell him about Jordy and me over the phone. I want to see his reaction—his eyes—because I'm pretty sure he's known all along about Jordy's feelings for me. He's had box seats to our relationship from the start.

I encounter him at the door of the restaurant.

"Alex! What are you doing here?"

"I was on the Upper East Side. I wanted to see if you were still here."

"I'm working dinner, but I've got an hour and a half. I was just about to get some pizza."

Jax takes my hand and we walk to Seventh Avenue. He buys two slices and eats them as we walk toward Rockefeller Center. The streets are crowded with tourists who walk too slowly and talk too loudly. Jax and I maneuver in and around the gawking visitors until we lose patience; we find seats in the outdoor plaza next to the Ziegfeld Theater. He lights a cigarette and offers me one.

"No, thanks. I'm down to four a day."

"What?"

"Yeah, Jordy and I are quitting."

"You're shitting me—for real?"

I nod. "You should, too."

"I love cigarettes. Cigarettes love me. We're a perfect couple."

"We're getting too old for bad habits, Jax," I point out.

"Some might say smoking dope is a bad habit."

"I'm detoxing, from now until Halloween."

Jax shakes his head. "No butts, no pot—don't tell me you're going to start jogging."

I laugh. "I don't run unless chased, you know that."

He laughs, exhales and steps on his half-smoked cigarette. "I guess I could take a few months off from pot. Friends that detox together stay together!" he sings.

He hugs me. I can smell his Kiehl's Lemon Verbena Body Soap.

"I have to tell you something," I say into his neck.

"It's about fucking time," he replies, pushing me out of the hug.

"What?"

"When you picked me up for the first day of the wake, something was different—the way you walked, the way you looked at things. I've been waiting for you to tell me."

I take a deep breath and stare at the movie marquee. "I figured out what the 'missing piece' is."

"You did? That's amazing. What is it? How do you know you're right? How did—"

"It's Jordy." This shuts him up for exactly ten seconds.

He slaps his thigh. "I knew it!"

"You did?"

Jax nods, then shrugs and smiles. "Well, I sort of knew it. I had a feeling she's in love with you, but I was never completely sure. When I first read Sam's note, Jordy immediately popped into my head. I thought about saying something, but if I was wrong . . . Plus, you know me, I think half the population is gay."

"One in seven, they say."

"*They* are usually all straight, so what do they know?"

"Jax?"

He turns his body so he's fully facing me. It's amazingly quiet in this little plaza. I can actually hear the small, scrawny trees sway in the wind.

"I think I'm gay."

Jax pulls me closer to him. "You think?" he whispers.

"I know I'm gay."

Jax hugs me. He breathes evenly into my hair.

"Why are you crying?" he asks.

It's just a single tear. "Because I feel like an idiot. I'm almost thirty and I'm just realizing who I am. Jordy's had these feelings for me for like, I don't know, a really long time, and I just realized how she felt two weeks ago. Sam knew. You knew. Even Tucker knew."

Jax doesn't say anything. I pull away from him.

"What's wrong with me?" I continue. "How come I couldn't see it? I really liked that guy Ben in college."

Jax folds his legs Indian-style and takes my hands. "First of all, you liked having sex with Ben. You had no desire to stay with him beyond college, and it never even crossed your mind to marry him. There's a difference between physical pleasure and emotional pleasure. You've always leaned more toward women than men. Look at your friends—every single person who's close to you is either a woman or a gay man."

I open my mouth to object but Jax gives me the hand.

"Not counting relatives," he continues. "And so what if you haven't been able to see Jordy's feelings until now? There's probably a reason for that. Correct me if I'm way off base, but until recently, you were pretty busy trying to get through each day without hating yourself or killing yourself. Now that you're better, your mind has other things to think about, to notice. And your sexuality just happens to be first on the list."

Jax hands me a tissue; I wipe my eyes and nose and shove it in my bag. "You mean there might be more?"

He laughs. "You never know. Maybe you're going to realize that deep down, under years of repression, you are actually an advocate of the NRA, or that in addition to being a lesbian, you are also dying to become a mail carrier or, better yet, a gym teacher!"

"Shut up, you lunatic." I try to slap him but he's got my wrists locked, held together in one of his hands, just as he used to do when we were kids. "This is not funny, you know. I didn't make jokes when you came out to me."

Jax's eyebrows shoot up. "Oh really? I seem to recall an immediate line of questioning regarding whether I was a pitcher or a catcher."

I forgot about that. "I was young and immature. What's your excuse?"

Jax releases my hands but joins our fingers together. "I just wanted to make you laugh. You looked so serious."

"This is serious, Jax. I have to tell Teddy and my parents, and my whole life is going to change and—"

"Alex, slow down. You don't have to tell your family yet. In fact, you shouldn't tell them until you're completely ready. Your life will change, yes, but you don't have to process all the changes today, or even tomorrow. Give yourself some time. You always want to deal with everything right away."

"Since when did you get so wise?"

"I know you better than anyone on this planet, Alex. You're my best friend. Jordy may love you now, but I loved you when you peed your pants during *The Dark Crystal*."

I slap his knee. "That only happened because I had a bladder infection!"

We're both laughing, and then suddenly Jax isn't laughing.

"Are you in love with her?" he asks.

I nod. "She's the only person I can imagine sleeping next to for the rest of my life."

Jax sighs. "Wow."

"I know."

We watch the people passing by on the sidewalk for a few minutes.

"What do I do now?" I ask.

Jax uncrosses his legs and stands up. "Nothing. You have fun, you write more books, you go dancing, you live your life."

He offers me his hand. I stand up and sling my bag across my chest.

"You make it sound so simple."

"It is, sometimes. Being gay doesn't have to define who you are, Alex. You're still the same neurotic, hilarious, intelligent person. You just happen to be in love with a woman."

We leave the plaza and walk westward, toward the sun, which is slowly starting to set over the Hudson River. He lights a cigarette and I fight the urge to smoke.

"How'd that meeting go with the agent who called you?" I ask.

"Good. I signed papers, and I'm recording two commercials next week."

"Congratulations! Tucker's father gave me the name of a literary agent who likes my books. She thinks my illustrations are good enough to get me hired to draw other people's books. I'm going to call her tomorrow."

"Excellent, babycakes! Oh, we never discussed how nice it was that Tucker showed up at my father's funeral."

"It was ridiculously nice of him. But I wasn't surprised. He's a good guy."

Jax nods. "He is a good guy. And a hottie. What a waste."

I laugh as we cross the street. "Not *all* the cool people are gay."

Jax laughs and checks his watch. "Shit, I've got to run some errands before dinner. What are you doing later?"

"Nothing, as far as I know."

"Maybe I'll stop by on my way home. I'm first cut, so it shouldn't be too late."

"OK. Jordy interviewed at Hunter today, so maybe we'll have something to celebrate."

"You mean in addition to the fact that you both just admitted you're in love?"

I nod. Jax kisses my lips and hugs me so hard I momentarily lose my breath.

"Oh, and Alex, don't think I'm not going to ask about the sex. I'm just giving you a day between momentous conversations. But I want details, and I want the truth!"

"'You can't handle the truth!'" I yell.

Jax shakes his head. "*A Few Good Men.* Give me a little credit, will you?"

He kisses me again and walks swiftly down the street. I stare at his back until he blends in with the colorful crowd, then hail a cab and head downtown. It's almost five o'clock—Jordy should be home.

"I got both jobs! I got both jobs!" Jordy yells as soon as I enter the apartment.

Somehow, I knew she would. The planets have shifted, and the cosmos agree that it's our turn.

"Congratulations!" I wrap my arms around her.

"It's basic American History—nothing specialized—and I'm only a Lecturer for now, but who the hell cares, right? I'm teaching two classes at Hunter College and two classes at Queens College!"

I toss my bag toward the open closet door and kick Teddy's shoes off. "You got two classes at each school? Wow, you can actually go shopping once a month!"

Jordy laughs. "Only at Target, until I get a full-time position. Maybe the Gap every once in a while."

I unbutton my shirt as I walk down the hall toward my room. "Yeah, right. Like you're not going to be first on line for the Barney's Warehouse Sale."

Jordy races ahead of me, her hair a beautiful mess. "A sale is a whole different story!" She collapses on my bed, laughing. "Oh, Carchie called."

"How's he sound?"

"Really good. He's going back up to Lake George to fish before the 'fucking fall foliage freaks' invade. He said he'll call you next week when he gets back."

"I told Jax about us."

"What'd he say?"

I step into the bathroom, grab a washcloth and clean my face while Jordy waits. I brush my teeth, smiling into the mirror, and return to the bedroom.

"He had a feeling about you, he had a feeling about me and he promised to take us to our first Melissa Etheridge concert."

Jordy laughs.

I get into bed. I suddenly want to close my eyes and fall asleep. "He's thrilled. And he explained a lot."

"Like what? Membership dues?"

Jordy lies down next to me and kisses my neck.

"Like how I shouldn't tell my family until I'm absolutely pre-pared to, and how it doesn't have to totally change our lives. I don't know—he just made me feel better, less worried."

"You're worried?"

"A little. Aren't you?"

Jordy sighs. "I guess so. I was consumed with finding a job, so I haven't been thinking about it as much as you. And I assumed we'd figure it out together. What is it you're worried about?"

"I don't know—nothing, everything. Sometimes it seems so big and overwhelming and all I want to do is talk to Sam. Then the next minute, it feels like no big deal—I'm in love with the person I love most."

Jordy sits up and looks out the window. The sun has just dis-appeared, and the moon is already up, waiting its turn to light the sky. I rest my cheek on Jordy's bare shoulder. She tilts her head until it touches mine.

"Alex?"

"Yeah?"

"Is this what you want?"

"Yes."

"Are you absolutely sure? Do you want to slow down? I could go back to sleeping in my bedroom."

"I don't want to slow down." I prop myself up against a stack of pillows; Jordy kneels in the middle of the bed, facing me.

"Maybe we should. I bet Sam would tell you to slow down, to take your time."

"Jordy, don't make my decisions for me."

"I just want you to be sure, and I want the timing to be right."

"The timing *is* right."

"But how do you know?"

I lean forward. "'When you realize you want to spend the rest of your life with somebody, you want the rest of your life to start as soon as possible.'"

Jordy stares at me for a moment, not knowing the line is from *When Harry Met Sally*. She leans into me and I kiss her.

Jax calls at midnight. Jordy and I are in bed, tangled up in the blue sheets.

"Sorry," he says breathlessly. "I had a table of six that wouldn't leave."

"Where are you?" I ask.

"Walking home from the subway. Were you asleep? It's barely twelve o'clock. Please do not tell me you're going to start going to bed early, too. I'm going to have to re-evaluate our friendship, babycakes."

"I had sex for a few hours and I fell asleep. Is that all right, Jax?" I smile, half-wishing I could see his face.

"Oh, OK—perfectly excusable. I assume you're not into having a drink with me, then, huh?"

"Tomorrow night?" I ask.

"Tomorrow night I have a date, but that will no doubt end early, and miserably, at which point I will call you, and you will cease fornicating and meet me for a drink. You can bring along your *girlfriend* and perhaps we'll even go dancing at Oblivion."

"Ah, just like old times." I shiver and snuggle under the covers.

"Exactly. Listen, keep next Wednesday open for lunch, around noon."

"I don't eat lunch at noon, Jax, and neither do you."

"I know, but our mothers do."

"What?"

"I invited my mother to lunch. She told your mother. They're taking the train in and we're buying them lunch."

I sit up and gather the sheet around my knees. "You invited your mother to lunch?"

Jax stops walking and plops down, probably on his stoop. "Yes, I invited my mother to lunch."

I hear him search through his bag. "If I light a cigarette, will you stay on the phone with me until I finish it?" he asks.

"Sure."

He lights one and exhales. "I was on the phone with her, and she just sounded so fucking sad, as if her best friend died, and it dawned on me that, for whatever fucked-up reason, my father actually was her best friend. Plus, the only role she can remember how to play is the one as his wife—the woman has absolutely no idea how to live without him. She's definitely not innocent in the whole 'you-can-be-straight-if-you-try-hard-enough' saga, but she's my mother. She's been calling me every two days. Should I turn my back on her? An eye for an eye? I don't want to live like that. So I invited her to lunch—I didn't think she'd say yes, by the way—and then your mother called and told me my mother is so excited, and this and that, and your mother is so proud of me and if she takes the train with my mother can she and Alex join us and blah blah blah. And now you and I are taking our mothers to lunch on Wednesday at noon."

I close my jaw. My instinct is to tell Jax to get me out of it, but then I remember my mother's face as she stood outside Jim's wake, smoking a cigarette for the first time in over two decades, and I realize I'm too old not to have lunch with my mother. She'll sense something is going on, of course, but I'll just smile and tell her how great things are, how happy I am, and no, actually, it has nothing to do with Tucker—he and I broke up. Afterward, Jax and I will put them in a cab heading for Grand Central, and we'll immediately find a place to sit. We'll both start talking at once and we'll vow never to invite our mothers to lunch again. But we will invite them to lunch again, because we represent both the best and the worst of our mothers.

No matter how much my mother screwed up with me—during my childhood, after Ashley died or when I was wandering around that hollow mental hospital in Massachusetts—I know she would give her life for me without a moment's hesitation.

"Alex? Are you there?"

"Yeah, I'm right here."

"Are you pissed at me?"

"No, no. It's fine. Wednesday at noon."

"Can we do this?" Jax asks.

"We can do anything," I reply.

"I love you, babycakes. I'll call you tomorrow."

"I love you, too. Good night."

I place the cordless in its cradle. As I settle into my pillows, it occurs to me I haven't been this eager to fall asleep since before Ashley died. I roll over and curl my body into Jordy's—we fit perfectly, naturally. I so wish I could tell Ashley I have found love (or did love find me?). I know he would be pleased, ecstatic, even. I know accepting this new life—who I am—won't make me miss him any less, or cease to regret those years I squandered, but I think I am now ready to acknowledge—and appreciate—the time we did spend together, the level of closeness we did, finally, achieve. I gaze outward, searching for the moon. It must be beyond my perspective right now. I lean forward and find a tiny star—it's not very bright, but in Manhattan, any star is a discovery. I'm about to make a wish when Jordy sighs in her sleep, pulling me closer. Instead of asking my little star for something, I close my eyes and silently say, "Thank you."

CLOSER TO FINE

Meri Weiss

ABOUT THIS GUIDE

The suggested questions are intended to
enhance your group's reading of
Meri Weiss's *Closer to Fine*

DISCUSSION QUESTIONS

1. There are a lot of songs discussed and/or played throughout the story. What role do you think music plays in the novel?

2. Do you think *Closer to Fine* is an appropriate title for the book? Why or why not?

3. Both Alex and Jax seek refuge in huge, loud dance clubs. Why do you think they find comfort in dancing? What is it about the gay club culture that they connect with?

4. Alex ignores the inheritance from Ashley for four years. Why doesn't she access his money earlier? What does the money symbolize to her?

5. What hints does the author give about "the missing piece"? Did you notice any of the hints as you read? What is the significance of the iceberg poster?

6. Alex is very much a New Yorker, yet she appears to be fulfilled and energized by her short trips to Washington, D.C., Lenox, the Hamptons and Cooperstown. Why do these trips reinvigorate her? Have you ever taken a physical journey that led to an emotional journey?

7. Family discord and conflicts with parents are important themes in the novel. Do you think this is a generational issue? Alex and Jax have both spent a lot of time in therapy—do you think this affects how they relate to their parents?

8. Carchie is much more than an uncle to Alex. Why are Alex and Carchie so close? What does Carchie offer Alex that no other character does?

9. Why is Tucker so certain he can fix Alex? Does Alex need to be fixed? How has Tucker's mother's suicide affected him? Do you think he and his father can repair their damaged relationship? Why or why not?

10. Do you think Tucker and Alex will remain friends? Why or why not?

11. Jordy has been in love with Alex for a long time, while Alex just realizes her love for Jordy at the end of the book. Do you think Alex and Jordy will last? Have you ever loved someone from afar for an extended period of time? Did you ever tell that person how you felt? What happened?

12. Alex and Jax have had a strong, supportive friendship since childhood. What does Alex learn from Jax throughout the novel? Does Jax learn anything from Alex? Why does their friendship work so well?

13. Alex seems to be acutely self-aware of her personality quirks and issues. Do you think this helps or harms her?

14. At the end of the novel, do you think Alex has made peace with Ashley's death? Is it possible for anyone to recover from the death of a sibling?

15. The book is full of both drama and humor. How does the author juxtapose solemn scenes with amusing scenes? Is the balance of light and dark moments effective?

16. Who is your favorite character in the novel? Why?